W9-CBH-274

LOVER UNDER ANOTHER NAME

By the author of

AT SUNDOWN THE TIGER

LATE HAVE I LOVED THEE

Ethel Mannin

LOVER UNDER ANOTHER NAME

"The artist, who is only the lover under another name . . ."

(Basil de Selincourt in his *Introduction to Blake's Selected Poems*)

G. P. Putnam's Sons New York

FIRST AMERICAN EDITION, 1954

ACKNOWLEDGMENT

In the writing of this book I have been deeply indebted to Mr. S. T. Lister, of the well-known Greenwich timber merchants, for much valuable information concerning timber; and to Mr. Alan Durst, A.R.A., for the sculptor's point of view in the handling of it. For assistance with proofs I am indebted as always to Mr. Gilbert Turner.

E.M.

Library of Congress Catalog Card Number: 53-8151

MANUFACTURED IN THE UNITED STATES OF AMERICA

For

ALAN ALLEN

Tho' thou art worshipp'd by the names divine
Of Jesus and Jehovah, thou art still
The son of morn in weary night's decline,
The lost traveller's dream under the hill.

(Epilogue to *The Gates of Paradise*.
William Blake.)

The Vision of Christ that thou dost see
Is my vision's greatest enemy.

(*The Everlasting Gospel*.
William Blake.)

Contents

Part One

HUNGER AND LOVE

I

FOR most people who don't live there Greenwich means, I suppose, the green wooded hill of the park rising unexpectedly from the river after the five-mile stretch of dockland grayness from the Pool—a green hill crowned by the Observatory globe, and forming a background for a Wren waterfront of domed and pillared buildings, with glimpses of colonnades and wide lawns and scarlet geraniums, and immediately behind and adjacent to all this, stately yellow houses with bow windows and a lost-nobility air.

But that Canaletto-*cum*-Regency façade, with the intimations of faded gentility behind, is not the whole of the picture. There is a hinterland about which the week-end trippers who flocked to Greenwich in recent years by water-bus knew nothing, and which is of no interest except to those who live there, or who, like myself, were born there. The trippers come to spend a few pleasant hours on the hill and round about; they climb up to the Observatory and admire the view and examine the twenty-four-hour clock and make little jokes about Greenwich mean time; they look respectfully at the Nelson relics in the museum, and admire the herbaceous borders of the well-kept gardens, the elegance of the faded Regency houses—"They knew how to build in those days! I suppose they're all flats now. . . ."—and at a cafeteria pavilion set among King Charles II's massive sweet-chestnuts they can get tea by courtesy of the L.C.C. Why should they go farther and fare drearily with mean streets of a Deptford drabness in unpleasant proximity to the gasworks?

When I was a boy I never thought Observatory Hill or the Naval buildings or the Queen's House so very wonderful. In common with all the other hinterland kids I was glad the park was there to play Red Indians in. Nowadays I believe the kids play gangsters and hold each other up with tommy-guns, but in my time, before the first bout of global warfare, it was Red Indians and cowboys and bows and arrows; comparatively speaking, it was the Age of Innocence. In the company of other snotty-nosed ragamuffins with dirty knees I scampered up and down the steep wooded slopes, lay in ambush in grassy hollows, hid inside hollow trees centuries old, and had a high old time. But any old piece of wasteground or rubbish dump would have served as well, and the strip of beach below the pier at low water was more exciting; you could paddle there, and you never knew what you might find among the washed-ashore garbage of old shoes, bits of wood, cabbage stalks, and seaweedy tangles of refuse.

For the boy that I was, the broad highway of the river running out to the sea was vastly more exciting than any green hill, and a tug chugging along with a string of barges sunk deep in the gray water was as alive for me as all the stately architecture was dead. My father had told me that when he was a boy a fishing fleet sailed from Greenwich to the North Sea, and that they would go as far as Iceland and Greenland. I would think of this when I saw the great red-brown sails of the barges spread against the sky; in my mind I would see a whole armada of tawny sails gliding down the river. Where they were bound for didn't matter; all that mattered to the boy that was young Tom Rowse was that they were off somewhere, which seemed to me, living down by the gasworks, a fine thing to be. I didn't want Iceland or Greenland; we learned about Greenland in a hymn at Sunday school—"From Greenland's icy mountains"—and Iceland sounded equally chilly. I certainly didn't want to go to sea like my brother Martin. He went as fireman, and it seemed to me he might just as well have gone to work at the gasworks like our father, as work shifts in the furnace heat of a boiler room in the bottom of a ship. Martin joined the Merchant Service because he wanted to travel. He saw a bit of India and Australia, it's true, but his traveling came to an abrupt end in 1917 when he was torpedoed and drowned. He was nineteen.

I just escaped the war, being only just eighteen when it ended. It was bad luck for my parents that if they had to lose a son it should be their favorite, and not even a grave for my mother to water with her easy tears, only the impersonality of his name on a war memorial. It was all the worse luck for them because young Tom turned out the way he did.

I am writing this book for my own son. I've walked out on him, it's true, but it isn't quite as the bare statement of fact suggests. Bare statements can mislead. You can state that Jesus was a Jew of Nazareth who was executed as a political offender. It is true, but most people would agree that the fact is a long way short of all there was to it. That I am a good deal concerned with "the little more, and how much it is" of the Nazarene story is part of the reason for recording my confused attempt at interpreting it. Or perhaps it is more accurate to say is the cause of all that made the recording seem necessary. I walked out on everything except one thing, which was an idea of something which for the sake of convenience we will call God. That hounded me down the labyrinthine ways all right.

But in my lost traveler's dream under the hill, in my particular labyrinth of living, I had a guiding star to make me a little moony night, and if his poetry was more obscure nevertheless the fiery, sun-in-splendor clarity of Bill Blake's ultimate vision was something of which poor Thompson was physically and spiritually incapable, in bondage as he was to the black-gowned ones on the one hand, dark preachers of death, "of sin, of sorrow, and of punishment, opposing nature," and his own neuroses on the other. For Blake, Jesus was the bright preacher of life, of creativeness; he was God, and imagination eternity.

One of the things you learn in the labyrinth, if you learn anything—and it is not uncommon to learn nothing—is that Love is both the Lion and the Lamb, uniting in itself both Innocence and Experience. But that the artist is only the lover under another name—that is esoteric. For that fiery particle of truth it is necessary to serve a long novitiate—sometimes a lifetime. I served the novitiate and received before I was forty the revelation, and the "firm persuasion" for its acceptance. Now all that remains is to "care not for the consequences but write"—for other lost travelers dreaming under the hill, not least the one who is flesh of my flesh, created in a night that had neither moon nor star, but only the cold darkness of a tenement room, in the last phase of the novitiate. Then I had not learned how to "love without the help of anything on earth"; materially I had something then, and having it had nothing. Now—but it were better to go back to that mean street under the green hill where it all began.

2

THIS IS my first book, and it will be my last. Writing is not my trade. This is the flesh made word, the wingèd life bound down to paper, and there is a sense in which both writing and reading are unnatural practices, a living at second hand. Yet there is the need for communication, and to be communicated with.

I have read a good many of the proletarian's-progress type of novel, and admirable many of them are, so painstaking in their creation of the working-class background and atmosphere, so accurate in detail, acute in observation—so photographically true in all particulars, material and spiritual. Nothing remains to be said about it; it has all been dealt with efficiently and exhaustively by Messrs. H. G. Wells, Arnold Bennett, D. H. Lawrence, and a horde of lesser writers.

I do not, therefore, propose to enter into the drab details of my childhood and boyhood in the house-in-a-row that opened onto the pavement in one of the streets where the visitors to Greenwich do not go. It was a home without culture of any kind. The only "literature" that ever came into the house was *Old Moore's Almanack* and the *Pink 'Un*—the former because my mother was deeply superstitious, and the latter because my father was "interested in sport"—that is to say, he backed horses without ever going to race meetings, and he enjoyed watching other men play football. I don't know what other interests my father had, unless it was what in our circles we called "the booze." As a child I feared him because with the drink in him he would shout and swear, and because my mother always held him over my brother and me as a threat—"You wait till I tell your father!" and "Your father'll take his belt off to you and tan your hide!" As often as not she *would* tell him, and he would take his belt off to us, or clout us over the head with his heavy hand and threaten to "knock the stuffing" out of us if he had any more of it. As a boy, when I no longer feared him I hated him; later still I despised him; but finally the contempt petered out into indifference.

I felt sorry for my mother because he often clouted her too when he was "boozed." I never managed to love her when I was a child because she was always betraying me to my father, and I was jealous, too, because she always favored Martin. When I got older I realized her stupidity and was irritated by her, though in later years I saw her as pathetic and discovered a kind of pitying love for her, and tried to make up to her a little for my youthful impatience. When I left home my father, from time to time, wrote me illiterate whining letters, the burden of which was that whereas he had hoped to have two sons to comfort him in his later years, here he was turned fifty and one son dead and the other might as well be, for all the help he was to him; it was no doubt his fate to work until he dropped, etc.

When I think of him I find it difficult to believe in what the Quakers call "that of God in every man"; it is much easier to believe in an overdose of what the orthodox call "original sin." He seemed to me both stupid and a brute. Yet my mother lived with him some forty years and would never hear anything against him, even when she was walking around with a black eye he had given her and deceiving herself that the neighbors really believed her story of how she had run into a lamppost, or something equally as unlikely. She always made excuses for him—Dad was "hasty-tempered"; or he had had a little too much to drink—it was his weakness, she would unnecessarily explain—and "wasn't responsible." He was her man, and as such demanded her loyalty, for better or worse, come hell or high water.

When I was fourteen I left the board-school and was apprenticed to the carpentry trade, because although I was stupid at lessons and was invariably at the bottom of each class, I was considered to be "good with my hands." There was a carpentry and a gardening class once a week for the boys, and a laundry and cookery class for the girls, and in both my classes I did well because I was interested; making things grow, and making things out of pieces of wood—all this was creative and exciting. The only classroom lessons I was any good at were drawing and painting, but we only copied things and were never allowed to design, so that the real creative impulse was frustrated. Still, I liked handling pencils and crayons and brushes, and though it cost me marks I did not always copy so exactly, but reproduced things, shapes and colors, my own way. I had a great feeling for outlines and colors and what could be done with them.

Fortunately, near the end of my time at school we had an intelligent art master and he recommended that when I left I should go to the Technical School night classes and what he called "study art properly." I had talent, he said, and should do something with it. When I told him that though I liked drawing I preferred woodwork, he said I could combine the two; I could make woodcuts and wood engravings from my own drawings; I might even in time be able to make a living at it, illustrating books and designing Christmas cards.

I was interested, but I still thought it would be more satisfactory to work in wood in a big way, not, as I thought of it, "niggle" with it. And my parents, of course, would entertain no "fancy notions"; there were certain accepted ways of earning a living, and "messing about" with something called "art" wasn't one of them. My father knew a cabinetmaker who could "do with" a lad, so I was apprenticed to him.

My employer, Mr. Snell, grandly called himself a cabinetmaker, but had any customer wanted anything as elaborate as even a modern bedside cupboard, he would have been hard put to it to produce it. He was little more than a jobbing carpenter who had worked for a firm of builders and decorators and was now on his own, earning on an average less than when he was an employee but released from the burden of having to get up early in the mornings and stay at a bench a regular number of hours. He was lazy and gloried in it.

"What we want is not more employment," he would assert, "but bigger and better unemployment! So that people have got time to live, see?" He was a natural-born anarchist, endemically agin the government—any government, all government. Governments, he would declare, are rods nations create for their own backs. His favorite book was Kropotkin's *Fields, Factories and Workshops*. He was fond of asserting that in a rational society, in which every able-bodied person did his share of work, no one need work much.

This I thought admirable. Unfortunately we did not live in a rational society, and it seemed to me that Mr. Snell extracted his money's worth from young Tom. My apprenticeship to the cabinetmaking trade included running to the "local" for jugs of beer, and to the fried-fish shop for the fish-and-chips off which my employer lunched. I would much rather have eaten my lunch as he did, from a greasy newspaper, seated on a form in the workshop among the sawdust and wood shavings and looking out onto the river, than go home to the "proper" meal my mother so devotedly prepared for my father and me every midday. Mr. Snell ordered me around a good deal, fetching and carrying, waiting on him, running errands, while doing as little work as possible himself; nevertheless I thought him a nice old man. In later years it was quite a shock to look back and realize that he couldn't have been more than forty at the time, if that. He was a medium-built man with bright blue eyes, a lot of untidy straw-colored hair, and a big gingerish mustache with long waxed ends. With his always neat collar and tie he was sartorially true to his trade. He liked leaning up against the door of the workshop watching me work, twisting the ends of his mustache and making humorous or philosophical remarks.

"You gotter be a philosopher in this life, young feller," he would say. "It's the only way of comin' to terms with it. Even then you won't get out of it alive!"

Just as his political philosophy was based on Kropotkin, his personal philosophy was based on Omar Khayyám. He was very fond of quoting from *The Rubáiyát,* and long before I obtained a copy for myself I learned quatrains by heart simply by hearing him quote them so often. He had a greater influence on my mental development than I realized at the time. I formed a great affection for him; he was the sort of man I would have liked for a father. He had a son about my own age, but he had won a scholarship for a secondary school, so would be, as Mr. Snell put it, "a few more years getting educated" before coming into "the business." He added with a chuckle, "Not that it's what you learn in schools that matters. In the end there's only one real school, and that's life itself. But you can't tell my old woman that. Women are mostly snobs and she's no exception. She likes the idea of her boy hobnobbing at school with the doctor's son and she never lets on her boy got there by scholarship. 'Stead of being proud that he's there because of his own brains and hard work, whereas the doctor's son is only there because his dad can afford the fees and probably wouldn't have got in if admission was by intelligence only!"

Mr. Snell was certainly a big part of my own education. I never acquired the art of cabinetmaking under his mentorship, but I learned to think a little, and my interest in wood as a medium was given scope. I learned to love wood of all kinds, and to "know" it. I was fascinated by the diversity of shapes and textures; I loved the almost fleshlike quality of smoothness when the bark was stripped off, and then I would think it almost a destruction of wingèd life to drive a saw into it.

Mr. Snell often sent me down to Lister's, the timber merchants in the Blackwell Lane, with orders for the wood we needed. I had nothing to do but hand the order in at the office, and was always commanded to "look sharp" on the getting back—"Look sharp now, young feller-me-lad," Mr. Snell would say. "We're all behind like the cow's tail!" Not that he ever did anything to help us get forward. The sawmill fascinated me, and when I'd handed in my order I would take myself off to the big shed where men fed long planks to circular saws, band saws, and planing machines, and others operated lathes. I liked to watch a man hold chisel or gouge against the revolving wood and see the shape of the thing he was making emerge. The man who did it, I would think, was in his own way an artist.

Everything about the sawmill fascinated me—the sight and sound and smell of it; the scream and whine of the saws in contrast with the deep roar of the planing machines, the smell of the sawdust, and the individual smells of the different timbers lying about there in the long shed and in the yard beyond. Sometimes I would be in luck and come across pieces small enough to slip into my jacket pocket when no one was looking. No doubt had I asked the foreman he would have given them to me, but I was hungry for wood, and I couldn't afford to have him say no and shoo me out. Besides, it was more exciting to "pinch"—"nicking" we called it at school.

I stole wood all my life. Even when I could afford to buy all I wanted I could never resist the satisfaction of nicking a bit. But I never took anything from Mr. Snell. It's true I never needed to, for he would occasionally give me an odd piece he had no use for, but I am convinced that even had he not done so I could not have stolen from him. I never even thought of it in connection with him. I needed all the wood I could come by for the little figures of people and animals I was always carving with no other instrument than a pocketknife. How else was I to come by the material I needed? The odds and ends Mr. Snell gave me were not nearly enough. I *needed* this material, because to make things in this medium was as much a necessity for me as eating and drinking. I tried modeling in clay, but it didn't satisfy me; it was too facile a medium; the edge of my creative impulse was whetted by the gentle resistance of wood.

I soon discovered that the pieces of wood I picked up in Greenwich Park were no good except as firewood—which was a bitter disappointment to me, for often they had interesting shapes and needed very little work on them to make them into something, had they only been seasoned wood. But these bits of branches were always either green or rotten, fit only for burning —though I always saved any which looked as though they had legs or a face, or part of a torso; they gave me a queer sort of pleasure.

At Mr. Snell's workshop, standing almost with its feet in the water, we "knocked up," to use his expression, all manner of things—cupboards, chests, "occasional" tables, bookcases, kitchen steps, garden gates. Sometimes I would be sent to a house to measure up for bookshelves or a new door for a hen run or tool shed, or something of the kind, so that I got about and saw a bit of the world.

Occasionally a girl working in an office to which I would be sent, or in someone's kitchen, would try to "get off" with me, give me what in those days was called the "glad eye," but even at seventeen I was still awkward and shy, half attracted, but also half frightened. I would go red and my hands and feet would suddenly feel enormous and all over the place. Martin, only a year older, seemed to have no such difficulties; but then, as my mother was fond of pointing out, he had all the looks in the family, and he had all the self-confidence that the knowledge of good looks gives. Whereas I was a funny-looking thing with lank, mousy hair and glasses—they decided at school I needed glasses; they seemed to think that bad sight might account for my "backwardness," despite the fact that I always got full marks for drawing and painting.

I didn't mind not having my brother's looks and charm. He had a job in an engineering works in Deptford, and as soon as he could get out of his overalls he would doll himself up and go off with a pal looking for girls to "click" with—like tomcats on the prowl, I would think. But looking back I think the need for adventure came into it, that it was all part of the adventurousness which made him eventually go to sea, because he wanted to travel. He was good-natured and lively, and we got along well enough, though he thought me slow and a bit dim-witted because all I seemed to want to do in my spare time was sit about and chip away at a bit of wood or read a book—poetry when I could get hold of it—and I thought him a nitwit because he seemed interested only in girls and never read anything except the saucy bits in the *Pink 'Un*.

I had had a feeling for books since I was six years old. I coveted the books I handled at school during the reading lessons. I was frequently in trouble because I soon became impatient of the slow pace of the class and was always reading something else, or was far ahead of the class in the set piece, so that when called upon suddenly to read I had difficulty in finding the right place. I discovered a number of things for myself in the class reader in this way—we never seemed to take the most interesting pieces, either in prose or poetry, during the lessons. We had to learn by heart boring poems, like *Ode on the Death of the Duke of Wellington*, for example, when in the same book there was the wild, strange, exciting *Kubla Khan:* and we had to learn dull and difficult passages from Shakespeare's plays instead of the Sonnets, and *Venus and Adonis*, and amusing little songs. Only of course the Sonnets and the poems of *The Passionate Pilgrim* weren't in our school Shakespeare; I discovered them for myself long after I left school; at school I thought Shakespeare a patriotic pompous bore.

There was a weekly literary magazine called *The Bookman* in those days. I used to read it in the Public Library. Just to sit there at a desk with books from floor to ceiling on all four sides afforded me a curious satisfaction. Well, there is nothing original about all that; it conforms to the usual outline of self-education. The only touch of originality about it, perhaps, is the discovering of Blake at fifteen; that's not so common. There was an essay on him, with a reproduction of an engraving from *The Book of Thel*, which of course I didn't begin to understand but which fascinated me nevertheless. Because I was interested in drawing it fascinated me purely technically; and it fascinated me by its strangeness, by its quality of a dream; it was something different, and a difference which though I didn't understand it seemed to have to do with something in myself. Why, I wondered, hadn't we learned about Blake, as a poet and artist, at school? Why had he not even been mentioned in our so-called studies of English literature? I found the courage to get out a book on Blake from the reference library, and because I could not take it away with me went evening after evening and copied passages from it—not what was written about Blake, but what was quoted of his. I didn't understand the half of it, of course, but some of it made sense—exciting sense at that. That bow of burning gold, those arrows of desire, are like flashes of light when you come across them at fifteen. The *Songs of Innocence* and the *Songs of Experience* were easy going, the bits that were quoted of them, but it was *The Everlasting Gospel* which was the real bow of burning gold, for I was by then already in revolt against the orthodox interpretation of the Christian doctrine. I longed to possess a volume of Blake's writings, and I hunted in the secondhand bookshops until I found in a box of battered volumes, all fourpence, a little pocket edition of Selected Poems. For a long time no one knew I possessed it. I hid it under my mattress at nights in case my mother should snatch my jacket to mend a tear or sew on a button, as she sometimes did; by day it lived in my jacket pocket. I hid it under my workbench at Mr. Snell's and brought it out in the odd moments when he was out of the way and I could escape from the humdrum, for a brief precious interval, in my own private chariot of fire. At week ends on fine days I would lie in the grass on the green hill above the river and struggle with *Jerusalem*, or indulge myself with the gnomic verses.

It was inevitable, since we shared a room, that Martin should eventually discover that I possessed the book. He never betrayed the fact to our parents, but he also never understood what I should want with such a book. It wasn't only that it was poetry, which he considered "soppy," that is to say the quintessence of unmanliness, but that it was incomprehensible at that. When I admitted that I didn't understand a great part of it he could only conclude that I was what he called "crackers," for why else would I bother with what I couldn't understand? It seemed to fill him with a kind of good-natured impatience which stopped short this side of contempt, though at times there seemed to be in his attitude to me a puzzled near-admiration. It was as though he could never make up his mind whether it was "daft" or "brainy." He was what is nowadays defined as extroverted. We were fond of each other. He had a quality of warmth and easy good-nature which I liked. I hardly know why he liked me; perhaps for no other reason than that I was his brother. We got along well enough together, anyhow; he had his girls and his football matches, and our mother's adoration, and I had Blake and the art classes at the Tech night school, which were all I needed.

When Martin was drowned I was angry and upset, because he was someone I had known and liked and it all seemed such a waste, so stupid; but I had no sense of personal loss; we had never been close enough for that. I had the feeling that my parents resented me after Martin's death. I felt that they would have respected me if I had joined up underage like some young fellows they knew—young Freddie Snell for example—"blamed young fool," said his father—instead of which I was safely at home in a civilian job while their favorite son only a year older was at the bottom of the sea—denying my mother even the comfort of a funeral for her ewe-lamb.

I left home the following year. I could have stayed on with Mr. Snell and got myself a lodging in the district, but I had a great need to get right away, as I explained to him. He declared himself "real cut up" at my going, and gripped my hand hard and gazed at me very earnestly with eyes that seemed bluer than ever. "Don't forget, son," he said, "there'll always be houseroom for you here!" He had never called me "son" before and it struck me as odd. But I was too young, and too unsettled and somehow wounded, at the time to realize the significance of it. Without realizing it I had grown up with him. He was the father I had always wanted, and though I didn't know it until I was about as old as he was then, I was the son he had always wanted. He gave me a suede-covered *Rubáiyát*—it was fashionable to case poetry in suede at that time—and a paper-covered copy of Kropotkin's *The Conquest of Bread*. "You'll find some stuff about art in it," he mumbled about the latter. I left him with every intention of going to see him from time to time; but I never did.

I went off into the Big City, where I'd got myself a job in the "stereo department" of a Fleet Street advertising agency and a cheap room in a squalid street off Tottenham Court Road. The job was inferior and the room dingy, but I had the feeling of having launched myself into the real world. I had served my apprenticeship not merely to Mr. Snell but to adult living. My father was good enough to call me an ungrateful cur for leaving home when I did, and my mother did an ostentatiously silent suffer which merely hardened my heart. "Good luck, son," Mr. Snell said, when I finally left. Which was more than either of my parents said.

Not that I cared all that much. I was off on my own; it was a little frightening, but it was also very exciting. And from that new start everything happened. Everything till then had been mere prelude.

3

HAD I chosen any other job from the Situations Vacant column, or had my application failed, my whole story would have been different; the Paris part would not have happened, and Paris was the foundation of my particular labyrinth. Paris was never on my agenda. I hadn't Martin's itch for travel. I was a born and bred Londoner like Bill Blake; I'd always thought that one day I would see more of England's green and pleasant land, and I'd already gone the rest of the way down the river to see what happened when it met the sea; but I had no desire to embark upon that sea. For me being off somewhere merely meant getting away from home. For me it was true that there was "no place like home"—thank God! But if I hadn't gone to work at Smythson's I wouldn't have met Carol Bayes, and if I hadn't had Carol to take me under her not-so-maternal wing I'd not have gone to Paris, and if I hadn't gone to Paris I wouldn't have met two people who played a very big part in my life, a middle-aged American woman, and a young Englishman.

I answered the Smythson advertisement because it said the applicant must have some knowledge of blocks. The only blocks I knew about were the blocks used in wood engraving and cutting; of these I could truthfully say I had had experience—from my night classes. I also added in my letter that I had had some training in drawing—in case Smythson's had an art department. I didn't quite see myself doing drawings for patent medicine advertisements, or toothpaste advertisements, but on the other hand to draw almost anything was fun, and the human animal was nothing if not adaptable.

Smythson's had an art department consisting of five men and a woman. These artists sat all day at their drawing boards doing neat pencil layouts for advertisements, and the lettering from which blocks had to be made; they also did rough drawings from which, when these were "O.K.'d" by the clients, they made finished drawings for the blockmaker, and to me it was all very interesting, particularly as I didn't think any of their work very good. It seemed to me I had seen as good at my art night classes, and could do better myself. I had a good deal to do with the art department, as I had to go into it with the "pulls" I had taken from the stereos in my own department, and to fetch lettering and drawings to measure up and send away to the blockmakers, and quite often I would stand by one of the drawing boards watching the artist at work. The artists were good-natured and didn't mind and offered me cigarettes, and when the manager was out of the way they liked to stop and light a cigarette and gossip. They struck me as a good-natured, lazy, incompetent lot, with about as much right to be called artists as any of the messenger boys who took their work off to the blockmakers in Fleet Street and the city. They could draw and letter all right; they could copy; they could carry out an idea; but even if they originated an idea there was never a spark of originality in it, that I could see, and when I had been three months with the firm and one day one of them told me he was leaving to go and work in a poster studio, I walked into the manager's office and asked if I might have his job; I'd spent my lunch hour doing a few specimens of lettering and a few rough designs for various of the firm's clients, and when I showed them to the manager he was impressed. He took me on at less than he'd paid the artist who was leaving, because, he said, I'd had no experience; still, he took me on, and at the end of the week I found myself bending over the drawing board at the table behind Miss Bayes.

She was about thirty-five, I suppose, tall and slim and golden and very elegant, and it was said in the office that she was paid about three times as much as anyone else because she was a friend of the managing director of one of the firm's clients, and the Boss had taken her on because he was asked to and daren't refuse for fear of losing the account. Certainly she dressed better than any other female in the office, including the Boss's secretary, generally regarded as "a smart piece of goods," and she was always ringing up people on the firm's time, or being rung up by them, and making luncheon dates for the Savoy Grill or the Waldorf Grill, whereas everyone else just went off to a Lyons or the A.B.C. or at the very most—if you were the Boss's secretary or the chief accountant—a Corner House. She and the Boss called each other by their Christian names, too, and she was altogether a cut above the general staff level. The Boss's secretary and the typists were jealous of her, resenting her, but the men in the department liked her; she was amusing, and without "side," and very free with her cigarettes—and she smoked a good brand. They all called her "Bayes" and treated her rather as though she were another man, and there was never a trace of flirtatiousness, or even sex-consciousness, in her manner to them. Perhaps, I thought, because she regarded them as so much lower in the social scale as to be unthinkable except as colleagues at work. And young Tom Rowse, a good fifteen years younger than herself, was a mere child. She did not hesitate to patronize.

The first day I took the job on, she came and stood by my table. She wore a green smock during working hours, tied at the neck with a big black bow—very much the artist. She stood with her beautifully waved golden head—her hair cut to the fashionable "shingle"—on one side, smiling critically.

"You can draw, Rowse," she said. "You're good."

I resented her condescension, and I told her, drily, "I'm the only one in this department who *can* draw!"

She replied no less drily, though she smiled.

"That's not quite accurate. If you're not doing anything this evening come along to my studio in St. John's Wood and I'll show you some drawings—real drawings."

"Thanks," I said. "But I'm not free tonight."

"Make it any night this week between six and eight—I never go out till eight."

I mumbled that I would come tomorrow. I was free that night. All my evenings were free, always. I would have a meal of sorts in a Lyons or A.B.C., then stroll along the Embankment or through the parks; occasionally I would go to the Victoria Palace, the Palladium, or the Coliseum, or to the cinema. I never went home, and at that time I had no friends. I liked the people at the office all right, and got along with them, but I didn't feel myself drawn to any of them. I didn't feel drawn to Miss Bayes, though I thought her good-looking and liked her style. But she seemed remote from me in every way—socially, and by reason of the difference in our ages, and what seemed to me then her huge salary. (I'd been told she was getting at least ten pounds a week; it was a lot of money in those days, and a big salary for a woman. Typists got only twenty-five and thirty shillings a week then, and the average wage of a workingman was three pounds a week.)

I agreed to go to her studio because I didn't know how to get out of going. I'd seen her work and I didn't believe she had anything better at home to show me. I wasn't all that interested in drawings, anyhow. What I longed for was to get my hands on a decent bit of wood again, a fine round smooth trunk or branch that I could make something of. The day I was to go to her I stayed on at the office after she had left. I had told her casually that I would "be along" about seven. I felt that I would give a lot not to be going at all.

I finally set off in a rather glowering mood to St. John's

Wood. I didn't see why she had to have a studio; she wasn't a real artist. I had more right to a studio; if I had a decent-sized room, properly heated, and with room for a bench, I could get down to some work in the evenings. I would like a studio in a garden, I thought, right away from everyone, so that I could work in peace and privacy.

And then, of course, she had exactly that, a studio at the end of a walled garden behind a big old house, and I resented her more than ever. There was a skylight, and a big ugly stove which gave out a great heat, and a divan strewn with brightly colored cushions of some rough material, great sprays of beech leaves in earthenware jugs, a number of oil paintings, and well placed on a pedestal in a corner something which caused me to catch my breath: it was a nude female figure carved in limewood, a tall slender narrow piece of the most exquisite flowing grace that made you want to run your hands down the lean slightly rounded thighs from the sheer compulsion of the rhythm. There was urgency and movement in the lift of the head, the tentatively emerging breasts—the creature was going somewhere, hurrying, eager. In that piece of tree, nature had given everything to the artist, even the lovely knot of the navel, and the material and the artist's dream had become one. I suppose I must have laughed aloud in my delight, for I heard Carol saying, "It's quite amusingly young and naïve, isn't it?"

I could have leaned my face against the gentle swell of the beautifully grained belly. It was like the flow of water over stones, or the wind moving over long grass.

"Heavens," I said, "to get a piece of wood like that, and to be able to do that with it!" God and Man, I thought suddenly, working together in perfect harmony.

But she said, carelessly, "It's a nice little thing. The young man who did it was killed in the war. Such a waste! He showed promise, I think. But if you like wood carving, that's nice, I think, Madonna and Child—I got it at Oberammergau before the war."

She indicated the usual little group, quite pretty in its roughly chiseled fashion, but nothing, nothing, no flow and rhythm, no movement, just a bit of wood chipped to a recognizable shape.

"It's the one thing I want to do, wood carving," I said. I felt restless. I wanted to be alone with the lovely thing, to gaze at it, stroke it, joy in it. But Miss Bayes was opening folios of drawings, spreading them out on a table, inviting me to look at this little thing, that little thing, a corner of Paris, a corner of London; pencil drawings, crayon and charcoal, some studies in gouache—quite nice, a lot better than the stuff turned out in the art department at Smythson's; she could draw all right. Yes, yes, it was all right; she had talent all right. I felt restless; my eyes kept going back to the lovely carving. There was something on the wall which I liked, a male back drawn in strong clear lines, with beautiful anatomy. There was the sense of rhythm and flow again.

"That's nice," I said.

She glanced up from the folio.

"That—oh well, yes, of course—Mike Angelo . . ."

I murmured something about planes and economy of line and turned back to the neat, efficient and essentially feminine drawings being turned over endlessly in the folio and went on murmuring suitable comments.

We got to the end at last, and I asked her, "Why do you work in an advertising agency? I mean—wouldn't you like to be a noncommercial artist?"

"There's no money in it unless you're first-class, and I'm not, and I like money. Money is delicious. Don't you think so?"

"I don't know," I said. "I've never had any."

"You're very young. You'd like to make money, wouldn't you—then you can buy pictures—or wood carvings, if you prefer—and you can travel—have lovely things—do lovely things. . . ."

"I suppose so. I've never really thought about it." I moved restlessly about. "I want to do wood carvings myself, not buy other people's. I don't think I want to travel—I like England, London. I would just like someone to give me a tree—a whole tree. I'd like an oak tree, but I'd be grateful just for a cherry tree. Or a pine—lovely sheen on pine when you've stripped it. I'd like a tree, and a studio like this to put it in, and leisure to work on it. Look, thank you for showing me your drawings, but I must go—I've an appointment. . . ."

If I couldn't be left alone with the limewood figure I wanted to be gone, where at least I could remember it and not have to make conversation.

But she wasn't deceived.

"Nonsense," she said. "Of course you haven't an appointment. I'm going to make you an omelette and open a bottle of Montrachet and you're going to tell me about yourself. Why *you* are working at Smythson's—that's much more important than why I am. I want to know about you—"

"It's not interesting, I assure you."

"Backgrounds and beginnings and potentialities are always interesting. Let me give you some sherry to start off with. By the time we've worked our way through a bottle of Montrachet we should know each other a lot better."

"I only drink beer," I said, stubbornly.

"There's no potentiality in beer. Tonight you're going to drink wine and loosen up a bit. Then we shall know what to do with you."

She went over to a table where there was a collection of bottles and glasses and poured sherry from a decanter and handed it to me, smiling. She had blue eyes and a mouth that was thin without being hard, and her little amused smile was reflected in her eyes. There was something quizzical in her smile. She poured sherry for herself and said, "You know, I don't really give a damn what becomes of you, but you interest me, and I've nothing to do this evening, and I'm trying to make up my mind whether to take you to Paris with me next week end or not."

"Thanks," I said. "But if I went to Paris it would be under my own steam."

She smiled. "How boorish the young can be! If you wait to go to Paris under your own steam as you call it you may have to wait for years, and it's now that the experience would be of value to you. In Paris you can see some more of Brenovska's work—that's the man who did that thing you like. . . ." She nodded to the limewood figure moving urgently forward from its corner. "They're in a private collection, and I happen to know the owner. And there are other things you should see. Apart from the fact that Paris is the most beautiful city in the world. And the most civilized."

I thawed a little. "I'll go one day, perhaps. Perhaps soon. I'd like to see more of—that man's work."

I walked over to the figure again with my glass and stood beside it, taking in every line of it hungrily. Carol went away to the other end of the studio and disappeared behind a screen, where I heard her beating eggs, and in a moment there was a smell of butter melting in a hot pan.

It was a very good omelette. I didn't realize then how good it was, only that it tasted all right, and the wine was cold and soft, yet golden and strong. We drank it out of glasses with long stems which reminded me of the marbles I'd had at school, with the twists of colored glass in them—the "blood alleys." We sat side by side on the divan, at a little low round table, and she kept pouring the wine, and after the omelette there was fruit, a great wooden bowl of it. She kept pouring the wine and I knew I was talking a lot. The words seemed to flow easily, and I told her about my home, my parents, about Martin, about working for Mr. Snell, and this passion I had for wood, and how that Brenovska thing excited me. . . .

I went over to it again while she was making coffee, and when she came back she found me running my hands over it.

"I can't get over it," I said. "It's so beautiful."

She looked at me with her quizzical smile.

"It's alive," she said; and then, abruptly, "You like women?"

I could tell her without self-consciousness then, the wine all a soft golden glow in my blood and in my mind, "I've never had to do with one."

I looked from the statuette to her and then suddenly I knew.

"It's you!" I exclaimed.

"Ten years ago. In Paris."

The wine made it possible for me to ask her, "Was he—I mean . . ."

She smiled, still. "Yes. We were lovers. For a little while. At the time he wasn't much older than you are now. I was a little older than he was."

"He was lucky," I said recklessly.

"We were both lucky." She turned away. "I'm afraid that if you're to get your last bus . . ." she said.

Incredibly it was nearly midnight. She was clever. I left her—that is to say, she got rid of me—without my having so much as touched her hand, though I was drunk as much with the scent of her as with the wine, and spent the greater part of the night lying awake remembering her—a nymph carved in limewood, but sweet with the intimations of mortality; and remembering her, knew myself a man. And that I would go to Paris with her; even without Brenovska.

4

In this episode my brief relationship with Carol Bayes was of little importance. What was important was not the introduction to the man-and-woman business but the introduction to Paris, and to the work of Josef Brenovska. I never for a moment believed myself in love with Carol. Love didn't come into it. I wasn't a romantic youth, and I had no adolescent yearnings either to love or be loved. Girls didn't attract me; if anything they repelled me; I didn't much care for the shape of them, physically or mentally; broad-hipped and narrow-minded, they struck me. I disliked their twittering preoccupation with clothes and "boys." I felt that I was not designed by nature to be any young woman's "boy." There was a dreadful expression in use in the twenties—"clicking"; in due course everyone at the office knew that I had "clicked" with Miss Bayes. Had I been in love with her the vulgarity of the expression, and of the attitude behind it, would have been intolerable; as it was I thought the word not much more squalid than the relationship itself.

Carol attracted me—powerfully. But she got into my imagination and my blood by way of the little Brenovska statuette. The excitement she roused in me was not entirely sexual—unless all aesthetic excitement is basically that, which could be. She took me to Paris and I felt like a gigolo, and as gigolos go I don't think she got her money's worth. If she expected that I would be worth my boyish weight in passion and virility she miscalculated, for I was a clumsy and ineffective lover, and she was not sufficiently interested in me to attempt to make anything of me.

When the week end was over I discovered that she was playing me off against the Boss, who had been her lover for the last six months. She had taken me to Paris because he had gone off to some advertising conference that week end instead of spending it with her, and she was piqued. Perhaps she didn't believe he had gone to a conference. Anyhow she let it be known in the office that we had gone to Paris together, and it appeared to afford her satisfaction that her lover—the big florid middle-aged man—was hurt and humiliated. I suppose she wanted to demonstrate to him that she could have a young lover if she chose—with all the implications of superior potency.

She told me triumphantly, soon after we got back, "The Boss knows about us! I hope you don't mind?"

Had I been gallant I would have said that on the contrary I would be proud for the whole world to know of our relationship, but instead I told her, with sincerity, that I found it embarrassing that the whole office knew, from the Boss down to the messenger boys.

She smiled her ironic smile.

"How conventional you are! Far from being embarrassed myself I wear our relationship as a feather in my cap!"

It wasn't, I thought, much of a feather: and at the end of the week I gave the manager a week's notice. He didn't want me to go; I was the best artist in the studio, and he offered me an increase in salary to stay on. I was grateful to him for that, it gave me confidence, but told him I had personal reasons for leaving and that I was leaving London.

When I told Carol she was extremely angry.

"You can't do that," she said, violently. "They all know about us and it makes me look a fool!"

"You'd sooner I hung on till the Boss sacked me out of simple jealousy?"

"He wouldn't dare—he knows I'd finish with him if he did!"

"Look," I said, "there's my point of view in this, too, and I don't happen to like this situation, everyone knowing that I'm having an *affaire* with the Boss's mistress!"

"How young and crude you are! I warn you that if you leave here I shall finish with you."

"It's what I want."

We had this scene in her studio; I had gone there to have it out with her. I had told her I wanted to talk to her and asked if I might come. I think she had hoped that when the talk was over we would make a night of it, and I had gone along feeling a little afraid that she might in spite of everything get round me. But what she said made me angry and hardened my heart against her and for once she failed to stir my blood.

"Haven't you any sense of gratitude?"

I was astonished that her voice broke suddenly in a rush of tears, and I was momentarily disconcerted, for I wasn't hard and

I didn't want to hurt her but only to extricate myself from a situation which I felt ought never to have arisen. And I didn't feel that I had anything to be grateful for, since she had taken me to Paris solely for her own amusement, not because she wanted to do me a kindness. I wasn't at all clear in my mind about this business of gratitude. She had been an experience for me, and so had Paris, and Paris had been the more important experience. Does one have to be grateful for the services people render one unawares? I didn't know. There was very little I knew at that time. I looked at the wood carving in the corner of the room; there was a tenderness in the carved wood lacking in the living model.

I said, helplessly, "I don't really know what you want with me. You have a lover—someone rich and experienced, and I'm neither, so not much good to you on either count, and it's not as if you're in love with me. I can't be used just to spite your lover!"

"With a little more intelligence you might have replaced him. I left a quite comfortably-off husband for Brenovska, who was penniless."

"Presumably you were in love with him."

"I might have fallen in love with you, given the chance."

Had she hoped I might replace him in her life? I felt bewildered and unhappy. Young and crude as I was I couldn't bring myself to say that whereas he had been in love with her I was not. I went on looking at the wood carving and reflected that he had evidently been able to evoke a tenderness in her which I could not.

"I'm sorry," I said, still helplessly, and then I told her, "I'm going back to Paris. I keep thinking of the river and the trees leaning out over it, and the old houses on the Ile St. Louis, and that house you took me to to see the Brenovska things—I can't get it out of my mind. I'd sooner starve in Paris than make a comfortable living here."

"Don't be ridiculous! How could you make a living in Paris, without a word of French?"

"I'd soon learn French if I had to. I'm determined anyhow. I've a few pounds in the post-office savings bank, and with that and my week's wages from the firm I should manage till I get something—even if it's only washing dishes in a restaurant!"

"You think that because Brenovska did it you can? At least when he came from Cracow he could speak French."

"Not because Brenovska did it," I said, "but because I want to do it."

I got up to go then because there was nothing more to say, and she made no effort to prevent me.

At the door I turned and looked back at her, caught again by a kind of regret.

"Thank you for everything," I said.

She flipped open the lid of a cigarette box on the low table in front of the divan where she sat.

"Oh, go to hell," she said.

5

So I WENT to Paris, and it was both heaven and hell. For about fourteen years. Paris in the twenties was full of Americans: American tourists, and young Americans, both male and female, studying in the art schools of Montparnasse and the Quarter; there were plenty of English, too. Most of them, both English and Americans, were backed by small allowances from their families, but a few got along as best they could sketching in cafés, dish-washing, giving English lessons, working as models in the art schools; while some lived even more precariously by cadging, or contriving to live with someone with an allowance. It was all very *vie Bohême*, and viewed in retrospect, from the fearful fifties, across the wasteland of the frightful forties, and the politically dirty thirties, assumes a curiously innocent air. It was the decade of belief: belief that despite all the rearmament, war had come and gone—anyhow for a lifetime; belief in the League of Nations; belief in art, the emancipation of women, sex equality, and above all in the importance of having a Good Time. So there were cocktail parties, tea-dances, dinner-dances, supper-dances, night clubs, cabarets, sexual promiscuity—and *rentiers* galore.

In Paris the *rentiers*, male and female, English and American, sat about at the Rotonde, the Dôme, the Coupole, the Deux Magots, the Select, the Flore, pretending to be painters, poets, writers. The painters had pavement displays of their works, and the walls of the Rotonde were plastered with framed daubs, all for sale. The poets and writers broke into print in various intellectual quarterlies—run by wealthy dilettantes, English and American, who fancied themselves as patrons of the arts. Those who could afford it went south in the summer and lay about on crowded *plages* made of imported sand, and at the correct *apéritif* hours drank at bars called Sunflower Sam's, and Jimmy's. Others went to fishing villages near Toulon and painted, or lazed the summer away. In those days it was possible to debate seriously the case for or against the Soviet Union, and the Russian Ballet reflected the genius of Diaghilev and was something to get excited about, and people got excited about it, unashamedly, and with reason.

And with all this it was the era of Vorticism and Jazz. Gin and sin were fashionable, and Negroes—Negro models in the art schools, Negro dancing places, Negro night clubs, and African wood carvings and masks for the decoration of studios. And studios, whether you painted in them or not, but more people than not painted in their studios in those days. Art flourished, sex flourished, good times flourished, and a touching faith that somehow good . . . In retrospect even the affectations were singularly naïve—a model would strut about a café in a Spanish shawl, young men with artistic pretensions conscientiously affected velvet jackets and beards; it was amusing then to be scandalous, and a "character." Individualism flourished, and brightness was all.

But with all this it was easy to starve, or live very narrowly on the bread line, and plenty in Paris did, and I was one of them. For a long time; for the whole decade of peace and plenty. There was a tall, thin, gaunt, bespectacled young man with bold features and lank hair frequently to be seen in cold weather leaning up against one of the radiators facing the zinc bar of the Dôme, hanging about with all the other down-and-out artists and "bums" waiting for someone to stand them a *café-crême*, hot and a bit nourishing; in warm weather the scraggy young man was to be seen with a portfolio of drawing paper under one arm pestering the tourists in the cafés to let him make a drawing of them—for a couple of hundred francs; though he would take fifty—gladly. Sometimes he would be hawking one of those pornographic books, published in France and banned in England, masquerading as highbrow literature; he would be working on commission then. He became one of the "characters" always to be seen about in Montparnasse and the Quarter. Sometimes tourists out to see the sights, which included the "Bohemians" of the Rive Gauche, nudged each other as he passed, for he was an odd-looking creature with his cadaverous cheeks and his air of hungrily prowling. He was considered a bit eccentric, but in fact his eccentricity was nothing more than a certain lightheadedness induced by continuous hunger, and his prowl was nothing more than the unending search for the means of subsistence. Portrait of the artist as a young man. *C'est moi.*

From the start I was determined to learn the technique of wood carving. By paring my living expenses down to the barest minimum, by renting an attic cupboard of a room without running water or heating, and by cadging meals wherever possible and subsisting always on the border line of starvation, I was able to save a few francs each week toward the cost of a course of wood-carving lessons. With the sketching classes, *croquis*, you could just go in any evening for a few francs, but the sculpture classes had to be paid for in advance, for the whole term, and you had to provide your own tools. Also whereas the Quarter abounded in art schools for painters you could not pick and choose if you wanted to specialize in wood carving. Sculpture meant modeling in clay, and there was not much interest in wood carving; it was considered a sideline to sculpture proper —which, as it was not working direct in stone, was not sculpture as I understood it. It took me a whole year to save up the money for the only school which seemed likely to give me the kind of tuition I was seeking.

I would have done better to have offered myself as a pupil to a sculptor who worked in wood, but I was young, and I had this idea of "classes," following on my art classes in London; and I had no real idea how to go about anything. I would have done better to have remained in London and worked in a regular job and gone to L.C.C. sculpture classes; I might even have saved enough to take me to the Slade, or the Royal College of Art. But I had this obsession about being in Paris, because Brenovska had lived and worked there, and because he had become for me a kind of patron saint. And because I was in love with Paris, and had a romantic idea of it as the cultural center of Europe. As perhaps it was, though why it was so important to be there at the source only youth knew. Anyhow, there I was, dedicated to *la vie Bohême* and the idea of myself serving an apprenticeship to art. The summer was the best time for the mooching and prowling variety of the struggle-for-existence, for then there were plenty of tourists about. In the winter there were odd jobs, dishwashing in restaurants and hotels, but I could only take temporary jobs because I had no permit to work in France. I had no *carte d'identité* either, because I had an instinctive resistance to officialdom in any form—the police, forms, permits, any kind of bureaucracy; it all added up to "the enemy," something contra the individual. I was the natural-born anarchist. I didn't know—and I still don't know—how any artist, any sincere artist anyhow, manages to be anything else. For all else is capitulation to Mammon—to money, power, and the domination of man by man.

Living the way I did I was often hungry, and occasionally even shelterless, part of the empty-bellied, unwashed, drifting population of down-and-outs, but also I kept clear of all the jumped-up *petit-bourgeoisie* of France's great army of *fonctionnaires*. It was always easier to get oneself stood a drink in the cafés than to scrounge a meal, but one always accepted the drink in the hope that an invitation to a meal would follow, but either the stander of the drink was prepared to do nothing but go on drinking all night, or else was "going on" somewhere. In that kind of life it was impossible not to cadge and sponge, but I confined all such self-help activities to the wealthy *rentiers* drinking too much and working too little on other people's money.

I got to thinking about the whole business of money—the absurdity of it and the immorality of it. Who is to assess the value of a poem or a painting or a bunch of violets? A thing is of value according to the arbitrary law as to what it will fetch in something called "the market," which in turn is determined by supply and demand, which is determined by fashion, fluctuating economic factors, press and advertising boosting, and none of it any relation to the intrinsic artistic worth of the poem or the painting or the aesthetic pleasure afforded by the beauty and fragrance of the flowers. And such is the immorality of it all that a film star may earn, by what was then called "sex-appeal" and is now called "glamour," more in a week than a miner, the most valuable member of the community, earns in several years, working in darkness, discomfort and danger. In those lean years in the wilderness in Paris I came to dream of a society that was both classless and moneyless, in which production was for use, not profit. It was of course an anarchist society, free of all centralized government and therefore of the curse of politicians and political parties; scrap money and you scrap power, scrap power and you scrap politicians, scrap politicians and you scrap wars. I did a lot of thinking at that time, in my hungry, lightheaded way, and I came to a conclusion from which I have never deviated, that every politician is an incarnation of the Devil, and every State is the hell the devils make for men to live in. Though perhaps men make it for themselves, since they make the politicians.

But this is no way to tell a story. Yet a man's ideas are as much part of his story as his love affairs and the ups and downs of his fortune. I got my money together for the wood-carving course, but it disappointed me from the outset, and I had no inclination to save up again for the next term. I felt that I made no progress with each successive class. I hardly know why. I had made progress with my drawing in the Technical School night classes I had attended in London, but in those Paris wood-carving classes I had the feeling that both the teacher and the students regarded wood carving merely as a sideline in sculpture, and there were times when I felt that the class was little more than an advanced carpentry class. None of the students—they were all young, about my own age—seemed to think of themselves as potential creative artists; when they had finished studying they hoped to teach. I did of course learn a good deal; I learned the handling and care of tools, and a great deal more about different woods than I had learned in the carpenter's shop; and I did of course learn how to carve in relief and in the round—that is to say, I learned the technique of it. But once I had acquired this elementary knowledge I felt that the classes could not help me any further. Perhaps the teacher lacked inspiration; whatever was wrong—for me—with those classes I felt they could not enlarge my vision as an artist; that merely looking at a fine wood carving would do more for me. A fifteenth-century Madonna in the Louvre could do more for me. I mooched about the Louvre looking for things and finding them. I explored the modern museums, too, and found something interesting or exciting occasionally.

Then one day I went to Chartres. I was so overwhelmed by the magnificence of the Cathedral sculpture that I went back to Paris resolved to scrape and save until I had enough to be able to go and live for a month in the ancient town spending my days studying the superb carving of the great doors of the Cathedral. It took me about a year from the day I first went to Chartres to save enough to carry out this dream, but I did achieve it, and it was the sweet month of May when I went to Chartres for the second time. I lived that month in a kind of delirium of aesthetic excitement and rapture. That was my real artistic education. I knew then that though wood would always be my most loved medium I would also one day carve in stone, because stone too had it own life, its own potentiality for the expression of ideas. What impressed me so profoundly, studying the sculpture of Notre Dame, at Chartres, was the perfection of harmony achieved between architecture and decoration . . . but I could write a long essay on this subject, and it is sufficient here merely to record the important part that month at Chartres, going every day to the Cathedral, represented in my artistic education. If all the years I spent in Paris were largely a waste of time, at least that phase gave me Chartres and the realization of the noble role sculpture could fulfill in terms of applied art.

But Paris gave me more than that. It gave me those personalities I needed for my artistic development, and in each case, strangely, there was the connection with the original source of my desire to create—Josef Brenovska. Whether I would have discovered his work and come to Paris without meeting Carol Bayes is a moot point, but with the feeling I had for London, and my disinclination to travel, it seems unlikely. Carol, trivial in herself, outlined the pattern—like the first charcoal drawing on the wood before the gouges begin their delicate chiseling out of the design.

There were a few *affaires*, of course. I don't know if they could be called love affairs, though none of them were of that hard caliber of the Carol Bayes *affaire*, and in one at least there was love, even if it could not be considered a great love. In my half-starved condition I had no very strong sexual impulse, and in each of the three relationships which had any kind of importance in those Paris years the initiative did not come from me. I had neither money nor inclination for prostitutes, and with neither money nor physical attractiveness the light, gay, brief encounters of the Quarter didn't come my way. Women sometimes felt sorry for me, and in some women pity breeds what passes well enough for love, and passion springs from compassion.

Some six months after I got back from Chartres I was collected —there seems no other word for it—by a plump little Armenian Jewess known in the Quarter simply as Helga. She was an artists' model and posed a lot in the schools; emotionally she seemed to drift from one down-and-out artist to another, and she took Tom Rowse in her stride. She was at a loose end, which she never was for long. She got into conversation with me one midnight when I was hanging about in the Dôme zinc on an ebb-tide of hope that late as it was something still might happen, for I had struck a bad patch, and it was perishing cold outside and I had nowhere to go. She stood me a coffee, and jokingly I asked her if she would let me come home with her and sleep on the floor. She replied simply, "Why the floor?" She was generous and kind; she also hated sleeping alone, especially on cold nights. And she had this weakness, which was part of her good nature, for down-and-outs.

She was so good-natured, throwing in her plump little body, as it were, with the excellent meals she prepared so proficiently out of very little, that it was a wonder she ever got rid of anyone she took under her warm and cozy wing. But get rid of them all she did, including Tom Rowse. A streak of hardness would suddenly emerge in her. "I'm bringing someone else back with me tonight," she would say simply, and that was that. She was quite right, of course; otherwise she would have found herself running a kind of stray dogs' home. She liked to give, but she couldn't bear being sponged on, she told me. But when I offered to go then and there, since not having a sou I couldn't do other than sponge on her, she wouldn't hear of it. She begged me to stay. "You're different," she insisted. "You at least get up in the mornings and go out and look for work."

Some of them, it seemed, were not merely spongers but quite willing to be pimps, but Helga had never sold herself, and what she had had the sense not to do at seventeen she wasn't going to start at twenty-seven, she assured me. Despite the fact that neither mentally nor physically was she my style, I got fond of her; not merely was I grateful to her, but I admired her honesty. When I landed a job at a picture framer's I suggested to her that we stay on together for a while longer, sharing expenses.

"In fact you needn't work for a few weeks if you'd like to take a holiday," I said. "The money's enough for both of us, and it would make a change for you to be kept for a bit."

But she wouldn't hear of it. No man was going to keep her. And anyhow she was interested in a Russian Jew—from Bessarabia, a very good painter who was having a very bad time. She wanted to help him. . . .

"You're incorrigible, Helga," I said. "Just for once why don't you take on with someone who isn't having a bad time and doesn't need help?"

I knew the answer better than she did, of course; she just wasn't interested in people who were getting along all right on the right side of the road; it was the ones limping along on the wrong side of the road that attracted her, and there was something in her which attracted them to her, just as some women attract neurotics and are attracted only by them. As soon as I had a bit of security and was able to shift for myself—and for her too, if only she'd let me—I was of no interest to her.

We parted very good friends, and I think of her with affection and gratitude. I missed her a good deal, and I envied my successor, for she can be said to have kept a very good bed as well as a very good table. Poor Helga! As she was never likely to be able to earn much, and handicapped by that particular psychological and sexual kink, she had no possibility of ever improving her lot—unless with the climacteric some emotional change overtook her and she developed a need to lean rather than be perpetually leaned on.

6

IN THAT Paris decade I seemed to do more leaning on women than was good for my self-respect. It's true I stopped leaning on Helga as soon as I could, and that I stayed on with her after the first night because she begged me to; but somewhere inside myself I was ashamed of the way I kept going back to her evening after evening, sometimes with a few francs picked up in a café, but as often as not with nothing at all. I should have had the self-respect to clear out; I thought so at the time, but it was bitterly cold in the streets, and it's not so easy to be high-minded when you are homeless and cold and your belly sagging with emptiness. The empty belly has no conscience; well, very little. As it was I was only too glad to creep back to her—the bare little room was "home," and Helga was wife and mother—and a bowl of onion soup, and, when the money would run to it, veal cutlets fried in breadcrumbs. I would think about the soup and the *Wiener Schnitzel* all day long, some days, voluptuously, as well-fed men think of women's bodies. My need then was for food and warmth, not sex. There were times when I couldn't think of Helga as a woman at all, but only as a provider of shelter, warmth, food. Warm and fed, then I could think of her as a woman, and I did. Desire destroys hunger only when the body is well-fed. Those who think otherwise have never been hungry. I don't mean hungry with the recurrence of the three-meals-a-day appetite, but hungry with the hunger of never having enough to eat for weeks and months. There's the difference, too, between the way the well-fed body reacts to coldness and the way the starved body reacts, seeming to fill up with the coldness in every vein and nerve and tissue.

I was with Helga only three weeks, but I got built up in that time, and with the regular job at the picture framer's I was able to eat regularly and to afford a room with a radiator in it, and I could work a bit at carving in the evenings with the wood I pilfered from the shop. I pilfered all the time I was there. I had no conscience about it; there was plenty of waste lying around in the yard, but Monsieur was a miser in wood. He hoarded it as some people hoard every kind of junk—in case it comes in useful one day. He wouldn't give a scrap away. So I helped myself, taking oddments away with me in the sagging pockets of an old raincoat carried over my arm. Encouraged by these successful operations I took to visiting timber yards and carpenters' shops on the pretext of finding small pieces of wood to buy; sometimes I would actually buy something, but I always left with more than I'd paid for. While the foreman of a timber yard was off searching for something I'd asked for I'd find some useful little piece on my own. I'd tried working with wood picked up in the Bois, but it was useless, as any wood carver could have told me. I ought to have known from my experience in the carpentry trade, but I was desperate for wood, and if I found a sizable piece tried to will it into being the seasoned stuff I needed.

I looked like seeing the winter through comfortably. I was "settled" for the first time since I had come to Paris; the work was not arduous and not uncongenial, and was reasonably well paid. I was able to add to my set of tools and buy a few additional items of equipment; I had a modestly comfortable room and was able to do the work I wanted; and for the first time since I'd left England my meals were square instead of oblong. Then my employer got worried about my lack of papers; he urged that I should go to the police and get them put in order. But the very word police did something to me—raised my hackles. I was damned if I was going to any police. In fact I felt that I would be damned if I did. I told Monsieur that to ask me to go to the *gendarmerie* was like asking the Devil to dip his fingers in holy water. Except that the Devil might be prepared to do it for devilment, which I wasn't. Monsieur was equally adamant, so I was out on the street again.

The year had turned the corner, but the warm days were far off yet, and March is a drafty month, particularly when you're not eating enough. I had nothing saved, of course, not a sou, for anything I was able to earn over and above my bed and board went on equipment and materials—and once in a way I had to get my hair cut and my shoes mended, though I begrudged money for these purposes. My hair I would chop at myself, very often, but my shoes it seemed important to keep repaired; once your shoes have gone you have finally joined the legion of the destitute. And once they have gone too far they can't be mended. It's not a question of respectability but of self-preservation; broken shoes mean wet feet, and colds, or worse.

And out of all telling I dreaded getting ill. I had a fear of French hospitals which was more than a fear of their methods; it was that, but it was also a fear of falling into the hands of authority, of officialdom. I had to be free, even if only free to die in my own way. If I got ill I wanted only to be left alone, to crawl away and hide in a corner, to live or die as the laws governing my animal body decreed, without the doubtful benefit of official healing. Certainly without benefit of clergy.

That I didn't get ill before I did was a miracle. But soon after I was thrown out from the picture framer's I got what I suppose was 'flu. I had fever, and pains all over my body, and no place to go. I had pawned my tools, but you can't live long on what a pawnbroker will lend you on a set of gouges. When I met people I knew in the cafés they told me I looked bad, that I ought to be in bed. There seemed no point in telling them that I hadn't a bed. I had had a bug-infested room in a ramshackle hotel up in Montmartre for a bit—I had moved there when I had lost my job, to save money—but you cannot stay indefinitely in even the slummiest of hotels without paying something after a time. As it was I had had to shoot the moon from the hotel in order not to forfeit my suitcase with my few clothes, drawing materials, Blake's poems and some precious bits of wood. I was fortunate then in having a ground-floor room and it was easy to escape without being heard or observed by the concierge in her room off the entrance hall.

After that I got a job as *plongeur* again, and had another squalid room, for which I was able to pay the first week's rent; but by then I was too ill to stand fifteen hours a day in a hot dirty basement kitchen, or anywhere else. I shot the moon again because I was terrified if I stayed on I would be forcibly moved to a hospital.

I had a third-floor room then, but I got my suitcase out by letting it down from the window by a rope to someone—the waiter from the restaurant where I'd worked, an expert on moon-shooting—waiting outside the house to receive it. We did it at three in the morning when there was no one about. I had taken the precaution of checking the time when the *gendarme* strolled past on his rounds. A few hours later I left the hotel under the ever-watchful eye of the concierge, who knew that I went out every morning at about the same time. I left the suitcase in charge of the friend who had taken it, and went to the Dôme, where someone stood me a coffee. Among all the people I knew there must be one who would let me sleep on the floor. The man who had the suitcase had always been willing in the past, but now he had a girl in his room. But there were people who lived alone; if only I could think. Only I couldn't think. The hot coffee gave me another little spurt of energy, and I dragged myself off to the gardens of the Luxembourg, where I sat on a bench in pale sunshine that had a little warmth in it. I sat there for hours, mindlessly, dozing. When the sunshine ebbed I left the gardens and made my way down the Boul' Mich' to the river, where I found a sheltered place under the quays and sat with my back to the wall and dozed again, for hours. At six o'clock or thereabouts by some sort of reflex action I got up and mooched off to a bar in a narrow street off the Boul' Mich'—it didn't open till six. It was a small, cozy, intimate place, with quite an amusing clientele, and I went there very occasionally to chat with the barman, an Englishman called, almost inevitably, Jimmy, and give anyone so minded the chance to stand me a drink. Jimmy was good-natured, and even if there was no one to stand me a drink he would let me hang around. He might even invite me to have a cognac on the house; he had been known to. Though my greatest need was to be able to huddle undisturbed in a corner.

The bar was empty when I entered, except for a colored girl in a red dress sitting up on a stool at one end of the counter. She had a glass of tomato juice in front of her and she was talking to Jimmy, telling him a story in a slightly throaty voice.

"The minister said to Mandy, 'Now where d'you think you're going to go when you die, getting drunk every night like this?' Mandy said, 'Sure I know where I'm goin' to go when I die. What I want to know is where I'm goin' to go tonight!' "

Jimmy was round and red and Yorkshire. He knew everybody and was liked by everybody. He didn't drink much, but with a very little in him would be loquacious and amusing, though never malicious. As the girl finished her story his moon of a face creased into a grin. He paid her the tribute of his guffaw and then turned to me.

"Evening, Mr. Rowse. You're quite a stranger. How you been keeping?"

"None too good," I said. "Touch of 'flu, I think."

His round blue eyes regarded me critically.

"You look bud," he observed.

"I feel bud," I assured him.

The girl chimed in then. "Try a rum punch." Then as her eyes took me in, swiftly, so that the time-lag was only just perceptible, "Have one on me! Unless mother told you never to take drinks from strange women."

"Whatever mother told her little boy he's forgotten it—it's so long ago. I could do with a drink, and I'm broke, so thank you kindly. I came in to try and cadge one off Jimmy, as a matter of fact."

Jimmy laughed, good-naturedly. "As bud as that, Mr. Rowse?" He explained to the girl, "Mr. Rowse is a sculptor, Miss Johns."

"My last job was that of *plongeur* at Chez Charles," I amended.

"He's going to tell you a hard-luck story, miss, don't mind him. I'll go and fetch the hot water—won't be a jiffy."

I turned to the girl, not because I wanted to talk, for my head was splitting, but everything has its price, and the price of being stood a drink is that one must be sociable.

"I think I've seen you at Les Antilles," I told her.

She smiled. "Probably. I've been one of the *attractions* there every midnight for the last three months. Ah, here comes Jimmy with the ingredients."

Jimmy made the punch and the girl paid for it. I raised the steaming glass in its metal holder and looked at her. What did one say? I didn't know.

"Good luck," she said, and then addressed herself to Jimmy. She was telling him another Mandy story. "Mandy said, 'Don't you come talking religion around here. Momma don't want no religion around here. Momma only wants *Jesus* around here!' "

I sipped the punch and watched her. She had a shabby brown fur coat slung around her shoulders, the empty sleeves dangling. Despite my bursting head I took in the slimness of her ankles and legs as she sat, her narrow wrists and long thin fingers. I liked the warm, polished-wood brown of her skin, the shape of her small head with its thick, crinkly, jet-black hair standing out around it like a black halo, the softness of her fine almond-shaped eyes with their translucent bluish whites. I should have liked to have drawn her—if I hadn't been feeling so damned ill. The hot drink increased my temperature, and I broke out into a sweat. My whole face was suddenly wet.

Jimmy regarded me anxiously.

"Eee, but ye do look bud," he repeated.

The girl laid a hand on my arm.

"Come and finish the drink at a table," she said gently.

Some people came into the bar, and Jimmy turned aside to attend to them. I've no clear recollection of how I got to a table in the corner, or how the girl came to be sitting opposite me. I remember her saying, "You ought not to be out. You ought to be in bed," and that what with my high temperature, and the drink on my very empty stomach going straight to my head, I laughed hysterically, telling her that that was all very well, only first you had to have a bed to go to.

Then somehow I was in a taxi with her, and she was trying to make me say where I lived, and I was trying to make her believe I didn't live anywhere, that under the Pont Neuf, or any other old *pont*, would be my address until further notice. I don't remember much about the drive except dark streets and the occasional blur of café lights, and of her hand on my forehead once, and her low husky voice murmuring, "You've a temperature all right," and then of stopping in a dark empty street with a high wall at one side, the sudden coldness of the night air, and the pavement coming up to meet me, and then stairs that seemed to go on forever, so that again I was a little hysterical and said something about a brace of pheasants, a pride of lions, and an agony of stairs, which at the time seemed to me extremely brilliant, so that I kept on repeating it, while the girl kept on assuring me that we were nearly there. Then at last there was a door, a room, a bed, and blessed collapse.

I suppose I passed out then on that soft bed—the first soft bed I had lain on in my life—for I remember no more until suddenly I was conscious and the room was dark, and I was alone. I had a rug over me and a cold cloth on my forehead. I groped in my pockets and found a box of matches and struck a light which revealed an electric switch beside the bed. It turned on a bedside lamp, with a shade of pleated parchment, and I lay for a while looking at the room.

It was a pleasant room, comfortably warm. There was a radiator, and on a shelf above it a clutter of paper-backed books —Tauchnitz—some French illustrateds, a couple of tarnished brass candlesticks with the candles guttered out and their grease spilled down the sides. The bed was a divan in a corner, against the wall, and above it, at the head and extending along the wall, was a shelf of books, English and French. On a table flush with the wall, facing the divan, was what looked like a kitchen table painted a dull red, with a couple of similarly painted chairs pushed under it at either end. Above the table was a spotted mirror in a shabby gilded frame, and on the table below it a hairbrush and comb, a bunch of Parma violets in a tumbler, and a carved and painted grotesque wooden figure which I took to be African. On the wall above the radiator there was an African dancer's mask in teak, a devilish grinning thing. There was a shabby cretonne-covered armchair, a threadbare red carpet, a washbasin. Long faded red curtains in some coarse material that looked hand-woven covered the window. The corner opposite the door was screened off by red cotton curtains. The room was worn and shabby and makeshift, but obviously occupied by a person of some taste and culture.

I removed the cloth from my forehead and got up. I was curious. Also I wanted to go to the toilet. On my way out of the room I peeped into the screened-off corner and found an improvised larder, with a primus stove. I found the toilet at the side of a spiral stone staircase immediately opposite the door. It was an arrangement usual in old Parisian houses—a hole, with "footprints" for the feet, and you had to rush out quickly when you pulled the chain lest the flood washed over your feet. I judged the house to be a students' lodginghouse, or it could be a tenement house; the walls and stairs seemed old, and it smelled old; not as old English houses smell, the mingled smell of mildewing books and insufficiently aired bedrooms, vaguely pleasant with a suggestion of *pot-pourri*, and sheets laid with lavender, but fugitively of drains, and of toilets ventilating into the house, all laced with the smell of coffee and French cigarettes and garlic. I had no idea in what part of Paris it was, but I guessed it to be somewhere in the Quarter.

I relieved myself and went back into the room. I washed my hands and threw some cold water over my face, and passed a comb through my hair. I still ached all over but was no longer sweating, and I had the weak feeling that follows a high temperature. I walked over to the window and drew back the shabby red curtains and looked out. There was a café across the road, but it was closed. It was no café that I knew. There were trees and a high wall. There was no sound of traffic. It must be very late. The girl was doing her number at Les Antilles, I supposed. I took off my tie and lay down on the divan again, pulling the rug—gaily striped and hand-woven, I now noticed—over me and closing my eyes. Now that the fever had left me I felt pleasantly relaxed. I switched off the light and closed my eyes, and in my relaxed state it was easy to slip into sleep.

I was wakened by the light going on; after a moment's confusion I realized that it was the bedside light and that the tallish slender figure of the girl stood beside the divan looking down at me. She had the shabby fur coat she had worn in the bar thrown around her shoulders, over a long scarlet evening dress; I was aware of the gleam of gold ornaments around her brown throat and on her bare arms—beautiful, I thought, their dark brown against her flame-colored dress.

She smiled as my eyes moved up from her wrists, so close to me as she stood, to her face.

"Feeling better?" she inquired.

"Very much, thanks. My temperature seems to have subsided. Is it very late?"

"It's four-thirty."

"I didn't know Les Antilles stayed open so late."

"It closes at two, but I go to a *bôite* across the river—L'Ange Noir. It's fashionable just now. It's a good deal more strenuous but they pay well, and request numbers bring in nice little *pourboires* from the people who request them!"

She threw off her coat and took a cigarette case out of a small handbag covered with gold sequins.

"Feel like a cigarette?"

"Thanks."

I took one from the case she offered, raising myself on the divan cushions. She held the match for me and I was aware of the pinkish insides of her slim brown hands.

She pulled the chair up beside the divan and lit a cigarette for herself, then leaned back, closing her eyes a moment as though utterly weary.

"Look," I said, "you must be dropping with tiredness and wanting to get to bed. I'll be clearing out."

"Where to?"

"Oh, I'll find a corner somewhere—some pal or other—bound to crawl in somewhere—"

"Don't be a fool. You've got flu and you must stay put for a few days at least. I get up around midday and make coffee. If you want it before then you make it yourself. You'll find everything you want in the corner behind the curtains. If you throw the cushions down there and take the rug and my coat you should be all right. O.K.?"

I could only say feebly, "You're very good." I felt too weak for anything but the line of least resistance.

"What's so specially good about being ordinarily decent?"

"Most people wouldn't consider ordinary decency demanded taking in a complete stranger just because he was sick and destitute. It raises the whole question of am I my brother's keeper."

She blew out smoke, smiling, the whites of her eyes gleaming with the slight backward tilt of her head.

"The answer is yes, isn't it, for Christian people? Shall we become more personal, though, and introduce ourselves? My name's Patricia Johns. Spinster, from Port of Spain, Trinidad."

"How d'you do?" I said. "May I introduce Mr. Tom Rowse, bachelor, from London, England."

"How d'you do?" she murmured, and continued, conversationally, "Have you been in Paris long?"

"Ten years. And to save you the trouble of asking, the reason I don't go back to London, where I could probably get a respectable from-nine-to-six job, is that I prefer starving in Paris. Not that I starve all the time, mind you, but the winter is always difficult—no tourists willing to have their mugs sketched in the cafés, or be carted around the night places."

"Jimmy said you were a sculptor."

"I do wood carving, when I can get the wood, and when I can take time off from the struggle-for-existence. Jimmy has a suitcase full of my things—I can't lug them around. I have to shoot the moon too often. I had a crazy idea I might get enough together for a show some day. Daft, of course. What I need is a nice rich patron. Or an introduction to a bishop with a taste for religious art."

We talked till our cigarettes were finishing, providing each other with potted biographies. I gathered that her father was a primary schoolteacher in Port of Spain, and had a deep sense of the wrongs of his people at the hands of the whites. Not only the economic exploitation of the Negro by the white man, but the imposition of white culture, religion, and ethics, so that educated Negroes were all the time trying to get away from their African origin—which in the West Indies meant trying to get away from the fact that they had been brought to the islands as slaves.

Patricia's mother, it seemed, was a case in point. The daughter of a Protestant pastor, she was desperately respectable and conventional, as though by a super-white morality—mid-Victorian, Patricia called it—she could somehow live down her black skin. Instead of living up to the challenge it represented—as Patricia was taught to do by her father. The affinity between father and daughter was very strong, the girl reacting away from her conventional mother and entirely given over to her father's idea of re-creating the folklore and culture of their people, and of presenting it—as a challenge—to the whites: a challenge to their superiority, and their right to dominate the colored races.

"Mother's dearest dream is that I should marry a white man and produce mulatto grandchildren for her. But of course I never would."

"Not even if you fell in love with a white man?" I asked.

"No. On principle I wouldn't."

"You don't believe in miscegenation?"

"Not at this stage. Not until we're a free people."

"I think you're wrong," I told her.

She shrugged. "Perhaps. Either you see my black viewpoint or you don't."

"I see it," I told her, with sincerity.

Well, then, it seemed her father encouraged her natural desire to dance and directed it into the channel of interest in African art generally. So as a young girl she had dreamed of going to Europe—which meant for her London and Paris—as an exponent of Negro dancing, the authentic un-Americanized article, a dream in which her father had encouraged her. But though colored dancers had a certain vogue in London and Paris in the twenties, the interest was confined chiefly to its misinterpretation in revue and nightclub numbers. Patricia Johns's dream had been to put Negro dancing on the map of serious art as Paul Robeson had put the spirituals. She saw herself leading a troupe of colored dancers with bookings in all the capitals of Europe and presenting authentic West Indian music, dancing and singing. You could put over a lot of useful propaganda in calypso, with its pointed sociological comment:

> A white man will love a Negro to the core
> As a brother but not as a brother-in-law.

White people would be amused by the humor, but because of the tremendous throbbing rhythm of words and music and dancing they would remember more than they realized.

She had a dream, too, of Negro ballet. But at twenty-five, after five years in Europe, she was still doing nightly cabaret numbers at places like Les Antilles on the Left Bank and L'Ange Noir on the Right—"stomach dances" at the one, and sexy songs at the piano at the other.

Her smile was rueful as she said, "And like you I could go home, of course, and earn my living respectably. I'm not doing any good here, but living in a pipedream that one day, somehow, I will find a way to combine doing what I want with earning a living."

For her to throw in her hand and go home wasn't easy, for her pride came into it. So long as she remained in Europe she was fulfilling at least part of her father's dream. He had no idea, apparently, of the purely cabaret nature of his daughter's dancing. She stubbed out the butt of her cigarette and got up.

"I must go to bed," she said.

I got up from the divan, gathering up the cushions. I arranged them on the floor and made myself comfortable on them, with the rug, and her fur coat, which she insisted on my having.

She went to the cupboard and took out a yellow silk wrapper with a jazz design of red and green all over it and went with it behind the corner curtains. I lay listening to her movements, and heard her use the washbasin and clean her teeth—her quite magnificent teeth. In a few minutes she came out from behind the curtains wearing the wrapper folded around her slim body. She stood a moment looking down at me, smiling faintly.

"You all right?" she demanded.

"I'm fine," I told her.

"You don't snore, I hope?"

"No complaints have been received to date," I assured her.

"Good."

She went over to the divan, yanked back the coverings and pitched in, switching off the light. There was a little sigh, and then such a silence it was as though she held her breath. I lay awake for a little time thinking about her and what she had told me of her background, but finally I slept.

At midday she was moving about in her wrapper making coffee. Our life together had begun.

I was content to stay around all that day and the next, feeling weak and shaky after the fever, but on the third morning I got up and went out while she was still sleeping. I was determined to get some money—just enough to be able to stay on with Patricia until I felt equal to going around first in search of a job, then for a cheap room. I was determined not to stay with her as I had stayed with Helga. Though there was more than that to it. It wasn't only self-respect and pride involved; I wanted to be able to do something for her. For Helga it had been enough that I just stayed with her and made love to her until she had had enough of me; with this girl, who had no sexual interest in me, and with whom nothing of the kind came into the picture, it was different. I wanted to express more than my gratitude to her—something also of my admiration for her courage, for the way she went on doing the cabaret stuff in the hope that one of these days she would get a chance to do what she really wanted to do; I admired her, too, because in spite of the fact that she must have been intensely attractive to all kinds of men she did not have *affaires* or allow anyone to keep her. She could, obviously, have had a comfortable, even a luxurious, life had she chosen. But the artist in her was too strong, and the sense of dedication to her own people.

We talked a good deal in the afternoons of the first few days, and I suppose we told each other all there is to tell. Certainly I told her all there was to tell about Tom Rowse. She was uncritical of the Helga episode.

"It was what she wanted," she said, simply. "You made her happy, and when you had some money and could have helped her she turned you down. Think what fun she had with her down-and-out artist! The sense of power it afforded her—the eternal mother!"

I took the opportunity to say, "I can't stay here on those terms."

"But the terms aren't the same, are they? She gave you half her bed, food, sex; all I give you is shelter—the right to doss down on the floor—and a cup of coffee at midday."

"And your friendship," I said.

"For what the lonely thing is worth!" She smiled, but there was a curious melancholy in her great dark eyes, even somehow in the smile itself. There was altogether a kind of soft dark melancholy about her; even, somehow, in her quiet graceful movements; the melancholy of the animal that walks alone, an innate, uncomprehending sadness.

"As from one solitary to another it's worth a great deal," I told her; and I meant it. She came and went, as a cat does, solitary, self-sufficient; yet somewhere in the world, I would think, there must be another creature, as feline and as solitary, through whom she could be fulfilled. She had had a love affair, it seemed, with a young man from Jamaica, and for six months they did a double number at a *bôite* in Montparnasse, singing everything from *Greensleeves* to *Frankie and Johnnie*, and accompanying themselves on guitars, in a dim light, she at one end of the room, he at the other, their audience crowded at low round tables in between, massed so close it was impossible to move between the tables, and latecomers sitting on the floor, their backs to the walls, some even accommodated on stools behind the bar.

"We were an immense success," she said, "but it was mostly Peter—he has all the looks and all the charm in the world, and completely no heart. There was a Swedish girl who came every single night and sat at his feet. She never sent up any requests, but she was always there, gazing at him. His voice is pure velvet."

But he was conceited and arrogant, and quarreled with the proprietor of the *bôite*, and when his arrogance began to extend to the clientele his popularity began to wane. He blamed Patricia, and gradually everything broke up, first the arrangement at the club, then their business partnership, then their personal relationship. He finally found another partner, and when Patricia last heard of him he was being a success at a smart place near the Opéra, and he and the girl were living together.

"What did you find to love in him?" I asked.

She smiled her sad smile.

"Does anyone ever really know why one loves? Isn't it a skin thing—an answering of the blood, outside of reason? And isn't that sufficient reason?"

"I don't know," I answered her. "I've never been in love."

"When it happens you'll remember what I said."

I couldn't tell her that already within a couple of days I was as near to being in love with her as made no matter. She attracted me enormously, and I admired her enormously. She was the most intelligent person I had ever met—perhaps the only intelligent one; certainly the only intelligent woman. If liking plus physical attraction signified being in love, then I was in love. Yet at the back of my mind even then I had an idea there was more to the whole business than that. But that she was my friend, and that I felt a deep affection for her, and that she powerfully attracted me—all this was certain.

I went around to Jimmy's that third day to find something in my suitcase to sell. With the idea of an exhibition eventually, when I had enough good stuff, I didn't want to have to sell anything before then, and had always resisted the idea before when I'd been down and out. But this time I positively had to have some money.

Jimmy had a small flat over the bar, all shrieking wallpaper—violent pink roses and black trellis—and nouveau-riche French furniture almost comic in its blue plush and yellow veneer vulgarity. I found him unshaved and looking tubbier than ever in a gaudy "art silk" dressing gown having his *petit-déjeuner* coffee and rolls. He greeted me affably, asked me how I was feeling, adding that I was looking better, and waddled out into his kitchenette to fetch another cup. Pouring out coffee for me he remarked that he hadn't seen Pat Johns since the night she took me off in a taxi.

"She used to look in for a chat and a tomato juice every night on her way to Les Antilles," he said.

"She's been stopping at home talking to me," I told him. Then I saw the look in his round blue eyes and added, "No, not what you think. If you know anything about Pat you'll know she's not like that."

"She's a right good girl——"

"So that in this case two and two don't make four, and I'm clearing out probably tomorrow. But first I must have some money so that I can anyhow make a gesture of repaying. I want to get a couple of small things out of my suitcase and hawk them around the cafés."

"You could take them to one of the antique shops along the quays," Jimmy suggested.

"And get a hundred francs apiece for them, and they'll sell them for five hundred! I'd sooner sell direct. With any luck I'll get two hundred francs apiece."

"Two hundred francs is two quid," he reminded me, reproachfully.

"Isn't the work of a man's heart and mind and hand worth a couple of quid?"

I was wrily amused. On the windowsill there was a completely hideous painted plaster figure of a semi-nude woman holding out a voluminous skirt suspended from her hipbones, a mass-produced horror which I knew cost two or three hundred francs.

"They're only wood carvings," he protested.

"Let's have a look at them, anyhow," I said, and when he waddled off to what he called his "boxroom," where he had my suitcase stored, I went with him.

He stood by while I opened up the case. I had a lot of things in there, carefully wrapped up in newspapers, and I unwrapped a number before I found what I wanted. I was looking for two items. The first I found was a nice little thing of a cat. It had real feeling to it, I thought, handling it after months and recalling the difficulties I'd had with it—a bit of elm I'd picked up cheap, with a knot in it in just the wrong place. I stood it on an upturned trunk, then unwrapped some more packages till I found the other thing I was looking for—a foal, a bit of wild cherry with a lovely polish to it, and a beautiful grain, the shape of it almost ready-made for the slender legs and the straight, taut back, and I'd given it movement and life; or so I thought. I would have liked Pat to have seen both before I sold them, but then if she had admired them I'd have wanted to give them to her, and they were the most likely pieces for a quick sale. I set the little foal out beside the cat, and it made me feel gay just to look at them both, they'd come off so well, they were so fully interpreted through their medium. Jimmy regarded them with a puzzled frown.

"I suppose it's hard to get a near-likeness to things, hacking them out in wood like that," he said at last.

I grinned. "That's about it, lad."

He picked up the cat. "You can make out that's a bird all right, though. I don't call that bud, though I'm not partial to owls meself."

"Thanks," I said.

"My sister's very artistic," he went on. "Pen-painting on handkerchieves and scarves, and that. And barbola work round mirrors. Very pretty. She made a loovely vase once, covering a jampot with cigar-bunds. It's a great gift, being artistic. But she was the only one of the family. My old mother had no patience with it. She said there was more money in being practical."

"Your old mother was right. Look, Jimmy, just in case I have no luck with these things right away, be a pal and advance me a couple of hundred francs—I can't go back to Pat tonight with nothing. I'm bound to sell these little chaps, but there's no guarantee I can do it between now and midnight."

He let me have it. It was the first time I'd ever touched him for anything, though he'd often given me the odd cognac and double-decker sandwich when he knew I was on the breadline. I hope people did as much for him later on, when the bad times came. But I don't know. I never paid him back, and I wasn't the only one.

I had no luck at midday; the affluence of alcohol makes itself felt more effectively as the long drinking night wears on, and I got back at midnight exhausted with so much trekking about in my convalescent state, but with four hundred francs in hand. Jimmy's two hundred I'd spent on a bottle of champagne *nature*

—still, quiet stuff that I knew Pat preferred to the sparkling—and a whole lot of things I knew she liked—olives and anchovies, and a great hunk of Gruyère cheese that was just the right degree of moistness; and a long crisp stick of bread I got, and some butter, and tangerines, and a couple of red candles left over from Christmas, and a bunch of Parma violets. The last were a wild extravagance, and cost damn near as much as the champagne, but my heart was set on them, because she'd said they were her favorite flower. She never wore them on the street—they were too much associated with Lesbianism at that time—but she liked them in her room. They were right for her, I thought; they were "different," like herself. She could only have them when they were given her, but admirers of both sexes gave them to her, so why shouldn't I—who admired more than her lithe, live brown body and the charm of her sweet melancholy smile—though my heart leapt with the thought of both. My ridiculous jumping grasshopper of a heart.

Because, of course, by that midnight I was mad for her. "*I am black but comely*." By God, she was! The sun had looked upon her all right. All the time I was doing things for the love feast I was arranging for her—scraping the grease off the candlesticks and polishing them up, arranging the violets, laying the table—the Song of Songs kept coming into my mind. "*Set me as a seal upon thine heart, as a seal upon thine arm. . . . This is my belovèd, and this is my friend. . . . How fair and how pleasant art thou, O Love, for delights! O thou fairest among women!*" So I thought of her, preparing for her with every kind of love, but that I might "lie all night betwixt her breasts," of that I did not dream. I was all humility regarding her—not because of my poverty, but because she seemed miles above me—intellectually, morally, physically, in every way. And there was her feeling about race.

I'd cleaned myself up for her. I'd shaved and put on a clean shirt, and a tie, and brushed my hair and flattened it with water. But before all that I'd stripped and washed myself all over, and I felt good, better than I'd felt in weeks—months. Years, if it came to that. I laid the table with one of her gay check cloths, and put the candles in the cleaned and polished candlesticks, and the violets in a tumbler; and I put out the food, and stood the champagne in cold water in the washbasin behind the curtain, then I lay down on the bed to wait for her. I thought I might sleep a little, but I was too excited. I lit the candles a few minutes before she came—she was unvarying in her time—and they were burning with a steady flame and intensifying the gleam of the candlesticks as she came in.

She came into the room in her long scarlet dress, the old fur coat thrown about her shoulders with such an air you'd think it was mink, her small black head tilted, the long almond eyes gleaming above the high cheekbones, and on her skin, her face, throat, breast, arms, hands, that lovely satiny sheen the skin of white people never has; she came into the room and the candles lit her face and the living flame of her figure; she gave a little cry of surprise and delight and looked from the candles and the flowers to me—tall, lanky, romantic, foolish me, with my old white shirt and my shapeless trousers and broken shoes, and ridiculously leaping heart.

"Why," she said, smiling. "What is all this? Is it someone's birthday?"

"I wanted to do something for you," I said. "I sold a couple of little figures—"

"But your exhibition—you were keeping them—"

"I can do some more. Ways and means don't matter. I've got some wine. . . ."

I went behind the curtains and drew the cork, and when I came back she had thrown off the fur coat and sat in the arm-chair. She had lit a cigarette and she was looking at the violets. The old sadness was back in her face. I filled a glass and brought it to her, and she smiled as she took it from me.

"You are sweet," she said.

I said again, awkwardly, "I wanted to do something for you." I wished, fiercely, in that moment, there could have been arm-fuls of violets instead of a mere bunch.

I filled my own glass and stood looking down at her. She reached out a hand and took mine.

"Let's drink together," she said.

"To what?"

"To us."

"Severally or collectively?"

"Both!"

So we drank, and then went over to the table and ate, and I was happy because she liked the things I'd brought, and the wine worked in her so that tiredness left her and she was a little gay, and I told her, "This is a farewell party, because I must go tomorrow."

"No," she said.

"Yes," I insisted. "I'm well now, and there's no excuse for my staying on."

"We're friends, aren't we? Can't friends share a place for a time?"

"Not if one falls in love with the other. Not in one room," I said. "It's too difficult," I insisted. "For the one in love."

She said in a low voice, "There's loving-kindness."

"Not when only one is in love. It's the last thing in the world one wants. It adds up to pity."

She got up then and stood by me and pressed my head to her breast.

"You're a fool," she said. "You're so sweet, but such a fool."

My arms went around her narrow waist, and I held her like that for a moment; then I stood up and gathered her to me, and that night I did not sleep on the floor, or on any of the nights that followed.

We stayed together a month, and when at the end of that time I left her it wasn't because I didn't love her but because I did, and it was all intolerably one-sided, because though in the first instance she gave herself to me with passion, after that it was kindness, and the inequality of it—my economic dependence on her—coupled with all the rest, was more than I could bear. I didn't want to take a regular job just then because I'd started working on a fine three-foot piece of pine I'd picked up cheap while I was earning regular money with the picture framer. It was the most ambitious thing I'd yet tackled—Negro girl dancing. Nothing less. I had to get all the intensity and lithe rhythm of her dancing naked body into it. *Nothing less.* I worked on it all day, and every day, forgetting to eat, forgetting everything except the feel of the wood under my hands, the delicate precision of the tools between my fingers. Into that wood in which the sap had long ago ceased to flow I had to instill the vibrant life of her young and powerfully rhythmic body. My hands would go over the smooth wood with the same tenderness that they went over her living flesh. The same tenderness and the same delight. Negro girl dancing. Negro girl loving. But that was where pain came into it, for she wasn't loving but merely being kind. After that first encounter I kindled nothing in her. She was the good friend, the loving friend, generous with herself as with her money.

She knew I would go when the work was finished, and she knew why I would go. I didn't resent it that she couldn't love me. I could see no earthly reason why she should, she who was young and vital and beautiful—why should she love the gaunt, skinny, unkempt, crazy thing that I was—the obsessed thing, with not a penny to bless itself with, let alone help pay the rent, or pay back Jimmy-the-barman, or supply any more flowers and candles and champagne. She made me promise that I wouldn't sell the statue to just anyone in a café, but only for a proper price, to someone who would appreciate it and be willing to lend it when I got an exhibition together. I promised. It was after all hers, dedicated to her. With all my love. My inadequate love.

Without being in love with me she loved me, but I think she was glad when I finally cleared out and she could be the cat that walked alone once more. She wanted that we should keep in touch, but I knew it wouldn't be possible—for a time, anyhow. She was too much in my blood, and I had somehow to get her out of it. For a time I thought I would go crazy with the memory of her and the longing for her, and I would have to fight the desire to go to Les Antilles and L'Ange Noir just to see her again.

Then it was Easter and Paris filled up with visitors and I was escorting them in twos and threes and happy family parties around the artists' and students' cafés, and the night places of the Left Bank and Montmartre, and resisting the temptation to go to Pat's *bôites*, and thankful for the nights when I dropped into my bed too exhausted to think or feel or do anything but sink into a black sleep.

Only I was never so intensely aware of the beauty of the Paris spring as that year, and I could hardly bear it. I thought a good deal about trying to save the fare back to London, but I could bear that even less. I wasn't ready to go back. Any more than Patricia was ready to go back to Trinidad. There was a thing to do, even if I wasn't very clear what it was, and it wasn't done yet. There is a time for things, and it wasn't yet time, and it's never any use forcing the pace.

7

THEN AROUND Whitsun I picked up with an American girl studying at the Sorbonne. That is to say I was picked up by her. She was attracted by me because she considered me "intellectual," which was something she liked people to be. Also, it seemed, she had come to Paris determined to lose her long-preserved—she was twenty-nine—virginity to an artist, and she was a girl who had the money to secure for herself almost anything she wanted.

I met her when I was doing the rounds of the student cafés on the Boul' Mich' one night. She was with a party of other young people and, primed with Pernod, they let me make some sketches of them. I made four, at a hundred francs each, and Joycelyn Carr—that was her name—paid for the lot. She also invited me to sit with them and have drinks and talk "art" with them. By midnight the other three were too drunk to be worth talking to. But Joycelyn was more sober at midnight than she had been earlier, which commended itself to me. It made her, to some extent, my kind of person. I knew all about that business of getting tight and coming right through it and out the other side. I liked to drink, and I liked other people to drink, but I liked people to become the better for drink, not the worse for it. Otherwise it was waste of good alcohol. When you had devoted a lot of money and time to alcohol it was a pity to get the wrong results.

Anyhow, Joycelyn and I walked away together at midnight neither tight nor sober, but in that in-between state which is all relaxation and euphoria. I wasn't so much attracted by her as attracted by the fact that she was so manifestly attracted by me. I knew by now that I didn't readily attract women. They more easily felt sorry for me. All except the first one, who had shamelessly used me. And Joycelyn wouldn't have been attracted by me had I been anything but an artist. But I was an artist, and as such endowed with romantic attributes.

We met a number of times. She invited me to meals in small restaurants, and I escorted her to various galleries and gave her highly individual lectures on her favorite subject—Art. I did, in fact, educate her quite a bit—more than she knew, for when I met her she had a whole lot of ready-made and conventional ideas about art, and I gave her a series of mental shakings and made her think for herself. I had a kind of Gauguin ruthlessness for her which fascinated her. Also she found me good company, which I could be when I wasn't half-dead with hunger gnawing in my belly. I wasn't the soulful, intense, poetic type. Good poetry or fine carving didn't send me into ecstasies; it made me want to get up and cheer, or laugh out loud with sheer happiness. I was what my mother called high-spirited and what later on the psychiatry boys got calling extroverted. I wasn't addicted to any "artistic" temperamentalism; when I was depressed it was no nameless sadness; I'd know all too well what the reason was—undernourishment, no money to buy materials with, no chance to do the things I wanted to do—that for me was a more devouring frustration than any sex frustration. Not that I underrated sex; after the Pat Johns interlude I realized for the first time my own potentiality, and I saluted human love, full-blooded and passionate, for what it in fact is: whether the world will have it or no, the essential generative flame, and the key to such meaning as there is in human existence. Denied it, I now acknowledged, one was an incomplete human being, but one's potentiality was a kind of flame in itself once it had known the revelation of experience, and every day was charged with delightful possibilities, so that the frustration was tolerable as an appetizer for the banquet to come some time in the not too remote future. But frustration on work was another matter; it deadened and destroyed. It was a kind of mental, spiritual and emotional castration; it was all deadness, emptiness, and despair; release from it depended not on any chance encounter but purely on material circumstances over which one had little or no control. At the time I met Joycelyn Carr I was having a bad bout of work-frustration, not having had my hands on a piece of wood since I had finished the Negro Girl, which was a great deal more tormenting than not having had my hands on a woman. The sexual frustration was still focused on Pat Johns; I went on wanting her, which was why she had had no successors in spite of the almost unbearable beauty of that Paris spring. I liked Joycelyn, but even if desire hadn't taken root in my memories of Patricia, I doubt if I would have felt much drawn to her, physically—she just wasn't my style; too bloodless. But I knew damn well I could use her money; that I could use it a damn sight better than she could. She had altogether too much, and she hadn't earned a penny of it; nor had the father from whom she got it; hundreds of people worked forty and more hours a week in offices, and stood by machines in factories, and sweated in tropic suns, in order to make money for that family. I had no scruples in deflecting a little of that money my way, which I did by the simple process of capitulating to her desire that we should graduate from being friends to being lovers. Left to myself, given, that is to say, no intimations of what I suppose is best called her infatuation for me, I would have made no advances to her and would probably have taken another route to make her a patron of the arts by endowing the genius of that down-and-out sculptor Mr. T. Rowse. But since she made it clear that my attentions would be welcome and meet with response I did, literally, cash in on the fact, and that without any conscience, since we were both getting what we wanted thereby.

She was thin and pale and blond, and I had fair women associated with the coldheartedness of Carol Bayes. She was self-consciously cultural, too, and that sort of thing always fills me with a wicked desire to debunk; but she liked me and wanted me, and her money made a pleasant change for me; it meant an end of creative frustration. Fundamentally she was a very simple girl, and when she laid aside the culture with her horn-rims and let herself get a bit tiddly, so that she relaxed and permitted herself to be humanly lowbrow, then I thought her a grand girl and warmed to her, and in time she got to understand that the highbrow line didn't work with me, and to accept that it was neither good thinking nor good living.

So that we might be together and enjoy the summer without the distractions of Paris she took—at my suggestion—a house on the edge of the forest of Fontainebleau. She had suggested a villa in the South, or on the Italian Riviera, but I wanted an atmosphere in which I could work, and I did not feel that the Midi offered it. I liked the idea of living near a great forest, and though I didn't admire the paintings of Millet and Rousseau—the Douanier was another matter—I had Fontainebleau linked in my mind with Barbizon and creative work. So I countered the Riviera idea with the suggestion that we make a day trip to Fontainebleau and have a look around, and there was a villa there, right by the forest, *à louer, meublé*, and before we even went inside I knew it was what I was looking for. And what was right for me was right for Joycelyn, hideous wallpaper, vulgar furniture, lack of plumbing and all. If the French have the best taste in the world—and generally speaking they have—they have also the worst. House and contents were equally vulgar and hideous, but there was a wild, neglected garden, damp and lush and green, with lovely flowering weeds running riot in it—tall sunshiny things like a whole bunch of golden daisies clustered on one stalk, drifts of pinkish-mauve bay-willow herb, and whole regiments of the spikes of purple loosestrife. The walls of the ugly house with its faded green shutters were festooned with bridal veils of a small creamy clematis, and in the garden there were broken stone steps where bushes of old damask roses fought a winning battle with the invading grass. The rooms were dark and damp, but at the back there was a bedroom with a balcony overlooking the garden, and downstairs a sitting room opening out into it. And all around there was the forest, sometimes deep and dense as an Henri Rousseau jungle, sometimes all delicacy and grace like a Corot landscape, both by day and by night. And within the house I had my own private trees, bought for me by Joycelyn, a really beautiful piece of mahogany with a wonderful grain, a useful piece of elm trunk, about eight feet, and a very nice piece of birchwood, just right for a bust. Also various odds and ends of small stuff, which I planned to take back to Paris with me; the big stuff I intended to work on there at Fontainebleau, and I did work on it, fixing up the long kitchen table as a workbench and using the room which opened into the garden, with the forest at the end of it, as a studio.

I had a wonderful time that summer. I had no worries, I had good food—Joycelyn was a good cook and did heroic things in the utterly inconvenient kitchen, where the fire drew badly and the cracked oven didn't heat properly and into which she imported an oil stove—I had all the leisure in the world and all the material necessary to enable me to put the precious long hours of daylight to good use. Joycelyn was a good girl and never begrudged the hours I put in at the bench instead of walking in the forest with her or accompanying her on her shopping expeditions to the town, and she never complained when I left her alone at nights because I'd feel a need to be alone and think about the figure I was working on, which was pretty often—much oftener than I felt the need to hold her in my arms.

I used the birchwood for a bust of her—a half-figure, to be

exact. She was too thin, but her small breasts were firm and prettily pointed, and she had nice shoulders and waist. She had good hands, too, and I used them to good effect, one lifted to brush back a strand of hair from her forehead, her head tilted back, her lips parted on an intake of breath, the other with the fingertips pressed upon the suggestion of windowsill which formed the base of the carving. I had seen her in this position one morning at the window, naked to the waist, her head thrown back and her face lifted, breathing in the morning air. I had been struck by the unconscious grace of the pose; she was a girl who had spent the night with her lover and wakened with the glow of gratified desire upon her, just as Bill Blake would have liked it. She was startled and a bit embarrassed when I said I wanted to make a carving of her like that, but as soon as I began making some preliminary sketches she became interested. We decided to call the figure "Morning," and what I wanted to get into it, and what I think I did get, was the exhilaration of feeling of great draughts of the summer morning drawn into a body glowing with well-being in all its nerves and tissues.

I used her tall thin figure again in a study of Daphne, tree from the hips downward, long hair entangled in laurel leaves, and the whole feeling of the taut straining body one of flight. Joycelyn didn't much care for it; it hadn't the charm of Morning, I knew, but it had the essential wild dryad quality, and I liked the flowing rhythm of hair, lean body merging with the tree, and the way in which I had used the straining hands as part of the whole movement of long flowing lines, and I felt the whole thing in harmony with the nature of the elm trunk from which it was made. I think her dislike of the figure was subjective rather than objective criticism—that she didn't like the accentuation of the thinness of her body for this subject, and thought it distorted and ugly—despite her resolute modernism, which did not flinch at anything, however hideous, however preposterous, when viewing it in an art gallery.

The wonderful piece of mahogany I left till last, rather in the way that a child will leave the piece of almond icing and marzipan on the top of a slice of birthday cake as a luxury to look forward to at the end. I knew from the first, when I had first set eyes on it at the timber merchants', what I wanted to do with that warm, brown, beautifully grained piece of wood. I wanted it for a bust of Pat Johns—just the lovely head downward drooped in the deep ancient out-of-Africa melancholy, the long slanting eyes half closed, the wonderfully modeled lips just faintly smiling. I spent the last three weeks of our stay at Fontainebleau working on it. It was September then and the forest was turning golden and the leaves fell in a Danae shower after a night of rain. The house began to feel the damp in its walls, and despite the log fires in the evenings the warmth never seemed to reach beyond a radius of a few feet from the hearth. Looking back I think that when Joycelyn shivered in those last weeks, when I was working on the bust of Patricia, it was more than physical. For one thing I never slept with her again once I had begun working on that. At the time, absorbed in re-creating a memory of passion and tenderness and despair, I didn't even notice my withdrawal from her. Only now, recalling it all, I remember the silence that closed around her, and how often she shivered. The light that shone in her that summer morning at the window was quenched, but she did not reproach me or complain, but waited patiently for the work to be finished, and took an intelligent interest in its progress. She asked me who the girl was, and I told her, and that I had lived with her and loved her. I might have spared her that, I suppose, but at the time it seemed natural to say it.

"She's a fine person," I said, standing back with half-closed eyes to squint at what I'd made of her in mahogany.

"She has a sweet face," Jocelyn conceded, and I remember the warm tone of her voice. She was a good girl.

We went back to Paris as soon as the work was finished, I to my old room in the Quarter, and Joycelyn to the expensive hotel she had been living in before on the Right Bank. She wanted that we should be married and go to New York together; she felt that her time in Europe had come to an end, and that she was overdue to see her folks again, as she put it. She put the proposition to me with commendable directness. We could have a studio apartment in Greenwich Village, she said—naïvely explaining to me that it was "where all the artists and writers live"—and as her income was enough for us both I would be free to do my Creative Work—one saw the majuscules as she said it—without being financially harassed. In due course I could have a show in New York. She knew a number of influential editors and critics who would help put me on the artistic map, I gathered.

Well, I hadn't minded being kept for a summer; in fact I'd

been glad of it; but for life was another matter. There was no principle in it; living with her for art's sake was one thing, for heart's sake another. For one thing I felt I would get very tired of having that thin pale pseudo-intellectual girl always at my side in our tastefully furnished book-lined apartment—in which, without a doubt, we should give nice little dinner parties to nice quiet cultural people Interested in the Arts, and I would be her tame-artist husband, Paris-bred but house-trained. I saw it all very clearly, but I didn't see it for me, so I thanked her kindly and presented her with the birchwood figure of herself, and cheerfully on my side and regretfully on hers it was agreed that the-best-of-friends-must-part, Love, and-so-must-you-and-I. . . .

She wasn't coming back to Paris, and she wrote to me for quite a time, still throwing out the suggestion of my going to America at her expense, with an exhibition of my work in New York, but I didn't respond to treatment and eventually she met a young Harvard professor to whom she became engaged, and then, astonishingly, she shipped the figure back to me because, she said, she felt it was "only fair" to the man she was going to marry, since it was rather more than head and shoulders. By which I could only assume she meant because I had reproduced her breasts, and her professor might be jealous that another man had seen them. *Quelle délicatesse!* But I didn't understand that particular form of delicacy and wondered how she reconciled it with her rigidly art-for-art's-sake attitude to aesthetics, but I was very glad to have the figure back, with the exhibition in mind, for I regarded it as one of my most successful pieces—though not as good as either of the things I'd made of Pat Johns—and I wrote her an almost model Nice Letter thanking her. I was quite sincerely grateful to her, though she did not bring to our relationship the warmth that Helga had brought, or the friendship and companionship of Patricia.

In one sense, though, Joycelyn did more for me, since she made possible a whole summer in which to work in peace, but then she wanted me, whereas Patricia's goodness to me was the sheerest altruism, and Helga included herself with the bed and board because she was incapable of being mean with herself. Both of them, in their different ways, gave because giving came naturally to them. If Helga was promiscuous—and I suppose in the generally accepted sense she was—there was nothing whorish about her. I have an idea Mary Magdalene was like that, and she ended up with a halo. Helga was sweet, and I won't hear a word against her. Human relations would be happier if there were more women like her.

8

THERE WERE others besides these three, of course; fourteen years is a long time, but some of them were one-night-only *affaires* whose names I can't remember, and of the few who stayed around for a little while none had the warmth of Helga, the intelligence of Patricia, the helpfulness, free of all possessiveness or demandingness, of Joycelyn. And those three, whom I remember with lasting affection and gratitude, came at a time when I most needed—and desperately needed—exactly what each gave. Through the years I learned that it was a general rule that the women who gave least demanded most—materially and emotionally and in every way. If you live in an attic—and I mostly lived in attics—the woman who would take it for granted you would go all the way down the stairs to see her off at the front door was the one who had been all but, if not completely, a waste of your time. Whereas the woman who would very sweetly insist that you mustn't dream of going down all those stairs, knowing you would only have the weariness of climbing them all again—"you poor dear"—was the one who had given a good time and had one. Such women go through life loving and getting themselves loved, giving pleasure and receiving it, with the happy simplicity, the simple happiness, of children receiving sweets and offering them. The bloom of innocence remains on such women, and if they get fat in middle age it doesn't matter, they are still better value, love for love, than many of the young ones, and somewhere in the sixties they end up as great old girls drinking stout in pubs and still with an eye for a man, which it is a first law of nature that it is right for a woman to have, to the end of her days, that the sap may be preserved in her.

But the women mean with themselves—they become skinny and acidulated in their middle-age, and by the sixties they are trees in which the sap long ago dried up, leafless boughs in which no birds sing, no cock-birds, anyhow. They command respect, which is a very arid thing to command. No man is ever going to be sufficiently interested to administer even a playful slap on their neat behinds—more's the pity.

All this and a good deal more I learned about women and love and sex in the twenties and early thirties in Paris, when I was getting along as best I could. There are those who make a living and those who do-the-best-they-can, and for all those years I belonged to that always makeshift often shifty company so frowned upon by the respectable-and-proud-of-it. It's one thing being poor-but-honest if you're just poor, but when you're destitute you can't afford to be so squeamish. Conscience can be a luxury article, and the down-and-out brigade get up to other tricks than dishwashing, and hawking pornographic literature disguised as art around cafés, and hanging about waiting to be "treated." Shabby tricks, some of them. Such as attaching yourself as guide to some tourists who don't speak the language, buying tickets and settling bills for them and charging them a little more than you pay out, and taking them of course, as far as possible, to places where you get a commission for bringing people.

Why didn't I go back to London and earn my living honestly? Honesty is a matter of definition. Was it honest to be part of the advertising racket in London? What is all that commerce of London, of all big cities, but a vast parasitism preying on the countryside, the only begetter and sustainer of life? In Paris I could get along without being part of the commercial racket, and in the process preserve my integrity as an artist. That sounds highfalutin' but it's true. I never lost the vision of Brenovska's little limewood figure. For me it was Absolute. Absolute Beauty; Absolute Truth. Nothing less.

I went very often and looked at the Rodins in the museum in the Luxembourg gardens. His passion and power moved me deeply. I was stirred by the intensity of emotion he conveyed in the stone, and by the sheer brilliance of the craftsmanship. The reaction against his romantic realism—but in some aspects he was purely Greek—had already set in, but I didn't care. Years later I discovered that Gaudier-Brezska had declared that we should never see a greater sculptor than Rodin, and that he was to France what Michelangelo had been to Italy, and I felt vindicated in my homage.

All that time in Paris I thought about England-home-and-Greenwich only when I received the periodic plaintive letter from my mother monotonously repeating the inquiry as to when if ever she was to see her sole remaining son again, and complaining of my father's shortcomings. I was sorry for her, as I had always been, but there was nothing I could do for her; I had no money to send her, and it was not really money she was short of, but her husband's love and kindness. I couldn't have gone home even if I had wanted, for I hadn't the fare, nor any chance of raising it. My chance of revisiting England had gone back to America. One of these days I supposed I would go, but it was impossible for me to predict when. I would go when life so arranged it, when the pattern shaped that way. There had been a time to go to Paris, and there would similarly be a time to return to England. I wrote this to my mother every so often, but it was of course impossible for her to understand. From her letters it was evident that she was convinced that I remained in Paris because of the wicked fascination of the "fast" life she imagined I was living there. She began to find in religion—High Anglican, all decked up with incense, flowers and choral effects—the solace her marriage denied her, and to pray for me. This hardened my heart; what right had she to haggle with her anthropomorphic Deity over the date of my return to England or the manner of my life? When religion set in and the praying began I left her letters unanswered. My anger was not because I was antireligion but because I had too deep a reverence for the religious spirit in man, as the creative spirit, the authentic Holy Spirit, to be able to tolerate its submergence in dogma and ritual. Straitjacket with trappings, was how I saw it. I had too powerful a preoccupation with the life and teachings of Jesus of Nazareth, whose astonishing and tragic career began in a carpenter's shop and ended in agony on a tree. It both sickened and angered me to come up against that supreme drama of sacrifice and expiation debased into a kind of pious superstition, and a sort of insurance policy for some disembodied future life on a vague astral plane. For me as for Blake God was Jesus, and so much that orthodoxy labeled sin "the loves and graces of eternity."

I did a great deal of thinking in those years of mooching in the narrow streets of the Latin Quarter and wandering along the quays of the Left Bank. I was concerned with the relation of art to life, and religion to both; and in the definition of God, Beauty, Truth. I had no friend with whom to discuss these first and last things. I knew a number of people; I could never pass a café or stroll through one of the big cafés without being hailed by someone, and there were plenty of people prepared to talk art, life, and religion, until the last waiter had gone home; but I knew all that kind of café talk—art for art's sake, art for life's sake, life for art's sake, art for God's sake, God for art's sake—and it wasn't what I was after. I was after some kind of prophetic vision which Brenovska had when he carved the little limewood figure, and Rodin when he labored on his Portal of Hell, and Blake when he wrote his Prophetic Books.

Oh, Blake! Blake! Such fulminations and flounderings! Such obscurities of mysticism! Such torrents and confusions! Such wildernesses of words! And such visionary gleams of the authentic dayspring from on high! I had begun reading him on the green hill of Greenwich Park as a boy; I read him in Paris garrets, and lying homeless under the parapets of the quays along the Seine. I shall read him so long as I have eyes to see with, and if blindness should come upon me read him in my mind.

> Can a poet doubt the visions of Jehovah? Nature has no outline,
> But imagination has. Nature has no tune, but imagination has.
> Nature has no supernatural, and dissolves; imagination is eternity.

Here he dedicates his vision to "Lord Byron in the Wilderness"; and in the same strain he addresses himself to "the Christians": *I know of no other Christianity and of no other Gospel than the liberty both of body and mind to exercise the divine arts of imagination—imagination the real and eternal world of which this vegetable universe is but a faint shadow, and in which we shall live in our eternal or imaginative bodies, when these vegetable bodies are no more. . . . What is the divine spirit? is the Holy Ghost any other than an intellectual fountain? . . . Is not God a spirit who must be worshipped in spirit and in truth, and are not the gifts of the spirit everything to man?*

And to Satan "the Accuser who is the God of this World":

> Tho' thou art worshipped by the names divine
> Of Jesus and Jehovah, thou art still
> The son of morn in weary night's decline,
> The lost traveller's dream under the hill.

I wasn't prepared to be a party to pawing Blake over at the cafés, with all that bogus knowledgeableness, and pretensions to having read the Prophetic Books—upon which boast Dorothy Parker's raised eyebrows and "You *have?*" is the only possible comment. If I was going to talk Blake with anyone it would have to be with someone who had a glimmering of what he was about, and humility enough to admit that the little moony night is easier to comprehend than the wheel of fire, whose name is Caiaphas, surrounding all the heavens, against which Jesus strove and did not escape. Caught inextricably in the current of the wheel, how shall we comprehend it? Yet there is—supremely for the artist, the apostle of creation, of life—the need to recognize it and strive against its devouring flame.

One of these days, I thought, there would be someone with whom I could profitably discuss all this, though I knew well that chaos dwells in the human heart and mind, and that both are "wall'd and moated round within."

In the meantime I walked about Paris, and sat about, and worked when I could and observed, and did not feel the time wasted. Sometimes I'd persuade a girl to pose for me; she would have to do it for love, since I couldn't afford to pay her—love of me or love of art, or sheer good-nature, or simple vanity. Usually it was either good-nature or vanity. I began to accept the fact that I wasn't really attractive to the general run of women. Apart from being gawky and odd-looking, I had no money, and there was no compensatory promise in my physique. In short, nothing much was to be expected of me in any way at all that could interest any kind of woman. Occasionally there was a woman or girl who liked me because she thought me "interesting" or intellectual—those were the arty ones, like Joycelyn; the others, the simple ones, like Helga, felt sorry for me, sometimes. A beautiful and intelligent and gifted girl like Patricia Johns, who had liked me as a person and for one wild lovely night been attracted by me as a man, might perhaps happen to one such as me only once in a lifetime. By the time I was thirty, I noticed, girls were inclined to regard me a bit askance: I could be amusing at times, but was too wild and crazy for most of them. And then, in turn, I was never very strongly attracted, generally speaking. Sometimes I thought I would never again be attracted by a white woman as I had been by Carol; yet I never went after colored women. I knew well enough it wasn't just "women" I sought, black or white or brown, but the "friendship lit by passion" I had found so briefly with Patricia Johns. But something beyond that too; some—*je ne sais quoi.* Some lost traveler's dream under the hill that went beyond women and love and sex; far beyond it. Something that had to do with loving "without the help of anything on earth." Sometimes, so little in general did women attract me after the Pat Johns episode, I would think that the capacity for that kind of loving had died in me, that the lean years had sapped my vitality, physical and emotional. I'd think sometimes that the only passion left to me was the creative one—to shape something with my hands; I'd get so wildly excited, sometimes, fashioning an animal, or a human body, out of a lump of wood, I'd think I knew how it felt to be God making Eve out of one of Adam's ribs. "O clouds unfold/Bring me my chariot of fire!" But back of all this was a sense of incompleteness and loneliness, an inner desolation.

Two good things happened to me at that time, when I wandered in the wasteland, not creating much and loving not at all—I broke my glasses and as I couldn't afford to get them repaired learned to do without them. It's doubtful if I ever really needed them. I had been told at school that I needed them, and my mother had supported the idea: she was a great believer in glasses; glasses and false teeth. "Have them all out—you're better without them!" was her slogan regarding teeth. If it had been possible to see with glass eyes she would undoubtedly have extended the slogan to eyes too. She had had her own teeth out in her twenties, when false teeth were "all the rage," and had never regretted it. False teeth were so lovely and white and even, and positively no trouble, unlike those provided by Nature, which sooner or later decayed and ached and had to come out in the end. Fortunately my one really good feature was my teeth, and in all the years when I could not afford to look after them Nature stood by me in that respect. When my glasses finally broke I discovered that I had been wearing them from sheer force of habit and was no worse off without them.

That was one thing; the other was that one day at a bookstall on the quays I picked up a battered copy of a book on anatomy—discarded no doubt by some medical student. I found the study of the complicated human joints fascinating, and I enjoyed making finely accurate pencil sketches to assist in memorizing the numerous bones. It seemed to me that no artist, whether painter or sculptor, could ever study form enough—minutely enough or lovingly enough, the way Leonardo did, and old Rodin.

And then quite suddenly, at the beginning of 1934, I felt that I had come to the end of the Paris interlude, or phase, or however one liked to term it, that it had nothing more to give me. I was suddenly tired of propping up the Dôme zinc, tired of all the daubs around the walls of the Rotonde, of all the Sunday exhibitions of bad paintings on the Boulevard Montparnasse, and under the scrawny acacia trees in the Place du Tertre at the top of Montmartre. I was tired of straight-haired, handwoven young women, and long-haired and bearded and corduroyed young men. Tired of all the intellectual and artistic pretensions of the "bums" and the *rentiers* equally. I felt that I knew down to the last delicately furred frond what the chestnuts would do in spring in the Champs Elysées and the gardens of the Luxembourg and the Avenue de l'Observatoire, and in the dark little Place Dauphine, like a cool leafy room between the Palais de Justice and the Pont Neuf. Paris was suddenly like a beautiful woman of whose beauty one is still aware but which no longer stirs one. I had a sudden longing for English beer and London pubs, a yearning for the dull rumble of London traffic in place of the shrill screech and scream of the Paris streets, and for the quiet, good-natured English crowds. I wanted a barmaid to call me "dear" again, and a barrow-boy to call me "mate." I thought with nostalgia of a pub on the waterfront at Greenwich where you could swig your beer looking down the gray-green water into the sunset behind Tower Bridge and St. Paul's. I wanted the muddy smell of the Thames—the living London river below the Pool; I wanted the smell of fish-and-chips, and the newsboys yelling *Star-News-Standard*, and good-naturedly facetious bus conductors, and the humor and mateyness of London streets, and public bars on a Saturday night, and great old girls who did Knees-up-Mother-Brown at closing time. In short, after fourteen years of exile I was suddenly homesick for my native heath.

But while I was feeling all this, but lacking either the energy or the cash to do anything about it, the political climate became such that I knew I had either to get out or fall into the hands of the police. Following the revelations of the financier Stavisky's goings-on, angry French citizens began tearing up the palings around the boulevard trees and demonstrating outside the Chambre des Députés against the Chautemps Government. Everyone was convinced that there was going to be a Fascist *coup*, a dictatorship. Sinister stories were flying about concerning the strength of the Royalist party. There would be a Fascist regime; there would be a Monarchy; it would be the end of the French Republic; the end of democracy. There would be civil war. Paris would go up in flames inside three months. The streets swarmed with *gendarmes* and the hated *gardes mobiles* in their steel helmets. The words "Stavisky" and "*bagarre*" were on everyone's lips. The *gardes mobiles* were thick on the Boulevard St. Germain, and the Place de la Concorde, and around the Hôtel de Ville in the evenings in readiness for the always expected *bagarre*.

I don't know to what extent they got it. There were stories of machine guns in the streets and of people wounded and killed. Café proprietors took their chairs and tables inside when rumors of a scrap, in progress or expected, went around: they were too handy as weapons—like the palings around the trees, which began to be systematically collected, those that were left. I don't know how much of all that was alleged happened, because I kept out of it. I stayed up in Montparnasse and had only secondhand stories of what was going on "down there" in the St. Germain-des-Prés area. I knew if I went down there I'd get swept up into it—the mere sight of the helmet of a *garde mobile* would be enough to make me snatch at the nearest paling and join in the *manifestations*. At that time even for people who hadn't any innate hatred of the police the sight of a posse of *gardes mobiles* or a vanload of *gendarmes* was enough to make them see red. I was entirely in favor of throwing out the French or any other government, but apart from the fact that I didn't see the point of throwing out one government only to put in another—and you couldn't keep up with the changes of government in France at that time—I didn't fancy being run in for having lived fourteen years in the country without a *carte d'identité*. I'd kept out of the clutches of the police and bureaucracy all this time and I wasn't going to dish myself just when I was all set to leave of my own accord for old England.

Communist-controlled trade union organizations were very active, and there were people who feared a "Red Terror" as much as a Fascist *coup*. There were also alliances of working-class organizations for resisting Fascism—Committees of Vigilance, they were called, but only later did the Communists co-operate with them. There was the united front against Fascism, and the stage all set for the *Front Populaire* which swept the country in the summer. It was exciting if you believed in party politics, clenched fists, and military alliances. But Blum was no more my cup of tea than Laval. I wasn't, you might say, a tea drinker.

On the day of the twenty-four-hour General Strike, called as a protest against the formation of a National Government, the gardens of the Luxembourg were closed, and the Boul' Mich' was empty; a number of cafés, shops and restaurants were closed, but more were open. And the complete stoppage of water, gas, electricity did not happen, nor the complete stoppage of trams, buses, trains. But the only paper published that day was the Royalist *L'Action Français*, which gave itself the gloating pleasure of announcing the fiasco of the General Strike. The *bagarres* continued throughout January, and by February had achieved the proportions of fully fledged riots.

I should have liked to have felt, as many did, that it was as exciting as the barricades of the French Revolution, and the last stand of the Communards, but I didn't. Whatever government was in power France would still not be a workers' republic; she would still hang on to her colonies, and the mass of people would still go on slaving to make profits for the few. The fine-sounding slogan of the French Revolution, *Liberté, égalité, fraternité*, would continue to receive lip service with no reality in fact.

The tension in Paris increased my longing for placid old London. I couldn't stay on in Paris swarming with police and *gardes mobiles*. There were groups of *gendarmes* at the entrance to every Metro, because people collected here, around the newspaper sellers, who did a roaring trade; lorry-loads of steel-helmeted *gardes* rattled provocatively down the boulevards. Sooner or later I'd find myself taking a bash at one of them. I wasn't safe at large in Paris, and Paris, which had never been really safe for me, was less safe than ever. It was all on my nerves, too, all this French excitability. I wanted peace. Somehow or other I had to get the money to clear out. I didn't know how, but I did know that the first step to finding a way to achieving it was wanting it enough.

But before I cleared out of Paris there was something I wanted to do; I wanted to see the Brenovska collection again. I had many times passed the handsome old house on the Ile St. Louis which housed it, and to which Carol had taken me that week end of my initiation. She knew the Englishman, a Mr. Graham Carlton, who owned both the house and the collection. I hadn't met him, as he had been away when we had called, but his manservant knew Carol as a friend of his employer and had admitted us. I had never been back, but had heard that the wealthy Mr. Carlton was still living there. I decided to call, using Miss Carol Bayes as my introduction.

The high handsome door of Mr. Carlton's house was opened to me by a small, slender, golden-haired young man who looked as though he might have strayed out of the Russian ballet. He was, in fact, the most faunlike young man I had ever seen outside of it. He could have been the young Nijinsky himself. And as the faun at that. He had slanting light blue eyes, and a sensitive feminine mouth. It was midday when I called, but he wore a very beautiful golden silk dressing gown, with a jade green silk scarf, matching the dragons on the gown, tucked in at the neck. I began addressing him in French, but he drawled in English, with an air of the utmost boredom, "You can talk English. I don't know a *word* of French. If you want Mr. Carlton he's not here, but you can see the collection."

"Thanks," I said. "I hoped I might. I've never met Mr. Carlton—I was brought here by Miss Carol Bayes ten years ago. He was in Cannes then."

"He's there now."

He stood back, and I entered. He took a catalogue from a side table and handed it to me.

"Will you come up?" he said, wearily.

He sounded so bored and dreary that I felt constrained to say, as I followed him up the stairs, "I hope I'm not being an infernal nuisance—"

He smiled, wanly. "Not unless you want to *talk* about the beastly things."

I said, startled, "You don't like them?"

"I can't *bear* them! I don't know what they're all *about*. Like that frightful person Epstein. It's a wonderful family, Stein."

I stared at him, my hackles rising. He drawled on, like a naughty child who is determined to say the forbidden thing.

"There's Gert and there's Ep and there's Ein—"

"Don't bother to finish," I said sharply, "I know that one."

We had come into the big studio room with its deep windows overlooking the river. A number of wood carvings stood on pedestals around the walls as I had remembered them, and on a black-lacquered table in the middle of the room was a tall Adam-and-Eve statuette in sycamore, with the most beautiful grain and polish. The nude figure of the woman melted into that of the man, who stood behind her; her head was turned against his shoulder; the arms of both hung loosely at their sides; it was as though she leaned against him, relaxed, secure; and the tall male figure was carved with a curious tenderness. The whole thing, though highly stylized, was imbued with feeling. I liked the sensuous rhythm of their arms and the woman's hair completed by her legs flowing away into the base of the tree from which they both sprang. I remembered it from before, but now it meant more to me. Much more.

"It was over in a corner by the window last time," I said.

"I *know!* It's only recently we've had the beastly thing out in the middle of the room. It's Graham's favorite." His voice was petulant.

I turned to him with interest now.

"Why do you dislike Brenovska's work so much?"

"It's such frightful affec*ta*tion." He dragged out the third syllable complainingly.

"I don't agree with you," I said, "but assuming for the sake of argument you are right, what's wrong with affectation? If it comes to that, all stylization is affectation—a deliberate artificiality. When the result is aesthetically satisfying the end justifies the means, wouldn't you say?"

"I don't find the end aesthetically satisfying," he drawled, in his bored voice. "I find it perfectly frightful. Like Epstein's revolting Genesis, and Gaudier-Brezska's beastly Imp."

"I would agree with you about those two things," I said, "though in general I admire both Epstein and Brezska enormously. But I suppose you like only the classical—Mike Angelo and Donatello and Cellini and Verrocchio—"

He replied devastatingly, "I can't bear *any* of them! It's all so *use*less! Like all the pictures cluttering up all the galleries—thousands of them, all over the world." He smiled, suddenly—a singularly engaging smile. "You think I'm doing an act, don't you? Graham thinks I do it to be shocking when I go on like this. But it all seems to me so *silly* painting pictures and making statues. What's the *good* of it?"

"What's the good of a poem, or a concerto, if it comes to that? Or can't you bear music and poetry either?"

"I'm very fond of both, as it happens."

"But what utilitarian purpose do they serve?"

He gave me an odd look from his soft, slanting eyes with their shaded lids.

"Would you say the purpose of art is to illuminate life?" he demanded.

"I would."

"Well, then!"

His smile now was mocking. He continued in his bored voice, "But I can't see that anything in this room illuminates anything! Art for art's sake! You'd think people would have something better to do, wouldn't you? But don't mind me. Enjoy your Brenovskas. Take your time."

He pulled some yellow tulips, elaborately arranged with blue iris and beech leaves in a large copper bowl, into what he evidently considered a more satisfactory composition, then turned to go. At the door he looked back, smiling faintly.

"What part of London do you come from?"

"Greenwich. Are you a Londoner, too?"

"You can tell by my accent, can't you? My *common* accent, Graham calls it. I was born in Clapham. Kleppem, dear."

"One has to be born somewhere," I said. I added, "Mr. Carlton sounds a bit of a snob."

"He leans over backward in trying to prove that he isn't! You know what I mean. Makes a point of being jolly with working-class people to put them at their ease. He'd never go on like that with anyone of his own class—he'd be thought very rude if he did—as I tell him. He never realizes how *patronizing* he is."

"What does Mr. Carlton do? Or doesn't he?"

"He doesn't. He patronizes the arts, gourmet restaurants, and talented young men. Ballet dancers, dress designers, interior decorators."

"At a guess I'd say you belong to the first category."

"You'd say wrong. The nearest I ever get to the ballet is when Graham gives me a ticket. I don't much care for it, anyhow. All those tights and codpieces, you know. And the ballerinas poised on their points and cocking their legs. So *silly*. When I go I shut my eyes and listen to the music. Can't stand all that jigging about when they're playing Brahms' Fourth. An outrage I call it! I don't do anything artistic. I just skivvy for dear Graham. He calls me his secretary because it sounds better. I cook for him and his boy friends when he eats at home, and wash the dishes afterwards, and press his clothes and clean his shoes and push the Hoover about."

"And arrange the flowers?" I was being a little malicious, but he gave me a quick look and smiled.

"Yes, I do the flowers, though he never likes the way I do them. He says I have no imagination and arrange them like a suburban housewife. I like doing them, though. I'd like to work in a flower shop. My favorite dream is that I take Graham his coffee one morning and find he's died in his sleep and left me a few hundred pounds. Then I'd start a flower shop. In London, not here. I hate Paris. It's so artificial."

He was being willfully provocative, I thought, but I didn't rise to it. He trailed out and I went around looking at the Brenovskas. I stood a long time in front of the Adam and Eve. It did illumine life, I thought. Poems had been written, whole novels had been written, to say with every kind of elaboration what those simple lines carved out of the trunk of a tree said with such immediacy. It was merely a matter of choosing your medium, I thought—words, paint, wood, stone. Poetry, painting, sculpture, music, it was all the expression of humanity's groping to elucidate the eternal mysteries of truth and beauty, to get at some meaning in the business of living—all the loving and suffering and struggling that went into it. What, I wondered, had a man like Brenovska, an artist like Brenovska, to do with a woman like Carol Bayes? Or was there more to her than the inequalities of our relationship permitted me to see?

As I stood in front of the Adam and Eve, and walked around it, there impinged upon my reverie the smell of coffee, and then a little later the sound of music. I knew nothing about music, but this music was strong and clear with the strength and clarity of a peal of bells or water running over stones, and when the melody entered and ebbed and re-entered, it had a morning sweetness, a cool sweetness, and gradually I found myself listening to it. When it stopped, which it did abruptly, without any crescendos or diminuendos, the young man came back into the room.

"I hope the music doesn't worry you. I won't put on another record if it does."

"I like it," I told him, adding, "I'm not what's called musical, though."

"Thank goodness for that," he drawled. "I can't bear musical people. They go *on* about it so. I just play a movement of Handel's Water Music, or something from one of the Brandenburg Concertos, in the mornings and late at night, to cheer myself up. I prefer Bach to Handel, really. Would you like some coffee?"

I thanked him, and he stood aside for me to enter his room. It was a small room with pale green-painted walls, long brocaded satin curtains in some soft peach color, white furniture picked out with gilt, a great many brocade and satin cushions piled on a divan covered with dull green velvet, the whole length of one wall lined halfway with books, flowers everywhere—blue iris, hothouse white lilac, pink tulips, beech leaves arranged in masses—old flower prints in gilt frames, a good deal of very charming bric-a-brac, rose-brocaded lampshades on electric candles, a very fine glass chandelier, an exquisite Venetian mirror. The coffee was set out on a low round table drawn up to the divan, and I saw that he had already placed two cups and plates. He waved me to a brocaded armchair and seated himself on the divan and began pouring the coffee from a handsome cream-and-gold coffeepot which matched the cups.

"You have some nice things," I said, picking up one of the cups and examining it.

"This set is Meissner. Graham bought it for me on one of his German holidays—to make up for not taking me with him. He hasn't taken me the last few years. He says I cramp his style. I'd much sooner he went without me and brought me things. Do help yourself to *croissants*." He waved a slim hand at the pile of *croissants* and a dish of butter. On the little finger of the right hand he wore an enormous lapis-lazuli ring.

We exchanged the usual preliminary biographical notes. His name was Lee Morton. Not that Lee was his real name, he said. He was christened Charles, but he was always called Charlie and he couldn't bear it; he didn't mind Charles, but felt it wasn't "right" for him, so when he got away from home he decided to be merely Lee. He was of lower middle-class family, the only child of middle-aged parents for whom he had not much affection—"I can never feel I've anything to do with them," he said. "It all seems so unlikely, somehow." His parents, apparently, were as baffled by what they had produced as though a changeling had been foisted on them. Mr. Morton, in fact, was thoroughly put out by the fact that at an age when other boys were playing football and "rugger" young Charlie was what he called mooning about reading poetry. His mother decided that he was "artistic"; his father that he was "sissy."

"He was always telling me that I ought to have been a girl—it was the most insulting thing he could think of to say, and it used to make him mad when I agreed with him and said I wished I had been, then I could wear dresses and put ribbons in my hair! There was a frantic row one day when he came home and caught me embroidering a teacloth—it was one my mother had begun, but she did it so badly and I took it over from her. In my father's eyes it was sheer depravity for his son to be doing anything like that. I left home soon after that."

He'd gone straight from the elementary school to a job in the gents' outfitting department of a local store, having failed to secure a scholarship for a secondary school, and at sixteen, after the big row with his father, he left home and worked in a gents' outfitters in town. Mr. Carlton came in one day and bought some expensive silk ties. He took the golden-haired young assistant to dinner that evening. A month later he took him to Paris. He was seventeen then. That was eight years ago. He went to England occasionally and his mother came to meet him in town; he never went home. He had kept on his cheap little basement room in Chelsea when he had gone off with Graham, and used it when he went to London. He had his mother to tea there, and he took her to matinees, and bought her the odd blouse and bunch of flowers; he was fond of her, in a vague sort of way, I gathered; as he said, she had, after all, stood by him. It amused him that she always referred to him as being a bachelor. "Of course you being a bachelor," she would say, looking around his basement, "you can manage in one room."

His face assumed a curious expression while he talked of her, half ironic, half rueful. He had a little picture of her in a silver frame on top of his bookshelves. When, later, I was looking at his books, he took it down and showed it to me. I saw then where he got his almond-shaped eyes from and his girlish mouth. "She's rather pretty," I said, with sincerity. "Yes," he said, "I suppose she is." He looked at the picture for a moment when I handed it back to him. "Poor thing," he said.

"She's probably happy enough," I suggested.

"No," he said. "It's an unhappy marriage. He doesn't drink or ill-treat her or anything. I don't think he's unfaithful, even.

It's just that they don't manage to make each other happy. If they had I might have been different. I don't know."

"Married or single, human beings don't seem to manage to be very happy," I said. "Did you ever meet a really happy person?"

"Yes. Graham. He manages it by being completely hard and never becoming emotionally involved with anyone. He has enough money to live exactly as he likes, have whatever he wants—even the people he wants. He's never loved anyone in his life."

"Have you?"

"Yes. Always the wrong people. The kind who don't love back, though they like having people in love with them because it flatters them and gives them a sense of power. They love to be able to say, carelessly, "Of course so-and-so's *mad* about me!" They go on doing it, even when they're old and *no* one's mad about them. It becomes a habit with them, poor dears."

He smiled suddenly, the half-rueful half-ironic smile.

"Well, no one's mad about me, and I'd like someone to be, and I'd like to be mad about someone, but I'm not. Every New Year's Eve the joybells ring in another year of sleeping alone, and I get so *bored* with it!"

It was the beginning of our friendship. We went around a good deal together, and I suppose people talked, but that worried neither of us. What I liked so enormously about that young man seven years younger than myself was his complete honesty. He was honest even with himself. He seemed quite incapable of self-deception. He told me once, "Of course I'm a parasite preying upon a parasite."

"Not preying," I protested. "You work for Graham."

"It's all quite futile, though. Pointless. The only thing which can be said for my existence is that if I were dead my mother would be that much lonelier and unhappier. Graham is actually less parasitic on society than I am—he is at least a patron of the arts. Because he helps artists a good deal you might even say he does contribute to society—at second hand. Whereas I make no contribution at all."

"You at least have the grace to acknowledge the fact!"

"But don't you see that that makes it much worse? If I had no vestige of conscience about it it wouldn't matter. Then at least I wouldn't be sinning against the light. But as I have a conscience that's exactly what I am doing, and I go on doing it because I haven't the guts to change an easy life for a hard one."

"You wear your sackcloth and ashes with a difference," I assured him.

"Naturally," he said, with his charming, rueful smile. "I have taste!"

9

I HUNG ON in Paris, when I was all set to go back to London, because Lee insisted that it was "important" I should meet Graham.

"He'll buy something of yours," he said. "Whether he likes it or not he'll buy something, as an investment. In case you should be a success one day and command high prices. He doesn't need any more investments, but he likes the feeling of having them, more and more of them—it makes him feel safe, and powerful. To give him his due, he doesn't sell the things he really likes. He hasn't sold a single Brenovska. He's not holding them in the hope of their commanding a bigger price in a few years. He thinks they're more likely to decline than increase. He'll buy something of yours for sure, and give you a high price for it—a thousand francs is nothing to him, and you might as well spoil the Egyptians."

A thousand francs meant a lot to me; it was ten pounds at that time. It would take me to England and leave me with enough to live on for a couple of months. It was important, all right, that I should meet Mr. Carlton. But I wanted to meet him for another reason—because he had known Brenovska. I'd got no picture of Brenovska from Carol Bayes; he had been her lover, and she hadn't been able to see him any other way. I wanted to know about him as an artist, and as a man other than a lover.

I lived around in Paris those last few months as I had always done. Lee had me do a drawing of him—he would give it to his mother on his next visit as a present from Paris, he said—and insisted on paying me five hundred francs for it. He gave me a suit of Graham's which he swore he would never wear again, and paid for it to be altered to fit me—Graham was my height, it seemed, but broader—as well he might be, considering the expensive food he stuffed into himself twice a day all over Europe, Lee said. He wanted to fit me out with socks and shirts from his employer's wardrobe, and showed me the piles of everything, a great deal of it unworn, in a huge fitted wardrobe, and in a long glass case like a shop showcase. But still I felt I could not steal from Mr. Graham Carlton. It would serve me well enough if he just gave me a thousand francs for something. When I refused to budge from this, Lee went out and bought me a couple of shirts and half a dozen pairs of socks, all of which I badly needed.

"You see what you cost me by being so obstinate," he grumbled. "You're always telling me about fleecing rich tourists, so I don't see why you have to be so particular about old Graham."

I couldn't bring myself to tell him that it had something to do with the fact that Graham Carlton had been the friend and patron of Josef Brenovska. I murmured something about feeling I couldn't pinch a man's shirts and then meet him socially. Lee gave me one of his odd looks and I knew that he knew I was making excuses, but I let it go. The truth was that I could hardly account to myself for the intensity of feeling I had about anything to do with Brenovska as an artist. The worst thing I knew about Carol was the fact that she had referred to the limewood figure as a "nice little thing" and said that its creator "showed promise."

In June Graham came back from the Riviera, and Lee wanted that I should take a selection of my figures along to the Ile St. Louis apartment. I protested that I was not a commercial traveler, and that it was bad enough hawking odd things around the cafés; let Mr. Carlton come to my place. I couldn't lug big things like Daphne and Morning about, anyhow. Lee said that Graham would never climb all those stairs up to my attic, or if he did would be in such a temper when he got to the top that he wouldn't be interested in anything I had to show him. We compromised by Lee sulkily going off with my smaller stuff in a taxi, so that, as he said, it could never be said that I had demeaned myself by going around to Graham's apartment like a commercial traveler. He would clear a space in his own room and set the things out and Graham could inspect them at leisure, and then we could all three meet in the American bar of the Coupole. If Graham liked any of the things he would tell me so, said Lee, and make an offer; and if he didn't we'd just have a few drinks and some polite conversation—"about art and life in capital letters, ever so cultural," and no one would be any the worse off; except Graham, who would pay for the drinks.

I never minded Lee's occasional irritabilities and sulks. He was a devoted and loyal friend, and we understood each other. For all his self-sufficiency there was something lost and lonely in him, the need to come close to some human being in mental and emotional intimacy. For a few months he had been lifted out of loneliness by Graham Carlton, but the illusion of closeness had been destroyed by Graham's essential coldness of heart. He never admitted this in so many words, but it was to be read between the lines of all that he did say, and for all his affection for me I felt that he never "went out" to me as he once had to Graham, and at the very point at which I would begin to feel that we were close he would be suddenly withdrawn, as though he had gone inside himself and closed a door. He could be difficult and tiresome, but never in any way which affected his fundamental integrity.

When I met Graham Carlton I realized immediately that I knew him very well by sight. He was the tall, gray, distinguished-looking man I had often seen in the Coupole Bar, either in the company of effeminate smart young men, or elegant not-so-young women; or as the center of lively, obviously amusing mixed parties at the Flore, which had a literary reputation at that time; or alone at the Select, his cold gray eyes searching the tables on the terrace or roving along the bar, where doubtful youths of all types and all nationalities hung about at all hours. That evening he had with him, besides Lee, an attractive red-haired woman dressed in purple and wearing a small round feather hat of the same color. She was of very striking appearance, with wide eyes and a high forehead and a rather large mouth upon which she used a lipstick that was too scarlet but which on her was somehow permissible. It was a good face, I thought, intelligent and full of character, not young—fortyish, perhaps—but all the better for that, I thought, because the fine webs of lines under the eyes, and the vertical lines between the brows and in the cheeks added to its interest. It was a strong face, but the eyes and the mouth suggested kindness.

I came up and Lee introduced me to Mr. Carlton, who in turn introduced me to the lady—Mrs. Shelmerley. I brightened, as one does in an introduction in which the name is familiar, and inquired if she was by any chance Helen Shelmerley, the painter. She smiled and replied that she was. I was able to tell her that I had recently visited her exhibition at the Lucien Gallery.

"That's fine," she said, then added, still smiling, "At least I hope it's fine and not an embarrassment to you?"

She had a pleasantly low voice, and her accent reminded me that she was American. It was one of the better American voices, the unobtrusive accent adding to its attractiveness. She was altogether attractive, both her appearance and personality, and instinctively I liked her.

I told her, "I hope it doesn't sound patronizing or raise any feminist hackles if I say I thought your work remarkably strong for a woman?"

She laughed, and I approved the strong even teeth. "I take the comment as characteristically male condescension," she said, good-humoredly.

"What women artists are there—of any importance?" I challenged her, but I also laughed, because it didn't much matter what we said; I felt she was my sort of person—the first I had ever met.

"Not many. But there are also not many male artists of any importance." She turned to our host. "Wouldn't you agree, Graham?"

"Oh, my dear," he said, "don't make me take sides! I never generalize. So far as I'm concerned there are only individuals, anyhow. I loathe both sexes in the mass and all their works. I like your work, and Mr. Rowse's and Brenovska's, and outside of the Italian Primitives, which amuse me, very little else among the visual arts." He turned to me. "What may I order you?"

Before I could reply, Lee, who had been looking more bored than usual, drawled, "At five to sex in an American bar he always drinks a dry martini."

Graham raised his eyebrows. "Really, Lee!" he murmured.

Lee giggled. He was a little tight.

"Really, Lee," he echoed, "what a common little boy you are!"

The cold gray eyes still held mine inquiringly.

"I would like a dry martini, please," I said.

Graham gave the order and indicated the champagne bottle upside down in the bucket on our table.

"You can make it a half this time," he told the waiter, then addressed himself to me again.

"I thought you would like to meet my old friend Mrs.

Shelmerley both as a fellow artist and because of your interest in Brenovska. Helen probably knows more about him than anyone living."

I asked her, eagerly, "Did you know him?"

"He was my first husband. We ran away together when I was eighteen and he was twenty-two. We were married in London, and we lived in a horrible room in Soho." She smiled ruefully. "He called it living down to his level. I hated it. But he hated all the alternatives."

"I can sympathize with you both," I said, "but more with him!"

The white-coated waiter brought the half-bottle of champagne and the dry martini.

"You two should go into a Brenovska huddle together sometime," Lee said, in his most bored voice. He got up. "I must be getting along. Half past sex. Be an angel, Tom, and pilot me through the swing door. Swing doors can be so complicated at times."

He smiled sweetly at Mrs. Shelmerley.

" 'Bye, Helen. Be a good girl."

She smiled at him, affectionately.

"I'm sorry you're going," she said. "Call me up soon and we'll have lunch and go to a concert."

"You're a poppet," said Lee. " 'Bye, Graham. Be seeing you."

"Unfortunately," Mr. Carlton murmured.

Lee swayed a little as he moved away from the table. I went with him to the swing door and bundled him through. Outside on the terrace I asked him, "Are you all right? Shall I get you a taxi?"

He laid a hand on my arm and smiled his half-ironic half-rueful smile.

"Taxis don't take you to the end of the night. You go there on your own little tottering tootsies and crawl back on all fours."

I said severely, "You're tight. Why don't you go home to bed?"

"Don't be such an old auntie! Of course I'm tight. After pouring all that expensive liquor down my gullet at the expense of His Nibs I ought to be! I'm tight, and with luck I shall be tighter. Tighter still and tighter. 'Tis a consummation devoutly to be wished. Hamlet. Go back to your cultural conversation with the grownups and leave little Charlie to the big black night —that coal-black mammy of mine."

He swayed down the terrace and out onto the boulevard and was lost in the promenading crowd. I went back into the bar and rejoined Carlton and Mrs. Shelmerley at the table.

"I'm afraid Lee's canned," I said. "I suppose he's all right wandering about on his own?"

"He won't be alone long," Graham said drily.

"Oh well," I said.

"Precisely. Lee showed me some of your work. It was good of you to leave it with us. I wondered if you'd consider selling the Negro dancer? I like it enormously. It reminds me of a colored girl who's having a success at L'Ange Noir just now."

I said only, "I'm glad you like that piece. Sometimes an idea comes off, and that one did."

"Had you thought what you wanted for it?"

"As much as I can get."

"You put me in a difficult position. Whatever I offer you, you might get more from someone else."

"Or less," I said.

"Precisely. Would five thousand francs seem an insulting or a fair price to you?"

"Five thousand francs is fifty pounds," I said. "It's more than I've had in my life. It's a fortune! Whether it's too much or too little I've no idea, but I should find it an extremely useful sum."

"How amusingly frank you are! Let's call it a deal, then. I'll leave it to Lee to arrange for you—he does fulfill the function of secretary occasionally. Have you ever tackled anything big?"

"Look," I said, "to be a sculptor in wood you need two things—to be able to buy good seasoned wood, and a proper workbench. So far, a good deal of the time I've never had a room, let alone a proper workbench! And I've only been able to afford small pieces of wood. With the money from you I intend to go to London and get a sizable room and a bench and a six-foot tree trunk—lime, if I can get it. Then I'll really make something."

I was excited, and I suppose I showed it, for his light eyes regarded me curiously; reflectively.

"Why London?" he asked.

"Because I can get a job there—a real job, not just dish-washing or touting. I'll get a job in a commercial art studio or the art department of an advertising agency. I came to Paris because I wanted to be free, but I've had fourteen years of being free—to starve. I'd like to eat for a change, and work. Really work. Then you'll see!"

"I shall be very interested to see. I should like to see your work shown at a good London gallery. I like your whole approach—the translation you bring to your work without floundering in a quagmire of abstractions. But as to eating we might inaugurate the new regime by going and have a good dinner now, the three of us—if you're free. . . ."

"I'm so free," I said, lightheaded on two dry martinis on an empty stomach, "that my belly is rattling round like the wind-on-the-heath brother!"

He gave me an odd look, then called for *l'addition*. What he paid for drinks would have kept me for a week—in comfort at that.

"Let's go, then," he said.

We went by taxi to a small restaurant on the Place Dauphine on the Ile de la Cité, a low-ceilinged place with windows at either end, facing one way onto the river and the other onto the little square dark with chestnut trees. One of those unpretentious-looking places which nevertheless cater to gourmets. Paris is full of them. They are always very plain inside; people go there to eat, not to admire expensive decoration. You don't pay for hothouse flowers and prancing waiters in such places; the prices are high, but what you pay for is fine food finely cooked. This place was like that, plain to the point of austerity, long tables, faded red leather benches running along the nondescript walls, and the only flowers a bunch of something on the bar counter as you go in. Madame sat high-busted, tightly corseted, black-clad, in the traditional manner, at the receipt of custom by the till at the end of the bar. We got a table in the window at the river end. I don't remember now what we ate because I was lightheaded when we went in and even lighterheaded when we came out—lightheaded but with a rich warm feeling in my belly, as though it had closed in gratefully upon everything it needed for comfort and strength. It was quite a new feeling, but it was fine.

The occasion had importance because it got Graham Carlton interested in Tom Rowse, and Tom Rowse interested in Helen

Shelmerley. Not in Helen Shelmerley the painter but in Brenovska's widow. Carol Bayes had never interested me in that connection, despite the fact that Brenovska had slept with her and idealized her in what was for me the most beautiful thing he had created. She had been an *affaire*, and an attractive model. This woman with the red hair and white skin and the strong intelligent face was the one he had married. I did not want to talk art with Mr. Graham Carlton—not even my own art. I wanted to talk Brenovska with his widow—who was also an artist, and one whose work commanded my respect.

I asked her eagerly, "What was he like to look at?"

She smiled. "Rather beautiful, in an odd sort of Slav fashion—dark hair and eyes and high cheekbones. Medium height and build. What was remarkable about him was his zest and vitality. Sparks seemed to fly from him. He brought passion to everything he did, whether it was working or playing, loving or quarreling. He was fierce and tender, violent and gentle. He could be so angry, and so gay. Even in his black moods you felt the fires banked up, smoldering just below the surface. The black moods came when the work didn't go well, and when we quarreled." She sighed. "He was difficult. He could be so sweet and so maddening. He had such a hatred of money. It was an obsession with him, and it made life very difficult."

"It's money that makes life difficult," I suggested, "not the objection to it."

"There are people who don't use money," Graham said carelessly. "Royalty and tramps."

"I'm on Brenovska's side," I said, "and Blake's. Money is the curse of art and the enemy of Christianity."

"But five thousand francs enables you to go to England, get a room, a workbench, materials . . ." Graham's smile was ironic.

"The curse lies in the fact that whether I am able to do the work I want depends on laying hands on those five thousand francs," I pointed out.

"You want art state-subsidized?"

"I want the state abolished, and money with it!"

Carlton laughed, but I saw her eyes kindle with interest.

"The state is a great evil, I guess. Wasn't it William Morris who said that the less people were governed the better?"

"*News from Nowhere*," I told her.

"You are an anarchist?" she asked, and her tone approved.

"Yes, ma'am. But not anti-Christ. Only anti the blaspheming Christians." I was a little drunk; drunk enough not to mind what I said, but not so drunk I didn't know what I said.

"Money propagates war and death," I went on, cupping the great brandy globe in my two hands, and breathing the powerful bouquet of it in like a flower. "Between lovers and between nations."

I felt full of prophetic fire, poetic genius. I swung the brandy around in my glass. "This," I declared, "is the authentic prophetic spirit."

"What do you prophesy?" she asked, smiling.

"Woe," I said. "A piteous sleep, a piteous dream. Can a poet doubt the visions of Jehovah?"

"You speak in riddles," she mocked me.

"So did Jesus. So did Blake." I was suddenly wildly excited, filled with urgent longing to be out under the stars, seeing them through the shadowy trees along the river and reflected in the dark water. I wanted to take her by the hand, the white-skinned woman with the flaming hair who had lain under Brenovska in the darkness of the nights, however much she might have fought him in the hard white studio northlight of the days; I wanted to rush with her through a darkness lightning-slashed by the flame of imagination. Talk about the visionary gleam, and intimations of immortality!

"Intimations," I said, "are all that are ever vouchsafed us! God had an intimation of mortality and created Man. Man has intimations of immortality and creates God in his own image. The creative impulse is God." I banged the table and glared at them both. "Can you doubt it?"

Graham giggled nervously, and murmured, "When a man bangs on the table I never dream of doubting anything." He called for the bill.

Helen smiled. "All the same—*in vino veritas!*"

"Blake wasn't drunk when he declared that art was the tree of life and science the tree of death," I reminded her. "And the only difference between Tom Rowse drunk and Tom Rowse sober," I continued, still glaring, "is that with enough drink in him he can lay his tongue round the words he's short of sober."

About noon the next day Lee came around in a taxi bringing back all my stuff—all except the Negro Girl Dancing which

Carlton had bought. He also brought me a wad of notes—five thousand francs. He had dark rings under his eyes and looked pale and a little puffy about the gills. He saw me looking at him and said quickly, "Yes, I know, I look frightful. I feel it!"

"Was it worth it?" I asked.

"Does one ever know?" His voice was weary and he went over and lay flat on my bed. "The things we do to keep on living!" He groaned slightly.

"I'm sorry," I said. "I'd help if I could. But I've a fair-sized hangover myself. It's the last I'll be having in Paris for some time—I'm off as soon as I can get all my big stuff crated up and its shipment arranged for. By the end of the week, I hope."

"In a hurry, aren't you?"

"I'm fourteen years late."

"Oh, I know! I know! It's always later than you think. Oh, well! You can have my Chelsea room if it's any use to you. Till Christmas, anyhow. The other people in the house are all the kind that get along the best they can, so you'd find the atmosphere sympathetic. It might tide you over for a bit. You could just about get a workbench in there if you didn't mind being congested."

I assured him that if I had a workbench I wouldn't mind anything, and I very gratefully accepted the offer. It seems there can be avalanches of good fortune as well as of bad. I had the feeling of owing everything to Brenovska. If I hadn't had the compulsion to go and look at his work again, before leaving Paris, I wouldn't have met Lee or Carlton, I wouldn't have sold the little figure, I wouldn't be going back to England. I wouldn't have met Helen Shelmerley, either, but the significance of that I had yet to realize. If the world's a stage, as far as Tom Rowse was concerned she still waited in the wings.

I got all my arrangements made according to plan, and Helen and Lee came to see me off the next evening at the Gare St. Lazare. We had a few drinks at the station and were all a bit "on," and the train nearly went out without me, because laughing so much we didn't hear the guard blow on his little tin trumpet. I don't know now what we laughed about; perhaps it was only that we felt gay and *en accord*. We all kissed each other on both cheeks. We agreed to meet in London. Life seemed suddenly rich and full, and that skinny old scarecrow Tom Rowse seemed to be moving already through the centrally heated corridors of success. I had fifty pounds; I was wearing a Savile Row suit—true it wasn't made for me, but it fitted me near enough—I had a furnished room awaiting me in London, and I was being waved off on the next stage of my promising career by two good-looking and intelligent and charming friends, one of whom was both a distinguished artist and a charming woman. Her perfume and the brief touch of her cheek, warm, soft against mine, remained, curiously, with me all the way to Dieppe—until the effects of the Pernods had worn off, in fact.

When the Newhaven Heights loomed up, blessedly green and white, blessedly English, through the gray drizzle of an English summer morning, she receded into the background, with the whole memory of the Paris decade. In a few weeks I could not recollect precisely what she looked like, beyond that she had red hair and a pale skin and was somehow striking; but I couldn't have made a memory sketch of her. Whereas Lee remained so vividly with me that often when I was working in the basement I would hear his weary-dreary drawl, or a sudden droll, caustic remark, half ironic, half rueful, as clearly as though he were there. But then it was, after all, his room, inhabited by his personality. Whereas she—the rich American who had for a short time been married to a poor and then unrecognized Polish artist, who had become even richer by her second marriage—so Lee said—what after all was I to Hecuba, or Hecuba to me?

10

LEE'S CHELSEA room was very different from his Paris one. A divan with a nondescript faded cover occupied the length of one wall; a shabby blue-painted chest-of-drawers in need of repainting stood against the wall opposite the window; a cupboard occupied one side of the fireplace wall, where a gas fire was fitted into the fireplace, and at the other side of the gas fire was a curtained-off washbasin. Books flanked the window, were piled up on the chest-of-drawers and on the narrow mantelpiece, and a shelf of them ran along the wall above the bed. There were dirty cotton curtains of some striped material from which the colors had long since faded—they had once, perhaps, been striped in red and white. Only the presence of the books saved the room from squalor. Not that I cared. It was a room, rent-free, and there was space for a trestle table which I bought cheap in the King's Road. Once the table was in it was possible to move around the table and no more, and the door would only partially open, making it necessary to edge around it to get into the room.

The stairs which led from the front door down to the basement were bare and dirty, with the grime of ages deeply ingrained into corners. A narrow passage led one way out into the area where the dustbins lived, and the other way to a flight of steps up to a square of walled garden so overhung by a plane tree that not even grass would grow in it. It smelled powerfully of tom-cats, but it was handy for pegging out a bit of washing in, and Miss Hopkins put her baby out there to sleep in its shabby second-hand pram. There was such a complication of pipes along the ceiling of the passage, and so many meters along the walls, that the general effect was like that of a ship's engine room. There was a windowless bathroom with an alarming-looking geyser and a rusty bath down in this dungeon, and conveniently opposite the door of Lee's room a W.C. with a window into the basement.

Miss Hopkins and her baby occupied the room at the foot of the stairs. She was so plain and sedate and matter-of-fact that it was difficult to imagine her foregoing formalities and getting herself a baby without first making sure of a husband. She did copy-typing and her machine spattered away all day and often far into the night. She had such an air of efficiency and self-sufficiency that I thought at first she must be one of those emancipated pioneer women who cherish the right to motherhood without benefit of marriage. But later on she told me her story, and it seemed it was the man and not she who had resisted the idea of marriage and she had been "very upset." She still saw him, occasionally—he paid the "maintenance" fairly regularly—but had "nothing to do with him—not after the way he let me down."

I said, puzzled, "But you said he was against marriage all along?"

"So he was, but he promised me it would be all right. Else I wouldn't have gone with him. I'm not a fool."

She was sensible, it seemed, even in passion, and when trouble came upon her, sensible in that too. For anyone who had no objection to dullness—and plenty haven't—she would have made a very good wife. She was industrious, and she kept her room, herself and her baby very neat and clean. She took the baby regularly to a welfare clinic and it flourished exceedingly. It was fat and pink and plain, and so well behaved that but for the pram and the daily line of napkins in the garden you would hardly know there was a baby in the house.

Miss Hopkins was very censorious of Miss Naylor who lived on the first floor, and had no visible means of support—unless you counted a wide circle of men friends—or acquaintances—with one of whom she arrived home after midnight most nights of the week. Miss Naylor never got up till past midday, and then "slopped about," as Miss Hopkins defined it, in a dressing gown until about six, when she dressed herself up very smartly, with blue fox furs thrown over her shoulders, and yellow hair fluffed out under hats frivolous with feathers and veils, and went out. Miss Naylor could be heard singing in the bath in the afternoons when Miss Hopkins was spattering industriously away on her typewriter. It was vaguely understood that Miss Naylor worked at a nightclub, though in what capacity was never defined. She was a pretty, smiling, friendly creature, but Miss Hopkins despised her.

"She's so untidy," she said. "And she uses such awful cheap scent."

"If that's all you have against her it's not much," I suggested.

Miss Hopkins regarded me solemnly behind her spectacles.

"Oh, but it is," she assured me. "That sort of thing stamps you."

"As what?" I couldn't help asking her.

"As common, of course."

"Is that a crime?"

She flushed slightly. "You know quite well what I mean. Everyone is liable to make mistakes, but there's no need to be common."

"Would you say that I was common? You can be frank."

"Of course you're not. You're educated."

"I left school at fourteen."

"All the same—you're gentlemanly."

"And you're ladylike?"

"I hope so. I try to be."

"I see."

Jesus, was he gentlemanly, and his Jewish mother ladylike?

Was Jesus gentle, or did He
Give any marks of gentility?

But the house wasn't entirely given over to spinsters of varying degrees of respectability. In the room across from me was an elderly widow who disapproved of the sedate Miss Hopkins—who was after all an unmarried mother—and the glamorous Miss Naylor—in her opinion "no better than she ought to be"—equally. I had not long been her neighbor before she confided to me that she had lost her husband—"poor Hilley" as she invariably referred to him—only a few months ago. She was not, however, downcast; on the contrary, after a few conversations with her I got the impression that she had bloomed since her bereavement, for poor Hilley, it seemed, had been a great "drag" on her, being always in poor health. So that when he "passed away" it had been, as she ingenuously said, "all for the best." She had sold part of her home and moved with the rest into the basement room, crowding into it furniture which had originally occupied twice the space.

When I had been in the house a few weeks she invited me in to give her my opinion of a picture which her husband had always believed to be a Morland. He had always intended getting expert advice about it, she said, and being as I was "an artist of sorts" she would like my opinion. Although I assured her that my opinion would be worthless she badgered me into inspecting the oil painting—a very dirty yellow-and-brown affair, so dark that it was extremely difficult to make out the subject. She had it, moreover, propped up among a great clutter of furniture, pictures, bric-a-brac, in the darkest corner of the room. I was aware that she stood unnecessarily close to me while I bent forward to peer at the cracking canvas. I edged a little away and she suddenly clutched my arm, gave a kind of gasp, and swayed, then lurched against me. I grabbed her and she sagged, but still clung. Fortunately there was a chair nearby and I dumped her into it; she remained motionless, limp, her eyes closed. But she had a good color, and I wasn't convinced. I went along to Miss Hopkins's room but she wasn't in. I then went upstairs to find someone.

When I reached the top of the stairs the front door opened and young Mrs. Tanswell came in carrying a shopping bag and a bunch of yellow roses. I knew her by name and by sight, but until then had no more than passed the time of day with her. She and her husband occupied a flat on the first floor, and were always referred to by Miss Kent, the housekeeper, a kind of concierge and rent collector in one, as "our better-class tenants" because they had a whole flat whereas everyone else had only a single room. Mr. Tanswell was a commercial traveler—ladies' dresses, Miss Kent said—and was away a good deal. I had had glimpses of him—stockily built, red-faced, a hubby man, a pubby man, such as prop up the saloon bars of town pubs all over England. Miss Kent described him as "very jolly" and Miss Hopkins considered him "coarse."

Mrs. Tanswell was saleswoman at a small West End dress-shop, and the word generally used to describe her was "glamorous." She was twenty-six or so, small, slim, and with that kind of dull gold hair that has streaks of brightness in it. She wore it sitting on her shoulders, where its straightness curled over like a wave rolling in to a shore. She parted it on one side and the heavy side of it curved against the line of her cheek and when her head was lowered swung out and hid her face tantalizingly. She had high cheekbones and singularly beautiful dark blue eyes. I suppose she modeled herself on Tallulah Bankhead—certainly she greatly admired that vivacious exponent of sex-appeal. For me she had the same essential quality: it was in the fall of her hair, the high cheekboned curves of her lovely heart-shaped face, and in something indefinable in her figure. She was given to wearing black suits beautifully tailored, with straight narrow skirts, and with them white blouses which fastened at the throat so that her head on its small neck seemed to rise out of the whiteness like a flower on a stalk, with the dull gold hair like downward-curling petals. She had a small slightly discontented mouth, the lips beautifully shaped but a little thin. Her whole expression was a little hard, suggestive of a smoldering restlessness, of something just below the surface that could break out in passion or rage, but which was now sullenly held in check.

Until the day I came up from the basement seeking first-aid for Mrs. Hilley I had never had more than brief, disturbing glimpses of her. Suddenly coming face to face with her like that I almost cried out with joy and relief. It was as though I had not known how intensely I had longed for just such an encounter. There was something about the narrow shoulders in the tailored black, something about the fall and curve of the straight gold hair, something in the smoldering eyes and discontented mouth—something which added up to that shock of pleasure which is produced by the impact of unexpected beauty. Only the purely aesthetic impact does nothing to the blood, and she did everything to mine.

There was no sweetness in her face; there was unhappiness in it, hardness, selfishness, bitterness, and a latent sensuality—like a portrait of one of Botticelli's beautiful, shallow Florentine youths—and yet it seemed to me the most beautiful face I had ever seen, including the many beautiful faces I had gazed at in paintings and in films. Her image had moved restlessly in my blood since I had first glimpsed her, then suddenly there she was, letting herself into the grimy hall, letting the sunshine of the shabby street in with her, and coming face to face with her like that she seemed the very arrowhead of love, and with all the heart's wild unreason I loved her, all in a blinding confusion of excitement and delight—while I babbled of Mrs. Hilley fainting down below.

Young Mrs. Tanswell laughed. "Did she invite you in to see her Morland?"

I grinned, and she added, "Another friend Mr. Morton let his room to some time ago was so unnerved after being asked to give his opinion on the Morland that he moved up to the attic where the rain came through the skylight but where he had the whole floor to himself. I'll go down. Perhaps you'd better wait here."

She put her laden shopping bag down, then picked it up again. "I'll take it in," she said, "and the flowers."

She went the few steps along the passage to the door of her flat, and I followed her and took the bag from her while she opened her handbag and extracted the key and inserted it in the lock. The door opened into a shabby, untidy living room. She went in and laid the roses on a table cluttered with women's magazines and some used tea-things on a tray. I waited at the door and she said, carelessly, "Do come in."

I went in and stood the bag on the floor, by the table.

She went on. "I'll just pop down and pretend to take her seriously about coming over faintified, as she calls it, then perhaps we could have a drink together—if Bill hasn't swiped it all."

"Thanks," I said. I added, "Perhaps you'd better explain that I'm no hand with faintified ladies, any more than my predecessor."

She laughed and went out, promising not to be long.

I don't know how long she was gone, but I seemed to wait a long time in that ugly room which even the disorder she had created in it could not make personal. Even the roses were somehow quenched by that impersonal drabness. I went over and stood by the window looking down into the garden where no flowers bloomed. A curious irrational anger smoldered in me because she had me wait in this place she shared with this Bill person—there was his blackened pipe on the mantelpiece, a raincoat of his on a peg on the back of the door, and presently if we had a drink here it would be by the grace and favor of his not having swiped it all.

By the time she came back I had worked myself into a suppressed fury. She was laughing and saying something about Mrs. Hilley, and for all she knew I had her in my arms, but she didn't know. I wasn't listening to what she said, only waiting a chance to cut in on her and say with a violence that startled her, "Let's get out of here and have a drink on neutral territory. Let's go across to the Six Bells."

"Not the Bells," she said. "It would cause too much talk. They all know Bill's away just now. Let's go to the Pier."

"Anywhere out of here," I said, and then, "Who are 'they'?"

"All the people in this house, to begin with."

I let it pass, but I knew that Miss Hopkins never went into a pub, not even with a gentleman, and that Miss Naylor always went straight to her nightclub, and Miss Kent prided herself on never touching a drop, and Mrs. Hilley though she liked pubs disliked the Bells for some reason.

She picked the roses up and carried them through into the kitchen saying that she would see to them when she got back.

We went out into the evening sunshine and walked down the shabby street and crossed the King's Road, and continued down to the Embankment. She asked me about my work; she had already heard from Miss Kent that I was a sculptor and had been living in Paris. I told her I was starting a job next week in a commercial art studio, and somehow we got onto fashion-designing, in which she was interested. She had done a little, she said. She would like to have been a mannequin but of course she wasn't tall enough. She adored clothes, she said. I thought the word extravagant but let it pass. She asked me was I married, and when I said no asked me had I ever been. When I again said no she remarked that I no doubt found safety in numbers. I thought the remark vulgar but I let it pass. I let everything pass, because it didn't matter what she said—not that night. Not for a time. Though even that night I like to think there was one thing I wouldn't have stood for. The one thing she did eventually—disastrously—say.

It was early and the Pier was empty when we arrived, so we got a corner seat. We were still there when the place filled up.

She didn't drink much. She was the kind that makes a drink last. At first I was disappointed, wanting her to drink, to talk, to melt to me. Then I discovered that a little drink went a long way with her, and on the second gin she was quite willing to talk about her marriage, and what a bore Bill was, so hearty, and always telling the same dirty stories over and over again until you could scream, and never wanting to go to a theatre or cinema, and how life with him was one long pub-crawl, and how of course there was nothing between them except friendship and hadn't been for years—how really their marriage was all over almost before it had begun, as you might say, five years ago.

Naturally I asked her why in that case she had married him.

"Case of have to," she said.

"You mean you were expecting a child?"

"Unfortunately. Of course if I'd known then what I know now—"

"Is the child away at school?"

She looked startled.

"The child? Oh, that. Oh, it came to nothing." Then after a moment. "A miscarriage, you know."

I asked her what had attracted her to him in the first place.

She shrugged. "I was only a kid. What does one know at seventeen?"

I was about to say that there seemed to be some misunderstanding somewhere, that I had understood her to say she was twenty-six and had been married five years, but in the split second in which there was that debate in my mind as to whether I would say it or let it pass it became too late to say it, because she changed the subject and began telling me an involved story about how the roses she had brought in had been given her at work that morning by the husband of a customer, and how she had not dared to walk out of the shop with them in case Madame walked in, and so another girl had taken care of them for her and they had met for a cup of coffee at Charley's in the King's Road and the friend had handed them over there. I didn't quite see why the wife of the donor should be expected to walk in, or if she had done so why she should have suspected that the roses came from her husband, nor did I see why the girl friend couldn't have delivered them to the house if she had to take them; it all seemed a great rigmarole to me, but being of no importance not worth trying to sort out. It was a silly, boring story, but she looked lovely telling it, with her golden wing of hair falling about her face. Every now and then she would throw the wing back impatiently with a small fine hand, and look at me with her beautiful candid eyes, which of course were not candid at all, which I realized even then. I think I did realize everything about her in that first evening, but I thrust it all into the background, deliberately. Nothing mattered, because she was both the bow of burning gold and all the arrows of desire. But all of them. Pat Johns had said when I finally fell in love the heart would have its reasons that reason knew nothing of, and by God she was right.

We stayed a long time in the Pier and then went out to eat. I left the choice of place to her. She told me of a restaurant in the King's Road where, she said, the food was good; she warned me that it was expensive, but I had five pounds on me and I didn't care if we spent the lot, and we damn near did, what with a bottle of wine and liqueurs. She knew a bit about food and wine, I noticed, and wondered whom she'd learned it from. Hardly from Bill, I thought. She didn't drink much of the wine, but when we left the restaurant she had all she could carry—perhaps rather more than.

Anyhow she took it for granted I was going into the flat with her, and was astonished when I firmly refused, adding that she was coming down into my cellar or there was nothing doing. She protested that Miss Hopkins and Mrs. Hilley would hear us; I retorted that that was up to her; personally, I said, I wasn't the rowdy kind. She was put out; no one had ever talked to her like that, it seemed. She was on her dignity when we got into the hall and said, "Well, good night. Thanks for the evening," but I grabbed her by the wrist and said "Oh, come on," and pulled her down the stairs after me.

I thought that once the door of my room had closed on us I would be down on her like a wolf on the fold, but when that fiercely longed-for moment came everything was immediately different, and just to have her lying there on my bed seemed most wonderful and peace in itself. I knew then that, clandestine like that, taking advantage of Bill's absence, whispering in case anyone heard, sneaking about on creaking stairs and getting her back to her own place before it was light, wasn't the way I wanted it. If I had been the lover she had expected that night perhaps—I have sometimes thought—she wouldn't have gone on with me; or anyhow not for long. As it was, in my adoration, I was something different, and she was fascinated—"intrigued" was the word she used.

She told me to call her Tansy; everyone at work did. Her name was Gladys, which she couldn't bear. Tansy was a silly name, too, if it came to that, she said, but it was better than Gladys. I told her I thought Tansy was a lovely flower name, but she hadn't realized it was a flower. She was "intrigued" when I told her it was golden like herself. But when I showed her some a week later in Battersea Park she thought it ugly, and the bitter-sweet pungency of its leaves crushed in her fingers horrible. Now she declared she would never like being called Tansy again and was glad Bill called her Gladys. I asked her, savagely, what the hell it mattered what Bill called her. She said I was jealous and stupid. We were only a week old and quarreling already. We walked together in the bright warm June sunshine, week-old lovers, with the river sparkling on one side of us and a herbaceous border gay with all the bright clear colors of summer on the other, and we had half of the day and the whole of the night before us, yet we spoke daggers to each other, and one of us at least was utterly miserable.

The whole business of her marriage had to be dragged up again. Why did she stay with Bill if he was such a bore and a boozer, I demanded. Then she flew to his defense. Bill was worth ten of me. He was decent; he loved her; he was her best friend; we couldn't all be so blasted artistic and intellectual—thank God! Why *shouldn't* she stay with him? What had I to offer? Bill gave her security; Bill was gentle and kind, etc., etc. We sat on a seat and the river flowed shining below us, and there was a scent of summer flowers, and Tansy looked so beautiful in a flowery silk dress that clung to her small lovely breasts and her slim lovely thighs, and there was such blackness in us both. She sat with her head down, the wing of hair hiding her face, and I felt her as cut off from me as though she were at the other side of the river, and a dreadful bitter silence fell on us. With that incident the whole pattern of our relationship was formulated.

We made it up, of course. I apologized, without being clear what it was, exactly, I was supposed to be sorry for having said, and that too, was part of the pattern.

I encouraged Miss Kent to talk about her better-class tenants, which out of her great admiration for them she was always glad to do. She "did" all the rooms; the service, such as it was, was included in the rent. She banged a worn-out carpet sweeper up and down the threadbare carpets and followed it with a process she called "flicking" a duster around. In this intimate association with all the tenants' rooms she was thus intimately associated with their lives. She herself was elderly, kindly, and platitudinous. Her favorite axioms were that kind hearts are more than coronets and that it takes all sorts to make a world. When it rained she declared, invariably, that it would "do more good than we shall," and any mention of cold hands always brought forth the exclamation about warm hearts. She was a great old dear, and a great old bore.

Out of curiosity I asked her, a few days after my night out with Tansy, "What is Mr. Tanswell like?"

"Oh, very pleasant," she assured me. "Very ordinary, of course, compared with her, but very pleasant. Always ready with a joke, and openhearted as they make them. Thinks the world of her, of course, but being married to a commercial traveler can't be much fun—you might as well not be married at all. It's dull for her when he's home, too, for he's the kind that when he's home he likes to stay home."

"I suppose they go to a pub occasionally?" I said carelessly.

"Very rarely. He likes to sit home and listen to the wireless. She has a better time, really, when he's away, going to the pictures twice a week with Miss Hopkins, and dancing with Mr. Gifford—Mr. Morton's friend that had his room for a time. Mr. Gifford works for the B.B.C. He's more her style, really, being young and lively. Not but what Mr. Tanswell isn't very nice, but he's not much at home. Marriage is a gamble, isn't it? Excuse me asking, but have you ever been married, Mr. Rowse?"

"No," I assured her, "I never have."

"I have. Though I don't go under my married name on account of me having left him twenty years and more ago, it being ambigamous on his part. I was very upset at the time, but time heals all wounds. But marriage is a kind of lucky-dip, if you ask me—you don't know what you're picking, and when you've had your dip and unwrapped your surprise-packet it's nothing much, as often as not. You're better off single, really, as I always say to Mr. Morton. You're so right, Mrs. Kent, he always says. He calls me Mrs. Kent knowing I've been married. I must say I can't see *him* as anyone's hubby, can you?"

I agreed that I couldn't. I wondered what he had made of Tansy, and wrote to ask him. He replied promptly, on Graham's elegant embossed notepaper:

My dear Tom,

I was glad to have your news. I'm glad you feel at home in my basement, and hope you find my bed comfortable—for all purposes. But you and your arrows of desire! She, anyhow, has never heard of Bill Blake. Or of old Bott and his Florentine youths. I suppose she's attractive if you like them a cross between Bankhead and Dietrich. Garbo's more my style. I daresay Tansy has s.a. for even Graham thought her rather fetching; must be the Florentine youth touch. Gifford fell for her first go. She told me she liked his "Oxford accent," and that he "danced divinely." I suppose what she falls for in you is the romantic idea of you as an artist. She's looking for what she doesn't get in her bore of a husband, but he represents security for her, and as he's away a good deal she can take the maximum from him and give the minimum.

Give me Gwen Naylor any time. Good honest old tart. Pinch her Rubens behind for me, bless her! And give my love to old Kent—she's a decent old troll. Why don't you carve a head of Ma Hilley looking like a lecherous gargoyle? Do be careful of those arrows—one of them might have a poison-head or turn into a boomerang, or anything. Hope I don't sound auntyish, but Gifford wrote me the same sort of letter about this sex-appeal-Susie when he went to live there, and now he's all bitter because she Doesn't Really Love him, and presently it'll be your turn, and it's such a bore.

There's a lovely Bach concert here at the Châtelet Théâtre on Sunday—three Brandenburgs in one program, and I am asking Helen to come with me. She took me to dinner at the Boeuf à la Mode the other night—wonderful food, everything à la some-

thing, ever so classy and expensive. She sent you her love, which is more than you deserve, flinging your spirit "all awhirl into the bosom of a girl," in that fin de siècle *fashion. If you had to fall for a female woman why couldn't it have been Helen? For one thing she is deliciously rich, and for another she's quite taken with you. Gladys Tanswell can't hold a candle to her—which is a silly expression, but you know what I mean.*

Graham has your hideous statue in his sitting room, and it's much admired by English, French and American intellectuals assorted. You'll be fashionable yet. Graham thinks you're a second Brenovska. I wouldn't be surprised, but you'd better make more money than he ever did, or you'll finish up as an also-ran in the Tanswell stakes, with Tony Gifford.

L.

But it wouldn't have mattered to me if Lee or anyone else had declared that this girl was Jezebel, Messalina, and Queen Thamar, all rolled into one. When she was in a good mood she was a good companion, gay and easily amused, and with a childlike capacity for enjoying anything and everything; then I adored her this side idolatry. I'd feel then that she was essentially my sort of person, and that she was good for me, balancing my seriousness, and enabling me to relax from my various preoccupations with the problems of art and life. At other times, when it would seem to be impossible to say or do anything to please her, and she would seem hostile to everything I was and stood for, I would feel I knew what Faustus felt in his damnation, when he cried, "This is hell, and I am part of it!"

Perhaps our extremes of mood, the ease with which we inhabited both heaven and hell, made us the same kind of people despite the lack of intellectual companionship. During the bad times I would think, wrily, that we had nothing in common, mentally and emotionally, that there was nothing between us but a compelling sexual attraction, natural on my part, odd on hers. In the good times I would ask myself what really is meant by nothing in common? Wasn't a mutual sexual attraction the most powerful thing two human beings could have in common, a bounty-of-God beyond comparison with the sterility of shared intellectual interests? What was between us was vital and living. When all the highfalutin stuff is cut out, what is life but the flow of blood? What do people mean by the "merely physical"? The physical cannot be mere. The warm animal life flowing in our veins is the essence of our being. Destroy the physical and you destroy all—all poetry, all passion, all intellect. We live in our bodies. Blake said it in *Heaven and Hell* when he vigorously declared "Energy is the only life and is from the Body," and "The lust of the goat is the bounty of God."

What, really, did it matter that the day we went to the Victoria and Albert Museum, and I gazed with fascination and delight at wood carvings of saints and angels and apostles, Tansy was bored, that the French 15th-century Angel Gabriel, painted and gilded, but its color so graciously faded as to be no longer an offense against the oak in which it is so exquisitely carved, was for her merely a worm-eaten religious figure in a glass case, and the finely wrought detail of a Grinling Gibbons relief worth no more than a brief disinterested glance? I hadn't really expected her to be interested—why should she be?—and her boredom neither surprised nor disappointed me. I had what I wanted—a quick look around to discover what was there, so that when I went back alone, to linger and to study, as I had at Chartres, I would know what to look for and where to find it.

None of the arts interested her; music, poetry, painting, sculpture, literature, meant nothing to her. She read a good deal of light popular fiction on the way to and from work; it wasn't trash, exactly, but also it had no pretenses to being literature. She never bought a book; she borrowed her books where she bought her toothpaste and aspirin; as often as not she did not know the authors of the books she read, even when she "raved" about them. She liked the theatre, provided it wasn't serious; she liked amusing well-dressed revues, and spectacular musicals with romantic love stories—she was "mad about" Mr. Ivor Novello and his productions—and next to him Mr. Noel Coward and his works. She did not so much love the cinema as take it for granted as part of a normal life. She was almost an authority on American and English film stars, both male and female. Gifford took her to an occasional French film, but she found them too realistic, and by not knowing the language she felt herself cheated by the subtitles—which of course she was. She was of her generation and did not think it in the least odd that when anyone said "There's a picture I want to see," a film was meant, not a painting; nor odd that whereas stars were once heavenly bodies they were now more commonly Hollywood ones. By art she understood the summer exhibition at Burlington House. She "went religiously" every year to the Royal Academy, she told me. I don't know why "religiously." Perhaps this annual patronage, in alliance with weekly or bi-weekly visits to the pictures that move, is a form of religion. She liked dancing but was not interested in dancing as an art, and was impatient when I said I did not consider the jigging about and walking about, belly to belly, of the Western idea of dancing anything but what Huxley had called back in the twenties "the imitative copulative article," and nothing whatever to do with the ancient art of the dance.

I knew she went to dancing places and to cinemas with young Gifford, and I did not mind; what I did mind was her lying about it. I assured her that I did not mind and that she could always tell me.

"Why should I mind?" I protested.

"You despise him—you despise everyone who isn't an artist or an intellectual—you despise me in your heart!"

I could only say, helplessly, "I am sorry you think that. The fact remains that not being a film addict I don't feel the need to act up to the pictures and register a jealousy or any other emotion I don't feel. If I thought you were in love with Gifford I would be as jealous as Othello, but since you assure me you are not in love with him, and that you are in love with me, why should I be jealous?"

"How can you believe me if I am such a liar?" she demanded, with a spurious bitterness she frequently assumed.

"I believe the evidence," I told her. "You can be so sweet."

It was true. In the good times she would put such a spell upon me. I would get the feeling I could hold her in my arms forever, or "die upon a kiss." Then I would think that if only I could keep her happy I could keep her all sweetness and gentleness like that; in happiness she would bloom; she needed the warmth of all that money can buy for feminine delight; if I could take her to expensive restaurants where she could eat and drink delicious things and gaze at beautifully gowned women, elegantly dressed men; if I could heap her with flowers and jewelry and furs and clothes and exquisite perfumes—all the riches of the rue Faubourg St. Honoré in fact. If, in short, I could keep her in luxury. She would insist that she didn't want luxury, only "nice things," only not a mean scraping—and saving—existence.

"Then why did you choose Bill Tanswell for a husband and

Tom Rowse for a lover," I asked her, "since we're neither of us likely ever to be able to give you what you want?"

"Bill is quite likely to be making several thousand a year in a few years' time, and you might suddenly get your name in the papers and be talked about and make money like the one there was all the fuss about not long ago—the one that did that awful Christ——"

"But why wait for Bill or me to make good when you could have someone really rich now, if you took a little trouble?"

"People like my boss, I suppose you mean, fat and bald! My trouble is I never fall for people with money. I'm too sentimental, and it doesn't pay. You have to be hard to get the people with money."

"You mean you have not to be emotionally involved?"

"I mean," she said impatiently, "you haven't got to be sloppy and romantic and care about people."

That she liked the idea of romantic love—by which she meant nothing more complicated than the passionate closeup of the screen, going just that step further not permitted to be depicted even in an A film—I was well aware, but as to the caring I was skeptic. She afforded no evidences of it. When she was happy she purred like a cat and was sweet—as a purring cat is sweet. It makes you feel good when a cat purrs under your caressing hand, and when it rubs its beautiful silky body against your legs in rapturous anticipation of milk or fish, but unless you are very sentimental indeed you don't deceive yourself that the cat is loving you; what it cares for is the pleasant sensation of the caress, or the food in the saucer. But it is a charming animal at such times, not a doubt of it, and tenderness and even love may flow in you for the pretty creature—but that is your affair. More and more I came to think Tansy was like that. I wanted not to blame her. It wasn't her fault if she hadn't it in her to love greatly. You couldn't draw out—or give out—what wasn't there. At what were for her the appropriate moments she would declare that she loved me, but I knew that we didn't understand the same thing by love. Sex she understood, and a kind of demonstrative affection—playful or sentimental according to mood and occasion—and good times together; bedtimes, and the times when I could spend money on her in pubs and bars and restaurants; being happy, she called it. I suppose for her it was happiness, that sense of euphoria produced by good food and enough alcohol to blur the hard edges of every day, and the satisfaction of knowing that at the end of it all there was lovemaking, as it were to round it all off. Her needs were only skin-deep, you might say.

But I would reflect—was it morbidly?—that one could be "happy" in that gay, affectionate, good-time way with anyone who attracted and amused one; with even a tart, if she were good-natured enough. In all the between-times a good-natured tart would care as much; that is to say, as little. And there was this deep need for caring; for being cared for as a vulnerable human being—a human being with a headache, or a bad cold; a human being worried about work or money; a depressed or tired human being; a human being suffering from the frustration which is far more disintegrating to personality than sexual or emotional frustration—the frustration on work. Then there was the need for tenderness, sympathy, patience—in a word, caring. I wasn't asking any more of her than I gave; I did care for her as a person. I worried endlessly about her, both her physical and her material well-being, the awful coughs she got every winter, the fact that she went to work on wet days in silly flimsy little shoes, her coffee-and-bun teashop lunches, the fact that so often vitality would ebb in her as though some spark were used up in her, and she would be listless and "dead" and I wouldn't know whether it was physical or psychological—or both. Whether all her moods and depressions and nerves and unspecified ailments weren't the result of some inner dissatisfaction in her, some unresolved conflict she was unable to communicate.

I suppose the word neurotic applied to her, but I shrank from it; it was something I didn't want to acknowledge; I would fight any idea of it, in her or myself. Whatever the material difficulties, I wanted everything to be right between us, uncomplicated, a normal man and woman in love with each other. I longed to come close to her, protectively, in mental and emotional intimacy, but though she chattered about the girls at work, about her boss, about the customers, the travelers, and the people in the house, I never really felt that she took me intimately into her life, because she talked only of what was unimportant. Concerning what was important and represented a major problem, her relationship to Bill in relation to her relationship with me, she talked not at all. She had a way of making any serious discussion between us impossible, and though I was the victim of her moods of depression and irritability—"nerves" she called it; she insisted that she was something called "highly strung," which meant that she considered herself a great deal more sensitive than most people, including her lover—I felt I knew very little about what really went on in her. In spite of all the love-making I had often the feeling of making no real contact with her, and that act which the yellow-press Sunday papers refer to as "intimacy" could be, I discovered, the most unintimate of all human relations. Carol Bayes had taught me that in the beginning, and it was bitter I should remember it now when I was so wildly in love. Tansy brought out all that I had to give of passion and tenderness; passion she gave back, but of tenderness she appeared to know nothing, except superficially. So that often there was pain and loneliness and despair where there should have been fulfillment and peace and hope.

Yet I don't want to give the impression she was hard; she was all tears and temper and impulsive good-nature. On a Saturday afternoon if Miss Hopkins had a "rush job" of typing she would always go out and do her week-end shopping for her, taking the baby in its pram. Or mind the brat while Miss Hopkins was out delivering or collecting some work. She was fond of kids, she said once, though she'd never wanted to have any. She was certainly good with them. Sometimes I would see her coming along the shabby street with what looked like half the kids of the neighborhood hanging onto her. She seemed as young as they were, laughing and skipping along with them and talking nonsense. In spite of her good clothes, when she was with these street kids she seemed one of them, and she never looked lovelier than at these times. That gamin quality which flashed out of her when with children was something I loved in her, and it made me desperately want to understand those other aspects of her which seemed contradictory and baffling. She was both generous and selfish; giving was a form of self-indulgence for her; she loved spending money, both on herself and others; buying things was fun, giving things was fun; but of giving in the real sense she knew very little. She was, I suppose, the complete materialist.

Her parents kept a combined tobacconist's and sweetshop in Battersea. By marrying the thousand-a-year Bill and moving across the river into Chelsea she had achieved enormous social progress. Her chief criticism of her mother seemed to be that she had "no idea how to dress herself," and of her father that he dropped his aitches and would go about in his shirtsleeves.

"They're all right," she said carelessly, "but not my style." She had a spiv of a brother who made a living out of "the dogs" and what he called the gee-gees. He was a good-looking young man a year or two younger than herself; he dressed loudly and had a cocky conceited manner. He called around occasionally to borrow a pound off her. She always gave it to him. Terry was all right, she assured me, just a bit wild, and he and she, it seemed, were "pals—always were, even as kids." I personally never set eyes on Terry without wanting to knock his block off. He was always smiling, and there was something self-assured and impudent about him, and when I saw them together and Tansy smiling fondly at him while he bragged and boasted and sponged I would get the feeling that she was fundamentally as worthless as he was. I would think despairingly that she had no sense of values, no principles; but just when I had succeeded in hardening my heart against her I would see her with the children again, as much a child as they were, and forgive her everything. Perhaps it really sums her up to say that she had the gaiety of a child, the warmth, the impulsiveness, the unpredictability and the charm—and the hard heart of a child.

Well, but there it was. I had no illusions about her and I loved her. Whether she loved me I don't know; I attracted her, in some odd way; I was romance for her. I planted myself in her nerves and she in mine. Putting the thing at its lowest level I suited her physically, and she me, and that is a very powerful bond between a man and a woman. Flesh is kind and forgives, and subdues the mind. She was nothing, and she was everything. She created at her will a little moony night and silence—stilling the tumult of the world, she the female, the "little tender moon," and I the male giving time and revolution to her space. . . .

II

I STAYED in Lee's room less than a month, for at the end of the month Bill was due home, and I was damned if I was going to be the lover in the basement with old hubby Bill up there on the first floor all tucked up in the same room as Tansy. There was a double divan in the room, but there was also a camp bed, and she swore that he slept on that, and I had to believe her. It was a case of "Lord, I believe; help Thou my unbelief." I hated the whole unsatisfactory bag of tricks. I wanted her to leave Bill and take a room of her own, if she wouldn't come live with me and be my love. When I suggested she should ask Bill to divorce her and that she should then marry me, she was quite indignant. She had no intention of throwing poor old Bill over like that, she declared. He would be heartbroken. She wouldn't dream of hurting him like that. What had I to offer in return for marriage, anyway? She couldn't see me supporting her if she got ill and couldn't work. We always got back to that. As though I were still on the bread line, whereas in fact I was doing very nicely, earning ten pounds a week. Doing very nicely so far as a regular job and earning money were concerned, that is; so far as being a sculptor went I was doing depressingly little, because most evenings I spent with Tansy, and the evenings when she was at the pictures with Miss Hopkins or dancing with Gifford I was too tense with waiting for her and listening for her step on the pavement above me to be able to concentrate to any purpose.

The people at work meant nothing to me; they called me Tom, and I called them Joe, Freddie, Elsie, Mac, and occasionally I had a drink with one or other of them, and they told me things—how their tomatoes were doing, and how one of the kids had the measles, and what they were backing in this that or the other race, and Elsie showed me the jumper she was knitting and asked me did I think it suited her, and so on; I got on with them. They knew I wouldn't stay long because I was a "real artist" and real artists never did stay in commercial work. They were good-natured and kind and ordinary, and they were as unreal for me as the faces that came and went on the screen in the endless succession of films through which I sat with Tansy, holding her hand—for that was an essential part of the romance. They asked me if I was married, and when I said no they made little jokes about escaping so far but being caught in the end. They were all right, only there was no real communication between us.

But except that it provided me with money to spend on Tansy there was no point in my working with them. It could only have point had I been saving money so that for a few months I could work at wood carving without having to worry about the rent and the rest of it. There was no point in my having left Paris if I was going on the way I was. Then Bill's return was imminent and I took a day off from work and went back to Greenwich like a homing pigeon. I went to see my mother before my father came in at midday for his dinner. She had got fat and aged a lot in fourteen years. She cried all over me with joy. Her prayers, it seemed, had been answered, and God had sent the prodigal son back to her. She wanted that I should come back home to live, but I told her I had to get a studio. I gave her a few pounds to spend on herself and left her, promising to come and see her again soon.

When I left her I had an impulse to go and look up old Snell. He still had his workshop down there on the waterfront, my mother had said. Dad saw him sometimes in the pub. He wasn't doing too well, it seemed. He had had some sort of paralytic stroke and walked very dot-and-carry nowadays, and his son hadn't stood by him like he should, so it was hard for him to manage; his family wanted him to give up "the carpentering" and run a little tobacconist's and sweetshop or something of the kind, but he was stubborn about sticking to his own trade. He'd do better of course, my mother added severely, if he did a bit more work. . . .

I found him, as I had seen him so often, leaning up against the door of his workshop, looking at the river, his blue eyes a little misty with his reverie, his mustache as trimly waxed as ever, his stiff collar as white, his hair as untidy. He seemed a little thinner in the face, a little grayish, and his hair and mustache seemed to have tarnished, but when he saw me and grinned and exclaimed, "Well, bless my soul!" it was as though I had parted from him only yesterday. I mumbled something confusedly about turning up again like a bad penny, and he was crying "Sit down, sit down," and waving me to a bench and explaining that the boy would be "back in a jiffy with the beer." When he moved to join me on the form I was shocked to see how one of his legs dragged. He grinned at the look on my face.

"Got a gammy leg now, son, but still get about. How's life been treatin' you?"

"So-so," I said. "I was hanging onto the bread line by the skin of my teeth for fourteen years, but I got a break here and there and managed to knock up a few wood carvings. I actually sold something for fifty quid—that's why I could get back. Got a pukka nine-to-six job now, for the time being—designing show-cards and posters in a commercial art studio."

"Better be arf get yerself taken on at Lister's or some such place—more honest trade."

I explained to him that I had to get some money together so that I could do the work I wanted. I asked him about himself.

"Your son never came into the business after all?"

He shook his head.

"Nope. He wanted something better—jobbing carpentry, he called this. The head of his secondary school said it would be a waste of his education and got him with a firm of engineers—he's a fully fledged pattern-maker there now. It's highly skilled work, mind you. I suppose when you've had a bit of education you can't be expected to be content with the kind of jobs we do here. Ah, here comes young Bert with the beer. Come right in, young feller-me-lad! Did you have to wait while they grew the hops?"

The boy laughed. He was a bright, cheeky-looking lad with that frank open expression which often graces delinquents.

"Fought I'd give yer time to work a first up, guv'nor," he said, winking at me.

"None o' yer lip," Mr. Snell said, and lifted an elbow as though to strike him. The boy ducked away, laughing. I got the feeling that they understood each other. Mr. Snell took an enamel mug down from a shelf behind where we sat and filled it and handed it to me.

I swiped it in a long draught and handed the mug back to him. He refilled it and took a swig at it, then seated himself beside me. Young Bert mooched off to the end of the shed and began planing a length of wood.

"Yep," Mr. Snell went on. "Already fixed up with the engineering firm young Fred was when he has to go and join the blinkin' army, passing himself off as eighteen. Young fool! He was only in it a few months. Then he went back to his apprenticeship. I always hoped he'd come in with me—kind of saw the sign up, you know—J. Snell & Son. Looked good to me in my mind's eye, but you know what old Omar says, 'The little dream men set their hearts upon, turns ashes or it prospers.' Young Fred was earning a good wage be the time I got the stroke, which was just as well, for I had to shut this place up, with no one to carry it on. The boy and his mother would like me to pack it up altogether, but no fear—catch me doling out the packets of Woodbines and the *News of the World*, a blinkin' middle-man, me that's been a master-man all me bloomin' life, direct from producer to consumer! You know what Kropotkin says—"

No, he hadn't changed, and all over again I wished that he had been my father. When I left him I promised to look him up again. It had been fine talking with him.

And fine being back in Greenwich. I'd forgotten just how good it was. The river at Chelsea hadn't that smell of the sea on it, and it was good to see homely-looking people and snotty-nosed kids again instead of all the Chelsea beards and corduroys and art-and-crafty handwoven females. The people sitting about on the shabby grass on the Observatory hill were as ordinary as the people I worked with at the studio, but socially humbler; working-class. I observed with satisfaction that though they littered the hill with their cigarette packets, greasy sandwich wrappings, orange peel, banana skins—bananas had not yet gone out and the great ice-cream era not yet dawned—in the railed-off park where the lawns are smooth and stately with cedars and silver firs, and the herbaceous borders are like the illustrations on seedsmen's catalogs, there they behaved with decorum, putting litter into the receptacles provided, keeping the children in check, and sedately viewing the borders with a speculative air, mentally transferring the general plan to their own back gardens, or observing to each other that fine as the tobacco plants were they were really no better than those they themselves had raised from seed, and how Dad's sweet peas down on the allotment took a lot of beating.

I mooched about on the green hill, wandering up and down its wooded valleys as when I was a boy, and I sat for a while up by the Observatory, looking out over London, right across to the Hampstead Heights, and away to the west where the dome of St. Paul's balanced exactly between the towers of Tower Bridge, and the city was misty with smoke, so that the sunlight came to it filtered, and tall chimneys down by the river belched forth, and the battered old volume of Bill Blake I had so often pored over as a boy on this hill was still in my pocket, and familiar lines ran through my head again, as they hadn't since I arrived back in England's green and pleasant land.

Lo!
The stones are pity, and the bricks well-wrought affections
Enamelled with love and kindness; and the titles engraven gold,

Labour of merciful hands; the beams and rafters are forgiveness
The mortar and cement of the work tears of honesty. . . .

To build such a house of the spirit, to build such a house of love, enameled with love and kindness, the beams and rafters of forgiveness.

And throughout all Eternity
I forgive you, you forgive me.

I began brooding about Tansy. She was angry with me for clearing out of Chelsea; she couldn't see any necessity for it; Bill was coming and going all the time. If I thought she was going to trek all out to Greenwich to see me I was mistaken. All right, I said, come live with me and be my love. She had declared I had the neck of a giraffe to suggest such a thing. She had thought I wouldn't go, that when she got back from work she'd find me in my basement as usual. But I had made arrangements to go, had written to Lee, and told Miss Kent, and got the day off from work, and I left, and did not return.

I got a room without much difficulty, in a dilapidated house in a comedown square looking onto a wasteground that had once been gardens. The room was at the top of the house. It was large, and it contained nothing at all, unless you count the bugs left in the wallpaper. I paid a month's rent and then went out and bought a few secondhand things—a divan bed, a cupboard, a scullery table, a couple of chairs, a washstand complete with crockery, a rag rug. I also bought a large tin of white distemper, a tin of red paint, some brushes, and a builder's trowel for scraping the dirt of ages off the walls. I telephoned Miss Kent where to have my workbench and my crate of tools sent. Then I spent the rest of the day, until it was dark, scraping the walls. The next two or three evenings when I got back from the studio I spent distempering, and then the workbench and tools arrived, and I could be said to have "got straight." I telephoned Tansy at the shop and asked if I could call for her next day after work, it being a Saturday, and take her for a meal, then bring her back to see my studio. She said at first that she didn't know, and told a confused story about something she had promised to do with one of the girls, and in the end she said yes all right. I told her she had better bring some things and stay the week end. She said, "Fancy your luck, don't you?" I said yes, I did, rather.

The first thing I noticed about her when she left the shop was that she was carrying a small suitcase. I waited on the other side of the road for her. She came over to me, unsmiling, and I took the case from her without a word.

"If it's a slum I shall go straight back," she warned me.

"It's a slum all right," I assured her.

"I suppose you think squalor's artistic!"

I knew better than to try to reason with her. Reason was the one thing of which she was supremely incapable. I took her into the nearest pub and bought her a double gin. It went straight to her head, which was fine, because it melted her to me. Also it meant that she wouldn't notice the dirt on the bare boards of the staircase, torn and dirty curtains at the windows, the balconies cluttered with mangles, zinc baths, dustbins, rabbit hutches, junk. My room was clean and bare and scrubbed as a ship. It looked fine with its white walls and red paint. Not a bug left for old times' sake; everything spick and span. I'd scrounged a few things here and there—odds and ends of crockery and cutlery and kitchen things from my mother, and a couple of blankets and old sides-to-middles sheets, and the Chelsea people had found a few things for me, bless them—Miss Kent produced some blue curtains, faded, it's true, "but you'll get some more wear out of them, dear," she said; Mrs. Hilley gave me a white linen tablecloth edged with some lace she'd made herself, hoping, she said, I would use it when she came to tea; Miss Hopkins gave me an old blue divan cover she no longer used; and Gwen Naylor got up early and went out before the shops closed and bought me —surprisingly—a desk lamp with a green shade, one of those snaky things you can bend in all directions. She felt she wanted to give me something useful for my work, she said. There was no plug for it in the room, and I didn't feel I could afford to have one put in just then, so I turned the shade around so that only the green showed and stood the whole contraption on the mantelpiece as an ornament. It bloomed there on its snaky stalk like a Rousseau jungle flower; or so I thought.

I was all shipshape by the time Tansy arrived for the house-warming. I'd put the rag rug down beside the divan so that she needn't step out in the morning on the bare boards, and I'd fixed up a washing-corner behind a screen I'd knocked together myself with a few odd strips of wood and some canvas, so that she could have a bit of privacy. I had to go down two floors to a tap on the landing for water, but I bought a brand-new enamel bucket with a lid for clean water, and I knocked up a small clotheshorse upon which I hung some brand-new towels. I wanted everything to be neat and nice for her. I put the old blue curtains up at the window, with its red-painted woodwork, and I had a red geranium in a pot standing on the sill. I had my workbench, with my tools set out on it, by the window. It all looked fine and dandy.

I kissed Tansy a good deal on the way up so that she wouldn't notice the dirty stairs and landings, and when I opened the door of the room and she stepped into its clean whiteness and brightness she gave an exclamation of appreciative surprise.

"Why," she cried, "it's quite a studio!"

She stood in the middle of the room looking around at everything, smiling, and I looked at her—I never got tired of looking at that lovely heart-shaped face with its high cheekbones and huge eyes. She wore a dark suit and a white blouse, very crisp; she never wore a hat in the summer, and the sun seemed to make a halo of her hair as she stood in the middle of the room. She went over to the window and stood behind the workbench looking down at the trees in the derelict gardens, then reached up and drew the curtains against the afternoon sunshine and came back to me, putting both arms around my neck and pressing close to me.

It doesn't matter what she said. We had our own private language of love. She could be so sweet. My lovely girl! It gave me a quite acute pleasure to see her trim jacket hanging on the back of one of my chairs, her skirt and blouse folded across the seat, and her underwear a small pale pink flurry on the rug, with her shoes and stockings all anyhow beside the little pile. Not just her presence in the room but these small intimate touches constituted the real housewarming.

When we had made love we lay relaxed and at peace, sharing a cigarette, and agreeing that we did not at all dislike the antiseptic smell of distemper, and the oily smell of paint, and feeling the room a haven in which to forget the world, dedicated to love and happiness and peace.

Before we went out we made tea on the gas ring and covered the table with Mrs. Hilley's cloth and set out the crockery, enjoying the transition from lovers to married domesticity. Then I took her out onto the green hill, and we sat on the grass in the mellowing sunshine of late afternoon and watched the barges going up and down the river and feeling the nearness of the sea when the wind touched our foreheads. She sat with her shining head against my shoulder and a hand in mine. Sometimes I would touch her hair with my lips, and there would be a small pressure of her fingers on mine in response, and she would murmur my name, with an endearment. At such times I would feel that she did add tenderness to the bounty we shared. Then I was her dear love, her darling Tom, and I would have the illusion of her being all mine, of there being no world but that which immediately encompassed us, no life but that which we created together through the body's rapture and its afterglow.

I was happy, too, because Tansy liked this place which meant so much to me, and because she was seeing it at its best in bright sunshine. She liked the hot scarlet glow of the geraniums massed around the old yellow walls and along the colonnade of the museum down below, the vivid green lawns of the grounds seeming to flow away into the river. She liked the city with its domes and towers and spires misty in the near distance, and when we got up from the grass and I took her up onto the terrace behind she was fascinated by the Observatory dome, and by the twenty-four-hour clock.

At opening time I walked her down the hill, where lovers lay in the summer-deep grass and in the wooded hollows, and past the pond where children scooted about in little paddle-boats, and through the high iron gates and down toward the river, turning up a passageway behind the old Trafalgar to a little pub with a balcony jutting out over the river. The evening was warm and we stayed there a long time watching the barges and the sunset and the people relaxing over their Saturday night drinks. Presently we walked back, hand in hand, and climbed the stairs to the white-walled eyrie, and laid the table with Mrs. Hilley's cloth again and had a cold meal with a bottle of beer I'd stood in a bucket of water to keep cool, and went to bed while it was still light.

On Sunday we had a late lunch in a small cheap Italian restaurant—not much more than a taxi-drivers' pull-up, but the food was all right, of its kind, and we were too hungry to be fussy, and afterwards I took her back to the hill and walked her away through the sweet-chestnuts to the flower gardens, where we sat elegantly on the lawn in deck chairs for a while listening to the band some distance off, outside the gardens; then we strolled about admiring the rose beds and the herbaceous borders, and I showed her the deer in the wooded enclosure behind, and when it was time we went into the town and attended service in the pub beside the church of St. Alfege. Then I took her to the Ship, where we had more drinks and a snack supper, then with our arms around each other's waists walked back to the place we'd come to think of already as "home," to bed. In the morning we got up early and she made coffee on the gas ring while I shaved behind the screen, and within an hour we were in a bus traveling together to the West End to work, and it was all over for another week.

And that, with variations, was the pattern of our lives for about five years. For I never left Greenwich, and she never left Chelsea—and Bill.

12

I CONTINUED working through that first summer at the commercial studio, because only seeing Tansy at week ends I could work at my bench when I got in, so long as the light held. I wasn't spending so much money, either, with these weekly meetings, so with the regular pay packet could save quite a bit as reserve for when I wasn't earning. I left the studio at the end of August, and Tansy, of course, thought I was what she called "crackers," also in some unformulated fashion unfair to her, though I was still able to pay for everything at the week ends and even occasionally to buy her a little present.

So long as I was working at the commercial studio in the daytime I didn't do much on my own in the evenings. For one thing I felt too jaded, and for another by the time I'd had a meal the light was going and I would have a sense of working against time. I modeled a few things in clay, and carved a few small things from the oddments of wood I'd brought over from Paris. But as soon as I was free of the routine job I went along to Lister's and had the good luck to pick up a beautiful piece of old English oak at a bargain price, because there wasn't enough of it for a commercial purpose and it had been kicking about their yard for a long time. It was exciting to have a sizable piece of wood to work on again, and I got to work on a figure of Eve, naked and unashamed, and every lovely line of her of course was Tansy.

The more the work developed the more I felt I was making a good job of it—that in the subject and the material I was achieving harmony not fully reached before except, perhaps, for the Negro Girl Dancing—though my Eve meant more to me. I got an immense tenderness into the figure, and the taut, nervous, wild-creature grace that was peculiarly Tansy's. She liked watching this likeness of herself emerge from the mass of the wood; that I could make it happen, chipping away, as she called it, seemed to her most wonderful, though as the figure grew and the likeness became less readily recognizable she began to take a dislike to it, deciding that it was crude and clumsy and ugly.

She was always on to me about cultivating Graham Carlton as as a patron—why didn't I "get after him" to buy more of my things? I told her that he probably would, in his own time, but first I had to make them. She asked me what he had bought. I told her, "A little figure of a colored girl I knew in Paris—a dancer."

"A nigger?"

"A Negro girl. She was lovely, and a very sweet person."

"You didn't sleep with her by any chance?"

"That's putting it crudely. I loved her."

She was suddenly flushed and angry. "I think it's disgusting to have an affair with a nigger."

Something rose in me then, too. "Look," I said, "white man, black man, beggarman, thief, we're all God's chillun, and don't you forget it, my girl!"

"I wonder you didn't marry her and have done with it!"

"She didn't want me long, even as a lover."

"What a pity! You might have had some nigger kids."

I had to keep a grip on myself. All the things I had ever let pass of the things she had said—wounding things, stupid things, contemptible things, lying things—seemed to gather in me, whirling round and round in me in increasing momentum. The conversation took place in my room shortly after she arrived one Saturday afternoon. She had arrived in a good mood, and I had been happy because she had shown some real interest in my work—my real work—for the first time.

"If you don't shut up," I said, "I shall hit you."

"You wouldn't do it twice!"

"I hope I wouldn't need to."

She got up from the divan where she had been lying propped up on an elbow, thrust her feet into the high-heeled shoes she had kicked off when she had flung herself down there as soon as she had come in, grabbed her suitcase and made for the door.

"Good-bye!" she said, violently.

I answered her quietly.

"Good-bye," I said. I felt flat and cold. The door slammed and I heard her running down the stairs. I sat down on the divan and picked up a small lace-edged handkerchief she had dropped on the floor. It smelled faintly of gardenias. A small expensive bottle of gardenia perfume had been my last present to her. She liked what she called "good scent," and this gardenia perfume from a small old-fashioned shop in Jermyn Street was her favorite. She always wore it when she came to bed, which I liked, because then for the rest of the week it lingered on my pillow. But now I sat there turning the handkerchief in my fingers, aware of the perfume but finding in it no evocation of "time passed in love's varying delights." My heart was quite hard against her. There had to be a limit to what one was prepared to stand for. There weren't many women, white or colored, of the caliber of Pat Johns, whereas the world was well stocked with Tansies, all sex-appeal and sexiness, and selfishness, and ready-made ideas, and not a shred of principle to cover their spiritual nakedness.

I dropped the handkerchief and got up and took my pipe from the mantelpiece and began filling it. I never smoked it when Tansy was around, as she disliked the smell of it, though I smoked good tobacco; in her company, to please her, I smoked cigarettes, which always seemed to me a little effete.

I smoked leaning against my workbench and looking at Eve, four feet of slender loveliness on her little turntable. I turned her gently around. There was still work to do on her, but she had emerged from the tree whole, complete, and if she was a little coarse-grained, was she not the mother of all living? I smiled at catching myself out in the sudden willing suspension of disbelief. Symbolically, reason amended. I turned Eve around, and puffed on my pipe, and took a gouge and worked on her base, and in my absorption thought no more about Tansy, who had what my mother would have described as "flounced out" on me.

I was so absorbed that I started when the door suddenly

opened; I had heard no steps on the stairs. Tansy stood there looking white and miserable.

"Oh, hullo," I said, "I thought you'd gone."

"Where am I supposed to go? You know damn well I can't go back to Chelsea without looking a fool, having announced I was going away for the week end."

I bit on my pipe and leaned back and looked at Eve through half-closed eyes for a moment before answering. Then I said, carelessly, "I suppose you could have gone to your family!"

"Gay that would have been, wouldn't it?"

She came into the room and sat down on the edge of the divan.

"Why must you be so horrible?" she demanded.

"I don't know about horrible," I said. "At least I don't refer to decent colored folk as niggers. What have you come back for? To apologize?"

"For calling that girl what she is? Why should I?"

I laid aside my pipe. "Tansy," I said, "get out before I throw you out."

She buried her face in her hands and began to cry, her hair falling over her hands—fine slim hands emerging elegantly from white ruffles under the black sleeves of her jacket.

"Don't be so cruel," she wept. "I love you! You know I love you!"

"Is that why you insult a dear friend of mine?"

"I was jealous. I can't bear to think of it."

"You don't have to think of it, but it bears thinking about a damn sight better than you rolling about with beery Bill!"

She flung herself down on the divan and wept more violently than ever, crying over and over again that I was horrible—horrible. . . .

The upshot of it all was that I finally went out and left her to it. I went to the pub by the church and threw back a pint of bitter and a couple of whiskies to chase it, and ate a ham sandwich and slipped one into my pocket in case she should still be there when I got back. Which of course she was, lying on the divan still, and sobbing with small hiccups like a child. The room was in darkness and I switched on the light brutally as I entered. She moaned slightly and covered her face with her hands against the glare. I went over to the mantelpiece and began cleaning out my pipe, scraping round the bowl and knocking it out against the fireplace, very deliberately. I was sadistically determined that the next move should come from her.

Her voice came half smothered from the pillow on the divan. "Tom, won't you forgive me?"

It was the best she could do in the way of apology, I knew. But had she made abject apology I don't know that it would have made any difference. The mind gives assent to forgiveness, but whether the heart forgives—that's another matter. In my heart I don't think I did forgive her, ever. She had meant what she had said; she did not really repent of it; all she repented of was the trouble it had caused between us. She was sorry about that, and she was sorry for herself; perhaps, even, she was sorry for having upset me; but she was not sorry for the offensive thing she had said, which, so far as she was concerned, was true.

When I held her in my arms that night I had a feeling of betrayal—of having betrayed something fine, and I felt bitter and ashamed.

13

THAT WAS the general pattern of our relationship. She came at week ends, except when Bill was home, and sometimes he would be home several week ends in succession, and I would fret and fume and swear to put an end to the unsatisfactory state of affairs, if she wouldn't change them. I'd think sometimes of ending everything and going back to Paris. At other times I'd have fantasies of going to Bill Tanswell and telling him the facts and asking him what he proposed to do about it. Tansy swore that if I did this she would never forgive me. I couldn't see what was so special about old Bill that when it came to a choice between hurting him and hurting me he had always to be the one to be protected—while my own sensibilities had to take their chance with every wind of expediency that blew.

I was full of resentment, but the less I saw of Tansy the more I turned to work, and I turned to it with a kind of savage energy. I got through the winter all right. I had enough money saved out of my commercial-studio wage earning to last me a few months, living carefully, with only one meal a day, and cutting out the spirits at the pub, and smoking a cheap shag instead of John Cotton. Not seeing Tansy sometimes for weeks on end was a saving, too. I went out after work, my own kind of work, in a way I had never done in Paris. After the ten pounds I had laid out on the big piece of oak for Eve I couldn't afford any more big stuff, but I had some small pieces on hand, and I bought a little, and made some nice little boxes with carved lids and took them along to a West End store which always carried a few handcraft things. The buyer, who was a pleasant young woman and knowledgeable, bought them and was interested in some little animals I brought along. It probably impressed her that I wasn't prepared to sell them but had only brought them along to show her; I told her I wanted them for an exhibition, but if she liked them I could probably turn out a few odd pieces between now and Christmas. I got her interested, and I sold her quite a few things in the next three months. She put in a word for me with the Christmas-card department and I turned out some wood engravings—the usual Nativity things, but treated a little differently—which went down well. I didn't want to niggle either with wood engravings or little animals, but I did want to keep busy, and I did want to get some money together so that I needn't take another job, which for me was being bound down upon a rock.

I spent Christmas at home—Tansy being bound down upon the matrimonial rock. It made my mother very happy, and I found myself on drinking terms with my father; that, oddly enough, made my mother happy too. She was anxious that we should be friends. She wanted that I shouldn't be too hard on Dad. He had this little weakness—she meant the drink—but we were none of us perfect. Her loyalty never ceased to astonish me. I suppose she cherished some tender memory of the days when he had been in love with her—or had believed himself to be; what she sometimes wistfully referred to as their "courting days." I didn't mind the old man rotting his guts with booze; people have a right to choose their pleasures; all I cared about was that mother shouldn't suffer on account of his pleasures—and she did, because he drank away money that should have gone into the housekeeping, and he never got the better for drink, only the worse for it—bad-tempered, and even brutal. My mother prayed for him unfailingly, night and morning, but evidently the Almighty was too busy to attend to the matter of keeping Mr. Thomas Rowse, senior, off the drink, which with the mess the world was in by 1934, not to mention the outsize mess it was very clearly heading for, was understandable.

Christmas, in the commonly accepted sense, meant nothing to me. I was all for celebrating the birth of Jesus, even on an arbitrarily fixed date. I would have liked to set aside a day for celebrating the birth of the Lord Gautama, and the Mahatma Gandhi, as well. Goodness and light, truth and beauty, cannot be celebrated too often or with too great honor. But though there was a certain amount of churchgoing by all denominations, and carol singing, I couldn't see that Jesus came very much into the general picture. He seemed to be generally overlooked in the enormous world-wide party being given in his honor. People went about giving each other presents and cards and standing each other drinks, and the manufacturers and shopkeepers did enormously well out of it—the "Christmas trade" they called it, significantly—but I didn't see any mass-conversion to Christianity, even for a day.

Was Jesus born of a Virgin pure
With narrow soul and looks demure?
If He intended to take on sin
The Mother should an harlot been,
Just such a one as Magdalene . . .

O Bill Blake, Bill Blake, O ruddy limbs and flaming hair—how bound down upon the rock of filial duty I was that Christmastide, and how I longed to be back at my workbench if I might not hold my love in my arms.

Well, but it was all over with at last, and Tansy came to me again, the old miseries and splendors were resumed, and the year turned the corner, as years do. Tansy brought me a fine woolen shirt in a loud check of red and green which, she declared, was "just the thing for an artist." It had the authentic Chelsea look all right. I was glad of it, and touched that she had thought of it, and grieved that I had nothing to give her—except my love. Except my love. . . . It hurt her that I had nothing to give her; she wanted to know what I had done with all the money I had earned in the last few months; I ought to be "flush," she said. I told her what was true—that I'd given my mother a couple of quid to get some Christmas fare, and bought her a pair of warm slippers, and stood the old man a few drinks, and I had to leave a little on hand for the rent, and to tide me over till I got some more work in. She criticized me for overspending on my parents, though it was typical of me, she said, always putting other people before her—which considering she had put someone else before me for the whole of Christmas was a bit much. So in spite of the fine shirt we started off with a quarrel. We made it up, and I had the illusion of peace, but neither heart nor mind was deceived.

I went to see the young woman in the crafts department of that West End store again, and she bought a wooden bowl I took along—a lovely bit of walnut I'd brought with me from Paris—and said she was glad to see me again, as a friend of hers who was getting married was wanting a big chest made, with some fine carving in the old English style, and she knew where there was a wonderful piece of cedar wood to be had at a reasonable price, and this friend was willing to buy it if someone could be found to do justice to it, and was it up my street?

It was right up my street, and I was so wildly excited that I went off then and there to look at the piece of cedar. Then I rushed back to start roughing out some designs for the chest itself, and for the carving for the sides, and for the top of the lid. Next day I went along to the Victoria and Albert Museum to renew acquaintance with the fine old 17th-century settle there. It was several days before I realized that no price had been discussed for the job; and also that I couldn't do it in that room at the top of that tall old house. It would be a sweat getting the huge piece of cedar up there, and an even greater sweat getting the finished job down all those stairs. I also realized that I would have to have some money on account in order to live while on the job.

While I was pondering all this and feeling rather worried, Lee turned up—he had waited till Christmas was over, he said, he couldn't *bear* the English Christmas, all that pudding, and the dreadful *jollity*. . . . He *quite* understood why Peter Warlock had committed suicide rather than face another bout of it all. He had come over, he said, to see me, and one or two plays, and to take old Kent for her annual New Year's treat to the Circus at Olympia. "It sets her up for the whole year," he assured me. But there was the familiar malicious glint in his almond-shaped eyes. It did me good to see him. I hadn't realized till then how short I'd been of someone to talk to; really to talk to. It was his first visit to Greenwich and he was greatly taken with it. The waterfront reminded him of Venice, and despite his aversion to the visual arts he wanted to go and look at the Canaletto painting in the Maritime Museum. I took him to the pub by the church and the one overlooking the river, and we dandered about on the terrace up by the Observatory, and mooched among the sweet-chestnuts stretching away to the south, and he told me what was going on in Paris—the moral and aesthetic lowdown as he called it, and I told him what I had been doing, and the problem of how I was to cope with the cedar-wood chest. He immediately agreed that I must have a ground-floor workroom somewhere.

We routed about together and found a big ugly old house standing in a neglected garden, all very obviously comedown, judging by the assorted window curtains which had only one thing in common and that was their griminess. Standing back in the garden a little behind the house was a large dilapidated-looking shed. "The very thing," Lee murmured, "a studio in the garden."

We marched in and examined the place. It was about the size of a largish garage; it had a tiled roof, but some of the tiles were on the slide; the wooden walls were rotting and had already been patched up in places with bits of old linoleum. The doors swung loose on rusty hinges, and we pushed them open and peered inside. It was full of quite indescribable junk—old tins, pieces of rotting fencing, wooden boxes, all of it with the appearance of having been there undisturbed for years.

"You ought to get it for five bob a week," Lee said.

We went to the house and interviewed a slatternly old woman who was completely bewildered by our request, and bewilderment made her suspicious. She would have to ask her husband, she said—they didn't own the place, only rented it and let out rooms, and she didn't know how they stood with the landlord about letting the "garridge." Though of course it was years since it had been used as such. What sort of a shop did we say we wanted it for?

"A workshop," Lee repeated, adding, "This gentleman does carpentry."

"I see," the old girl said dubiously. "If you come back around dinnertime Mr. Tilley will be in then and you can explain to him."

We went back around one and Mr. Tilley proved to be a crony of my old man, and he remembered me from some fraternizing we'd done on Christmas Eve. He was small and seedy-looking, with watery blue eyes, and his manner was at once timid and cunning. He walked over to the garage with us and stood gazing at it speculatively. We could rent it, he said, provided we didn't "muck abaht wiv it; arf a quid a week it would cost, and cheap at that."

"Five bob," said Lee, poking a finger into the rotting wood of the door.

Mr. Tilley's creased and sagging face assumed an expression half aggrieved, half truculent. "Trying to be funny, son?"

"Not in the least. I thought you were! The place is falling to bits, as you can see, and Mr. Rowse will have to spend *pounds* on it. But *pounds!* Then when he goes you'll have a place you can reasonably ask ten bob a week for. You can't expect him to pay you that *and* do it up for you! Five bob a week's all it's worth as it stands—a collapsing old ruin!"

Mr. Tilley looked almost baleful. "It's a very 'andy toolshed, and properly speakin' I got no right to let it at all."

Lee's face was cold and unrelenting. "Exactly! So you're very lucky to get anyone to pay you a brass farthing for it. It'll cost Mr. Rowse pounds just to get the junk carted away. Simply pounds!"

Mr. Tilley raised his hands palms outwards each side of his face and vibrated them, crying, "Vot you vant, eh? Vot you called, eh? Ikey Moses! Vish I might die!"

After his little pantomime he dropped his hands and grinned, revealing three or four widely spaced yellow teeth.

"All right, you win. You can't get blood out of a stone. Being as it's for me old pal Tom Rowse's son—five bob a week, and no monkey tricks."

"But none," said Lee haughtily. "Why should there be?"

I paid a week's rent in advance, with an extra bob for luck money, to seal the transaction amicably. And walked away the possessor of something I had wanted ever since the first evening I visited Miss Carol Bayes—a studio in a garden.

Lee and I worked for a week turning out the junk, which we disposed of in the garden, burning what we could and burying the rest. We patched the roof with a bit of corrugated-iron sheeting we found among the junk, and put in a skylight; and we plugged the walls with bits of old timber. It was a proper shanty-town shack by the time we'd done with it, but we made it weatherproof and when we swept it out we found a good cement floor. All this rough and dirty work Lee tackled as though he had been doing manual work all his life. He sweated like a pig, got sawdust in his honey hair, knocked his beautiful hands about, but gave every appearance of thoroughly enjoying himself. He was also quite remarkably capable.

"How come you're so handy at this kind of odd-jobbery?" I asked.

He gave me one of his odd, ironic glances.

"As the curate said to his bride next morning, I'm glad you think I'm good at it—I taught myself! Really, Tom! Can't any ordinary intelligent person turn a hand to most things?"

"Not hands which spend most of their time making soufflés and arranging flowers," I said curtly.

He took it in good part. He was completely unoffendable. It was one of the many things I liked about him.

We found a haulage man with a horse and cart to move the workbench and the big crate of tools in, then we went off to arrange about delivery of the cedar wood.

At the end of the day Lee took me to dinner at an Italian restaurant in Soho. Over a flask of Chianti we talked this and that and finally got around to Tansy.

"You're a fool, Tom," he said. "She's nothing. Just a body. Everything you say about her confirms it. I say it again—the woman for you is Helen Shelmerley."

"No," I said.

"Why *not?* She's rich, intelligent, talented, and handsome. And gone on you into the bargain. She's also a widow. What more do you want, for God's sake?"

"Someone who needs me."

"And you think Tansy does?"

"More than she knows. She's never had anyone really care about her as a person. They 'fall' for her, and she needs more than that; she needs to be cared for. She needs to be liked as well as loved—made to feel she's more than just a lovely face and body."

"What is there to her, more than that?"

"She has her own qualities."

"For example?"

"Warmth, generosity, and her own kind of courage. Emotionally we're the same kind of people."

Lee smiled ironically and poured more wine.

"When people say that they usually mean they suit each other in bed."

"I mean more than that. We laugh at the same things and are moved by the same things."

Lee held his wineglass in his right hand and looked at it, thoughtfully.

"That you share the ordinary human compassions, I don't doubt—the lowest common denominator. But the big things that move you, Tom, everything you feel about social injustice, religious hypocrisy, your excitement over Blake, and over your creative work—she doesn't begin to be moved by such things, and if you weren't leaning over backwards to try and make a great love out of a physical attraction you'd acknowledge the fact. I don't know why you can't just accept it as that, an *affaire*, instead of trying to trim it all up—kidding yourself. I always find it such a pathetic spectacle—intelligent people deceiving themselves. Making fools of themselves is all it amounts to, really." He sounded inexpressibly bored. "She has charm, of course," he added. "I do admit that. Not that charm is much. Most people have charm, if it comes to that."

"I don't agree with you," I said. "I hold with Voltaire—that charm is a form of genius."

"Make it evil genius and I'll agree with you. People with charm can get away with anything. They're a menace. All charm corrupts. Great charm greatly corrupts. You know it. Why don't you admit it, and that you fell for the charming young Mrs. Tanswell just like everyone else?"

"I do admit it. Initially I did. But it's become much more—"

"You mean you sentimentalize it all—to justify it. Supposing something happened to her—an accident, or some serious illness, so that sex between you was ruled out completely? Would you still love her—as you call it? Would you? Could you really love as your old Bill Blake puts it, without the aid of anything on earth? Don't bother to answer. You like to think so. Naturally. The old *amour-propre* demands it, doesn't it? But you don't know. You can't know."

"There have been heroic loves—selfless loves," I suggested. "Great selfless devotions."

"There have been. I'm even prepared to accept that there are. But it takes more than a Gladys Tanswell to inspire them, don't you think?"

"What makes you sure she's all that ordinary? If I overrate her, don't you think you underrate her? Girls all that ordinary aren't attracted to human oddities like Tom Rowse, surely!"

"On the contrary I think it's quite astonishing how unusual men attract very ordinary women! The wives of great men all remind us—that there's no accounting for human nature. Look at Keats and Fanny Brawne! But you can leave the poets and artists out of it and just look round at the general run of people—at all the wives positively dedicating their lives to eliminating in their husbands' make-up anything the least bit unusual—like the woman in the Rhys Davies story—don't you remember, '*Ordinary* I have tried to make you!' Let them be like everyone else—let them conform! Work on them till every bit of individuality is purged away. 'Improving' them, they call it. I've known wives who have improved their husbands out of all recognition—turned them into tailors' dummies, and something called a 'hubby.' Horrible! Don't tell me Tansy hasn't set out to improve you—you're much tidier than you ever were in Paris! She'll start on your mind next, and tidy that up, and before you know where you are you'll be making lovely realistic sculptures fit for the Royal Academy. What exactly do you get out of a girl like Tansy—apart from beddy-byes with an attractive young woman, which isn't very difficult for a normal man to come by?"

What did I get out of her? All the joy in life, and all the pain. All that flesh and spirit crave for in the loveless nights and the harassed days. But it's not easy to put all that common human experience into words for someone remote by nature from such experience. I said only, "I thought we were assessing what Tansy got out of me?"

"That's easy. The romantic interest of her lover being an artist. It's the next best thing to having him a film star. Than which there is *nothing* more romantic. Nothing. But more importantly, do you think this Hitler person means business? That is to say war?"

"Not if he can get what he wants without it. It's not important."

"What *do* you mean?"

"Balance of power between nations, national territorial ambitions—how can all that claptrap of statesmen be important?"

"Whether we live or die is important—whether hell is let loose in the world or not."

"Nothing lets hell loose quicker than talking about it and thinking about it."

"What's your idea of what is important, then?"

"My idea of what is important? Creation, of course. Everything contained in that. The whole cosmic idea. Order out of chaos. In the Beginning was the Word, and the Word was God."

"Another world war would bust the cosmic idea wide open."

"No," I said violently. "The need to create order out of chaos will persist until the human race returns to the primordial slime. And then it will begin all over again. That's man's immortality. The resurrection of the body and the life everlasting! The primordial slime and the dancing star! The return of eternal Adam to create new heavens and new hells—but heaven or hell to *create!* The angels keep their ancient places—you don't suppose they bat a single wing tip for any upstart earthly dictator?"

"I don't know," Lee murmured. "I hope you're right. I hope the angels stay put when the bombs start falling, but I seem to remember that the original archangel ended up as the devil. . . ."

14

Lee came and went between London and Paris. And the wars came and went. There was the Abyssinian war, and everyone getting hot for or against sanctions against Italy, and jokes about Highly Salacious. But when it came to Spain no jokes came out of that. It looked altogether too much like the dress rehearsal for a major war. Lee, of all people, dragged me, protesting, off to an anarchist meeting. It wasn't that I didn't take sides; I hated the guts of "the gallant Christian gentleman" of Spain as deeply as I loathed his Nazi and Fascist cronies. But I wanted to be left alone with my creative preoccupations, not to have active evil impinge upon it. Lee rated me for adopting what he called an above-the-strife attitude, but the truth was I didn't want Spaniards murdering Spaniards even for an idea. Mass homicide was ugly enough, but mass fratricide seemed one degree worse. Lee was mad with me because I wouldn't sign a petition for the lifting of the arms embargo.

"I don't want *any* of 'em to have arms," I said. "I don't hold with these rough games."

He stormed at me. "That's all very well! Franco's getting all the arms he wants from the Germans and the Italians. All the embargo does is rob the Republican side, and don't tell me they're getting supplied by Russia, because it's not true!"

I told him I didn't care if they were. I wasn't interested in what they got or didn't get. So far as I was concerned there was a third front—the anarchist revolution in Catalonia. I wouldn't mind giving the anarchists five bob toward a machine gun . . . as a gesture. And they could please themselves whether they shot up fellow Spaniards under the Falangist, Republican, or Communist label. Though if I had my way no one would shoot up anyone. Not even for an idea. Not even for the idea of grinding the faces of all politicians in the primordial slime and abolishing all conceptions of the State for good and all, though that was a better idea than most, and one even a place-keeping angel might conceivably bat a wing tip for.

Lee's impassioned partisanship in the Spanish war surprised me as much as his capacity for rough manual labor. Just how much of it was reaction to Graham Carlton's vehement pro-Francoism I couldn't be sure. Mr. Carlton, it seemed in common with many of his class, was pro-Franco—while at the same time being anti-Hitler and anti-Mussolini—because of an immovable conviction that the Republican government was "Red"—that is to say, Communist. And even the palest pink shadow of the common ownership of wealth and the means of production is the shade of death to the possessing classes. Is now and ever shall be; Capitalism without end. Shareholders of the world, unite! You have nothing to lose but your risks, and a world to gain. It was anyhow to Lee's credit that in his anti-Francoism he had got round to the anarchist struggle that was part of and yet deeper than the anti-Fascist struggle in Spain. I suspected Helen Shelmerley's influence, as well as the reaction against Carlton. I had suspected from our conversation in Paris that she was a philosophical anarchist, which it is natural for an artist to be, and it interested but hardly surprised me when Lee said that she was taking the chair for a public meeting organized by old Emma Goldman, "Red Emma," whom she had known in America and who was an old friend of hers. The object of the meeting, Lee explained, was to make known the facts of the anarchist revolution behind the anti-Fascist struggle in Spain.

"It'll be a lovely meeting," he assured me. "Two great old girls like Emma and Helen, and all the East End communists and Mosley boys knuckle-dustering each other at the back of the hall, and all of them against the anarchists—the *wildest* fun! I'm bringing old Naylor along—"

"Naylor?"

He giggled. "It makes her feel all interleckchual, dear, to go to a meeting. She loves it. I took her to one on legalizing abortion last year, and one on voluntary euthanasia the year before, and we've been to any number on sex reform."

"Does sex need reforming?"

"Oh, my dear, you've no *idea* the things people get up to! And there's always the old boy at the back of the hall who gets up at the end and demands whether we want birth control or self-control—*such* fun!"

"Spain will hardly provide such gaiety," I suggested.

"But think of the thrill, the place bristling with invisible machine guns, and real live *señors* on the platform—well, one, anyway, they've been keeping one specially for the meeting."

"I bet he's never been anywhere nearer Spain than Buenos Aires!"

"Well, never mind, he'll have a lovely Spanish name and lovely Spanish black eyes—and there'll be all those fascist-communist black-eyes at the back of the hall, and everyone will be so worked up and we'll all wave pound notes in the air for arms-for-Spain and feel splendid! Afterwards we'll carry old Helen off for a nice din-din somewhere. You'd like to see Helen again, wouldn't you?"

"I'd like it fine," I said, "but couldn't I just meet you and Helen afterwards?"

"Certainly not! You're going to hear Red Emma, Queen of the Anarchists, and like it! Bring Tansy along—it would be good for her."

"She'd hate it. Anyhow she wouldn't come. Besides, what would she and Helen have to say to each other?"

"They'd admire each other's clothes. They could get together on that."

"Not for a whole evening. Besides, after the meeting Helen won't feel like talking clothes. No, we'll keep Tansy out of this."

I said nothing to Tansy about the meeting. It wasn't necessary to do so; the meeting was on a Friday and I was expecting to see her the next day for the week end, anyhow. I met Lee and Gwen Naylor in a pub near the hall, and we had a few drinks before going along. Gwen was all got up like a Wardour Street tart, silver fox furs and all, and the reek of cheap sweet scent all about her was enough to suffocate a horse. Her lashes stood out black and stiff around her big gray eyes, the lids heavily shaded, and a greasy scarlet cupid's bow had been drawn above the short straight line of her upper lip. Large pearl beads roped her smooth white throat, and the coffee-colored lace blouse under her black velvet suit jacket was aglitter with *diamanté*. I thought all over again what a very sweet face she had, in spite of the tartish make-up. She was on her very best behavior, little finger of her gloved hand stuck out elegantly when she lifted her gin-and-it, and listening with a serious expression to the most trivial remarks that fell from Lee's lips and mine. Between whiles she flicked her starry eyelashes at us both and was obviously brimming over with happiness at being in the company of two such intellectual gents, and going off to a political meeting with them for all the world as though she were a member of the intelligentsia herself. She and Lee flirted with each other in a pretty pretense of neither knowing a thing about the private life of the other.

When we were well primed we went along to the hall at the other side of the square. By the entrance blackshirts, communists, anarchists, pacifists, and independent socialists of various denominations were handing out leaflets and hawking their party papers—undersized spotty youths dolled up in the Mosley rig-out complete with jackboots, aggressive-looking communists and socialists with red ties, bearded anarchists, gentle-looking pacifists, all out to build Jerusalem in one form or another in England's green and pleasant land, and all of them as evangelical and sincere as the Salvation Army, and all of them, so far as I was concerned, as putting-off.

People were pouring into the hall, and we only just succeeded in getting seats. The floor and gallery were full, and people were standing along the walls at each side and at the back. The platform was draped with red and black, the anarchist colors, and across the front of the platform a banner carried the slogan *Viva la Fai*. Lee explained that the initials meant Federation of Iberian Anarchists. Gwen smiled and nodded, all aglow.

The meeting, advertised to begin at seven-thirty, started at eight. Then the door at the back of the platform suddenly opened and a procession of people entered, an unhappy-looking little middle-aged man carrying a bunch of papers, a dark handsome young man of Spanish appearance, then a short thickset scowling elderly woman with gray hair and thick glasses, then Helen smiling and looking radiant in her purple dress. There was some scattered uncertain applause as the speakers took their places behind a table covered with a green cloth. Helen seated herself immediately behind the water bottle and glasses set in the center of the table, with Red Emma on her right hand and the Spaniard on the left, and the dim little man at the end. She arranged some papers, murmured something to the queen of the anarchists, who sat glowering ferociously at the audience, and got up amid further, and stronger, applause. She spoke easily and clearly in her slightly throaty voice with its soft American accent; she smiled a little, and her whole manner suggested warmth and sincerity and cordiality. She referred to the long anarchist tradition in Spain, particularly in Catalonia, mentioned the achievements of the anarcho-syndicalists, and indicated that Red Emma, "the veteran anarchist," recently returned from Spain, would give firsthand information of what she had herself seen. She then called upon "our old friend," and sat down amid mild applause.

Then the fun began. "Our old friend" arose to a tumult of clapping, cheers, boos, catcalls. Some rowdies at the back of the hall began singing the *Internationale*, but far from it uniting the human race a young man in a black shirt threw a chair into the midst of the singers, and the fun grew fast and furious. There were cries of "throw them out" and "call the police," and from the platform Red Emma's voice roared that we anarchists had no truck with the police, we anarchists believed in free speech which it was clear our comrades at the back of the hall didn't except for themselves. Helen arose and besought a fair hearing. Her voice was drowned in the uproar. But Red Emma roared on, announcing that she had had fifty years of dealing with mobs and no one could shout her down. And by God, she was right; no one could. I couldn't keep some lines from *The Marriage of Heaven and Hell* out of my mind:

> Rintrah roars, and shakes his fires in the burden'd air;
> Hungry clouds swag on the deep.

I always liked that word "swag." Red Emma's voice swag on the waves of opposition. What she said was no doubt true, and proper to be said, but I could not keep my mind on it. I took out my notebook and made little sketches of Helen—she shifted her position so often she was as good as a model at a *croquis* class. I felt that she was bored with the booming, hammering, inescapable voice, which went on for a solid hour, by which time the opposition had either grown too weary to jeer or had gone out to wet throats parched from heckling. When at last the old war-horse sat down Helen rose and made her appeal for money-for-arms-for-Spain, adopting the tactic popular at that time—the communists were said to have invented it—of asking for five-pound notes first. She got quite a few; some had been "planted," and some were genuine. Then she took only pound notes, and they sprang up thick as weeds after rain, waving wildly in the air. Lee and Gwen both waved them, I noticed. Their faces were flushed with excitement, their eyes bright; they were enjoying themselves hugely. After the ten-shilling notes had been taken there was a general silver collection. I put in five bob. The price of a couple of gins toward a machine gun for Spanish anarchists to spatter away at Spanish Fascists, Republicans, Communists . . . 'ooray!

When the collection was over Helen introduced the seedy-looking little man who gave some semi-inaudible information about the Spanish anarchist organization in London, and about a woman's paper which he called the *Moojers Leebers;* he also announced the date and place of other meetings at which, he said, our-comrade-'ere will speak. Our comrade in the meantime sat scowling mightily. When the little man had finally drooled himself to a standstill and sat down, Helen rose and announced from a slip of paper which had been passed up to her that the collection amounted to two hundred and forty-three pounds eleven shillings, and wouldn't someone make it up to the nice round sum of two hundred and fifty. Someone did. Then she made a bid for three hundred, and after a combination of bullying and coaxing finally succeeded in doing it. She then called upon the Spaniard, recently back from Barcelona. Señor Gonzalez rose smiling and at ease, but his speech was in such strangely accented English that it was almost incomprehensible, though the phrase, "Franco's henchmen" and "hirelings of Moscow, Rome, Berlin, and Burgos" recurred with attendant cheers and boos. He went on for a long time, over forty-five minutes, and the audience was tiring, and some went out. Helen rose for the chairman's closing remarks, but before she could get going the queen of the anarchists rose, elbowed her aside, and began pitching into the audience for its smallness—though the hall was packed—and the paltriness of its three-hundred-pound contribution to the cause for which the Spa-aa-nish people, she yelled at them, were giving their life's blood. "You English people," she abused them, her Eastern European accent vibrating with unutterable contempt, "you think because you give a few miserable pennies you can shake off responsibility like water off the chicken's back. . . ." The audience which had waved its pound and ten-shilling notes in the air, and many of them given twice, sat enchanted under the attack, and when she had finished applauded wildly. Then Helen said her few closing words and it was all over. Lee turned to me flushed and happy.

"She's a marvelous old girl," he said rapturously, and added, "I thought Helen wonderful the way she extorted the money."

Gwen settled her silver foxes and smiled over his shoulder.

"Did you enjoy it, Mr. Rowse?" she inquired, as though we had been seeing a film or a play, and before I could reply had declared, "I was so thrilled when the collection reached three hundred! I felt I couldn't bear it if it didn't! I'm so glad I came. I do think Miss Goldman was wonderful the way she shouted those horrible communists and blackshirts down! Do tell her how much I admire her, won't you, Lee darling? Now I must get along to work."

"Sure you can't stop and have a drink with us before you go?" Lee asked.

She smiled at him affectionately, her lashes in full play.

"No, ta, dear, I'll have lashions when I get there! Good-bye dear. Thanks ever so for bringing me along. Bye-bye, Mr. Rowse. So nice seeing you again."

She moved off with the general mass movement toward the door, and Lee and I worked our way upstream in the direction of the platform.

There was a crowd of people in the speakers' room behind the platform, and it wasn't easy extricating Helen.

"Hullo, Tom," she greeted me. "It was nice of you to come along. Come and meet Emma, both of you."

"It's twenty minutes to closing time," I pointed out.

"Thirst things first," Lee murmured.

We got her away from all the after-meeting hangers-on by bursting open an emergency-only side door, and came out into an empty side street, on the corner of which the lights of a pub swang on the unburdened air. I swung around a lamppost from sheer exhilaration that Rintrah no longer roared, then did a Charlie Chaplin run and walk in through the swing door of the saloon bar of the pub. And there was Tansy standing up at the bar with a tall young man with wavy hair. I all but stepped on her as I came in, and she turned, and we were mutually startled.

"Good Lord, Tansy!" I said, and then Lee just behind was exclaiming, "Good gracious and fancy, if it isn't our Gladys, with the griffin in attendance!"

"Hullo, Lee," the young man drawled. "Have you just come from the meeting?"

"Yes, let me introduce Madame Chairman."

He introduced Helen to Tansy and Gifford, and me to Gifford and while he was ordering drinks I remarked to Tansy how surprised I was that she had been at the meeting, and had I suspected she was the least bit interested I would have suggested her coming along with Lee and me.

Before she could reply Gifford turned around and said in a B.B.C. snooty voice, "Why shouldn't she be interested? Aren't all intelligent people interested in Spain?"

"But you see, darling, he never thought of me as intelligent," Tansy said, with an edge to her voice.

"I just didn't think politics were up your street," I said, in a conciliatory tone.

She gave the familiar toss of her head, throwing the wing of hair back from the eye it was perpetually shading.

"You don't know the half of what is up my street," she said, and smiled up at Gifford.

"Apparently," I said. "You must tell me during the week end."

I turned to Lee to give him a hand with the drinks.

"There's a table in the corner," he said, and I took Helen's elbow with my free hand and piloted her across to it. I heard Lee inviting the other two to join us, and Tansy's quick "Tony and I are going to the West End, dancing."

They passed our table just as Helen was settling into her seat. Tansy said a careless, collective good night, and the young man merely nodded.

Lee said, as we both sat down, at either side of Helen, "I *said* you should ask her!"

"Who is she?" Helen demanded. "She's very attractive—like a young Tallulah. I wouldn't mind painting her. White blouse and black skirt, straight and narrow. Wide leather belt round that lovely narrow waist. The young man appears to be in love with her."

"They're all in love with her," Lee murmured, "including our Mr. Rowse."

Helen looked at me with surprised interest.

"Really, Tom?"

"Really, Helen." I added curtly, "We've been lovers for the last two years."

"I noticed she wore a wedding ring."

"She's married, and lives with. Fortunately he's what as a boy I always thought was a merciful panther." I raised my glass. "Here's to the downfall of our enemies, coupled with the name of General Franco."

Helen and Lee raised their glasses.

"And the merciful panther," Helen added gravely, though her eyes were amused—damn her.

15

WELL, THEN, so Helen knew about Tansy, and Tansy knew about Helen. Helen said when we parted that night, "D'you think she'd come and sit for me while I'm in London?"

"No," I said. "Why should she? She's not interested in art, and she has more amusing things to do with her spare time."

"If she's not interested in art, why is she interested in you?"

"I don't know," I said bitterly. "I often wonder."

"May I come and see you? I'd like to see what you've been doing since you left Paris."

"I'd like you to come," I said, and we fixed it for Monday.

The next day I saw Tansy and of course she was unpleasant about Helen. She was deliberately offensive.

"Who was the elderly party in purple?" she demanded.

"Look, Tansy," I said, "I'm not prepared to discuss any friend of mine in those terms."

"One of your Paris flames, I suppose."

"I only met her twice in Paris. She's a painter, and a friend of Lee and Graham Carlton. She interests me chiefly as Brenovska's widow."

"Brenovska? Oh, the man who did those hideous sculptures you showed me the pictures of—I suppose you went to the meeting on her account."

"Very largely," I said. "Why did you go?"

"Tony was mad to hear Red Emma. He fancies himself as an anarchist. Apparently it's the intellectual thing just now. Where did you go when you left the pub?"

"Lee took us both to dinner at the Eiffel Tower—a gourmet place in Soho."

"Where all the other anarchists eat, I suppose?"

"I can't say that we saw any others there. When I have some money I'll take you there, if you like. Helen wants to paint you, by the way, but I told her I didn't think you'd be interested."

"Helen?"

"Mrs. Shelmerley."

"Of course I don't want her to paint me. Why should I?"

"That's what I said. She thought you were attractive, that's all."

"I'm sorry I can't return the compliment."

"That was cheap, Tansy."

"I am cheap. You should know it by now."

And so it went on. It's not worth recording. She went on until I got really angry, then she collapsed into tears. We made it up and I forgave her, since if you are lovers you've either to kiss or part. And we were lovers; inescapably. But as over Pat Johns, innerly I did not forgive her. The following week end she wanted to know if I had seen "that woman," and when I said if she meant Helen Shelmerley the answer was yes, she did a jealousy act and sulked. I pointed out that she went dancing with young Gifford and shared a bedroom with old Bill, and I didn't make a fuss, though I wasn't all that taken with either idea, and surely I could have a woman friend with whom I was on considerably less intimate terms than she was with her young man and her old one.

"I don't clasp Helen in my arms and jig about a room with her," I pointed out, "nor do I share a room with her at nights."

"There's nothing immoral about dancing," she said, "and Bill is after all my husband."

She got right under my skin with that, of course.

"If I really believed that," I said, "I wouldn't be your lover!"

"Legally he is, you can't get away from it."

I let it go. What was the use of trying to make her see that the terms husband, wife, had more than a purely legal connotation? She was incapable of reason because she was impervious to logic. Any attempt to sustain a reasoned argument with her brought one sooner or later—usually sooner—up against some incredible *non sequitur*, rendering the whole process of argument as futile as it was exhausting. But then as against all this there were the times when she would slip a hand into mine, or lean her head against my shoulder with a sigh of content, assuring me how much she needed me, how I understood her better than anyone, how I was the only man she had ever been able to like and respect, and so on, and I would feel reassured in our relationship. And there were the worrying times when she was listless and tired and vaguely not well, yet always refusing to take medical advice. She had very bad times every month, and she always said it was because she had "never been right" since she had had the miscarriage. Sometimes I believed her, and sometimes I had the feeling that it was a way of attempting to impress and a little frighten the male with feminine mysteries. Anyhow it succeeded in focusing attention on her femininity and in mystifying and troubling the male.

I took to taking her to see my mother on either the Saturday or the Sunday afternoon each week end we were together. My mother accepted her as my "girl" and was sorry we couldn't be married. She prayed for us that it might be possible one day. She knew that Tansy stayed with me in my room those week ends, but I had the feeling that she never allowed her mind to dwell upon the implications of that. She drew down a convenient shutter at that point. The old ostrich-act. She and Tansy got on famously. I don't quite know how or why. Except that generally speaking Tansy in her careless good-natured way did get on with people. Had she met Helen independently of me she would have got on with her famously, too, particularly when she knew Helen considered her a young Tallulah.

I wasn't doing too badly at that time. I was selling a few things to the West End store, and one thing led to another. I got an odd commission here and there, like the cedar-wood chest, and I did a bit of night-school teaching. I rubbed along fairly well; I was able to give my mother an occasional ten bob or pound here and there, take Tansy to the pictures once a week, and buy her drinks and an occasional Soho restaurant meal, and most times a flower to wear—gardenias when they were in season, because we both liked the strong spicy perfume, and because they looked well on her trim black suit. I fulfilled my obligations as best I could, and on the whole not too badly; my greatest problem was to be able to find the money for the sort of wood I needed for the things I had in mind to carve. The piece of oak for Eve had cost me ten pounds; that had come out of the money I had from Graham Carlton, saved from the wreck of my Chelsea squanderings on Tansy. I'd not been able to buy anything but small stuff since then.

When Helen came to see me I showed her all the work in my possession, everything I'd brought from Paris, and all I had on hand of what I'd done since. I couldn't show her the cedar-wood settle, but I showed her the designs for the carving on it, and a photograph I'd taken of it before I let it go, and she looked at everything with obvious interest and appreciation. It was fine to see her there in my high bare room, and afterwards in my shack of a workshop; she was like a light, somehow, with her flaming hair and pale strong face. I was fascinated by her hands as she handled drawings and touched the things I'd made, lovingly, sensitive to their line and the feel of the wood—strong-looking hands they were, paint-stained, the unpolished nails cut short and only roughly tended—ugly hands, Tansy would have thought them, but they were sensitive, too, craftsman's hands. I thought her beautiful, as I had in Paris. The greasy scarlet lipstick clumsily applied to her large mouth was aggravated by the mauves and purples she commonly wore, but somehow it didn't matter; she was altogether vivid, striking, and a bit preposterous. And all over again I liked and admired her so enormously, the big, handsome, intelligent woman with the cool appraising eyes and generous mouth; her vitality stopped short just this side of flamboyance; it was the vitality of an artist, held in restraint. She looked at my work, and I looked at her, and the air was quick and alive with mutual admiration.

She had seen my Negro Girl Dancing at Graham Carlton's house in Paris and been impressed by it, she said, but Eve, she thought, was an advance on it, was more mature work—didn't I agree? I told her I didn't know; the Pat Johns thing meant so much to me that it was impossible for me to be objective about it. Helen looked for a long time at Eve, thoughtfully, then said, "I want to have an exhibition in London next spring, about May—how about making it a joint-exhibition, if I can get a gallery interested, and I'm pretty sure I can. Finstein, for one, is always on the lookout for new talent. It's thirty-three-and-a-third per cent for him, of course, but still, his is a very good gallery to show at—perhaps the best. You don't have enough for a one-man show, but if you got back the Negro Girl on loan, and a few of the other things you've sold here and in Paris, you'd have a good representative collection, don't you think?"

She went on gazing dreamily, with half-closed eyes, at Eve, not listening to my confused mumbled thanks and agreement. She continued, thinking aloud, "But you need one more big thing—something bigger and more powerful than either Eve or Daphne—something that would be a focusing point for the critics. A debating point, if you like, like Epstein's Genesis. There's your own conception of Genesis. And your own particular vision of Christ—remembering your *in vino veritas* conversation that night in the little restaurant on the Place Dauphine I'd say you have something to say on the Christ idea—or the debasing of it. . . ."

She opened her eyes and turned to me, smiling.

"There was something you quoted that night in the pub after we'd had a few drinks. You said it was from the *Everlasting Gospel*—there was a couplet that stuck in my mind—

> In dark pretence to chastity,
> Blaspheming Love, blaspheming Three—

That's your *motif* perhaps. . . ."

My mind immediately flamed with the idea. "The naked Human Form Divine"—the vision of Christ that was the enemy of the world's vision.

"I'll make him swarthy—black," I cried. "Why should he

always be represented as white-skinned? He was an Oriental Jew. And I'll make him short, strong, thickset, a Jewish workman—a man who worked with his hands in a carpenter's shop. A man with a terrible anger and pity in him, and a fierce and terrible beauty of suffering and forgiveness and expiation. He died upon a tree, and I'll make him out of lignum vitae, the wood of life, he who was the tree of life. . . ."

"You're choosing a hard medium," she said.

"I know the difficulties and I know the limitations," I told her. "The piece of lignum I'll want will weigh about half a ton—"

"What will it cost?"

I stared at her in sudden horror.

"The earth," I said bitterly. "More than I could possibly afford. Damn near thirty quid, probably."

I continued to stare at her, wretchedly.

"You don't think you could persuade your pal Finstein to express his faith in genius to the extent of subsidizing it, do you?" I asked despairingly. "He could still collect his thirty-three-and-a-third per cent on the sale price to balance the philanthropy and square the accounts."

"It would be simpler," she said drily, "if you would accept the material you need from me. The important thing is not who pays for it but that you get it."

I didn't have to think whether I could let her make me a present of the wood. I was so excited by the idea that ways and means didn't matter so long as I found the right stuff for carrying out the idea. In a curious way I didn't even feel gratitude, though I was indebted to her both for the idea and for the means of expressing it. It was as though in the wild rush of inspiration she had released in me I couldn't stop for gratitude—was swept beyond it; it was as though she had touched off in me something a great deal bigger and more important than that.

"You're an angel!" I cried, and grabbed her and whirled her around the room. When she succeeded in breaking away from my crazy dance she said, between laughing and calling me a fool and trying to recover her breath, "Well, then where do we get what you want?"

"Lister's," I told her. "They'll sell you anything from a deal plank to a whole rock-elm log. They know me, but I know them better than they know me. I was sent to them by my boss when I was a kid apprenticed to the cabinetmaking trade. I've bought odds and ends of stuff from them since I've come back here to live. I've also pinched odds and ends when no one was looking—same as I did when I was a boy. You'll have to do the talking—they'll never take me seriously for an order this size."

"Why don't we go now?" she said.

We went, and so far as I was concerned we reached the Blackwall Lane in a series of hops, skips and jumps, and Charlie Chaplin running-walks, which would have driven Tansy frantic with embarrassment. Helen rocked with laughter, pelting along beside me like a girl, clutching her purple feather toque with one hand against the leafy autumn wind and holding on to me with the other, breathless and panting and laughingly protesting that she couldn't keep up and that I must stop it; but she did keep up, all the same, near enough, and I didn't stop it. People turned and looked at us and thought us crazy—well, why not? An odd couple we must have made, the tall shabby gaunt shock-headed scarecrow that was me, and the handsome red-haired purple oddity that was Helen, and the two of us careering along the frowsy pavements of the Trafalgar Road, past the pawnshops, the old-clothes shops, the fried-fish shops, the dingy little shops that were combined newspaper-agents', sweetshops and tobacconists'; we chain-danced between drab women carrying dreary shopping bags, swung around the lampposts, waved to the trams rocking by like ships on a choppy sea, and to wall-faced babies in buggy prams. All in the staid September sunshine, with a wind that had the smell of the sea on it larking along the river and invading the squalid street like a brass band. We marched along to the stirring music of the invisible band, breaking into runs to keep up with its energetic rhythm, blaring and drumming unheard by all but the riotous two of us at the heart of the bright cool morning. It was so I had longed to run with her, exultantly, hand-in-hand, laughing, along the Seine that night in Paris when we dined in the Place Dauphine.

And of course when we got to Lister's, and the invisible band marched off with its unheard melodies to lose itself among the docks, they could offer us from their stocks—on hand, in mill or yards, in wharves or docks—everything but the large log of lignum vitae I needed. Plenty of slender stuff they could supply, of nine or ten inches in diameter, but I calculated that I needed a foot and a half at least, and I knew it was to be had. But other than this they could offer us woods whose very names were a vision of apes and ivory and peacocks, a poetry of Lebanon and Damascus, and the city that men call Tyre; teak they could offer from Indian thickets where the tiger took cover in a Rousseau-green shade; and balsa logs from the jungles of the Andes; and mahoganies from Tabasco and Cuba and Honduras. Ebony they could offer us, and Japanese oak; and tulipwood, and hemlock, and hickory . . . but not a sizable log of the wood of life, of guaiacum, lignum vitae, or lignum sanctum of the pale blue flowers and the pubescent sepals. But they were expecting what they called a parcel of timber, which included some exceptionally large logs of lignum vitae; it should arrive at the West India docks within the next ten days. If I would let them know the size and quality of the log I was looking for a suitable piece would be selected for me and brought up to the yard by the first available lorry.

I got worried then. "Look," I said, "I'm not running a factory. I'm not slicing this wood up to make skittle balls. I'm carving it, God help me! I can't do with just any old tree trunk!" I was getting excited. "I've got to see what I'm taking on—I'll need something sizable—"

Helen laid her hand on my arm, smiling.

"Sure you shall see, honey." The smile she turned on me was gentle and soothing; the smile she turned onto the stock clerk was radiant; it enveloped the entire office and swept like a searchlight down generations of timber-merchant Listers, invoking their consent. I was suddenly aware of her perfume in the little office, of the singsong American lilt of her soft voice, even of the sheen of the purple feathers of her hat. She was all charming woman, confident that nothing could be refused her. She was sure that Mr. Lister would be very happy for Mr. Rowse to go along to the docks when the shipment arrived and select the piece most suited to his sculptor's requirements. It wasn't usual? No, of course not, but it wasn't usual for a sculptor to be planning to carve a large figure of Christ in lignum vitae. If she might have a word with Mr. Lister himself . . .

Mr. Lister was fetched, and introduced to "Mrs. Shelmerley, the well-known American painter"—I did the introducing. Mr. Lister was surprised, interested, and curious; but above all he was charmed. It was not, after all, every day that so striking, distinguished, and gracious a lady graced the sawmills in the Blackwall Lane. Not every day or every year. Laved by the subtlest of perfumes, the most compelling of smiles, and a soft voice murmuring appreciation and gratitude, it was no trouble at all to write out a memo with the name of the ship and the particulars of the wharf and shed where the timber would be landed.

I felt a little dizzy while it was all happening, and I looked wildly around the office to see was there the odd bit of wood lying about that I could slip into the pocket of my raincoat, so that I would feel more at home, the transaction rendered more normal. But there was nothing, only tiny samples of wood, like railway tickets, minutely labeled, pigeonholed along one wall. My eyes ran over the tiny printed labels—satin walnut, teak, cocus, cedar, rosewood, pitch pine, ebony . . . No earthly use to anyone, things like that, no bigger than dominoes. I pulled out the cocus and it had a little border of sapwood, cream against the brown; I was quite taken with it and slipped it into my pocket automatically. I couldn't get over it at all, being in that office and ordering half a dozen hundredweights of timber, honoring the firm with my most magnificent custom, the importance of which, mere businessmen that they were, they would not realize. It's a fine feeling, once in a way, having delusions of grandeur.

Then we were being shaken hands with and bowed out of the office and escorted past the long shed where the circular saws screamed and the planing machines roared with a familiarity that was dear to me, and out into the drear of the Blackwall Lane. I no longer wanted to skip and run. I felt dazed. I had a curiously solemn feeling that between us we had achieved something tremendous. Helen slipped an arm through mine.

"I guess we've earned a drink," she murmured.

We went into the first pub we came to, in Trafalgar Road. We went into the public bar, where men wearing caps and white chokers stood about drinking bitter beer. They all stared at Helen. She turned her charm on them all like a light, and called for drinks for them all, because, she said, it was a birthday. They wanted to know if it was the lady's or the gent's. She told them "both." They thought her crackers, no doubt, but still she was a lovely lady, and a drink is a drink, 'specially when it's buckshee. They raised their glasses to us with their "best respects," solemnly. The English know what is important. She stood them all a second round, and there were many more of them by then, and then we got out.

She was still holding my arm as we went along to the Ship.

"It's a birthday all right for me," I said, "but how is it yours?"

She laughed and pressed my arm.

"It's too complicated to explain on one drink," she said.

In the Ship I asked her again, but then she laughed and said it was too complicated to explain with so much liquor under her belt; I must remind her some other time.

When we left the pub I saw her into a taxi to take her back to the West End, and when next I saw her I had a great deal more important things to think and talk about, and as it turned out it was ten years before we got back to the subject. And it would have been better for us both if we hadn't.

I couldn't sleep at nights, while I was waiting, for thinking what I would do with my half-ton or so of lignum vitae when I got it. I made endless sketch notes, of Christ-figures whole, and details of hands and feet. I felt myself particularly concerned with the hands. Sometimes the vision was of Christ crucified; at other times of the man of sorrows. And constantly recurring was the vision of Christ driving the money-changers out of the temple, his face twisted with anger and disgust. I knew that what I eventually decided on would be determined by the shape and size of the wood itself, what it was most suited to express of its own nature, but I was feverishly impatient to see and touch and come to "know" the wood and allow it to direct the vision.

Lee went back to Paris shortly after the Spanish meeting, and Helen went off touring the provinces with the queen of the anarchists, and but for Joe Snell I would have been lost for someone to talk to. I couldn't bring myself to discuss anything with Tansy. I knew that if I told her I was burning up with a vision of Christ she would say I had "gone religious," and if I told her that Helen was supplying the material for me to carry out the idea, which was anyhow hers, it would produce a stupid and wearisome jealousy. I didn't even tell her I planned an exhibition with Helen in the spring. I just went along teaching and doing odd jobs, and going after jobs, and making drawings of a Christ-figure, and reading *The Marriage of Heaven and Hell*, and *The Everlasting Gospel*. I pondered anew over the assertion that "The reason Milton wrote in fetters when he wrote of Angels and God, and at liberty when of Devils and Hell, is because he was a true Poet, and of the Devil's party without knowing it." Knowing Blake's hatred of orthodoxy and the world's perversion of good and evil, so that God became the Devil, and the Devil

God, I felt I knew what he meant. I liked the vision of Blake "walking among the fires of Hell, delighted with the enjoyments of Genius, which to Angels look like torment and insanity," and the Devil inscribing in corroding figures on the face of a rock a piece of Infernal wisdom:

> How do you know but ev'ry Bird that cuts the airy way
> Is an immense World of Delight, clos'd by your senses
> five?

I felt myself to be with Blake, of the Devil's party, whether the world will have it or no.

Then at last the days and nights of waiting were lived through and finished with, and Lister's notified me that the shipment had arrived and they would be glad if I would go along and make my selection. Clutching these tidings of great joy I rushed out into the morning and went haring off down to the Trafalgar Road to get a tram for the docks, the tails of my old raincoat flapping in the wind—looking, I suppose, more like a scarecrow than ever, but all but prepared to eat anyone who got in my way or argued with me. I was sweating as much with excitement as from hurrying when I finally fetched up at the dockyard gates and explained my business to the copper on duty.

After a bit of blundering about I found the yard I wanted, and with the help of someone from the yard foreman's office finally located the precious "parcel" of lignum vitae. In all the wharfside activity of cranes and ships and motor lorries, of loading and unloading, I was aware only of those great trunks of guaiacum, fine big logs all of them, straight as pines—and one huge trunk, bigger than the rest, had the good foot-and-a-half diameter I needed into the bargain. I stared at it, my heart pounding. It seemed too good to be true.

"Found what you're looking for?" the man at my side inquired. I nodded. It was already mine, as Tansy had been mine before I had so much as touched her hand. It was less than six foot—five-foot-eight, I judged, and the heartwood rich and dark, and patterned like marble. I could have cried out for joy. I had forgotten how beautiful a wood it was. And this one piece alone had the qualities I needed. It had a shape. O sweet Christ, it had a shape. . . . A kind of mist formed as I gazed at it, and through the mist the shape of the tree took on human shape. The human form divine. Christ in the temple driving out the money-changers, not with the small whip of knotted cords, but by the moral force of that honest indignation which is the voice of God —the spirit kindled to white heat. The Christ-symbol of Mercy, Pity, Peace and Love, translated in terms of the human heart, the human face, the human form, the human dress.

I felt very queer. I "came over faintified," like old Ma Hilley showing her Morland. The next I knew I was sitting on a pile of planks in a corner of the shed and the foreman's clerk was asking me if I felt all right. I hadn't passed out; just everything had blacked out for a few moments. I mumbled something about having felt a bit dizzy on account of hurrying. Then somehow I was back in the office arranging for the great log to be earmarked for me. I left the docks in a kind of daze and turned into the nearest pub, where I bought myself a brandy. I kept thinking of the noble trunks of lignum with their heartwood like dark marble, and how they would be sold for commercial purposes, ordered by the ton and taken to factories and turned into skittle balls and mallets and God knows what. And I thought about the trunk of the tree of life which by a holy miracle, it seemed to me, had been entrusted to me, that I might carve the living truth out of it . . . the Way, the Truth, and the Life.

16

I DIDN'T say anything to Tansy about the wonderful tree resting on the bench in my workshop. I was short of money again, because now I begrudged every minute away from my real work, and I had only the money from the three-evenings-a-week teaching. I told Tansy I was getting my work together ready for an exhibition in the spring. She never asked to see any of it; she wasn't interested. Except for a few little animals she thought everything I did hideous. She had been bitterly disappointed with the finished Eve. She hated and resented it as she would have hated and resented a bad photograph of herself, and could never forgive me for it. She regarded poor oaky Eve as a travesty of a representation of herself. I could not make her understand that there had never been any intention of making a photographic likeness, and that certain concessions had to be made to the medium in which one worked; that my Eve was of the nature of the oak from which I had fashioned her; she was also of the nature of her creator's intention, which was genesis. . . . But it wasn't any use trying to explain; for the Tansies of this world works of art are either ugly or beautiful. To qualify for the latter category they must be smooth and all their qualities readily recognizable; anything strange or subtle, or touched with abstraction, is ugly; in short they must realistically represent something, not express anything.

So I said nothing about the strange dark figure slowly taking shape in my dilapidated old shed. Old Tilley came and had a look at me working a few times, but he couldn't make head or tail of what I was at, and he and my father discussed me over their nightly beers and came to the conclusion—I learned from my mother—that I was "not all there," even if not certifiable. My poor mother came to see what I was doing, and when I told her that it was Christ driving the money-changers out of the temple she was pleased that I had, as she put it, "turned to religion," but she had all her life from the age of six or so thought of Jesus as tall and pale and slender, with a sad gentle face and moving in an aura of madonna lilies, and I could tell by the troubled bewilderment with which she gazed at this stocky dark figure carved in a wood that looked like stone that she feared her poor son was not succeeding very well with his commendably pious subject.

Sometimes I would go down to the waterfront, taking a couple of bottles of beer with me, and sit and drink and chat with Joe Snell. Sometimes we shared a paper of fish-and-chips together, which we sent young Bert out to buy. And one Sunday when I was working on the Christ because I couldn't be with Tansy, I looked up and there was the carpenter standing at the door in his Sunday-best—ready-made blue suit, rather bright, very clean white collar and shirt, and a ready-made bow tie, blue with white spots. With all this finery he wore a shabby trilby hat, which he had had, in his own vernacular, "for donkey's years," and was only worn on Sundays, when he ceased to be Joe Snell, jobbing carpenter, and became Mr. Joseph Snell, cabinetmaker.

He grinned at me from the door.

"Caution, man at work!" he observed.

"Come in," I said, and jerked my head at the great wooden figure. "It's coming on," I told him.

He hobbled in, dragging his leg, and stood leaning on his stick and gazing up at the strong, angry mass.

"Not much gentle-Jesus-meek-and-mild about that, son," he said thoughtfully, running a hand along his lip under his mustache. "They ought to set it up in the Stock Exchange," he added, with a chuckle. "Or outside one of those smart West End churches where if Jesus and his fishermen pals were to turn up the congregation wouldn't give 'em houseroom! More power to your elbow, son!"

"Thanks," I said grimly. "I'll need it before I'm through."

I wasn't thinking of the hardness of the medium. I had a flash of intimation of all the sweating of blood still to be endured before I would be through with my particular vision of Christ.

The queen of the anarchists went back to Spain, and Helen was released from touring the provinces and coaxing money from the good-natured unspeakable English people and returned to London. She spent only a few days there; she wanted to get back to Paris to finish the work for her exhibition; the Spanish cause had lost her a lot of time; but the few days in London she spent mostly with me.

She would arrive about noon at my workshop and sit around smoking and talking or just being silent while I worked, till I was ready to knock off and go and sit in a pub for a beer-and-sandwich lunch. Afterwards we walked and talked on the Observatory hill. To please her I spent an afternoon in the Maritime Museum with her, though gazing at things in glass cases isn't much up my street, unless they are carvings in wood or ivory. Museums, generally, give me the feeling that there are too many *things* in the world; the world is cluttered with things, in museums, stores, people's homes, as though the planet were just one vast repository. We had picnic meals in my room, sharing a bottle of wine with the bread and fruit and cheese I chiefly lived on. Once Helen came with all manner of packages from some luxury place in the West End where you buy birds already cooked and encased in jelly stuff called aspic, all done up very fancy, with strips of anchovy and stuffed olives and asparagus tips and God knows what, and I was mad with her, and threatened if she did it again to throw the whole lot out of the window for the benefit of the local scavenger cats. Which I reckoned is what Brenovska would have done.

"If you eat with me you eat with a poor man," I told her, "and you needn't come any of the Lady Bountiful act. I provide the grub and you provide the wine—that's fair enough; from each according to his ability." It wasn't pride with me; I could take from her; well, I had. But here a principle was involved.

"Do we have to be all that communist?" she drawled, dipping a finger into the aspic.

"Yes, we do," I said, fiercely. "All that anarchist."

"In my Utopia," she murmured, dreamily, "everyone shops at Fortnum and Mason's. They've got them everywhere, like Woolworths."

"Compulsory caviar! The masses in this country prefer fish-and-chips."

"Not when we've built Jerusalem. Then they'll all be enlightened and educated, and eat wonderful food and wear wonderful clothes and possess all they want of everything beautiful that money can buy."

"There won't be any money in a stateless society!"

"In mine, there will be. Stacks and stacks, and sacks and sacks, and *sacks* of it, for everyone! Money is delicious!"

"That's what your first husband's mistress told me when I was a young man."

"It only shows how sensible Josef's women are!"

"Apparently they didn't succeed in converting him!"

She laughed, and her eyes were full of mockery. She looked very beautiful like that, the big made-up mouth oddly attractive. Her front teeth projected slightly and were spaced, and it made the mouth when smiling unexpectedly provocative.

She maddened me at times, with her wealth and her unrepentant attitude to it, contradicting her anarchism, and I'd roar at her like Rintrah, but she'd take it all in a spirit of amused tolerance so that it was as impossible to quarrel with her as with Tansy it was easy. . . . There was nothing ostentatious about her wealthiness; but it was there. She'd wear the same purple dress over and over again, but the coat she wore over it was mink; her strong, paint-stained fingers carried platinum and diamond rings; the necklace round her throat was simple and neat, but it consisted of the most exquisitely matched pearls. Her powder box was gold set with turquoise, very beautiful; and so on. It would strike me as fantastic that I could have lived for several years on what her coat had cost, and I'd think of Brenovska and how impossible it must all have been for him, and then I would feel angry.

She could have come back on me, of course, by saying that

but for her money I wouldn't be carving my Christ in six hundredweight of lignum vitae; but then I'd have retorted that only in a corrupt society must the artist depend on private charity for the material he needs. She would have agreed with that, of course; it was just that I did not accept her premise that money was not in itself evil but merely debased by the system of society it was called upon to serve. I found the premise itself corrupt, and a product of that society. Money as I saw it degraded art and life and made mockery of Christian precepts. I held with Blake that where any view of money existed art could not be carried on, but war only, and that for every pleasure, in the real sense, money is useless.

But when I had Helen in my bare room, eating the food I had bought with the money earned by the labor of my hands and brain, and when afterwards she kicked off her shoes and lay back on my divan smoking my cheap cigarettes while I made coffee on the gas ring, then I could forget about her money and her views on money, and we could be two good friends and two artists together, with no damned artificial inequality rearing its ugly—not to say vulgar—head between us. Once she had suggested that after we had had our evening meal we should go and have coffee in her suite in the Dorchester; it would make a change for me, she said, and be saving my gas into the bargain. She meant, I thought, that we should be more comfortable, and I told her, sharply, that I knew my place, or anyhow had a rough idea of it, and it wasn't in any gilded halls. No, ma'am. But if she didn't like being here I would escort her to her bus—not that she ever went anywhere by bus. She told me not to be a fool, that she was very comfortable where she was; it was only that for a moment she had seen my gas fire as a kind of voracious monster devouring my poor pennies, but if I didn't see it that way why should she worry? To which I murmured in reply, Why indeed? and changed the subject.

It was the ancient enemy coming up between us, as it had between her and Brenovska. So long as she stayed around in my world I could forget about it; we could be equal; then suddenly her own centrally heated luxury world would impinge, and she was no longer Brenovska's widow and good old Helen, a fellow artist and a pal, but the wealthy Mrs. Shelmerley, layered around with almighty dollars. No wonder, I would think, that life with Brenovska hadn't been easy; no wonder they had fought; I would fight her, too, if I saw much of her. I wouldn't have her running with the hare and hunting with the hounds, like that. The money-hounds with the smell of death on them, harrying everything that was wild and free and uncorrupted. As an artist she was in the wrong camp, on the wrong side—fettered when she should have been free.

They were fine, our times together, with a great talk of art and life, and at times a sense of communion flowing between us beyond need of words, so that we were not less articulate in silences; we liked each other hugely; there wasn't any doubt about that; and we found each other good company, and amused each other. But I hated the endings of those times together, for then we would go down the gray dirty stairs together and out into the shabby square that smelled of cats and dustbins, and walk to the Trafalgar Road and find her a taxi. It was the moment when she stepped into the taxi saying "the Dorchester" to the driver that I hated; an impalpable wall seemed to rise up between us then, and I would walk back all bitterness, anger, and resentment. Till I climbed up to my room where the smoke from the cigarettes we had smoked together still hung, and wreathed in with it her perfume. Then I would forget about the Dorchester and remember only what we had said and how good it felt, the flow of soul, or whatever it is, and old Bill Blake would dart into my mind with his piece about friendship not being able to exist without continual forgiveness. I had to forgive her ideas, she mine; we anyhow sought the same ultima Thule of the Good Life, here and now, on the Good Earth, though we journeyed by different routes.

17

I HADN'T intended that Tansy should know about the days Helen and I had spent together; there seemed no point in telling her something which would only produce tiresome comment. But the last time Helen was in my room was a Friday, and when Tansy arrived on Saturday afternoon and made herself comfortable on the divan, the cushion which by night was my pillow behind her head, she suddenly sprang up as though she had spotted a snake.

"Scent!" she exclaimed. "Chanel! It's that woman! I remember noticing it on her in the pub after the meeting. She's been here!"

"More than once," I told her. "She was here last night. It's nice scent, isn't it? I noticed it when I went to bed. When I have some money I'll get you some." I wanted to get any discussion of Helen onto a normal, rational level, but I knew by the color draining out of Tansy's face and by the sudden quiver of her lips that hysteria was on the way up on the emotional escalator, and even as the realization came to me it was released, with all its wild irrelevancies, recriminations, and absurdities. There is no point in detailing it. It was the usual regulation jealousy act, during the course of which the most fantastic charges were made. They were so fantastic that they were not worth refuting, I felt, for if she really believed them she would believe anything, and our whole relationship was futile and absurd. Often in these scenes I wondered whether she believed, even at the time, the astonishing things she said. It is commonly held, I believe, that in rage as in drink people speak the truth of what they think and feel; perhaps grudges and resentments can work such havoc in the human heart and mind as to twist the truth inside out. I don't know. I only know that if Tansy believed the things she said when she was in the grip of rage she was for the time being insane, for at such times she was capable of asserting that black is white, and apparently of believing it. That she should accuse me of being Helen's lover was understandable; every friendship between a man and a woman is open to the sexual suspicion. I could accept that. The sort of thing that baffled me was her declaration—and she made it more than once—that I was evil, that my work was evil, and that she had seen my own mother shrink from me in fear and horror . . . which considering the way my poor mother's face lit up every time she set eyes on me, and how happy she always was when I took Tansy along and we'd have what she called "a little party," and how always when I left she'd cling to me with tears in her eyes, begging me to come again soon, and always giving me a little parcel of homemade things, a few sweets or cakes she'd made, to take away with me, was nothing less than astonishing.

At first I'd protest in incredulous amazement and ask her what on earth she meant; but as time went on I'd just let the flood of hysterical insanity wash over me and wait for it to be done. It always ended in violent sobbing and despairing appeals for forgiveness. "I get overwrought," she would say, afterwards, stroking my face and hair, all tenderness and sweetness. "Half the time I don't know what I'm saying. I get beside myself." The expression always struck me as odd. As though all the nonphysical part of oneself detached itself, became unrelated. All very interesting, psychologically speaking. They have fancy names for it nowadays—schizophrenia, and things like that. Tansy called it being "highly strung." My mother called such conduct "creating." She would tell me how my father would "create" when he came home the worse for drink and quarrelsome, or how the woman next door "created" when her line broke one morning when she'd pegged all the washing out and the backyard was muddy from recent rain.

Well, Tansy "created" over Helen having visited me, and when she had finished creating she wept, and finally I comforted her. In the beginning I would pet her and make love to her a little at such times; there would be passionate reconciliations. But as time went on I became weary of the repetitiveness of such scenes, and I'd feel merely exhausted when it was all over, and oh well, I'd say, what about a nice cupper, or, if it was fine, come on, tidy up the old face and let's go out and get some air. "Let's contend no more, Love/Strive nor weep/All be as before, Love" —anything for a quiet life.

We went out and walked hand-in-hand on the hill after the great row over Helen. It was a fine sunny afternoon and the trees were so beautiful in their golds and browns that I had a sudden longing for Fontainebleau. I began telling Tansy about it, and weaving a dream of how one day we'd go there together. Her face lit up at that and she smiled and pressed closer to my side, twining her fingers more tightly with mine, exclaiming that that would be lovely, that she had always wanted to go to Paris; the shops must be wonderful; perhaps we could go next Easter —she had heard that the spring was the time to go, when the chestnut trees were all in leaf in the Champs Elysées—the fashionable dress shops were all round there, weren't they? She wondered if Parisian women were really as smart as they were made out to be.

She ran on, eagerly, and the dream died in me. I knew then it wouldn't be any good our going together. Paris for her meant fashion, clothes, elegance, gaiety. I had nothing to do with any of that. Paris for me meant the narrow streets of the Quarter, rooms full of shabby red plush in small dark hotels that smelled of privies and coffee and onion soup, *bistros* with sawdust on the floor, the poplars leaning out over the Seine, and fishermen and bums letting time flow over them under the walls of the quays; it meant the fusty smell of the Metro, and the Dôme zinc, and the old houses of the Ile St. Louis, and the Luxembourg gardens. And the restless tormented ghost of Josef Brenovska.

Tansy snatched my dream from me, breaking it without knowing, and replacing it with one of her own—something at once much gayer and more ordinary. She wanted to know if I had ever been up the Eiffel Tower, or to the Opéra—"it must be terribly elegant"—or the Folies-Bergère, and was astonished that I should have lived so long in Paris and done none of those things. So that I knew that in spite of all I'd told her she still hadn't the slightest conception of my decade in Paris, lived mostly on the bread line; or even what sort of person her lover really was. But we would do all these things together, she said happily, and it would be fun.

Meanwhile we walked on the Observatory hill with the great gray sprawling city of London spread out below us, and the great S loop of the murky Thames; that was all right; I was fundamentally more part of all that than of Paris and the Seine, and my wave of nostalgia wasn't for Paris but for the forest of Fontainebleau in its autumn dress, only I wanted it with Tansy who was beautiful and whom I loved and desired in place of Joycelyn who was not beautiful and whom I did not love in the romantic sense and for whom I had had very little desire. Even if one had the time and the place and the loved one all together there was no guarantee of happiness, since the loved one's idea of the ideal place might be something quite other than one's own.

"Why don't we go out into the country while the trees are so beautiful?" I said suddenly. "Epping Forest, or somewhere."

She was quite startled. "Whatever for?" she exclaimed.

"Just to see the trees."

"What's wrong with the trees here, or in Kensington Gardens and Hyde Park?"

"Parks are one thing, forests another," I suggested.

"The country's all right in the summer, but not at this time of the year—all so muddy and damp. I always think the autumn's a depressing time of year."

Well, so that was that. Nothing like knowing, I thought. Love is like a game which there are various ways of playing; the problem is to find someone who plays it one's own way. But in every love affair, it seems to me, there is always one who is more romantic than the other, or more sentimental, or more sexual; and always one who loves more intensely than the other; and when love dies it seldom dies in the two people at the same time; so that there must always be one who suffers, both during the relationship and at the end.

There were times when I would have the illusion that this girl, whose chief interests in life were clothes and having what she defined as a Good Time, did play the game my way. Times when I could sweep aside as unimportant, irrelevant, all our bickers and quarrels and differences, and deceive myself that this really was the many-splendored thing the poets have dreamed of down through the ages. Her beauty put a spell upon me. The beauty of women has been enslaving men ever since the capacity to think and feel so disastrously evolved in the human animal. Men both more and less intelligent than Tom Rowse have been put in thrall.

I don't want to give the impression there was little or no happiness in this particular human bondage. Often and often I would feel, holding her in my arms, that just to have these brief intervals of happiness and peace was worth all the rest; that she was all my joy and all my pain, and would be till I died.

18

I WORKED all through the autumn and winter on the Christ-figure, and there was still quite a bit to do to it by Christmas. The extreme hardness of the wood, and the continual blunting of the tools as a result, meant that the work was slow and laborious. I was working, too, under difficult conditions in that old shed of a garage. So long as the weather was mild I could leave the doors open and get the maximum light; but by November it was too wet and cold, and with the doors closed the light from the window Lee and I had put in was pretty poor. I brought Gwen Naylor's snaky desk lamp along, finding a use for it at last, and most days in the winter I worked with that fixed upon a ledge above my bench. The workshop was cold, too, with the cement floor and the wind whistling under the ill-fitting door, and the heat from the oil stove seemed inadequate. During a spell of very cold weather in December I had to give up for a while, my hands got so cold I couldn't hold the tools properly. But despite the slowness of the work I never lost sight of the vision. I knew quite clearly what I wanted to express, and little by little, tortuously, the "human form divine" did emerge, and I brooded over it with the loving care of a mother for her babe.

I got some of "the boys" in the house to help me upend the great log when I had finished bosting-in. I had rigged up a shear-legs for the weighty job, since the roof of the shed would never have stood the strain of a pulley. Old Tilley came and looked on, giving useless advice.

"What's it going to be, chum?" one of the men asked derisively, when we'd got the dark mass standing firm on its own base.

I told him, "Christ driving the money-changers out of the temple," and he exclaimed, "Lumme!" to cover his embarrassment.

Tilley grinned fatuously. "You ain't got no religion," he observed.

The other man reddened. "I was brought up High Church," he said defensively.

Tilley's grin broadened. "Was you now? Low publican was more my style!"

The general laughter dissolved the embarrassment that had invaded them all. Christ was an oath, or something mumbled in a church, or a gracefully sorrowful figure on a cross, quite unrelated to the horror and agony of nails driven through living flesh. Christ belonged to Sunday school, and Salvation Army rantings at street corners, and a fancy business of bobbing and bowing in a church. Christ was an exclamation of anger or impatience or pain or physical ecstasy. Not a name to be said out loud like Baldwin or Chamberlain, without self-consciousness. Had I been able to tell them I was making a statue of a politician or film star they would have studied it with interest, but Christ . . . oh Jesus, let's get out! Even my mother, who being conventionally "religious" was not embarrassed by the Holy Name, could not look at my carving without embarrassment, not because of the subject but because of what seemed to her its badness—its ugliness, that is to say.

Christmas repeated the pattern of the previous year, and I was more than ever glad when it was over. My poor mother thought that as I had "turned to religion" and was carving a figure of Christ I might like to go to church with her on Christmas morning, and didn't understand when I refused. I didn't see any point in going into it; I just told her to go off and enjoy herself and I'd see to the dinner. She thought my remark about enjoying herself irreligious, and was baffled when I said, "Why not? Christmas is a celebration, isn't it?" But you celebrated, apparently, by stuffing turkey and pudding and mince pies into yourself when you got home, and if it was a birthday party, divine or otherwise, nobody mentioned the guest of honor. I longed intensely for it all to be over, and on Christmas night, when the parlor was full of relatives sitting around yapping about nothing and drinking grocer's port, I slipped off back to my workshop.

There were lights in most of the windows of the big old house; blinds and curtains were left undrawn, so that through the steam on the panes tawdry colored paper chains looped across ceilings were visible, and in some of the rooms there were Christmas trees. But there was only one tree I was interested in, and it awaited me leafless and unlit in a cold darkness.

I let myself into the shed and closed the door behind me and switched on the light. The figure stood facing the door with the lamp on its snakelike stem immediately above it. It was so cold in the shed that my breath rose like smoke. I went over to the corner where the oil stove stood and groped in my overcoat pocket for matches. I found them and my fingers also came in contact with a thin candle. My mother had asked me to get her some colored candles for her little tree, and this one had spilled out of the package. I had already noticed it in my pocket and intended giving it to her, but there it still was. I got the oil stove going, then on an impulse went over to the figure and set the candle at its feet and lit it, half ironically, half with a kind of bitterness. Poor lonely Jesus, with no part in all the guzzling and the humbug, the forgotten guest at the party. The flame of the little candle wavered and steadied, and the blue wax glimmered starrily against the dark mass of the figure. I switched out the electric light and brought an old kitchen chair and sat in front of the figure and studied it.

It had the essential quality of passion, I thought. There was suffering as well as anger in the furrowed face; anger at the profanation of something holy, the debasing of the temple into a den of thieves, anguish over the moral ugliness with which man debases the Jerusalem within himself, his pretenses to art which destroy art, darkening where they should illuminate; his pretenses to liberty which destroy liberty, bringing destitution and mutilation and death where life should be increased and enriched; pretenses to religion which destroy religion, substituting the outward forms for the emanations from within—

> . . . calling that love which is envy, revenge and cruelty
> Which separated the stars from the mountains, the mountains
> from man
> And left man, a little grovelling root, outside of himself.

I felt suddenly despairing and alone. It was not that I considered myself so remarkable, so unique, but that the few people I might have got along with weren't around any more. William Blake, Josef Brenovska, Henri Gaudier—what did he want to tack her name onto his for? He was the artist, not she. She was a tiresome thing, pretentious, and he was honest as the day, all passion and power and light. Like Brenovska he believed that sculpture was the supreme expression of the reality of ideas. He believed that art was emotion, the emanation of passion. But emotion, not disciplined by art, led them both full tilt into war, that is to say into destruction and death. Gaudier in the trenches in 1914 carving a little Maternity statue out of the butt-end of a German rifle, cutting the walnut wood with an ordinary knife. Gaudier in common with other French soldiers calling his bayonet Rosalie because it dipped into the rosy blood of the "fat bellies of the Boche". . . War could do that to an artist who believed in life, and in art as its illumination. Gaudier had called himself an anarchist; he had evaded military service; he had been dedicated to creation and life, but the forces of antilife had overtaken him in the end, and he had become part of the holocaust. Belatedly he had remembered his love for France, but its expression had been in terms of revenge and cruelty and hate. His anarchism had become anti-Christ. Christ was love, pity, forgiveness, and the artist who practices the arts of death betrays the sacred citadel.

I sat brooding in this way, looking at the dark powerful figure I had carved out of the wood of life; no one would like it, I thought; probably not even Helen. It would anger most people, in the way that anything which disturbs traditional ideas angers people. They would hate because they feared—without knowing that they feared. Only what is new and strange menaces the old and familiar—the safe. Early on in life most people make up their minds about things—life, love, morality, religion—and they don't want them unmade; it is too disturbing, too uncomfortable. Why think, when thought is already done up in neat little packages for consumption in schools and universities and churches, or may be taken in tabloid form through the columns of the daily press? Shut your eyes, pinch your nose, and down it goes—what to think on all occasions, no intelligence needed, live and die with your brains as good as new, very little used. . . . This dark angry Christ, this scourge of God, is very inconvenient; we need our money-changers, and if they tend to encroach upon the holy places—business is business. Had Jesus not been a carpenter and consorted with fishermen he would have had a better money sense, but he was poor and identified himself with the poor and the dispossessed, the socially outcast.

I had given my Christ no whip of knotted cords. Two out of three gospels make no mention of it. St. John may have been right, but it hardly matters. One man could not by physical force have turned the crowd of merchants and money-changers out of the temple; the real scourge was the voice of honest indignation, and the real temple is the temple of the mind. My Christ had his right arm raised in the gesture of driving out, and there was suffering as well as anger in his face. Such a figure, I thought, should stand in the porch of some big church in a rich and fashionable parish, as Joe Snell had said. Brompton Oratory might be a good place for it. Or St. George's, Hanover Square. Though in fact such a figure does stand at the entrance to all churches, invisibly. Unfortunately most people are unaware of the invisible. Truly

> The Vision of Christ that thou dost see
> Is my Vision's greatest enemy.

My vision of art, of life, of love, of Heaven and Hell—those states of being which, like God, exist within us. There were the two aspects of being defined by Blake as the Prolific and the Devouring. To the Prolific belongs all creative impulse, whether of art or of love; to the Devouring all that destroys, materially and spiritually; thus wars belong to it, all production for profit, all money evaluations, all ready-made thought, all orthodox religion, all that seeks to reconcile these two, which never can be reconciled—and whoever tries to reconcile them seeks to destroy existence, as Blake said.

Always I came back to him, he who was "such a burning and a shining light," and bound up inextricably with my preoccupation with a vision of Christ as the scourge of God.

I sat with my thoughts until the little candle finally guttered out in a tiny pool of blue melted wax, then I went out into the darkness and down to the Ship. In the public bar it was hot and crowded and noisy, all smoke and hubbub and heartiness, people were wishing each other "Merry Christmas," and a drunk was mournfully singing *Annie Laurie*. At one point the din was pierced by the shrill voice of a woman toasting "the king across the water!" A man's voice retorted, "Coupled with the name of Wally Simpson!" In Spain the bombs still fell, the guns still pounded, but it was something that wherever Franco had heard Mass that day it hadn't been in Madrid. . . .

19

When the Christ-figure was finished, finally, which was not until the end of January, I did no more work of any importance for a long time. I resumed my classes, and I did a few odd things to keep going, even a bit of commercial wood carving—a set of banisters—which I came by through Lister's. Creatively speaking I was drained. For the time being I'd said all I'd got to say. I was marking time, I wanted the exhibition over with, for good or ill. Sometimes I'd think of it with excitement—the feeling that Rintrah having roared the world must hear and heed. At other times I'd despise myself for wanting this recognition. The function of the artist was to create. The world could take it or leave it. Mostly it left it. What of it? It wasn't art for heart's sake, or art's sake, or for the sake of cash or kudos; it was art for life's sake, a shadowing forth of emanations not otherwise communicable.

I had to let Tansy see the figure in the end. She was curious about it. I warned her beforehand that she wouldn't like it. Her reaction to it was what I had expected—a mixture of horror and bewilderment. I watched her face while she gazed at it, and it was all written there. Inside her head something scuttled to and fro like a mouse in the wainscot; there must be a way out, something to say, if only she could find it. I could see it all going on.

Finally she said, "Well, of course modern art isn't really up my street, and frankly, if I hadn't been told I wouldn't know what it's meant to be, and I don't think many people will—not the ordinary people."

"They'll be able to look it up in the catalog," I told her grimly.

"Even if they do no one will buy it!" Her tone was truculent.

"Probably not."

"Then what was the idea of doing it?"

I laid a hand on her arm, then.

"Let's go," I said. "There's no point in discussing it."

We did discuss it, of course; she saw to that. And it was all futile—futile.

Another thing we discussed as the spring advanced was the trip to Paris I had so rashly suggested. Her heart was set on it. I told her I couldn't afford it—which was true: I was only scraping along at that time. She persisted that if I sold something at the exhibition then we must go. We would cross that bridge if and when we came to it, I thought, but I wasn't crossing any Parisian *pont* with her—not if I could help it. We quarreled a good deal that spring, and Helen's return to London aggravated the strain between us. But by then I was too busy with something new I was working on to have much time for Tansy and her tantrums.

As a result of my classes, and the few commercial enterprises—the banisters for Lister's, and odds and ends for the West End stores—and living very abstemiously, I'd got a few pounds together again and felt free to let an idea which I'd been keeping damped down in my mind till then develop. I wanted to carve old Rintrah, and once I let the idea grow it grew all over my mind and all over sheets of paper. I didn't have to consider the medium—it would have to be teak. I knew this as certainly as I had known that Christ had to be in lignum vitae. Teak is a lovely wood to carve and by its nature would permit of the broad planes in which I had conceived the idea. It's good sizable stuff, too, and I saw old Rintrah as thickset, powerful, energetic: but he was reason as well as energy, a fiery spirit as well as a roaring lion. He was the enemy of the "mind-formed manacles" of conventional morality, and religion manacled by the churches. Within Blake's terms of reference he symbolized the whole Marriage of Heaven and Hell. With fiery limbs and flaming hair he roared the Song of Liberty, spurning the clouds written with curses, stamping the stony law to dust, "loosing the eternal horses from the dens of night, crying: Empire is no more! and now the lion and wolf shall cease." . . . All that had to go into the carving I would make of Rintrah.

Lister's found me a nice log of teak, about three feet by ten inches by eight, which would give the stocky figure I wanted. I blunted a good many tools on it, but I had a grand time. I was still working on Rintrah when Helen turned up. "No one will make head or tail of it—literally," she said, but she smiled as she ran her hands over the broad planes and I had an idea she, anyhow, knew what it was all about, and the Christ moved her instantly.

"It's exciting!" she murmured, gazing at it appraisingly, with half-closed eyes. "You have the authentic Poetic Genius all right." She added, "The critics may turn and rend you, but they won't be able to ignore you!"

"Oh, the critics!" I said. I had to get used to the idea that people who knew no more than Tansy what I was up to would nevertheless say their little piece, smugly, with professional self-satisfaction, people who wouldn't know a fluter from a fret saw, people with no conception of the difficulties of working in lignum vitae.

"You'll probably also be criticized for limiting yourself to wood."

"Grinling Gibbons—" I protested.

"There's his James II in bronze—"

"His reputation's carved in wood," I persisted.

"You might like to turn your attention to stone next," she suggested. "It couldn't be a harder medium than lignum, I imagine."

"It isn't," I assured her. "Some stone is a good deal softer. But I'm wedded to wood."

She did not pursue the matter. It was one of the things I liked about her, that she knew when to let go. Tansy, once she'd fastened on a subject, would worry it to death. Helen did not so much start up something in my mind as confirm a feeling that had been growing in me since I finished the Christ. The medium would always be secondary to the desire to carve. Sooner or later, I knew, I would come to stone, and lignum vitae was perhaps the natural transition to it. Though I had the feeling that wood would always be what I can only call the more "instinctive" medium for me. I had heard sculptors declare that stone was a beautiful medium, but it had no smell, and part of my joy in wood was the smell of it, every tree with its small individual smell, like the individual skin-smell of people. Sometimes I thought that what so strongly attracted me to Tansy was the clean smell of her skin, like that of a newly bathed infant. Sexual attraction, I have an idea, is fundamentally a skin thing—that smell is the real *je ne sais quoi* of mutual attraction. As to carving, I'd got to love the subtle smell of lignum in the past months, and it seemed to have spoiled me for the time being for any other wood—as Tansy had spoiled me for any other woman—so that my thoughts circled around the possibilities of stone. I enjoyed carving Rintrah in teak, but it was a minor experience compared with the excitement I had brought to creating Christ from the wood of life.

I worked away at Rintrah and Helen fussed with organizing the exhibition—the compiling of the catalog alone was quite a business. Helen insisted that there must be an introduction written for it by some well-known person; she could easily arrange that for herself, but something must be said about me. I didn't see why my work couldn't be allowed to say all that was necessary, but both Helen and Mr. Finstein insisted that there must be at least a biographical note, which must include something about where I'd studied. Paris, it seemed, was always a good thing to mention. . . . It amazed me that Helen could take all this seriously. A very distinguished art critic wrote a very handsome piece about her, recounting where she had studied, and by whom her work had been acquired; it made impressive reading—studied under Sickert, associate of this, fellow of that, showed at this that and the other gallery, London, Paris, New York, then a lot of the jargon that always is talked by critics about painting, designed to make themselves sound knowledgeable and to impress the public. I learned that Mrs. Shelmerley's work was characterized by dense color masses within clearly defined contours; but when I asked her what it meant, and where one would expect to find the color other than within the contours, she told me not to be tiresome. She wanted that the Distinguished Critic, who was a pal of hers, should come and see some work in what she was pleased to call my studio, with the idea of writing up something about me, but I wouldn't have it. Why had people got to be told about my work—or anyone else's for that matter—couldn't they see for themselves? Did she really think that a lot of professional jargon was really any help to understanding what an artist was trying to shadow forth in his chosen medium? I couldn't even see what interest such facts as my age and place of birth could be—what relevance they had to my work. People were *interested*, she said impatiently. I protested that I didn't want them interested in *me*, but only in what I had to communicate.

In the end Mr. Finstein himself wrote a piece giving all particulars, with an astonishing bit about the strength and power of my work—all the more astonishing because at the time he wrote it he hadn't set eyes on the Christ, which was the only work to which the terms might conceivably apply.

Then there was all the business of sending out the invitations for the Private View—it seemed that the Press had to be invited, and the art critics, and all manner of important persons, the more the better, all gathered together in the interests of publicity. The gallery also employed a press agent, a Miss Flora Blomberg, whose function it was to glean tidbits of personal information about the artist and get them published in the press, the gossipy paragraph linked up with the current exhibition. "For instance," said Helen, "the trouble you took to find the right piece of lignum vitae, and how you came to conceive the idea of making that particular Christ-figure out of it—there's quite a little story in that. You ought," she added, "to get some press photographs taken, and of course some photographs of your Christ. Flora's quite smart at getting pictures into the press, and of course it all helps."

"What does it help?" I asked, bewildered.

"The artist, of course. You in this instance. Getting yourself known. You want to be known, I suppose?" There was the sort of edge to her voice I'd so often heard to Tansy's on this theme. I was silent because I didn't know the answer to her question. I wanted what I had to say about Christ driving the money-changers out of the temple to be known. Was that the same thing? I felt confused. I found it difficult to think in terms of press photographs and Miss Blomberg's chatty paragraphs. I began to wonder whether the whole idea of an exhibition wasn't a mistake. It seemed some big-pot must be got to open it. Helen wanted the American ambassador, whom she knew personally. Mr. Finstein favored a celebrated writer or theatrical person, as more likely to interest the general public. Also as it was a joint exhibition, and Mr. Rowse wasn't American, he felt that in this instance the American ambassador wasn't the right person. He and Helen wrangled slightly, and I said why need we have anyone, why couldn't we just open the door and let people walk in? In the end an R.A. with a title was decided on as having both art and snob value. So the cards were printed that the Exhibition would be opened by Sir Thingummy, R.A., a selected list of people to send them to was compiled, and the energetic Miss Blomberg set to work securing what she called "advance publicity."

The day we moved our stuff in Helen seemed to become as temperamental as the traditional prima donna; some framers had let her down, an important loan picture had not arrived, some pictures from the previous exhibition were still cluttering the premises. Mr. Finstein when he was not on the telephone seemed to be all the time yapping around her heels like a fractious little dog. For my own part, once the big figure was moved in and placed against the wall at the far end of the smaller of the two rooms that composed the gallery, the rest was easy enough. Helen had brought my Negro Girl Dancing over from Paris, and she looked well against the gray wall, on the right hand of Christ. Eve looked good, too; and I was glad when I saw it on the pedestal that Joycelyn had sent back the birchwood Morning bust of herself. I set her up opposite the mahogany bust of Pat Johns. The elm-tree Daphne I stood opposite Eve, and the roaring rampageous old lion, Rintrah, I had on the end wall facing Christ. Between these seven major works I had some animal figures, and in the middle of the room I had my carved settle.

It looked good, I thought, when I'd got it all arranged, though it didn't look much for all the years it represented; but all my life was there; all I'd felt and all I'd thought—Pat Johns, Joycelyn, the Dôme zinc, Chartres Cathedral, Bill Blake, and all. Helen, when she'd done running round in circles with her own work, thought it looked good, too. Lee, who had come over with Graham Carlton specially for the exhibition, looked in for what he called a "pre-preview." He looked disapprovingly at the female figures—"all those bosoms!" he complained—and decided that the Christ was "Epstein at his most frightful," but to my surprise liked Rintrah, who he decided was "a pet."

"What do you like about him?" I asked.

"He looks so deliciously wicked!"

"He's all intellect, energy and rebellion," I said.

"He shakes his fires in the burdened air—I know! I shall make Graham buy him. What does he cost?"

"Mr. Finstein thought he ought to be priced at fifty pounds."

"Good heavens!"

"I know. He's a nice piece of teak, though, and I blunted some good tools on him."

"With Rintrah priced at fifty pounds, what price Christ?"

"Two hundred and fifty, but don't worry," I added, "no one is going to buy him at any price. I don't even want to sell him, though I'd like to give him to anyone who liked him enough. But no one will want him even as a gift."

I wasn't bitter; I knew what I would have liked done with my Christ figure, and I knew it wasn't likely to happen: Rintrah roared against the churches, their self-righteousness, their perpetuation of war and glory, their raising up of mysteries, and Rintrah roared in vain.

"What will you do with him? It's not like a painting—artists can always wash over their paintings and use the canvases again. . . ."

He was being willfully provocative and I let it pass.

"He can just *be*," I said. "My function was to create him. His is to be." I smiled. "Like a tree, you know. After all, that's what he is."

Lee gave me one of his odd looks.

"You're a funny devil. I'll be going now. I'll look in tomorrow—I got the invitation."

"I'll rely on you for a firsthand report. Helen will be too busy being social, and I won't be here."

"What do you mean? You must be here! People like to meet the artist at this sort of do. You've got to meet the press, and," he giggled slightly, "your public."

"I'm not interested in meeting either. All I'm interested in is that they shall meet my work."

"May Helen and Mr. Finstein forgive you!"

"They won't miss me in the crush."

"Seriously, Tom, I think you should be here."

"Seriously, Lee, I don't intend to be. But don't tell Helen. I'd sooner the balloon went up when it's all over."

Helen came out to see me after the Private View. She came all the way by taxi and she was in a raging temper. I was having a bit of supper, with a book propped up against the pickle jar, when she came stamping up the stairs. I'd picked the book up second hand in the Charing Cross Road. It was called *Savage Messiah*, and it was all about Henri Gaudier, with a number of his letters, and I was enjoying it hugely. I had just got to where he was telling old Sophie off for saying color and design did not require much thought, and he was writing her that art did not lie in the dream, but in the marriage of the dream with the material, and I was just about to grope for a pencil among the litter at my elbow, to underline the passage, when the door burst open and an angel of wrath confronted me with blazing eyes and flaming hair.

"What the hell do you think you're up to?" the angel demanded.

"Having me supper, ma'am," I told her. "Won't you join me?" I pulled out a chair for her.

She continued to stand by the door.

"Is this how you repay all the trouble I took to fix this show for you and get all the most influential people along to meet you—"

"The exhibition wasn't organized solely for my benefit," I pointed out. "Presumably all the most influential people were of some use to the other half of the show."

"Is that all the gratitude you're capable of?" Her voice was intensely bitter, and I, too, felt intense bitterness.

"I didn't understand," I said, "that there was to be this accountancy between us—so much given in return for so much gratitude received. I understood that what you did was not done for Tom Rowse, but for something we both believe in, and which we call art. There's nothing you can do for Tom Rowse. He's quite content with his pint and his bread and cheese and pickles and the particular tenement in which you find him."

She came over and sat by the table, resting her chin in her hands. She looked very handsome in dark-green velvet, with some heavy antique silver jewelry at her wrists and throat. Striking and beautiful she looked, but very tired. I was suddenly moved by her and laid a hand on her shoulder.

"Don't let's fight each other, Helen," I urged. "We don't look at things the same way. You've got a commercial slant on things that I'll never have."

"You mean to tell me you don't care whether you sell anything or not?"

"If anyone buys anything because they really like and appreciate it, that's fine, but if not I really don't care. I can always make a living in one way or another—I did in Paris; I can here. I can go back to the cabinetmaking. Look," I said, "let me pour you a glass of beer, and then you tell me how it all went."

"I've got a taxi waiting," she said.

"All right, give me the cash and I'll run down and pay it off. Then we can talk."

She fished in her handbag and brought out a pound note.

"That should take care of it," she said.

When I got back after paying off the taxi driver she had taken off her feather hat and kicked off her shoes and lit a cigarette.

I sat down opposite her, smiling.

"Was there a good crowd?" I asked. "Did all the big pots come? And was the press there in full force? And did your pictures sell like hot cakes? And were they all horrified by my Christ?"

"The crowd was so thick it was almost impossible to see the pictures. It even overflowed among the Rowse sculpture. Graham has bought Rintrah, and you've also sold Morning and the bust of Patricia Johns, and as far as I could see all the animals. But you're in for it over the Christ, judging by the evening papers. Finstein is overjoyed. He considers you're made.

After this attack, the gallery will have a steady flow of people until the exhibition is withdrawn. I've got the papers if you want to see them."

"Not just now," I said. "What's the general line?"

"Oh, just a general charge of blasphemy coupled with the willful cult of ugliness."

"Blasphemy," I murmured. "Odd."

"What did you expect? Your vision isn't theirs."

"Tell me about the painting part of the exhibition," I said.

It seemed she had done very well, and expected to do better in the next few days when, the crowds thinning, people would really be able to see the pictures. "You'd better go in and see Finstein in the morning. He can arrange for the exhibition to be repeated in New York, but the cost of shipping everything would fall on you. If you sell a few more things you should manage it all right. You're welcome to use my studio-apartment if you go over. . . ."

She stayed till nearly midnight and we fought all over again because I was opposed to the idea of an exhibition in New York. I wanted the money from the things I sold to live on while I did a year's work on stone; I'd been having fantasies of great blocks of marble and alabaster. I had begun to feel the need to carve anything and everything after my long apprenticeship to wood. I was more interested in the idea of an exhibition in Paris than in New York, if I *had* to have another.

"You'll make more money in America," she said firmly.

So that we were back where we started. Helen was an artist, but money seemed to have eaten into her like an acid.

"But why *not* make money when you can?" she demanded.

"Helen," I said, "we've had all this. An exhibition of art isn't a circus to be taken on tour——"

"Plenty of exhibitions are taken on tour, I assure you, and very successfully too!"

"I dare say. But it's not for me. My ambition is not to have more exhibitions in the future but to contrive to do without them!"

"You're hopeless," she said, and Tansy herself could not have said it more impatiently.

When I saw her into her taxi at midnight and once again heard her say "The Dorchester," I had a sudden impulse to kiss her hand.

"You know," I told her, "I do feel gratitude to you, though not for the things you feel I ought to be grateful for."

She laughed, embarrassed.

"It's not like you to make pretty speeches, Tom!"

"I know. The good old Rintrah rant is more my line. But old Rintrah knows an angel when he sees one!"

There was a moment's quick pressure of her fingers, then she withdrew into the dark interior of the taxi. She waved through the little window at the back, and then I walked back to my tenement to read the abuse Christ driving the money-changers from the temple had brought upon me.

20

TANSY WAS very upset by what the popular press said about my Christ. She wasn't upset by the attack on the work itself, but because I had what she called "perpetrated" so foul a thing as to bring all this on myself. As all the girls at work knew that I was a friend of hers she felt terribly embarrassed. Tony said the whole thing was a stunt just to get publicity, but what good would publicity of that kind do me?

We quarreled very bitterly. It's no use recounting it. She said some extremely stupid things, and some extremely insulting things. I don't think she knew how insulting she really was. It was the worst quarrel we had ever had. It took place in the small Soho restaurant to which I took her to lunch when I met her from work, the Saturday of that week in which the exhibition opened. When we came out into the street I told her, "There's not much point in coming back with me, after all you've said. You can't possibly want to spend the week end with so depraved a creature."

She protested that she couldn't go back to Chelsea; that she had given out that she was going away for the week end and would look a fool. Not looking a fool was all that seemed to matter to her. I told her that she was welcome to stay at my place till Monday morning, but that I wouldn't stay with her; I would go and stay with my parents. She stared at me in complete amazement.

"You mean you don't want me?"

"I mean," I said, "exactly that."

She leaned against the wall of the restaurant and began to cry. Passers-by looked at her and then at me. It was clear I was doing her some great wrong. Had got her in the family way, probably, and was refusing to marry her. She had tried this kind of blackmail on me before and got away with it, but this time it didn't work. I had the strength of will to leave her. I walked away and left her sobbing there in the street. I walked away and I got a bus, and I got a tram, and with my heart still hard against her I got home. I found her sitting at the top of the stairs waiting for me. She had taken a taxi all the way, it seemed, because she felt "so ill and done for."

"You mustn't send me away," she said. "I have a terrible pain in my heart. I've always felt it when I've been upset, but never like now—like a knife!"

I didn't know whether to believe her or not. I let her into the room and she lay down on the divan. She looked ill, but then she very often did, when she had her periods, and when she had been upset, even when she was overtired, which she quickly became.

"When you feel better I'll take you home," I said. "You can easily say you came back because you weren't well."

"No," she whispered. "Don't send me away. Even if you don't love me let me stay with you at least till tomorrow. I hurt you. I know I hurt you. But I love you. You must believe I love you."

I stood looking down at her and I could have seized her slim shoulders and shaken her till she cried out the truth—because even then, with such pain between us, she would lie and pretend. I turned away from her for dread of laying hands on her. She would lie, I thought, even in whatever was for her the moment of truth.

"Love is being on the other person's side," I said, "and you are against me in all that I do."

She protested, of course, that she wasn't, that I misjudged her. She had said it all before, many times, and it's not worth repeating. Presently she exhausted herself and fell asleep. I went out and over to my workshop and pottered about. It seemed very empty without the great mass of lignum vitae. When the pubs opened I went to the Ship and I stayed there till closing time. I was pretty drunk when I went back to my room and pitched into bed beside her. I know nothing of the night, but in the morning I wakened with a brass band hammering in my head and with Tansy in my arms. She raised a hand and stroked my forehead.

"Poor darling," she murmured.

"O God," I groaned, not because of the thumping hangover, but because with the soothing touch of her hand and the soft small smell of her skin in my nostrils again I felt the old slow processes of seduction beginning anew.

What did she want with me, for God's sake? I would ask myself that over and over again, and I can only conclude that for her, too, the subtle skin thing existed, and that it was all as much a bondage for her as for me. Perhaps there was more to her than I ever discovered. Perhaps she had more depth of feeling, was less trivial, than I thought. Perhaps I never took enough trouble to understand her. I don't know. I just don't know. I only know that she clung to me—I who had nothing from her point of view to recommend me. I had no money, I dressed badly, I was odd; we didn't share each other's tastes; I liked pictures on canvas, in frames; she liked them celluloid, and to move. She knew nothing of any of the arts—we had, as they say, nothing in common—except the inability to get away from each other. But that she should hold me in bondage was not so strange, for she was physically attractive to me. But then I evidently was for her, and why? why? I would ask myself—and her. I never got any sense out of her in reply to the question; I was a poppet, she would declare, and an old darling, an old funny; or I was "sweet"; or because she liked being loved, and no one had ever loved her so much. "Plenty would," I would say, "given the chance. Chaps with money, good-looking chaps, well dressed, chaps you could be proud to be seen with. Bill loves you, what's wrong with Bill—why can't you love Bill?" She would say because he didn't attract her, because he bored her, and good-looking men with money were always bores, too; I was different, an old funny, and she loved me. . . . So we would be back where we started, and that I was different seemed to be the heart of the matter. I would fall back on the Pascal *pensée* of which Pat Johns had reminded me—that the heart had its reasons that reason knew nothing of.

When, to my astonishment, a provincial art gallery, the committee of which prided itself on being progressive, bought my Christ Tansy was genuinely delighted. This in her opinion established me as an artist of importance, whatever anyone else might say—ever. She was convinced that I was now well on the road to fame and success. The mere fact of anyone paying hundreds of pounds for a great carved mass of wood which she thought hideous proved that there must be more to it than she was able to appreciate. Money speaks. It certainly does.

I had such confused feelings about the sale of the Christ-figure. If some priest—of any denomination—had come to me and asked me for the figure as a gift to put in the porch of his church or chapel I would have been delighted, and proud. I would have counted it a great honor. Everyone seemed to think this gallery was doing me a great honor, but I couldn't overcome the feeling that it was somehow all wrong. In the first place the carving didn't belong in a gallery; it didn't belong anywhere but in a church, or just outside one; and then how can what has been produced in passion and love have a price put upon it as though it were some impersonal mechanically produced object? It seemed that the gallery committee had been induced to buy the carving as a result of some very generous things said in praise of it by various distinguished artists and critics—all the abuse had come from the popular press, apparently. Finstein had all the cuttings in his office and was eager for me to read them, but after skimming through a few both the praise and abuse seemed equally uninformed, beside the point. It all seemed so much jargon to me. The abuse was too stupid to be worth considering; the praise seemed so much highfalutin art talk such as I had heard times without number in the Paris cafés.

I was quite happy about Graham Carlton buying Rintrah because I felt that he really liked it and understood what it was about, just as he had liked the Negro Girl Dancing. That was all right. He was welcome to both carvings, and the same with the other sales; perhaps some people bought them as an investment rather than because they liked them; I don't know; but they were anyhow simple things, and though I'd liked doing them I had no special feeling about them; I didn't mind taking money for them, since I lived in a money system of society and had to have the stuff. But the Christ thing was different; quite different. I was troubled; I was even in an odd sort of way upset by the sale. I couldn't have refused to sell it; Finstein had shown everything on the understanding that it was for sale, except, of course, for the two loan things. He wanted his pound of flesh; his thirty-three-and-a-third per cent; and why not? Business is business. He wasn't running the gallery purely for art's sweet sake. After the sale of Christ was announced I sold everything else, and Finstein clamored for me to bring along any drawings I had, any wood engravings, anything at all I had. . . .

When my father read about the purchase of the Christ and the price paid for it he tried to "touch" me at the earliest opportunity.

"Cleaned up a tidy sum on the jolly old statues, eh, son?" was how he put it.

"I've made enough to enable me to work at what I want for a year," I told him firmly. I didn't tell him I was giving mother a pound a week privately for her own pocket out of it: I had made her swear not to tell him.

"You wouldn't think of helping the old folks at home a bit now you're on the up and up? It takes your old man a year to earn what they paid you for that blinking wooden image!"

"But you could drink it a damn sight quicker, couldn't you?"

He grinned affably. "Now you're talking!"

"Nothing doing, Dad," I told him. "I've better uses for the money."

The conversation took place in the public bar of the Ship. He had gone there specially to look for me; he normally used a pub much nearer home. I looked at him, trying to feel that I was related to him, sprung from his loins, but I could feel no such relationship. As a boy I had feared him; as a young man I had hated him for the way he treated mother; now I found I was merely indifferent to him; he was just a boring old soak best avoided. He was a tall thin gaunt man. I had got my height from him, but I couldn't find any other resemblance to him; I had my mother's long mouth, and was generally considered to "take after" her. I suppose there must have been something of my sire in me, but I couldn't see what it was—unless it was that I had it in me to drink too much; his height and a tendency to alcoholism—only I'm not altogether convinced I got that from him. If he had been a teetotaler I think I should still have been a drinker. It goes with the temperament. There must have been something lovable about my father when mother married him, I suppose, but whatever it was I had never glimpsed it, and I doubt very much whether she did after the first few months. If there is really "that of God" in every man, as the Quakers say, I can only say that in my father it was packed away well out of sight. Perhaps he drank from some sense of personal failure. But that, I think, attributes too great a sensitivity to his nature. My own feeling is that he drank because he was bored and empty. I suppose I should have felt sorry for him, but there was nothing, as it were, to hang pity on.

So we glared at each other balefully, like a couple of fighting cocks, and in the end I gave him a couple of quid—and begrudged it for the waste of money it was.

Tansy thought we should go to Paris out of the money. I tried to make her understand that if I was to work in stone and marble for a year as I planned, buy the materials I needed, and do the work I wanted without the interruption of having to give lessons or make things for ready cash, there was no money to spare. I put her off with the idea that I might have an exhibition in Paris the following spring and we could go over together then. Actually I didn't plan another exhibition for at least a couple of years; I couldn't possibly have material enough within twelve months. But I took her out to dinner at an expensive restaurant, and I bought her a few things—her favorite perfume, and flowers, and a Georgian silver necklace we'd seen in an antique shop, and she was content.

The fact that she was at last interested in my work made our life together a lot easier. She was prepared to respect, now, what she couldn't understand. Obviously what could command a purchase price of several hundred pounds demanded respect.

21

THE GREAT green tide of spring washed over the earth, and when it retreated the colored tide of summer crept up. Scarlet geraniums replaced the beds of scarlet tulips in the Museum gardens at the foot of the hill, and Malaga had fallen to Franco. It was the Coronation summer, and the summer of the blockade of Bilbao, and the bombing of Guernica by German planes. The Spanish Plot was now an open secret.

I had a block of alabaster lying in my workshop for weeks

before I did anything with it. I would sit looking at it, trying to get to "know" it. We were like a couple who are engaged to be married but do not know each other very well. There were times when I thought we should never get on together, and when I yearned for the return of my first love. Eventually it came to me that I would get my hand in with a bas-relief—and then immediately I saw the eternal horses in the dens of night charging across the stone. I got to work on some drawings, and immediately the old excitement stirred in me. My betrothed, it seemed, could arouse desire in me; as soon as I had pointed-in the design I was in love with my new medium. My horses came along beautifully, spurning the clouds, stamping the stony law to dust, tossing their manes and neighing that empires should be no more. . . . I enjoyed myself hugely.

I finished it somewhere near the end of the summer, just when Tansy had a fortnight's holiday from the shop. My excitement had spent itself, the work was finished, and I felt drained. I had a feeling I would like to go off to Cornwall with my love and visit some stone quarries and look at the stone-built houses and at a wild rocky coast and listen to rough seas, and relax. Tansy and I had never had a holiday together; she had always gone off on a sea cruise with Bill. The first year she had done it I had been sick with jealousy and resentment, though she had worked hard to convince me that in a double-berthed cabin for a fortnight at sea her relations with her husband were as "platonic"—as she called it—as at home. For my peace of mind—almost for my very sanity—I dared not not-believe her. She sent me postcards from Lisbon, and from ports in the Canary Islands; and next year from places in the Mediterranean. I got more resigned and therefore less jealous each year. Last year they had "done" the Norwegian fjords. This year Bill was thinking of a cruise to Madeira it seemed. But this year I had a little money, for the first time, and I was in revolt. Why couldn't we do something together for once, I demanded, and outlined my Cornish plan.

That produced all the old stuff about how she couldn't hurt and disappoint Bill; how much this annual holiday with her meant to him, and then the real reasons—how it was her only opportunity to get abroad, and how it was an annual replenishing of her wardrobe, because, of course, for a cruise she had to have a number of day and evening dresses, and Bill always paid for the things she needed. . . .

When she had finished I said, bitterly, "So that unless Bill leaves you or dies we shall never have more than a Saturday to Monday week end together if we live to be a hundred?"

There was the usual toss of her head and tightening of her lips.

"We have to accept each other's terms," she said.

"The terms might be subject to revision," I pointed out.

She did not answer, and I went on despairingly, "Are you content for things to go on like this for the rest of our lives?"

"You never know what may happen. Nothing goes on the same all one's life."

"You mean Bill might be run over by a bus or go off with a blonde. But the chances are just as likely that he might decide to go and live in the north or emigrate to Canada. Or just go on like this till we're all too old to care one way or another."

"What's the good of talking about it?" she demanded. "We have to take what comes."

"I might decide I'd had enough and leave you," I objected.

Again the arrogant toss of the shining head.

"So much for your great love!"

I knew what she meant. I had shown her once the passage in Corinthians—"Love suffereth long and is kind . . . vaunteth not itself, is not puffed up . . . beareth all things . . . never faileth" . . .

She had retorted, "Oh, that! We learned that at school!"

As though that somehow made it less true. The upshot of it all was, of course, that she went off on the Madeira cruise with Bill and a lot of new dresses and a lot of last-minute impassioned protests that Bill should not so much as kiss her on the brow, and that she would think of me all the time and long for me; and I listened to all she said, grimly, unable for the willing suspension of disbelief. Once or twice I even grinned, it struck me as so damned funny.

I had the chance of a block of stone cheap and took advantage of it, but I had no ideas for it, and felt as though I'd never have ideas again. I'd have to get away—even without my love. So I bought a secondhand rucksack and had my strongest shoes thickly soled and heeled and set off for Penzance. I had it in mind to walk around the coast, anyhow as far as St. Ives. I might turn inland a bit occasionally—I had a good map—and cut off corners, but in the main I would hug the coast. I would get put up at cottages and sometimes doss down in a barn. It was the first holiday I had ever had. It seemed a pity to be doing it alone, but there it was.

There were times when I was soaked to the skin on the shelterless cliff tops in a driving rain, and times when I was blinded with white sea mists. Times when I sat in the sun with a screen of gorse bushes, honey-sweet and a-hum with late bees, and the sea thundering below, brilliantly blue and crashing on tall rocks; then I would eat my bread and cheese and swig beer out of a bottle and smoke a pipe and say to hell with Tansy, there were other joys, other satisfactions. But after a day like that, of sun and wind and sea, relaxed at night in some cottage feather-bed, I would long for her intolerably. Sometimes leaving a village pub at closing time and going back to bed I would think of her dancing in the ship's ballroom, or laughing and talking animatedly in the bar, or leaning on the rail of the ship, with Bill or some other male done up in a boiled shirt and looking like a penguin. For her the night would be still young, I would reflect, and her crazy sculptor lover, Tom Rowse, somebody she had known in another world, long ago . . . if, indeed, she ever gave him a thought. Sometimes I'd be so lonely I'd be on the point of getting the next train back to London, where anyhow I could lose myself in work. At other times I would feel that I could never go back, and indulge a fantasy of somehow acquiring a tiny cottage, however primitive, and starting a different sort of life, without Tansy—grow a few spuds, raise a few hens, and earn my daily bread on a violet farm or as a common laborer or jobbing carpenter, doing a bit of wood carving in my spare time, and when I could afford the wood.

But I was in stone country, and it brought my thoughts back continually to stone and the hundredweight block awaiting me in my shed at home. After that I wanted to make something in marble. Stone of all kinds was beginning to fascinate me with its potentialities; though I thought I would never love it as I loved wood.

I took Bill Blake along with me in my pocket on my walk around the Cornish coast, but I read only his small light things:

Never seek to tell thy love
Love that never told can be;

For the gentle wind does move
Silently, invisibly.

Well, but I had told my love, had told her all my heart; sometimes I wondered if eventually some traveler would come by and silently, invisibly, take her with a sigh. Perhaps that was the alternative to Bill getting run over by a bus or going off with a blonde. . . .

I should have left Cornwall one day earlier; just one day earlier would have made all the difference—not so much to my own story, for that would have shaped the way it eventually did anyhow, the design having been roughed out that day in Carol Bayes's studio when I was first brought within the orbit of influence of Josef Brenovska; but it would have changed the whole destiny of another person. Fate gets up to odd tricks—dirty tricks, some of them.

After several consecutive days of sea mists I was striding over the cliffs in the direction of Porthcoe, where I hoped to find a room for the night, and had made up my mind that in the morning I would make for the nearest main line railway station and take the first train back to London. I was tired of feeling myself the only substance in a shadow world, tired of the wet cling of mist to my face, the wet grass under my feet, and the crash and boom of a hidden sea. There were still some days to go before Tansy would be back, but in London, I told myself, I would have more to distract me from the intolerable longing.

Christ, that my love were in my arms
And I in my bed again!

was the whole of my mood.

I reached Porthcoe in the late afternoon. It lies in a hollow in the cliffs; its gray granite houses descend in terraces to a rocky cove where the fishing boats lie up on a shingly beach which at low tide gives onto a stretch of sand. I got a room for the night at the first cottage at which I inquired—the Williamses'. It perched on the top terrace, where the houses have small gardens running steeply down to the terrace below. I was given a small clean upstairs room looking straight out to sea, and though I asked no more than a place to sleep I was also given the neat crowded parlor immediately below. Mrs. Williams lit a fire for me there because though it was summer the evening was chilly from the sea mist. She was small and clean and neat like her rooms. She gave me a good tea, with eggs and bacon and homemade bread, and fell to chatting a little; she asked me where I was from, and was interested when I said London. She volunteered the information that her youngest daughter worked there—the other one was married and living in Penzance—in a part called Golders Green; perhaps I knew it? When I said that from where I lived I could look right across the river to it she was quite excited. "Well, fancy that now!" she said. "Norah'll be ever so interested when I tell her. She's nurse to two children there. We're expecting her home for her summer holidays tomorrow evening—it's a pity you're not staying on. She comes home every summer to see Dad and me, but she finds it very quiet here after London."

She indicated one of several framed photographs on the mantelpiece. "That's Norah," she added. I studied the features of a plain, kind-looking girl, and not knowing what to say observed that she had a sweet face.

"She's a sweet-natured girl," her mother assured me warmly, adding, "Her lady thinks the world of her—treats her almost as if she were her own daughter."

I made noises of appreciation and approval and she chatted on for a bit, telling me that her husband shared a trawler with two other men, and how he was one of the best, and how when he was not at sea he pottered in the garden and had taken prizes for his early potatoes and his tomatoes. In the course of the chatter she managed to shoot at me the inquiry as to whether I was married or single. She was good-natured and kindly, but I was glad when she went out and left me to my tea.

Afterwards I was glad to take off my wet heavy shoes and stretch out my legs before the fire; I had done a good eight hours' rough walking that day and was sufficiently physically fatigued to enjoy the rich luxury of relaxing in warmth and comfort. I lit my pipe and slumped in my chair and for a long time gave myself up to a reverie that was all Tansy. I kept the mental image of her shipboard life with Bill away from me, barricading it off with a host of memories, the whole thing firmly laced with dreams.

I was glad to be returning to London in the morning. I would somehow feel less far from her there. There might even be a letter from her. . . .

But the morning broke sunny and windy, with not a trace of mist, the sea bright blue and sparkling in the sunshine; Porthcoe seemed to me the most attractive place I'd been in, and certainly the Williamses' cottage was the most comfortable accommodation I'd yet found.

" 'Tis a pity you're off back to London just when the weather's cleared," Mrs. Williams said, when she brought in my breakfast. "You wouldn't think of waiting over another day or two?"

Whether she had any ulterior motive in the suggestion I don't know, whether she thought it would be nice for me to meet Norah, or for Norah to meet me, or both; for my part I had forgotten that by staying over I would meet the girl, and had I remembered it would scarcely have affected my decision one way or the other. Looking out of the window at the gray huddle of houses in the hollow brimming with sunshine, with the shimmering poster-blue sea beyond, my desire to return to town melted away as the sea mists had melted. There would probably be no letter from Tansy, I told myself, probably not even a postcard, and with no work in progress, and no incentive of inspiration to start anything new, the days would drag interminably. So long as the weather held I might as well finish out the time here.

On my way out I noticed in the narrow passageway something I had not noticed when I arrived—a well-made old cedar-wood chest. I paused to admire it.

"That's nice," I said, and ran my fingertips along the grain.

"Cedar wood," Mrs. Williams said, with a ring of pride in her voice. "Lovely smell when you open it."

"I know. I know a bit about wood—I was apprenticed to a cabinetmaker as a boy."

"Fancy!" said Mrs. Williams, and added, "You must have a chat with Dad. He thinks the world of that chest. His dad brought it home from some place abroad—he was in the merchant navy. It's always been seafaring, one way or another, in the Williams family."

Mrs. Williams had cut me some sandwiches and filled my flask with tea, and I went off with my rucksack for the day. It was a grand day, and I walked for several hours, had a swim in a sunny cove, sun-bathed, slept, and got back to Porthcoe in the evening tired and hungry, and glad to be returning to clean and comfortable quarters where I was sure of a good meal and a good bed. The homecoming daughter was so far from my thoughts that when I walked in at the open front door of the cottage and into my room I was startled when the girl of the photograph looked up from the fireplace where she was laying a fire. She was like her picture, but the warmth of her coloring and the soft brightness of her eyes gave her a gentle attractiveness which the dull flatness of the photograph denied her.

She scrambled to her feet as I entered, blushing a little, and murmuring good evening, and something about getting the fire going as it was chilly in the evenings. She added that she was Norah Williams and that she had arrived soon after I'd gone out in the morning, having traveled by the night-train from London.

"You've brought the sunshine with you," I said, conventionally.

"I hope it lasts," she answered. "It's so gloomy here when it rains. Not like London where there's always something on to pass the time. Mother says you're from London!" There was a kind of awed admiration in the statement, as though to be from the Big City was to be the shining emissary from some earthly Paradise.

She went on to ask me if I knew Golders Green, and where I lived myself, and to eulogize Hampstead Heath, the London tube system, the shops, the cinemas.

"But for Mum and Dad I'd never come back here," she said. "I get so bored after the first few days."

"It depends what you're interested in," I said.

She looked puzzled. "What is there to be interested in here?"

"Cromlechs, monoliths, stone circles . . ." I smiled at her, teasing her.

"Stones!" she pouted.

I laughed. "She asked for interest and he gave her a stone! I'm sorry! But there's swimming and sunbathing and walking—"

"They're all right if you've got anyone to do them with, I suppose, but I haven't, and anyhow I can't swim and I don't care for walking, and if I lie in the sun I just get red as a lobster."

"What do you like to do?" I inquired.

Her face brightened the moment her mind dwelt upon her pleasures.

"I like to sit in Lyon's Corner House—the big one in Piccadilly—and eat a tooty-frooty and listen to the band and watch the people. I could do it for hours! Then I like to go to the pictures and see a good romantic film. I like wandering about in big stores and having tea in a nice old-fashioned-style tearoom." She sighed. "I always say there's nowhere like good old London!"

"Paris has still more to offer," I told her.

"Funnily enough I've no desire to go abroad. My lady and gentleman go there a lot and rave about it—they go everywhere. But I always say England's good enough for me."

"You've no curiosity about other countries?"

"Not in the least. For one thing I don't much like foreigners."

"If you went abroad it's you who would be the foreigner," I pointed out.

She looked puzzled. "How could I be? I'm English." Then recovering herself, "Oh, I see what you mean. But all those people from other countries—they seem to talk so funny. At least compared to us. Though I suppose they're quite nice, really, when you get to know them." Her tone, however, implied doubt. A dull girl, I thought; more than dull, stupid. Yet was she—really? More than Tansy? Only I always had the feeling with Tansy that she was not really stupid; it was only that she never bothered to think; and she had a liveliness of imagination this girl completely lacked. Norah Williams was ordinary—a dull flat level of ordinariness. Whereas despite all that was commonplace in Tansy she was somehow far removed from ordinariness, by reason of something vital and flamelike in her personality and nervous energy. This girl Norah, it came to me, would make someone a good wife; she would be good and kind and sweet, a good housewife and a good mother. In bed she would acquiesce, no doubt, in a spirit of duty.

I was thinking along these lines after supper when she came in to clear away and ask if I wanted the fire made up and if I would like a "hot jar" in my bed, as the night had turned chilly.

What I wanted in my bed was Tansy, and I declined the "hot jar." At the back of my mind was an uneasy feeling that this girl, out of the frustration and loneliness that her days at home meant for her, wanted to come close to me, not consciously—she was too essentially simple for that—but with a birds-of-a-feather instinctive feeling for my own loneliness and frustration. She had been so quick to take over from her mother where I was concerned, and was obviously eager to talk. Shaking the crumbs from the tablecloth into the fireplace she said, "Mother and I were wondering whether you'd care to come to Trewelyn tomorrow with us—the Summer Show is on. It would be something to do." Her voice was eager.

"What happens there?" I asked her, drawing on my pipe and watching her, covertly, through the smoke.

"Oh, there's prize cattle, and cart horses, and pony trotting, and flowers, and homemade jam," she said. "Just the usual country show. There's a tent where you can get tea, and there's fortunetelling and lucky-dips and things. Mother has some bottled fruit she's showing, and Dad has some tomatoes, as usual."

"How do we get there?" I asked.

"There's a bus at the crossroads at three."

When I agreed to go she looked quite incredibly happy. She lingered a little longer in my room in a pretense of making up the fire. She had rather nice hair, I thought, chestnut, with a kind of light "grain" in it. There was something eager and childlike in her face that was quite touching. She was about twenty, and the bloom of youth and innocence was still on her. She was what my mother would have called a "good" girl, but I had the feeling that the emotional antennae were alert in her, quivering upon the waiting air.

I watched her making and remaking the fire and let her chatter on. When she could do no more to the fire she still lingered, crouched on the rug beside the fender, looking into the flames, the fireglow making her unpowdered cheeks shine like red apples. It struck me how much homelier the room was that night, with her presence, than it had been the previous night. She was the sort of girl who would create a homely atmosphere wherever she went, I thought, and where men were concerned it would always be her undoing, because a man does not wish to be handed buttered toast when he would rather be kissed, but when that happens, then he would rather the toast.

The next day, of course, Mrs. Williams had a blinding headache and did not feel equal to going to the show, but strongly urged that Norah and I should go without her. I say "of course" because I should have known that it would happen; not for nothing had Mrs. Williams elicited from me the fact of my bachelorhood.

In the bus Norah sat bolt upright on the window side

looking out as eagerly as though she were seeing the flat fields of stubble, of cabbages, of cauliflowers, for the first time. She wore a very clean blue cotton dress, very clean white shoes, and silly little white net gloves. She wore a twisted necklace of pink and white coral which she explained that her lady had given her last Christmas, and over her arm she carried a rather grubby and dowdy fawn-colored mackintosh, because she was the sensible sort of girl who would never take a chance with the weather. She had, as Tansy would say, "no style," but she was fresh as a flower and happy as a child at a school treat, and with a straw shopping basket containing homemade jam—which her mother was belatedly entering—on her knee, and her warm happy air of general well-being, she created all round her on the bus her own peculiarly homely atmosphere.

The show was as dull as most such affairs usually are. We looked at all the prize exhibits, the massive cart horses, all manes and tails and "feathered" hocks, the bulls prodigiously equipped, the dairy cows with enormous udders, the ponies harnessed to light traps and trotting daintily around the ring; we gazed at fabulous marrows, bottles of fruit, jars of jam, arrangements of prize sweet-peas, collections of potatoes and tomatoes. We looked at needlework, embroidery, knitting. We drank strong lukewarm tea in a marquee, and watched some children in charge of a black-coated parson run an egg-and-spoon race. Norah reminded me of Tansy by the smiling tenderness with which she watched the children. And all the time a brass band played popular airs—*The Foggy Dew*, *The Rose of Tralee*, *Billy-Boy*, and *Shenandoah*—all of which Norah hummed and la-la-la'd as we wandered about over the worn grass.

By the time the pubs were open I was so exhausted I could think of nothing else. She didn't mind coming in with me but she insisted that she would only have a lemonade. I asked her what she thought a drink would do to her. She declared, confusedly, that even a glass of ginger wine at Christmas went to her head. I demanded of her, roughly, what if it did? Was she frightened of being sick, or did she think it immoral to be a little bit on?

"I like to know what I'm saying and doing," she said.

"On one port you will," I said grimly, and ordered it for her.

I got myself a stout and carried the drinks to a corner. She sat sipping her drink fearfully. I thought of Tansy and how she would relax over a stiff gin and become animated and gay and amorous, and my longing for her swept over me again, so that I took a swig of the stout and then announced that I would be going back to London tomorrow. There was once again the feeling that I would be that much nearer Tansy.

Norah looked at me dismayed.

"Must you really?" she said.

"I must really," I said firmly.

She took another cautious little sip of the port, then said diffidently, "Perhaps we could meet in London sometime—on my half day?"

"I don't have a half day," I told her.

"You're a carpenter, aren't you?"

"What makes you think that?"

"Mother said you told her you'd been apprenticed to a cabinetmaker."

"Well, I am a carpenter of sorts, I suppose. I've carved banisters, and I once made a cedar-wood chest like your Dad's."

"It's a nice trade," she said. "I always think it's lovely to be able to do things with your hands. You know what I mean—to make things. I do a lot of needlework—you know, drawn-threadwork tablecloths and things like that. I do a lot for the lady I work for—she likes anything like that, and she's good to me so it's nice I can do something in return, isn't it?"

She was a good girl all right, I thought, and I liked it that she approved of manual work. I should have liked Tansy to have said all that. If the psychologists were right and there was the creative impulse in everyone, what, I wondered, was Tansy's? The creation of beautiful clothes, I suppose, only she had never developed her flair for them. Perhaps frustration was the root of all that was difficult and unsatisfactory in her. Perhaps I had never tried hard enough to understand her and help her, never loved her enough. . . .

"You must let me have your address in Golders Green," I heard myself saying to the girl at my side, though I knew in my heart I would never seek her out.

After one drink each we left the pub, as we had to get the evening bus back. I asked her how she felt after imbibing what the bylaws call intoxicating liquor. She said she felt a little giddy, and that she seemed to be lifting her feet very high when she walked. I told her that all that on one port was matter for congratulation. I spoke harshly, but I dragged her arm through mine. I hardly knew whether I wanted to shake her or kiss her. On the whole I think I was more inclined to shake her.

When we got back to Porthcoe there was a broad silver path of moonlight on the sea, and the gray houses rising in tiers from the hollow of the cliffs seemed swathed in a fine gauze. We walked up from the crossroads, climbing up to the top terrace, and when Norah shivered I suggested she should put on her raincoat—I was anyhow quite tired of carrying it, but she said she wasn't cold, "just someone walking over my grave," she said, with a little laugh. I pulled her arm through mine again—a nice rounded girlish arm, it was; I wouldn't have minded making it in alabaster. When we paused near the top of the hill for breath we looked out over rooftops glittering like water with moonlight, and there was the strong honey-scent of the gorse on the cliff sides, and a strong sweetness of tobacco plants from a garden below us. Norah leaned heavily on my arm for a moment, her eyes on the sea, and sighed.

"It's been such a lovely day," she said, "I don't want it to end. I wish we could go on walking through the moonlight all night."

"I thought you didn't care for walking?"

"I don't in the ordinary way—this is different." She leaned her head against my shoulder. "I can't bear for you to be going back to London tomorrow," she said. "It'll all be so empty without you."

I felt I had somehow to extricate her from this emotional morass—before she dragged me into it.

"What's so special about funny old me?" I demanded.

"You're not funny and you're not old!" she declared vehemently.

"I'm going on for forty," I pointed out, "and I know quite well what I look like—which is something vaguely related to a scarecrow."

"I don't care how old you are, or what you look like—I've never liked anyone so much or been so happy—ever!"

Still with her head against my shoulder she looked up at me. I don't know if she was very pale or whether it was just the moonlight.

"You think I'm a little fool, don't you?"

"I think you're very sweet," I said, "and I'm glad you enjoyed today, because I did, too, but now we must be getting back or Mum will be cross with us for being late for supper."

Quite firmly I drew her on up the rest of the way. But when we were close to the house she pulled me suddenly into the shadow of a plum tree in a garden at the corner of the terrace and flung her arms around my neck and pressed her lips to mine. I was too astonished to respond, and before I had recovered from the shock she had moved away from me and was declaring that she wanted to say good-bye to me there, like that, not in front of the others in the morning.

"Will we meet in London?" she demanded.

I told her I didn't know, that life was unpredictable.

"You're not married, are you?"

"No, I'm not married—officially."

"You mean you've got a girl friend?"

"Yes, I have—a girl friend."

"Are you going to marry her?"

"Norah," I said, "stop third-degreeing me! I want my supper. Come on!"

We achieved the remaining few yards without further emotionalism, and when we reached the cottage I went straight into my room, where a fire burned cheerfully, a small table was laid, and an oil lamp had been lit and turned low. I turned up the lamp, and in a moment Mrs. Williams came in with a laden tray. There was the heartening smell of hot tea and fried sausages.

I inquired if her headache was better, and she asked how I'd enjoyed the day. Norah, she said, was "dead beat" and had gone straight up to her room; she was going to take her up some hot milk in a few minutes.

"She enjoyed herself, but it's all that walking about," she explained.

I replied that I was pretty tired myself. It was a relief not to have to see Norah again that night. Poor little Norah! If only I had kept to my intention of returning to London yesterday morning before she arrived.

In the morning she was composed and matter-of-fact and walked with me to the bus stop. She made no reference to last night. When we reached the crossroads she produced a slip of paper with her Golders Green address written on it.

"If you're ever up that way perhaps you'd call," she said. "My lady wouldn't mind at all."

"Thanks," I said. I tucked the slip of paper away in an old notebook I kept for sketching-notes. I couldn't imagine that anything would take me to Golders Green, though, as I said to her, "You never know."

When the bus came into sight I bent forward and took her face between my hands and kissed her forehead.

"Good-bye, Norah," I said. "Think of the old tramp sometimes but not sentimentally, then no one will get hurt."

Which of course made her sentimental at once, and the tears started to her eyes.

"I'll think of you as the loveliest person I've ever known!" she declared passionately.

I laughed and patted her cheek.

"Go on with you, sweet-and-twenty," I said. "You haven't got started yet!"

Then I climbed up into the bus, my rucksack the antisocial nuisance a rucksack always is in a bus, but I managed to do a half-turn and give her a wave. Poor Norah! I suppose she walked back feeling miserable . . . but she hadn't got started yet, though I wasn't to know it at the time.

22

BECAUSE I was so eaten out and in by my reunion with Tansy that whenever I sat down to study the block of stone I could see only her, soon after I got back I decided to use it for a straight portrait of her. She mistrusted me after Eve, but she sat to me nevertheless. What I wanted to bring out in the portrait was that quality of life—of sex, if you like—which made even the fall of her hair, the lift of her head, significant. She was in a good mood after her holiday, affectionate and full of bright chatter. She looked well, too. It came to me all over again that she was a very clear example of the principle of "be happy and you will be good." But I had no means of keeping her happy. I hadn't the money.

Our lives continued in the same pattern. Later in the year Lee wrote inviting me to spend Christmas with him—*Christmas is less grim in Paris than anywhere else*, he wrote. *Graham and Helen have forgiven each other about Spain and gone to the south together and won't be back till the spring, so come and stay as long as you like.* I went, and stayed a week. But for Tansy I would have stayed longer, but longer than that I could not bear to be away from her.

It was fine being back in Paris. I was excited by the familiar smell of coffee, strong cigarettes, garlic, drains, the moment I stepped out of the overheated train at the Gare du Nord. And excited by the café lights when we came out of the station, and the familiar shrilling of the car and taxi horns. It was fine walking the familiar streets again, crossing the familiar bridges, sitting at the same cafés and *bistros*. I liked it fine. And being in Graham Carlton's beautiful old house on the Ile St. Louis, the loveliest spot in all Paris, and seeing and touching the Brenovskas again. And fine being around with Lee again, someone of mine own fashion, someone I could really talk to with the feeling of speaking the same language. But I wanted my lovely girl. Alone at nights on my bed I sought her. We belonged. Cornwall had taught me that.

So I came back and there was one more reunion. And now encouraged by the success of my portrait bust I wanted to carve her in marble, but more than a portrait this time, something which would convey all I felt about her and which would express "the lineaments of gratified desire," according to the gnomic verse, and I would make it in Blake's terms in which exuberance is beauty, with "the head Sublime, the heart Pathos, the genitals Beauty, the hands and feet Proportion." Tansy would not like it because she would not find a waxwork likeness in it—even the bust, which was recognizably like her, she criticized as not being "exactly" as she was. I warned her that the shape into which I wanted to work the marble would not be a photographic likeness of herself, but only an interpretation of an aesthetic mood, inspired by what I felt for her. In that case, she said, she need not sit for me for this piece of work. I told her that I needed her there for inspiration. She made a good deal of fuss when she found I wanted her to pose naked. It was not nice, she protested, being looked at "cold-bloodedly" like that. Also she did not want to be portrayed in the nude even in marble. I told her, grimly, "No one will know it's you!" Yet I longed for her to be "with" me in its making, because what I planned was starry and glorious, like the Daughters of Los, with bright loins which were a beautiful golden gate opening into Paradise. She was still for me the bow of burning gold, and all the arrows of desire, and in such terms I dreamed she should be shadowed forth from the cold marble.

I was still working on it in March, when ex-Corporal Hitler marched his men into Austria; and in September when Chamberlain flew with his umbrella to Berchtesgaden, securing for the world a breathing space, and peace without honor. I did not go away that summer, and Tansy went with hubby-Bill to Venice, then down the Dalmatian coast to Dubrovnik, from both of which places she sent me charming cards saying how she missed me.

Soon after "Munich" I finished the piece of sculpture which I had decided to call Daughter of Los; around the base of it I had chiseled the words, *For everything that lives is Holy*. Tansy, as I had expected, thought it hideous and wanted to know what it was supposed to represent, and she was scandalized because I had carved the genitals. The big row about Epstein's Adam had yet to come. She considered that I was merely being disgusting when I asked what was wrong with genitals and where would we be without them? I hadn't set out to design a sexless tombstone angel.

I was as exhausted when I had done with the Daughter of Los as when I had finished with Christ driving the money-changers from the temple. But I had very little money left, and I had to buy some small pieces of wood and make a few things and tout them around again. I got back my wood-carving classes three nights a week. I longed now to try my hand at ivory, but I hadn't the money to spare for anything so expensive. For the time being I had come to an end. I hadn't enough money to go on making big things for an exhibition and no means of selling what I had already made. I didn't, anyhow, want to sell the Daughter of Los. I thought now that I must get some more money together and get back to wood.

I stayed in England for Christmas although Lee invited me again. For one thing I hadn't the fare to Paris, and for another I hadn't the heart for it. I longed for a few days-and-nights-in-a-row of peace with Tansy. I wanted the blessedness of sleep with her, unharassed by any necessity for counting the hours, watching the clock, free of the gray menace of Monday morning imminent. "Sleeping together!" How debased the term has become, stripped of its tenderness, made a euphemism for sex at its most vulgar. It seemed as though we would never have this boon of days-and-nights-in-a-row. I had, as she said, to accept her on her own terms.

I was lying on my bed on Christmas Eve thinking all this and feeling pretty damn miserable when I heard steps clumping up the bare stairs. A slow, firm tread it was, a little heavy, not like Tansy's quick running steps. There was a knock on the door and in the instant in which I called "Come in" it opened and Helen walked in, all black velvet, chinchilla, flaming hair, and parma violets. The room filled with her presence as with her perfume.

I leaped up and embraced her, kissing her on both cheeks and demanding how she had got here and when, and why.

"I arrived at noon, by plane," she said, throwing back her furs and seating herself on a chair. "I'm sailing for New York in two days' time. Everyone's getting out of Paris. Graham is coming over with me."

I was bewildered. "But why this exodus?"

"It can only be a matter of months before all hell is let loose. In Paris they're already digging air-raid shelters and piling up sandbags."

"They're doing that here too. I don't see why it has to get people on the run. What about Lee—is he going over with you and Graham?"

"Graham wanted him to, but he's coming back to London after Christmas. Says he would far rather be bombed than go to America. He may think differently when the bombs start to fall. Graham and I think you should come over with us, Tom. We could ship all your new stuff and you could work there and get an exhibition together."

She offered me a cigarette from her beautiful case.

"It's all right for you," I said, taking the cigarette. "Your family is over there. My mother is here, and Tansy. You're not suggesting I should run out on them?"

"You could bring your mother, and Tansy's husband will no doubt evacuate her to the country. But it's you who are important, Tom—you're an artist, a quite considerable artist, and that's a rare species. We've got to save our artists alive. You're an anarchist, too, so it's not your war. You're entitled to get out. You're not one of the stand-up-to-Hitler boys."

"Plenty of the stand-up-to-Hitler boys will run out too, leave others to do the standing up, don't you worry! Nothing like being patriotic from a safe distance! But I'm neither standing up nor running out. I'm staying put—along with all the millions that will have to stay put whether they like it or not. Why should being an artist entitle me to privilege? No, ma'am, count me out, but thanks for the offer."

"You're being quixotic," she said. "Also a little tiresome. A great artist is irreplaceable, and you know it. The artist who made that Christ out of lignum vitae is a great artist. You know that, too. He's a great deal more valuable than the millions of clerks and salesmen and factory hands who will stay put perforce. They're expendable. You're not."

"*For everything that lives is Holy*," I murmured.

"Well, it's not going to be holy much longer," she said shortly. "It's going to have the daylight bombed out of it! What's happening in Spain is only a try-out—a dress rehearsal. You know that."

"Helen," I said, "it's no good. There'll be plenty of fly-boys without me adding to them."

"You won't be able to work here—you realize that? It'll be an end of all creative work. You'll be set to work in a munitions factory or raked in for the army—either way you'll become part of the general destruction."

"Not Tom Rowse," I said quietly.

"The alternative will be prison."

"It'll be an experience. At least I'll come out of it with my hands clean. Let's talk of something else. How about coming over to my workshop? I've got several things to show you—all stone."

I couldn't keep the eagerness out of my voice, I suppose, for she looked at me with an oddly affectionate smile.

"You're pleased with them?"

"They've come off—especially a Daughter of Los in marble!"

"And you don't mind whether she's smashed by a bomb or not?"

"I do mind. If the war happens I'll take steps to evacuate her. When is this war of yours likely to start?"

"March, probably. The fatal Ides of March. Last March the *Anschluss*, next March the general conflagration—"

"You could be wrong," I said. "Germany's Problem Child Number One has been good enough to say he has no further territorial ambitions."

"Except the Polish Corridor!"

"No one is going to war about that!"

"You could be wrong," she said, and got up. "Let's go and visit your Daughter of Los, then perhaps we can have a drink and a snack at the Ship."

My beautiful white marble emanation of Tansy looked good when I switched on the light in the workshop, and I saw the admiration in Helen's face. She ran a hand down the gleaming thighs and smiled up at the tilted-back head, wild hair flying like the manes of the trampling horses in the bas-relief. The vitality of the figure, with the lifted breasts and tense lithe torso, was tremendous. The figure strained forward, and there was a suggestion of wings in the backward-flung arms. The bright loins were powerfully naked and unashamed, true gates to the Paradise of the senses.

Helen said, smiling, "It's a pity that the artist who made that doesn't feel he has a responsibility to his creative power—enough to want to save it alive. Or anyhow not to risk being destroyed."

"Risks!" I said. "We might go straight out of here and get run over by a bus!"

"It's possible, but not probable. The degree of probability is considerably higher in the matter of bombs falling on London in the near future—and on this part of London. Isn't there a big arsenal just up the river from here?"

"You're being morbid, Helen," I said. "Just take a dekker at the bas-relief and then let's go and have that drink!"

But she looked first at the bust of Tansy.

"Your lovely girl," she observed. "Is she pleased with it? I remember you said she hated the Eve."

"She likes it well enough," I said. I didn't want to talk about Tansy. I wanted to forget her. Until Helen had walked in on me I had wanted only to sleep the intervening days away. But now Helen was here and we could talk and I could forget—if I was allowed to. I indicated the horses. "Stamping the stony law to dust," I said.

She smiled and murmured, " 'Crying Empire is no more.'

Wonderful lines, and you've made a wonderful job of it. You're an artist, Tom—you stubborn fool!"

"Thanks," I said. I pressed her arm. "Let's go."

23

I DIDN'T see Helen again after that Christmas for seven years. She was wrong in prophesying the war would start in March, but there was a tragedy on the last day of that month: the Spanish "Christian gentleman," having bombed and blasted his way into Madrid, became "master of all Spain."

Lee arrived back in London before the end of 1938. He was quite content, he said, to live again in his Chelsea basement, leaving all his charming Louis-Quinze effects behind in Paris. Graham had taken all the Brenovska figures to America with him, and the bulk of his most valued possessions, including the two Tom Rowse pieces—Rintrah, and the Negro Girl. Lee had transported from Paris all his clothes, his phonograph and records, most of his books, and his Meissner coffee service. Within a fortnight of being back he had got himself a job in an antique shop in Knightsbridge. It was kept by a ladylike young man who between customers did *petit-point* embroidery in the Regency drawing room behind the shop. "He says his name is Gabriel," Lee said, "but it's probably George. I'm sure we shall get on famously." He giggled.

Throughout that spring and summer he spent his week ends with the anarchist refugees from Franco's Spain. The Republicans and Communists were well looked after, but the anarchists were not popular with the general refugee committee; they were considered to have sabotaged the anti-Fascist war effort with their Catalonian revolution. In response to an appeal made by Red Emma at a public meeting to raise funds for the refugees Lee had gone along on the Saturday to the S.I.A.—*Syndicado Iberian Anarquistas*—office in Soho with a bundle of blankets and towels and to offer his services in any capacity. He had believed himself to be volunteering, he told me, with a smile which was half amused, half rueful, but found himself conscripted. He turned up faithfully every week end and did clerical work, addressing envelopes by the hundred—"*Such* a bore!" Nevertheless he did it week after week, month after month, on whichever day he was not entertaining batches of the refugees to coffee and cigarettes in his basement, or taking them on conducted tours to see the sights of London. Part of his clerical duties at the office consisted of running out for cups of coffee and nips of whisky for the Queen of the Anarchists, who rampaged about the office cursing "Stalin's henchmen" and "Franco's minions" equally, in Central European English or good plain Yiddish. "She's an old terror," Lee said, "but you can't help *admiring* her!"

One week end when I couldn't see Tansy because she had gone off somewhere for a week end with Bill I went to one of Lee's refugee parties. The Spaniards had very little English, and neither Lee nor I nor any other of the English contingent had any Spanish at all, but with an Esperanto of good will sufficient communication was established. The Spaniards lolled about on the divan and sat on the floor, and Lee put rumba and flamenco records on the phonograph, and supplied quarts of coffee and hundreds of cigarettes. Ma Hilley came in with plates of homemade cakes, and while Lee busied himself with the phonograph Miss Hopkins and I handed around the cakes and poured coffee, and the Spaniards amused themselves coaxing smiles out of Miss Hopkins's solemn little boy. Before she went off to her club, Gwen Naylor came in for an hour, wearing a terrific hat with sweeping ostrich-feather plumes; she sang some French songs and was an enormous success—the heated and interminable political arguments were dropped—and where there are twelve Spaniards gathered together there will always be thirteen different opinions—and the dark eyes of these defeated and exiled men, politically, emotionally, and sexually frustrated, glowed and flashed with admiration, attraction, and much else. After a few attendances at these parties Gwen had an *affaire* with the handsomest of them—quite a love affair, I gathered from Lee, but that is another story.

I often wondered what these woman-loving and woman-hungry men made of this slender, golden youth, so effeminate, decadent even, who yet devoted all his spare time and a good deal of his small salary to their service, either at the S.I.A. office or on their entertainment. There was no ulterior motive in anything he did for them; he did, quite simply, profoundly admire and respect them. His manner to them was warm and friendly, but impersonal; he never met any of them other than collectively. He admired all that they stood for, he told me, and their courage, and a kind of fierce pride which, in the face of the Franco onslaught, had bred the *No Pasarán* stand and the impassioned declaration that it was better to die on their feet than live on their knees. "Personally," he added, relapsing into his bored, drawling tone, "I would rather live on my knees, but I do admire people who can take the heroic line."

"The life-at-any-price line takes courage, too," I pointed out. "Heroism, even. It might even be necessary to die for it!"

He gave me one of his quick, sidelong looks; he made no comment, but I felt we understood each other.

I didn't see much of Lee that year, between his working at the shop and his week-end activities with the Spaniards, but I was glad he was in London—in an odd sort of way it was a comfort. I had the feeling about him, as about Helen, that our friendship did not need to be continually bolstered up with correspondence, telephone calls, meetings; that it would remain as strongly and permanently there without these aids, that we would always be there for each other, and even if we did not meet for years could pick up the threads of the friendship where we had last laid them down. Occasionally Lee would come out to Greenwich on a weekday evening to have a drink and a chat; occasionally he would invite me into the West End to a meal with him in some small restaurant; but increasingly he gave his evenings as well as his week ends to the Spaniards—to work in the office, to attendance at Spanish-relief meetings, to the Spaniards themselves. Occasionally, bravely, he took Red Emma out to dinner to cheer her up. He was always wanting me to join him on Spanish outings or his indoor parties; I could bring Tansy along, he said, adding maliciously that it would do her good; but, selfishly, I felt that our time together was too short and precious to be spared. I squared my conscience by giving him a few shillings occasionally to buy cigarettes for his parties.

The talk that spring was all of the Danzig issue, and conscription posters appeared everywhere. In May, Germany and Italy formed a military pact "to contribute to the assurance of peace in Europe." In June the *Thetis* submarine disaster pushed Danzig into the inside pages of the papers. There were also Fleet Street rumors that the press had been ordered to pipe down on the war talk, as it had bad repercussions in the city. . . . But in July, Danzig was back in the news again—until it was ousted by the *Thetis* inquiry. On September the 1st, German bombs fell on Warsaw. The roads out of London streamed with cars loaded with people and bedding getting out in good time before the bombs started falling on London. The hospitals filled their ambulances with surgical cases and evacuated them to the country. Two days later, on Sunday, Chamberlain broadcast the declaration of war. Tansy and I heard it together in our usual Sunday morning pub. A woman exclaimed "O God!" and Tansy burst into tears. Soon after that the siren sounded and everyone believed the bombing had begun. Tansy clung to me, sobbing hysterically that she couldn't bear it. . . .

In the afternoon we sat on the grass on the Observatory hill in the mellow September sunshine and Tansy declared that when the bombs really fell she would never be able to stand it, that she would have to ask Bill to arrange for her to go to the country.

"Perhaps you could come and live somewhere near and work on a farm or something," she suggested, "and we could still see each other at week ends?"

"No," I said, "I'm staying here."

"But why?"

"My mother is staying in London, and Lee."

"Are they more important to you than I am?"

"You know they're not. But I can't run out on things, that's all. My workshop is here. I want to go on working so long as ever I can afford to buy materials. It's my way of boycotting the war. It's right for the children to be evacuated, and for women with children to clear out, and old people, but as all the people who keep the wheels going around will have to stay, whether they like it or not, why shouldn't I—and you?"

"My nerves won't stand it! You saw how it was when that siren went off for no reason at all!"

"Your nerves will get used to it. I expect a lot of people were scared when the siren was tried out, but most of them will still be in London at the end of the war."

"Those left alive!"

"Most people will survive. You and I have as much chance as anyone else."

"Bill is sure to want me to go."

"And what Bill says goes," I said bitterly. "If you go," I went on, "it will finish us. We shan't be able to meet. How can I come to you, wherever you are, one week end, and your lawful husband the next? How are you going to explain us to your hostess or landlady?"

"I could meet you at a hotel some distance off."

"You'd better not go far out, then," I said, still bitter. "I can't keep raising the fare to Devon or Cornwall."

We spent a miserable Sunday, with this deadlock of our wills, and we parted miserably, without having been reconciled, on Monday morning.

24

No one can walk a tightrope forever, or even for long, without falling off—certainly not the kind of tightrope Gladys Tanswell had been walking for years, ever since we became lovers. It was hubby-Bill who shook the wire, and into whose accommodating lap she fell. They spent that Christmas in Dublin; Bill was already over there on business, and what simpler than that his wife should join him there? Why spend Christmas in wartime in England when you could spend it in neutral Ireland? There was, as Bill put it, of the land of saints and scholars and poets, much more grub in Ireland. . . .

Tansy came back very worried. She could hardly wait to tell me the bad news. I had fixed up a reunion lunch at my place, and sparing no expense for the occasion had bought half a bottle of gin. She broke the news to me after the first couple of sips.

"I don't know what on earth we're to do," she said. "Bill's got the idea of taking a cottage outside Dublin for the duration. In fact"—desperately—"he's taken it. He wanted me to move in then and there, not come back after Christmas. But of course I had to come. I made the excuse that I couldn't let the firm down—that I must give proper notice, not just not come back. I don't know what to do. I haven't been able to sleep all this week for thinking about it."

My heart beat very fast.

"I'm surprised you needed to think twice. Obviously if you go to live in Ireland we can't meet. Assuming you want us to go on meeting you obviously can't go, and must tell Bill so."

"I thought perhaps you could come and live over there too."

"We've had all that. I've already told you I'm not running out.

I could have got clean away to America if I'd wanted, all expenses paid by Mr. Graham Carlton. So could Lee. We're both staying. But all that apart, what do you suppose I would do in Ireland?"

"I suppose you could get work."

"Do you really? Why, then, do you suppose the Irish flock over here?"

"You could probably go on being a sculptor over there—everything is going on just the same in Dublin—art shows and all that."

I said, grimly, "Do you really see my Daughter of Los, bright loins and all, being publicly shown in that narrow, provincial, Jansenist atmosphere? Ireland! I'd suffocate there among all those priests! After Spain it's the most priest-ridden country in the world. No fear! It's me for good old London and whatever bombs may fall!"

She said, with intense bitterness, "You may not feel so brave when they start falling."

"There's nothing wrong in feeling frightened. The thing is not to *act* frightened. I'll feel frightened all right. But I'd sooner be frightened out of my wits some of the time than have them smothered all the time."

"What do you propose then?"

"That you tell Bill straight out you're not prepared to live in Ireland for the duration. He can't force you to. You're not dependent on him, and you're long overdue for leaving him, anyhow. Tell him the truth, for God's sake, once and for all! Now's your chance!"

The conversation shuttlecocked to and fro on these lines for a time, each of us accusing the other of lack of love for not doing what the other wanted.

Finally I demanded of her, "What do you *want* to do? If you could have everything exactly as you liked with no repercussions from either Bill or me, how would you yourself arrange it?"

"I should have thought it was obvious what I would like. I would like to go to Ireland, to the place Bill has taken, and have you come there week ends when it worked out that way."

"I see. The best of both worlds, as before. But as that's not possible, what are you proposing to do—taking into account my firm refusal to leave London?"

"I shall go to Ireland, and hope you'll join me when you can."

"You think my love and longing will wear me down? But they won't, you know. You don't really think I'm going to spend week ends with you in the cottage Bill's paying the rent for—dodging in and out when his back's turned?"

"I suppose you could get a place in Dublin like you have here, that I could come to."

"Dublin's not London. There's no privacy in small provincial cities where everyone knows everyone. You and Bill would soon get to know people in Dublin; so would I. It would only be a matter of time, and short time at that, before people would begin spotting that we were together whenever Bill wasn't around. And people living cramped narrow lives love a bit of gossip—it's the breath of life to them. For me it's the "pale religious letchery" Blake had such a contempt for. No, my love, the choice is yours—it's Dublin with Bill, or London and your lover, and no two ways about it. I'm very willing to go and see Bill and explain to him."

Her eyes widened with terror.

"Don't you dare! I should deny everything! And he'd believe me, not you."

"What are you going to do?" I insisted.

"I must go—you know I must."

"Because of Bill—or because you're frightened of the bombs?"

"Both, if you want to know."

"I do want to know. I want to know one hell of a lot more. I want to know just how much Bill means to you—then perhaps I'll know how little I really mean!"

It came to nothing, of course. It was just beating the air. She insisted that she loved me, but that she couldn't hurt Bill. That Bill was a part of her life. It was where I came in—six years ago.

Presently she assumed another tactic—despairing passion, clinging to me and pleading wouldn't I wait for her? Perhaps the war wouldn't last long—some people even thought it would be over before Christmas—and in wartime there were always separations, and when people loved each other they waited for each other for years if need be. She would be faithful—she swore it.

"And if this war lasts as long as the last, am I expected to live like a monk for years?"

"So long as you don't *love* anyone else," she murmured.

"Unfortunately I'm not much good where I don't love, and it's too late to change now. Or are you suggesting I should take to tarts? Not that I think I'd be any good at that, either."

It was a disastrous week end. I quite deliberately got drunk at midday on the half-bottle of gin, and as soon as the pubs opened went out to continue the good work. I took Tansy with me and I suppose she had too much to drink, too, for I seem to remember looking at her once, near closing time, and seeing the tears rolling down her cheeks.

"You've had too much to drink," I said censoriously, though I hadn't been sober myself since she'd arrived at my room. The next day I felt horribly ill, and Tansy who wouldn't admit to a hangover complained of a bad headache. I was sober that night, but I still felt like death, not merely in my body but inside myself. My impotence was emotional as well as physical, and there was nothing I could do about it.

Tansy clung to me in the darkness—that dreadful dead darkness—and she cried very bitterly, accusing me of no longer loving her. But her tears and reproaches could not move me, I was so dead; they were like rain on stone, and the stone could not help being the cold pitiless thing it was.

I saw her off to work on Monday morning, then I went to Chelsea to call on Miss Kent. I wanted to find out when Mr. Tanswell was expected home.

25

I HAD to wait three days before Bill Tanswell was back from Manchester, but my determination did not waver in that time. I was only impatient for the time to pass. I had a complete obsession about the matter. My only regret was that I hadn't acted six years earlier.

Miss Kent had recommended that I should call on Mr. Tanswell at about nine in the morning. He had his breakfast with Mrs. Tanswell at eight, and she left at half past. He very seldom left before nine-thirty. I got there at nine. I noticed that in the basement Lee's curtains were still closed. I didn't blame him; getting up early is an abomination, like going to bed early.

I felt pretty grim when I knocked on the door of the Tanswell flat. I had slept badly, going over and over the impending interview in my mind, and filled with dread for its outcome; only I knew that if it meant I never set eyes on Tansy again I would have to do it, because I had reached a point which was a dead end of impotence and despair.

The door opened by Tanswell himself. He was just as I had remembered him from the glimpses I'd had of him years ago when I'd lived there—of medium height, heavy, red-faced, with thinning hair and the beginnings of a paunch. It was a pleasant enough face, I suppose, the sort of face you can see grouped around the saloon bar in pubs all over England—he looked exactly what he was, married, and commercial-traveler-doing-rather-well. He wore a good-looking dark-blue pinstripe suit, with a breast-pocket handkerchief, and a blue-and-red-and-yellow-striped tie.

He smiled pleasantly, and I was surprised that anyone so obviously doing well wouldn't treat himself to a better denture.

"Good morning, sir," he said amiably. "What can I do for you?"

"My name's Rowse," I said. "I'm a friend of your wife's, and I'd like a talk with you, if you can spare me a little time."

"Not Tom Rowse, the sculptor?" he inquired, his blue eyes bright with interest.

I nodded, and he exclaimed, "Come in, come in, Gladys has told me about you. Mah'vlous show you had last year, I believe—proper clearance sale, what?"

I followed him in, as I had once followed Tansy—the only time I had ever been inside the flat. He led the way into the living room, where the remains of his breakfast were still on the table.

"Care for a cup of tea?" he inquired. "It's still hot. There's some toast too. Or perhaps you'd like an egg? Have you come far, sir?"

"From Greenwich," I said, "but I don't want any tea or anything, thanks."

"Greenwich, eh, where they have all that mean time?" He laughed heartily at his joke.

"Care for a drink, perhaps?" he suggested.

"No thanks."

"Sit down," he said. "Sit down. No charge."

I sat down at the end of the table.

"What I've come to say to you may be a shock," I felt bound to say.

He looked startled. "No accident to Gladys?" he said quickly.

"Not that I know of," I said. "I haven't seen her since Monday morning, when she left for work after spending the week end with me."

His red good-natured face was all bewildered incomprehension.

"We've been lovers for the last six years," I said. "I wanted her to tell you from the beginning, but she always said she couldn't hurt you."

He went on staring at me. He licked his lips and his head jerked as though his collar had become too tight.

"I—I—" he said. There was a dreadful kind of helplessness about him.

"I'm sorry," I said. "I wish to God she'd told you in the beginning. I've pleaded with her to. This week end I asked her to for the last time, but she still said she couldn't, and she defied me to. But I had to. I couldn't go on. If she goes to Ireland with you for the duration it finishes everything. She can't have her cake and eat it—not all her life."

He licked his lips again, then he said, "What—what's the idea in telling me? What—do you want—exactly?" The words seemed to come with difficulty, and he never took his eyes off me.

"I want you to tell Tansy that you know, and that she must choose between us," I said. "It sounds like a novelette, I suppose, or something in a bad film, but there it is. . . ."

He got up and went over to the sideboard and took the cork out of a decanter. His hand shook a little as he poured himself a drink. He drank it neat and came back to the table. He sat down heavily.

"All this beats me," he said. "I'm out of my depths."

He stared at me in that helpless way.

"I'm sorry," I said.

"Yes. You should be. My wife and I are very devoted. I won't say I haven't had a bit of fun here and there. When a man's on the road, you know! And I never asked her any questions about this fellow she used to go dancing with. So long as nothing interfered with our marriage, if you understand. Naturally a man doesn't want his wife sleeping around—"

The flow of words stopped suddenly.

"I understood you were very semidetached. Platonic was the word she used."

"She told you that?" The incredulousness in his face and voice seemed to pierce me.

"She was always insisting on it," I said, and now it was I who was helpless.

Rage and misery seemed to be struggling in him now. His blue eyes seemed to burn.

"What the hell do you take me for—a blasted eunuch?"

I got up. "I've been a fool," I said.

"Yes," he said heavily. "Yes. It looks like it."

Then suddenly he seemed to go to pieces; his face sagged and his lips trembled and he seemed to shake.

"God dammit!" he suddenly shouted. "She didn't have to do that! I worshiped every bone in her little body! I know I was away a lot, but she had nothing to complain of when I was home. God dammit!"

He buried his face in his thick hands with their clumsy fingers —that fondled Tansy. Loud animal noises came from behind his hands. I suppose he was crying. I went out, closing the door upon him, closing the front door of the flat, closing the street door. Closing all the doors. Forever.

26

It wasn't the last I saw of Tansy. Bill went away again in a few days and she came out to my place one evening. I wasn't there and she went to my workshop, and not finding me there went looking for me in the pubs. She found me in the Ship, sitting in a corner, pretty well on. I hadn't seen her come in and I was startled when she pushed her way through the people standing near me and confronted me across the table. She was very pale, and blazing with anger.

I looked at her without smiling. She was not my lovely girl, my love; there were no more arrows of desire. She was Bill Tanswell's wife; Mrs. William Tanswell; Gladys Tanswell.

"I've been looking everywhere for you! I've got to talk to you," she said violently.

I moved a little along the bench to make room for her.

"We can't talk here," she said.

"There's nowhere else," I said.

"Why can't we go to your place?"

"No," I said.

She sat down beside me, then turned to me angrily.

"What was your idea in trying to wreck my marriage?"

"Until I got there I didn't know there was any marriage to wreck. I knew you were legally married to Bill, but you always insisted there was nothing between you. Your poor old Bill looked kind of astonished when I told him that."

"You believed him rather than me, of course."

"I don't always know when people are lying, but I know when they're telling the truth. Bill was telling the truth. It was written all over his homely mug."

"You're calling me a liar, is that it?"

"Yes," I said. "I'm calling you exactly that."

She struck me in the face then. Her ring caught my lip and cut it. I pulled out a pocket handkerchief and dabbed at it.

She went on, her voice unsteady, "I've denied everything to Bill, and he believes me! I convinced him you were potty!"

"Then you are a self-confessed liar."

"I couldn't bear him to be so unhappy."

"And you lied to me to keep me happy too, I suppose?"

"I didn't lie to you."

"It's no use discussing it," I said. "What did you want to talk to me about?"

"The future. What's going to happen?"

"You're going to Ireland with Bill—for the duration. I'm staying here."

"I know all that." Her voice was impatient. "I mean about us."

I stared at her in amazement.

"You don't really imagine that we're going on just as if nothing had happened, do you?"

"I can't see that anything has happened, except that you caused me an upset with Bill."

"Look, Tansy," I said, "we don't speak the same language. Let's not discuss it any more. There's nothing to discuss. I'm through. I should have thought that was obvious."

"You mean you're throwing me over?" Her lips quivered, and

all over again, even then, I thought what a lovely childish mouth it was.

"Unless you'd like to get a divorce from Bill, or anyhow leave him, and come and live with me."

"You're being ridiculous!"

"All right, I'm being ridiculous. There's no more to be said. You'd better go. People are taking an interest in us."

"Dab your lip," she said, "you've got blood on your chin. I'm sorry I did that, but you provoked me."

"Please go, Tansy," I pleaded. "I've been through heavy weather these last few days, and I can't stand any more."

"You don't want ever to see me again?"

"No," I said, "not as things are. I don't even want to think about you."

"It's awful to be parting like this—after so long," she said unsteadily.

"For God's sake *go!*" I said, violently. Did she really think I was going to play sentimental farewells, both of us dissolving into tears, and eventually sinking into each other's arms, and all-be-as-before-Love?

She gathered her gloves and handbag together and got up. I also got up and moved over to the bar.

"Good-bye, then," she said bleakly.

I answered curtly, without looking at her, "Good-bye." I didn't see her go out of the door; out of my life.

The rest was silence, grubbing for a living, bombs. For six years; for as long as Tansy and I had been together. Only it seemed longer in the living. But then at the end of it instead of a door closing a door opened.

Part Two

MERCY, PITY, PEACE

I

THERE seems no point in writing at any length about the war years. Bombs became the common experience in that bigger and more frightful world conflagration. The "England can take it" slogan could have been adapted to Russia or Germany with even more justification, and they had, no doubt, their equivalent morale-raiser. It was something to have remained in London during the war, but it was even more to have remained in Berlin or Warsaw or Stalingrad. People of all nationalities can take all-Hell when there's no choice. The human capacity for endurance is as deep and persistent as the instinct for life itself. Japan took the ultimate horror that human ingenuity could contrive—to date—and a new era was inaugurated, and another dress-rehearsal successfully carried out.

Greenwich had the distinction of being involved in the first big raid on London in September, 1940. The good old Ship copped it in November. Mum and Dad stayed down there by the river, in the little house-in-a-row, with the ruins all around them, popping out from under the stairs to make pots of tea between bombs and find out how their neighbors were faring. A good many other Mums and Dads did the same. It was a fine feeling running out when the all-clear had sounded to see who was left alive, and what was left standing, and if everyone else was all right. Most people never knew such exhilaration prior to that experience, nor have they known it since.

My mother had a certain amount of trouble with my father owing to his habit of rushing out of the house when he was drunk during a raid and capering about on the pavement, waving his arms at the stars where death trundled with black invisible wings, and shouting, "Send it down, David!" This would not have mattered in itself, except that when he rushed out he let a flood of light escape into the street, so that indignant air-raid wardens came steaming up terrifying my poor mother with threats to report her and have her most fearfully fined. It was a wonder she didn't die of pneumonia rushing out into the snow of that bitter winter in her nightgown and tin hat to drag my hilarious father back into the house.

As it turned out it would have been better if she *had* died of pneumonia. There was a Sunday night in December when a mine tied to a parachute came drifting down from the frosty stars. It took away Lister's, and the blocks of working-class flats opposite, and fifty little houses. Some of the people were in shelters. Mum and Dad were at home. Dad had left the pub before closing time when the siren went, so as to be with mother. He hurried home to keep his appointment with death, along with my mother, in one of the fifty little houses. Mother would have been glad he came home earlier; she didn't like being alone during a raid, but she would never go to a shelter; she felt safer in her own home, she always said. Dad didn't run out and shout "Send it down, David!" that night. He didn't have time. No one knows what happened in the little house. But one thing is certain —in death they were not divided.

I'd given my workshop up months ago, for the very good reason that all that sort of work came to an end. Artists are a luxury in wartime unless they can turn their art to some form of war work, and I wasn't prepared to do that. Lee arranged for my Daughter of Los, the bas-relief, and the bust of Tansy to be evacuated to some rich friends of Graham's who had found a safe retreat in the West Country. I struck a bad patch for a while. I didn't know what to do, for once again I was without the regulation papers. With my horror of officialdom and regimentation I hadn't been able to bring myself to take out an identity-card. I had the same old feeling that I'd had in Paris about it being a negation of one's personality. It meant that I couldn't get a ration book, of course, but that didn't worry me. With bread, fruit, vegetables, fish all unrationed I could manage well enough, and I could always get the odd cup of "cha" at a coffee stall.

I suppose that even without an identity-card I could have got a job of some kind in a commercial art studio, with all the younger men away at the war, but I didn't know what I'd be required to do, and I didn't anyhow fancy working with people who had all the right papers and the right patriotic ideas. I had the curious notion that so-called Christian countries had no business to be bombing the daylight out of each other; that when the Founder of their religion commanded them to love one another, and do good to them that spitefully used them, he didn't mean them to do it by blowing each other to hell, civilians and fighting forces alike. The pious contention that killing in war is not murder, as the black-coated ones of all denominations, with a few honorable exceptions, insisted, was a bit of humbug that turned my nondenominational stummick. So far as I was concerned the foulest governmental regime that human power-lust and megalomania could contrive was a considerably lesser evil for the mass of humanity than any war however lofty its aims. I had no more use for Hitler than I'd had for Franco; all the dictator big-boys were incarnations of Satan so far as I was concerned, but I couldn't see that letting all hell loose was a way of destroying the Devil—particularly when he inhabited an idea. Violence never yet destroyed an idea, good or bad.

So there I was, in the minority as usual, but I was with the narrow stream of life while the majority was swept along on the broad stream of death and destruction, and I'd read a bit of Chinese philosophy somewhere that so long as people remained in the stream of life they would survive, or anyhow what they stood for would, because in the last analysis life itself is indestructible. But to keep up my strength to go on swimming in the narrowed stream of life I had to find a way to earn my bread—not to mention the rent, and the odd cups of "cha." I went along to see Joe Snell to discuss the problem with him, and see if perhaps I could earn the little I needed with him for the duration.

Characteristically he assured me that I was "welcome as the flowers in May." He had no one helping him. He had been bombed out on the waterfront in the September raids and had a workshop and yard now in the town. Labor was hard to get; all the lads were making big money in the munition factories, and all the skilled men were in the forces.

A good deal of the work I did with Joe was boarding up windows after nearby bombs had blown out the glass. Wood was scarce for domestic purposes, and our cabinetmaking and carpentry was more makeshift than ever. Lister's threw up temporary premises on their bombed site, following some mathematical principle of the laws of probability which persuaded them that a second bomb was unlikely to fall in the same place. A good deal of their timber was looted after they were bombed, but I had not the slightest desire to "nick" even as much as would go in my jacket pocket any more. It wasn't just because I wasn't doing my own work, nor even only that I was grieved to see a good firm like that smashed up, but because it broke my heart that so much fine timber should be lying about like that, buried under rubble, at the mercy of vandals who wouldn't know hard wood from soft and who would take home a fine log of some precious wood and saw it up for the fire or use it to make a door for a hen run. I wouldn't have abused like that anything I looted, but I'd have identified myself with the vandals, and that also was something for which I had no stomach.

I had no desire to create anything, even had the material been obtainable—and I could have got something, small stuff, from time to time, I knew that—because inside myself no angry clouds swagged on the deep, provoking ideas; all was a moonless night created by the death of love in a world in which all other light had been extinguished. The first few months were the worst. There was no sharp, searing anguish, no tearing sense of loss; only a flat level of destroying deadness—the authentic death of the heart. I drank a good deal at first, but as it's impossible to get drunk and stay drunk, alcoholism doesn't serve—not unless you have the money continually to renew your condition, and I hadn't the money, and spirits were increasingly hard to come by.

It was a great comfort to me that Lee was in London during those years. I had old Joe Snell, but he liked to talk, to exchange ideas, and at that time I didn't much want to talk; the world of ideas seemed as dead for me as the world of love and the world of art. With Lee I could be silent and still feel the flow of communion between us. He knew I had broken with Tansy, and I was aware that he regarded it as a good thing and believed I would come to realize it in time, but he also knew that in the meantime I suffered, and without any need of words I felt his sympathy. He was "on my side," as no one else was, and I was on his, and we each of us knew it. I dreaded the time when he would be called up. It wasn't only that I would miss him, but that I felt his becoming part of the war would drive a wedge between us. I had the feeling he would go into the Air Force—because the uniform would appeal to him, its colors matching his forget-me-nots-under-water eyes, and because he moved in Air Force circles at that time. My heart sank when over dinner in a little Italian restaurant in Soho one night he told me he had received his call-up papers. I asked him what he was going to do. He replied in his most bored voice, pouring Chianti and not looking at me, "Register as a C.O., I suppose. What else?"

It was as exciting to me as a declaration of love. In a sense it was that: his love of life, and for his fellow man.

"I didn't know you held strong pacifist views," I said.

"I hold the strongest possible views about not getting mixed up in wars," he assured me, with his small ironic smile.

"Why didn't you go to America with Graham, then?" I asked.

"Because I wouldn't *like* America! The accent, and all that gum-chum. I don't really mind the bombs all that much. I get frantically frightened at the time, but it's so lovely finding yourself alive when it's all over! You can't imagine how many cozy cups of tea I've had with old Kent and Ma Hilley at all hours of the night and early morning since it all began. And Hoppy comes in with the kid, and Gwen comes in from entertaining the troops, and generally a bit on, and then we're quite a tea party, all girls together! It makes up for the Spaniards."

His group of Spaniards had all been housed in a house rented for them in North London. He no longer saw them regularly; they had most of them made various domestic arrangements for themselves "for the duration," and settled down to a wait that for them was to last long after the war had finished.

I pointed out to Lee that he couldn't just go before a tribunal and say he objected to getting mixed up in wars. "You've got to have a strong case—religious or ethical," I told him. "You've got to prove your pacifist conviction. Otherwise you'll just be struck off the register."

He gave me a droll look.

"You don't really think they want people like me in the forces, do you? They'll take one look at my beautiful eyes and give me unconditional exemption, I assure you!"

"They'll more likely give you land work or hospital work—the menial kind, emptying bedpans—or order you into Civil Defense."

"No one is going to order me into anything. I may join the Civil Defense later on, if they'll have me, but not if I'm ordered."

"Then they'll just bung you into a nasty old jail."

"Really, Tom, *must* you be so morbid?"

"All the same they might," I insisted.

"Didn't you once say that all the best people down through the ages had been in prison at some time or other?"

"Yes, but—"

"Then what are you worrying about? I'm not one of the best

people. I've made up my mind I'm to be given an unconditional, and later I shall join Gabriel in the Civil Defense and learn to do *petit-point* between bombs."

Which is exactly what did happen, except that he didn't have as much time for the *petit-point* as he might have expected, because between raids he was always busy cleaning windows, sweeping floors, attending first-aid classes, and doing all manner of odd jobs. When Alsatian dogs were introduced for rescue work he volunteered for training with them. I met him in Chelsea after the Guinness Trust block of flats had received a direct hit; he had been working with his squad and some American soldiers who had volunteered getting bodies out from the rubble. After hours of work in pouring rain, so that, as he told me afterward, everything was mud and blood, the Americans took the squad off to their canteen and fed them with bread spread with butter, and strawberry jam with whole strawberries. Lee got the jam all over his fingers. "It was the last straw," he said. "I can't bear *stickiness!* It nearly drove me *mad!*"

During the middle years of the war I had an *affaire* with a girl in Civil Defense. I had gone to meet Lee in the Six Bells and she came in with him. He introduced her as Janet Clyde; we had drinks, and afterwards a meal together in some small place nearby, and then Lee had to go back to the depot. She took me on to some nightclub she knew—one of those drinks-and-dance places that sprang up in basements during the war. She was attractive in the same way as Tansy, but both more amusing and more intelligent. She attracted me powerfully, and she was the first woman who had done so since the break with Tansy. She seemed to be attracted to me for the same reason that Tansy had been—because I was an artist. She had worked in a commercial art studio and lived in Chelsea for the last few years. She said she had often seen me in various pubs, but I'd always had a girl with me. She had noticed me, she said, because I was "unusual-looking." I told her curtly that Chelsea was full of unusual-looking people, and upon the girl I cast no light. She took me back with her in the small hours of the morning when we were both shot full of liquor. She had a small flat, full of books, and I stayed the night with her.

And after that many nights. She attracted me and I liked her; she was good-looking and good company, and she had a curious masculine detachedness about the whole affair. She was fond of me, but no more. She had a husband somewhere overseas, but they were already separated before the war. Before me she had had a "free French" *affaire*, and after me there was an American officer. She was having a good war. I finished with her when I got a dose of clap from her. I didn't hold it against her; it seemed to me I had only got belatedly what ought to have come to me years ago when I was batting around Paris. I had no right to expect fidelity from her; it wasn't, as it were, in the contract. I took no more risk with her than she with me. I was unlucky, that was all. I finished with her because while I was attending the clinic I was obviously out of action, and when I was cured I had lost interest in her as a result of the enforced separation. A "dose," I discovered, is a very salutary thing: for one thing it is very humbling; no man with clap can give himself airs. For another it is sexually very sobering. But more importantly than anything else it is an end of smugness. It can happen to the most chaste wife, the most faithful of husbands; it can happen to the most morally straitlaced who falls only once, while allowing the promiscuous to tread the primrose path all their lives unscathed. The man who prides himself on never having contracted it is a fool; he has merely been lucky; one lapse on the part of his lady-wife or fiancée or mistress, quite apart from any promiscuity on his own part, and he could find himself in what the kindly but very disillusioned doctor who treated me at the clinic called "the pendulum parade."

When it was all over I was almost grateful to Janet for the experience, but I was no longer interested in her or anyone. I was becoming war-weary—physically weary of the bombing, of the broken nights and the continuous nervous strain, and weary of the endless frustration of creative inspiration and impulse. Nothing unique in that, of course. By 1944 a good many people everywhere were exhausted from lack of sleep and being frightened too often, and living one way or another lives unnatural to them. "Victory year" was horrible with "fly-bombs" and rockets, a terror by night and by day, and 1945 was horrible in a different kind of way, being the year when Buchenwald and Belsen were liberated, frightful things revealed, and atrocity stories rampant. And as if all that were not enough the atomic era was ushered in with a single word streamlined across a London evening paper concerning a Japanese city—OBLITERATION. It was the year of the infamous Potsdam Guzzle, and starvation in defeated

Germany. And as passionately as they took sides in the Spanish war people took sides as to whether the ex-enemy, living in cellars and among the rubble, should be fed. Those who wanted them fed sought permission to be allowed to send food from their own rations, but it was not immediately allowed. Meantime there were trials of "war criminals," and hangings and the promise of more to come—and the horrors of peace were, generally, in full swing. There was the collective guilt of the ex-enemy, but there was also the collective guilt of the victors.

By the spring of 1946 I was back in Paris. I went with the intention of staying for a long week end. I was there for a short two years.

2

I WENT back to Paris at Helen's invitation. She had taken over Graham's house, since the postwar currency restrictions did not permit him to live there himself. It was agreed that she, with her dollars, would pay the expenses of the place and he would go there occasionally. He had brought his art treasures back to England, and the room in the house on the Ile St. Louis in which he had displayed them now served as her studio. The little room Lee had occupied was now the guestroom; it was no longer exquisitely *recherché*, but a simple affair of a narrow divan covered with a gay striped Mexican blanket, a similar rug on the floor, a kitchen chair and table painted red, a shelf of books, and a highly abstract Helen Shelmerley painting over the bed. In place of Lee's peach-colored brocade curtains at the window, which looked into a well, she had dragged a couple of lengths of unbleached handwoven woolen material across the glass: as curtains they had a curiously temporary effect. Helen was like that; she wore expensive and elegant clothes, but threw them on any old how. Any room she inhabited or arranged took on the impatient quality of her personality; all her care and patience was reserved for her work; only there was she sufficiently interested to take trouble; the minimum of thought and energy had to be expended on anything outside it so that the maximum time could be devoted to the thing that for her really mattered.

The rest of the house had been left intact with Graham's

furniture and decorations—the handsome Louiz-Quinze dining room on the ground floor, the long beautiful drawing room above the studio, and at the top of the house his bedroom with its small fourposter bed covered with a white bearskin, and eighteenth-century flower prints decorating the pale green walls. But the first floor, with the studio, where Helen slept on a divan which during the daytime was completely hidden by art magazines—English, French, American—canvases, newspapers and junk of all kind, and the bare little guestroom, was all Helen—workmanlike, untidy, makeshift. Lee's charming furniture and effects she had heartlessly sold at the flea market. "He didn't really mind," she assured me. "The dollars I sent him for it were much more useful to him."

Highhanded she was, as always, I thought, dollar-handed. But the same vital, vivid person, too, not much touched by the years which had intervened since she walked in on me that Christmas Eve after Munich. She had had a couple of exhibitions in New York. She had spent some months in Mexico, and a year in California, painting all the time. She would be ready for an exhibition in Paris in the autumn, and she wanted that I should come in with her again. I could show the Daughter of Los as the major work of the exhibition, she urged, and I had the alabaster and marble things, and the bust of Tansy, and by autumn I should have a number of sculptures in wood, and perhaps try my hand at a small ivory or two. There was a ground-floor studio I could have up by the Observatoire—it was to discuss all this she had sent for me. Wouldn't I like to work in Paris again, after being a "prisoner of the war" in England for five and a half years?

I told her I would like it fine, but I had no money, and the old life I had lived in Paris, touting around the cafés and propping up the Dôme zinc, was as dead as a lot of other aspects of Paris life. Then, of course, we were back where we started with all the old arguments about money. She had more than she needed, and the greater part of it unearned, and since I maintained that money was all nonsense anyhow why couldn't I help her redistribute some of her surplus by taking it to live on and work with?

Rationally there was nothing against her proposition, and I reckoned to be a rational person, yet the idea of being entirely dependent on her generosity, for rent, work materials, sustenance, not to have two *sous* of my own to rub together, galled me. In London I knew I could earn money, get a job of sorts, and there was always teaching; but in postwar Paris it seemed unlikely I would get even the sort of thing I had contrived for myself before the war. Yet I did long to live and work in Paris again; it wasn't only that the old enchantment was upon me, but that I was weary of London with its bombed sites and fish queues and tired irritability. I also dreaded the thought that now that Tansy was back in England we should one day run into each other. That she was back I knew from Lee. Bill had kept on the Chelsea flat. They were back but they were looking for a house, Lee had said, because they now had a child—a little girl, four years old, and "quite horribly like its father," Lee assured me. I didn't want to think about that, with all its implications, and in London I did think about it, endlessly. So that again at nights on my bed I sought her, my Beloved, and found her not, and suffered various kinds of hells.

It was good to be with Helen again, and it was fine the first night when we stayed at home and she prepared the meal in the kitchen, all white enamel and red paint, with a kind of snack-bar at one end where Graham and Lee used to have light meals when they were alone. Helen was a good cook, and we sat up at the little bar and opened a bottle of wine, and were gay. But the next night she wanted that we should dine at a gourmet restaurant on the quays, and overruled my suggestion that we should eat at a taxi-driver place, a *bistro* up by the Dôme—I had a little money still and could have paid for that for the two of us, and the *vin ordinaire* would have been *compris*—which is how wine should always be. Why shouldn't we eat good, she demanded, to celebrate our reunion and the fact that the war was over, and that I was about to start a new life in Paris—my career in earnest she called it. I gave in and we ate good, and it cost about five pounds, which I could have lived on for a week or more. Everything on the menu seemed to cost five hundred francs—which by then was ten shillings—and it spoiled the taste of the food for me. I couldn't see why the best steak in the world had to cost that much, whatever way it was cooked. Helen said, impatiently, that one paid not only for the food and the fine cooking, but for the atmosphere and service. *Merde!* I said, and meant it. It was that to me. A steak was a steak, and a belly was a belly. All else was flummery and pretension. In the back streets of Paris, in the tenement houses out by the Lion de Belfort, people were trying to bring up families on as much per week as we had blown on that one meal. The whole thing was immoral. I watched Helen pay the bill and reflected that at the place I knew by the Dôme where there is paper on the tables and sawdust on the floor, two people could have had a whacking great meal for the price of the tip alone. . . . I resolved that in future when we dined out we'd do it at one of my places; she might hate it, but it would give her a glimmering of money-sense, perhaps.

We had been that day to see the studio around the corner from the Observatoire, in the little rue Cassini, and I had liked it fine. I liked the leafy darkness of the Avenue de l'Observatoire running straight up from the junction of the Boulevard Montparnasse and the Boulevard Port Royal, a wooded cul-de-sac ending at the gates of the Observatoire. The rue Cassini goes off to the left just before you get to the Observatoire. It is a district of hospitals and convents and old shuttered houses and double rows of chestnut trees with benches underneath. Behind a small private hotel and sharing the same courtyard there is a modern studio building. The studio which was to let opened into the courtyard and was flanked at one side by a high wall, but it had huge modern windows and there was plenty of light. It had been used by a sculptor friend of Helen's; he had gone off to Cagnes for the summer to paint, and in the fall, she said, he was going to New York for an exhibition of his paintings and sculpture, and he was anxious to let the place furnished for a year; it might even be possible to get it for longer. It was what Helen called very simply furnished but it seemed luxurious to me, with a small modernly equipped kitchen, the floor and walls all white tiles, and a tiled bathroom with a heated towel rail. In the studio itself there was a workbench and a turntable, a divan bed, a chair and table, a cupboard—all anyone could want. The room was high and light and beautifully warm. Helen must have seen the hungry look on my face as I took it all in, for she laid a hand on my arm and smiled at me.

"Be sensible, Tom," she urged. "You could work in peace here and get a fine lot of things ready for an exhibition in the fall."

The centrally heated smell of the place affected me powerfully. It is as much the smell of Paris as the smell of coffee and cigarettes in the street, the smell of garlic in the Metro. It had the familiar chemical effect on my blood, like love or fear. I longed to accept. I'd had enough of coldness and makeshift and discomfort; enough of "the hard way" and being pushed around. I could work in peace there, as she said, and I could exorcise the memory of Tansy—Tansy with her husband's child: that child which confirmed everything which deep down and suppressed in me I had always known about her. I could accept the year's tenancy of the studio from Helen, I felt, if only I could find a way to earn my own bread. Perhaps I could borrow some money from Lee and pay it back after the exhibition; if I did as well as last time I could pay it back very easily. I could borrow it from Helen, but that I didn't want to do. I had a few pounds on hand, and if Lee would come over for a week end bringing all his basic allowance—we were allowed a hundred pounds at that time—and lend me as much of it as he could spare, about ninety pounds perhaps, I felt I could manage—by eating only once a day, until I began to sell my work again. I would have to let Helen pay for my materials, but that I did not mind, so long as I did not have to be dependent on her for my bread.

When I outlined this plan to her she declared that it was all nonsense, and why couldn't I accept from her in one sum enough to live reasonably comfortably on for a year, and thus not have to think about money but be free to concentrate on my work. It was no use, though, I couldn't bring myself to accept the offer. In the end it was complicatedly arranged through a French friend of Helen's who was going to London; she collected a hundred thousand francs from him for me, and arranged with Graham to let him have the equivalent in English money when he arrived. So that I started off my second Paris phase owing my patron about a hundred pounds. I didn't mind that, though; I was confident I would be able to repay it after my exhibition, and the money was lent by someone who couldn't possibly miss it.

I moved into the studio immediately, but it was some time before I could get back to work again. I had to recapture the feel of Paris; I had to settle into my environment again. I spent whole days just wandering about. I liked to stroll under the chestnut trees of the Avenue de l'Observatoire down to the Carrefour, past the Closerie de Lilas, gone grand now with an American bar, and a *coquillage* stall with a man in an apron standing guard over its array of oysters and sea-urchins decked out with lemons, and snails stuffed with a bright green paste of butter and garlic; a trelliswork with ivy growing on it still screened the terrace, but it was all smartened up, with prices to match, so I went on past it, and past the Atlas fountain by the entrance to the gardens, and I was always glad when it was a clear enough day to see from there the Sacre Cœur perched on the old Butte at the other side of the city, startlingly white and Oriental and drifting like a mirage against the pale blue of the sky. I liked to walk down past the children's playground, flanked by the avenues of tall close-trimmed chestnut trees, and come into the gardens proper, with the little twisted hawthorn trees on the terrace above the round pond, and children in bright clothes running about, and lovers sitting on little iron seats and holding hands and kissing—nothing seemed changed. War and occupation and resistance had come and gone, but Paris was still Paris. There was still the kiosk where "windmills" of colored paper could be bought for children, and colored balloons straining on thin strings for the upper air, and paper sunflowers which could be spun on a stick. Elderly shirtsleeved men still solemnly played bowls on pitches under the trees while the young looked on. It was all still there, the things, the people, and the life. The people were shabbier, but there they all were—playing bowls, or watching bowls played, strolling in the early spring sunshine, or sitting on benches reading newspapers, or watching the children, or merely sitting, and all around them, beyond the high iron railings and the trees and the pleasant ugly unmatching towers of St. Sulpice, Paris whirled and shrieked and shrilled—the high-pitched feminine voice of the Paris streets.

In those first days of return I liked to sit a while in the sun looking at the children and the lovers and the strollers and letting the first warm sun of the year flow over my face and hands, everything in me insisting that it was good to be back. Then I would go out through the big gates into the rue des Médicis, drop in at the *pissoir* for old times' sake, and continue on past the dolphin fountain and down the Boul' Mich'; the student cafés seemed less crowded than when I'd last seen them, but the gents' outfitters called the 100,000 Chemises was still there. Then down to the quays, where the bookstalls carried the same prints as in the twenties, the inescapable lady of *Le Rêve* sleeping with the bolster between her legs, the mottled and yellowing flower prints, good, bad and indifferent, the little colored maps of Paris two hundred or more years ago. Even the books seemed not to have changed; there was the same predominance of paper-backed books dealing with every aspect of *l'amour*—flagellation, fetichism, and even simple sentimental romantic passion. I took a stroll through the back streets and came suddenly upon the little alleyway of le rue du Chat qui Pêche with its overhanging upper stories and its one lamp thrust out from a dark wall, and the single, meaningful word *Hôtel.*

Another day I walked up the Boulevard Montparnasse; it seemed much the same, only shabbier, but I wasn't prepared for the deadness of the cafés I had always remembered as packed, outside and in, at all hours of the day. The Rotonde, which had been packed in the twenties and tailed off in the more sophisticated thirties, was busy again, and across the road the Coupole seemed anyhow alive, but the Dôme seemed as dead as a popular seaside resort pier in midwinter. All that end of the boulevard had changed a lot: bright, garish new cafés had sprung up, with strip-lighting and streamlined staircases and outlandish mural decorations. I felt alien there, and left it, cutting back down the Boulevard Raspail to St. Germain-des-Prés. There were plenty of people on the terrace of the Deux Magots, I noticed, and also at the Flore, and I went on past the church and down the rue Bonaparte and back to the river. I crossed by the Pont Neuf on to the Ile de la Cité and made my way to the little Place Dauphine where I had had the memorable dinner with Graham and Helen. The low-ceilinged restaurant with windows at one end onto the river was still there. I sat on a bench under the budding chestnut trees and listened to a canary in a tiny cage hung out of a window on the first floor of a house behind me singing with a wild bursting sweetness.

I had the feeling of having come home. I was both happy and melancholy. I had a studio and a little money, but I was empty of ideas. It was spring, and my heart was empty of love. In all my years in this city I had never been as alone as then when I had a good friend there, and security. In the down-and-out days the tide had always washed me up somewhere: there had been the little Jewish *boule de suif* Helga; there had been the dark flame that was Pat Johns; the pale flame that was Joycelyn. My loves of yesteryear. *Ou sont les neiges d'antan?* What, I wondered, had happened to Pat when the war came? But she might have been in America, or back in Trinidad—anywhere. I roused myself and began walking back to my studio, but when I got as far as the great stores, *La Belle Jardinière* and *La Samaritaine*, which with lights in all their windows were somehow like great ships, I had an impulse to go and look Helen up, and turned back along the river to the Ile St. Louis.

I hadn't seen her since I moved into the studio a week ago. She had said that she would not "intrude" on me; I would want to settle in and get started on a new piece of work, she said, and she would leave it to me to look her up when I was ready, and if a long time went by she would merely assume I was working. But in that sudden wave of loneliness which washed over me it already seemed a long time since I had seen her, and when I pressed the bell of the yellowing old house I hoped quite desperately that she would be at home—and alone.

She was in, working on the first pencil sketches for a mural for a restaurant being refurbished somewhere up in the Etoile district. She wore slacks as always when working, and answered the door with a cigarette dangling from the corner of her mouth, her face twisting a little away from the smoke. She removed the cigarette and exclaimed at the sight of me and commanded me to go on up. She asked me what I was working on, and I told her nothing. In the studio she poured Pernod for me, leaving me to add the water. I told her I would go if she wanted to continue working, but she said she had been working all day and was glad of the excuse to knock off. She helped herself to Pernod. I watched the water clouding it in the tumbler, then told her, "The truth is I'm lonely, and I lack inspiration because of it."

"Give yourself a little time," she suggested. "You've only been back a week."

"The world is different," I said. "The Pats and the Helgas and the Joycelyns aren't around any more, and I'm too old for the tough girls who have grown up in the Resistance movement. A man would starve to death propping up the Dôme zinc today before anyone would stand him a cup of coffee, let alone take him home to share a bed."

She gave me a quizzical smile from behind a screen of smoke. "I'm sorry," she said.

"You should be! I'm not earning my keep. I'm living rent free and on borrowed money. I've got that life-is-but-a-water-closet feeling, God-pulls-the-plug-and-down-we-go. I've done nothing creative for over five years, and it seems I've forgotten how. I took a stroll through the sculpture gallery of the Luxembourg museum this morning to look at a few things and see how it was done, but it's left me more hopeless than ever. If I went to the Rodin museum I should probably take the next boat back to England, home, and the carpentry trade."

I hadn't eaten all day and the Pernod had gone to my head, so that I was excited and angry and said more than I meant. I ranted against war that destroyed creative effort, and love that betrayed it. Tansy and the war had between them finished me off, I declared. Helen said nonsense, and that probably all I needed was a square meal; I probably wasn't eating enough to make all the blood necessary to stimulate the brain cells. I got angrier still and pointed out that I'd done some of my best work when I'd been half starving. I brought out the old one about privation and suffering being an artist's best school. Helen retorted that plenty of artists who had never known either had done some pretty good work. So there we were quarreling again over the old bitch-goddess money. Presently Helen brought out half a cooked chicken and some salad and a bottle of *vin rosé*. I ate ravenously and felt calmer. We finished the bottle of wine between us, but I drank more than she did, and on the Pernod basis it took effect more strongly than it might otherwise have done, so that I plunged back into the past and our London days together and went right back to the day we ordered the lignum vitae and sat in the pub in Trafalgar Road and celebrated birthdays without any very clear idea of what had been brought to birth.

"For you it was the birth of an idea," she reminded me. "Your idea of Christ driving the money-changers out of the temple."

"More than that," I said. "It was the birth of new inspiration, faith in my own powers, belief in the future—my artistic future. But you wouldn't say what it was for you. First you said you hadn't had enough to drink to tell me, and then you said you'd had too much."

She laughed. "And now it's too late."

"Too late for what?"

"To be of any interest. What was born in you that day came to something—your greatest creative effort. What was born in me was—still-born."

"Riddles are a bore—particularly when they're highfalutin,"

I said impatiently. "The way to say it is to say it. Out with it!"

She looked momentarily embarrassed, then sent up a smoke screen between us, and said bravely, "If you must know—I realized that day that I was in love with you."

I was so astonished that I could only exclaim, "Good Lord!"

She smiled now through the smoke.

"I don't know why you should find it so ridiculous. You were a reincarnation of Brenovska for me. You are still."

"But you no longer feel for me what you felt for him?" I was completely fascinated by the idea she had revealed to me—ten years late. It presented her in an entirely new light—more precisely it took me back to the day I had left Paris after selling Graham Carlton the Negro Girl Dancing and had carried the memory of Helen Shelmerley's perfume, and the touch of her cheek briefly against mine in the moment of station farewell, as far as Dieppe—until the effect of the farewell Pernods had worn off, in fact. After which I had thought a great deal more about Lee than about her. Now again we had drunk Pernod together and I was seeing her again as I had seen her then.

She took a final puff on her cigarette, then pressed out the butt in an ashtray.

"After years of firmly stifling an emotion it's difficult to know if it's still there. Your question's complicated, too, by the fact that I didn't stay in love with Josef. We quarreled too often and too bitterly. But it's a pointless discussion between two old soldiers like ourselves. Why don't we walk up to the Select and see if anyone interesting or amusing is around?"

"One good reason against it," I told her, "is that I don't think I can walk anywhere, and if you want to send me back to the rue Cassini you'll have to get me a taxi."

It was not quite true. I was fairly tight, but I could have got back all right, with a little concentration. Only I didn't want to be turned out into the night like a stray cat. I wanted the "pointless discussion" to continue until it finally fetched up somewhere.

"You'd better stay the night, in that case," she said.

Whether she was glad, regretful, or merely philosophical about it, I couldn't determine, and afterwards when I asked her point-blank she refused to commit herself, saying only that she didn't know—that she just went with the tide, or some such metaphor.

As I was staying she made coffee and we ended up at midnight with cognac. After which, of course, we didn't sleep. Though, as it turned out, we'd not have done so anyhow.

3

In our two years together I never quite got over the feeling that it was all wrong for Helen and me to be lovers. I don't mean morally wrong but that the sexual relation didn't really belong in our friendship, which was complete and satisfying without it. For us, becoming lovers instead of deepening and strengthening our friendship intruded upon it and spoiled it. She resented the fact that though I loved and admired and respected her, I was not really in love with her. I resented the fact that she, who had brought the relationship upon us, expected more of me than I had to bring to it. I resented the fact that every time I tried to break away from her she fastened her will and her personality more closely about me. She insisted that we "belonged," intellectually and emotionally; that we were the same kind of people. Perhaps it was true. I didn't know then, and I don't know now. I remembered the dinner party in the restaurant on the Place Dauphine when I had wanted to run out into the night with her, hand-in-hand through the starry darkness along the quays, lit by the feeling that she was my kind of person. And how we had run hand-in-hand the day we raced down through the grayness and squalor of the Trafalgar Road to Lister's, in search of lignum vitae, chain-dancing between drab housewives, swinging round lampposts, Helen clutching her little purple feather hat and laughing like a girl, all in the mellow September sunshine, with a leafy wind skipping along the river, larking along the pavements, and invading all the meanness and grayness like a brass band. Then afterwards the hours we spent together walking and talking on the Observatory hill, and in the pubs, and in my room and the ramshackle workshop—there had been all that, and a fine sense of communion between us. But it belonged to friendship, not to love.

She was the better lover of the two of us; she brought more *finesse* and imagination to it. She wore lovely clothes for me, and then declared they were wasted on me. Which was both true and untrue. I was very well aware of the beauty of the color and texture of the materials—there was a wonderful green brocade housecoat which made her look like a sixteenth-century Venetian of the Palma Vecchio school—and the brilliance and elegance of design and line—there was a spring suit the color of Parma violets which did everything for her hair and skin; she would be elegant in a *tailleur*, or romantic in black velvet; and always beautiful and distinguished. I was aware of it all; there was nothing wrong with my aesthetic appreciation. But all the time I would be aware that it was all possible only because she had so much money. Given Helen's money and Helen's dressmaker, Tansy could have achieved as much—or more. Then I would think of my lovely girl in her simple black suits and white blouses; Tansy in my room in a white blouse and narrow black skirt, a wide belt at her narrow waist; Tansy so slim my two hands would meet around her middle. I would picture her in that black velvet dress of Helen's, its rich darkness bringing out the pale gold of her hair . . . and then I would look away from the brilliant beautiful woman standing before me awaiting my praise, and say curtly that it was a nice enough dress all right but it probably cost the earth, and she would accuse me of being a bore and a boor—which I was.

Then in the same resentful mood I would make Helen put on her working clothes and come out with me and eat in some *bistro* full of steam and clatter, and where they served the roughest kind of *vin ordinaire* in carafes and dumped it down in front of you with thick tumblers. I was always at home in these places; I'd have a quarter of *vin rouge* and some onion soup and a piece of bread and feel I'd done fine. Helen hated these places and urged that it was ridiculous to eat in them when we could afford to eat better food in a more congenial atmosphere. To which I would retort that she could afford it but that I couldn't, and that as we couldn't level up there was nothing for it but to level down. She would try to get out of going to these places by suggesting we eat at home, by which she meant at her place; then I would counter with the idea that we eat at my studio, and if she didn't like garlic sausage and dry bread and *pinet*, so much the worse for her, but that was how the poor lived. Sometimes she would give in good-naturedly, declaring that "picnicking" in my studio was "fun." In other moods she would protest passionately at what she called my "puritanism," and we would quarrel —sometimes quite bitterly.

My power over Helen in our new relationship astonished me; it also distressed and angered me. What right had she to allow me to humiliate her like that? It horrified me that I could reduce her to tears. Tansy crying had always seemed natural enough; she was the completely feminine woman who, defeated in argument, invariably takes refuge in tears. But that Helen should do it was intolerable. She should have come back at me with her tongue, man to man, or picked up something and heaved it at my head. She did not weep wildly and hysterically as Tansy did, like an overwrought child who intends to go on until it is comforted. She would cry in a quiet unostentatious way, and usually alone. I would only know by the look of her that she had been crying. Or come upon her in the studio painting with the tears rolling down her face. When she could she would deny that she had been crying. Caught at it she would simply blow her nose, give her eyes a final dab with a sodden handkerchief, declare herself a fool, light a cigarette and suggest a drink. Well, she was a woman and had a right to her tears, I suppose. But it made me feel a monster.

"Look, Helen," I would say, "this can't go on. I'm no damn good to you. I merely make you miserable."

She would drawl in her soft American voice, "I guess in love we all have to take the rough with the smooth, honey."

It would be no use demanding whether so much rough was worth the little smooth; for her it was. As it had been for me with Tansy. As it is for all people who greatly love. In every love affair must there always be one person who loves more than the other? I had asked myself the question in times of unhappiness with Tansy, and I asked it again now, grieving because I could not love Helen as she loved me. Time and again I would urge that she would revert to being ordinary friends, but, "Honey," she would plead, in that soft lilt of hers, "don't be unkind!" Unkind with three syllables in that sort of soft beseeching singsong can be very undoing.

I did a great deal of work that first year in postwar Paris. Helen got me some portrait-bust commissions. I didn't want to accept such jobs at first, but she pointed out that if I did them for a few months I would earn enough money to spend the next six months doing what I wanted to do, and I was bound to admit the reasonableness of the argument. Modeling was an interesting change after carving, and I must admit I had fun expressing in clay the personalities of my sitters, or, more usually, some aspect of a personality. Only the very conceited ones objected to my interpretations, though some of the others looked a little dismayed, or anyhow startled. Some of the things I brought out in those faces I modeled I myself hadn't realized were there. There was a nice American boy studying at the Sorbonne; he was very good-looking and had an immense amount of charm. I liked him and enjoyed working on his portrait. When it was finished he looked at it wonderingly.

"Do I *reely* look that way?" he asked. He was disconcerted, but not offended; merely puzzled.

"To me you do," I told him. "If you want an exact superficial likeness there are plenty of photographers. Also painters who specialize in photographic likenesses."

He came back a few days later with the girl he was engaged to marry.

She was clearly startled by the portrait. "You've made him look kind of—queer," she protested.

I asked her in what sense she used the term. She flushed a little and substituted the word "odd."

I heard from Helen some time after that that the engagement was broken off and the young man had gone off to Cyprus with an English novelist, notoriously homosexual. I hadn't thought of the young man as that when I was working on him; I had only felt that he was not as simple, as uncomplicated, as his surface boyishness might lead one to suppose.

There was a plump little Jewess who claimed to be Russian and a princess by marriage. She was very wealthy and had a palatial house on the way out to the Bois. She used to arrive in a cream Rolls-Royce, and was all sables and Cartier jewelry. I judged that she had run to fat before she was forty from sheer idleness and self-indulgence, as though she lived on chocolate éclairs. In the bust I made of her she looked like nothing so much as a pig. She took it very well.

She looked at it a long time when she came to see it after it was cast.

"I can accept that as a portrait of myself," she said. Then she added, smiling—and in spite of everything she had a singularly sweet smile—"It had better stay here. My husband will hate it." But she paid for it all right—handsomely, at that.

Then Lee came to Paris for a long week end with Graham Carlton, and they visited me at my studio and were amused by the bust of the princess, whom they knew, and Graham commissioned me to do a portrait of Lee.

He commanded me, in Lee's presence, to "Bring out the viciousness in the little brute."

I didn't find any viciousness in Lee, but I did make him —quite unintentionally—look extraordinarily wicked. When Graham saw it he laughed and said all I had left out was a necklace of flowers and then I could call it the afternoon of a faun. So I modeled a few flowers around the base of the bust and called it simply The Faun, and Graham was delighted. We had it cast in green bronze, and it was one of my best pieces.

I didn't tell Lee that Helen and I had become lovers, but we all dined together one night *chez* Laperouse—a favorite gourmet place of Helen's and Graham's—and what is between lovers reveals itself in innumerable small intimacies of which the people concerned are unaware, and once I caught Lee's eye speculatively on me, and then he smiled faintly. When we were walking back together along the quays to the Ile St. Louis, Graham and Helen ahead of us, Lee asked me suddenly, "Why don't you marry Helen?"

I told him that the reasons I gave him years ago still held good—she had too much money.

"It's not as though she has to earn it," he pointed out.

"Money that's earned is the only morally gotten money," I said.

"What would you have people do with inherited money then?" he demanded.

"There's plenty to do with it," I told him. "The world was never fuller of the victims of man's inhumanity to man crying out for help."

"You mean refugees and displaced persons and so on, I suppose. But," he went on, "don't you want struggling artists—painters, sculptors, writers, composers, and all such—helped? People with large dollops of inherited money like Helen can help all manner of artistic stray dogs over all sorts of stiles. Why shouldn't people like Graham and Helen help people like you, for instance?"

"No reason at all why they shouldn't and every reason why they should," I assured him. "But it's not to be done by private charity. Let them endow funds for the assistance of struggling artists of all kinds. Let the whole thing be freed from any suggestion of anyone 'keeping' anyone—all suggestion of sponging and pimping and gigolo-ism."

"You're too fussy," Lee drawled. "If you married Helen, apart from helping yourself you'd probably get some control over her money and be able to help other artists."

"I don't see myself as a rich woman's tame artist husband," I told him. "If I had I could have married a very nice rich American girl years ago."

"I know. Your Fontainebleau dryad. But she was too skinny, I remember. Helen has lovely Botticelli curves—a proper Juno!" He giggled slightly. "You're a fool, Tom," he added finally.

I sighed. "I expect so," I said. I wanted to add that I wasn't, anyhow, in love with Helen, but it seemed disloyal, so I let it go at that.

But it was true that beautiful and brilliant, and tender and ardent and kind, as she was, she hadn't the power to create for me at will *a little moony night and silence*

> With spaces of sweet gardens and a tent of elegant beauty
> Closed in by a sandy desert, and a night of stars shining,
> And a little tender moon and hovering angels on the wing.

It was sad, but there it was. And I'd long ago come to the conclusion that life was mainly that—a sad business. What poor old Oscar Wilde defined as "a series of bad quarters of an hour, with some exquisite moments."

4

As THE spring wore on it became obvious that I couldn't have enough work ready for an exhibition in the autumn, and it seemed better I should go on doing portrait busts for as long as the commissions continued to come in and then start some important work for the exhibition. By August Paris would be "empty"—in spite of the millions still walking its streets, serving in shops and cafés and restaurants, driving buses, and the Metro trains, working in offices, the hoi-polloi who make the wheels go round. But the privileged minority with the money and the leisure, those not bound down upon the rock of daily labor, would be gone—to the Riviera, or to the Channel seaside resorts.

I was kept pretty busy with people Helen sent me, and people recommended to me by "satisfied sitters," till well into August. Then I did a head of the concierge's little girl, aged four, which is a charmingly unself-conscious age. She was quite my most satisfactory sitter, though she did not sit much. She liked to kneel on a chair up at my workbench with a piece of clay and pretend to be modeling the funny fellow that was me. We did not understand each other's French very well, but we got on famously all the same. She was a comical pug-faced little thing with short tight plaits with red bows at the end sticking out at each side of a round football head. At first the mother attended the sittings anxious that little Niki should behave as Monsieur wished; then the child sat fidgeting and looking bored and sulky. Next time they came I suggested that Madame should not derange herself but leave us alone together. Then we had fun, Niki with her ball of clay at the workbench, I with the droll little head and face emerging from the considerably larger ball on the stand. Madame was so delighted with the finished work that I let her have it for the cost of the casting.

That was the last of my portraits, and it was by then September, and I went out along the Boulevard Denfert Rochereau to a timber merchant's I had dealt with before the war in search of nothing more complicated than honest oak. I had been turning over an idea in my mind for some time; all the summer it had been shadowy; now it was clear; I intended to carve "The Doors of Life and Death." Nothing less. The idea had started in me in the early summer when Helen had said Paris would be empty in August, and I had thought of the millions who would remain and keep the wheels turning. I had thought a good deal about them and all that that wheel-turning involved —driving trains through the dark tunnels of the Metro, to and fro, hour after hour, day after day, with no glimpse of the light and sun; adding up columns of figures in offices; standing at benches in factories and making parts of machines—"machines for making more machines"—never a whole thing, but only parts of things, which is of all forms of human labor the most soulless, for even the columns of figures add up to something. It shaped in my mind with Blake's "arts of life" changed into "the arts of death":

The hour-glass contemn'd because its simple workmanship
Was like the workmanship of the ploughman, and the water wheel
That raises water into cisterns broken and burn't with fire,
Because its workmanship was like the workmanship of the shepherd;
And in their stead, intricate wheels invented, wheel without wheel,
To perplex youth in their outgoings, and to bind to labours in Albion
Of day and night the myriads of eternity that they may grind
And polish brass and iron hour after hour, laborious task,
Kept ignorant of its use, that they might spend the days of wisdom
In sorrowful drudgery, to obtain a scanty pittance of bread,
In ignorance to view a small portion and think that all,
And call it demonstration, blind to all the simple rules of life.

That was what they were all doing nowadays in the mass-production factories, I thought, doing monotonous jobs for a pittance, concerned only with a part, never with the whole, both in their jobs and in their living. And everything was plastic, tabloid, synthetic. Combs and cups were made of a milk substance; stockings and shirts of glass. Food came in packets and tins. It was dehydrated, or it was frozen; it had to be thawed or "reconstituted"; the goodness was taken out of things—out of the flour, out of bread—and sold separately, by chemists, in packets. Human beings were pepped up with aspirin and kindred drugs, and the earth with chemical fertilizers; there was soil erosion and soul erosion because all the simple rules of life were held in abeyance. My Door of Life would show the simplicities—an hourglass, a water wheel, a horse-drawn plough; my Door of Death would be a complication of machines, wheels within and wheels without, and the hands of men and women bound upon the wheels.

Helen wanted to know who I thought was going to buy a couple of oak doors like that, and I said I didn't know and I didn't care. They could be set up as panels somewhere, perhaps.

Or someone could build a house to fit them. What did I care? I was tired of all the talk about art in relation to life; let life bear some relation to art, for a change.

I was very happy working away on these bas-reliefs. The chestnuts threw all their clothes down in the Avenue de l'Observatoire, and I hardly noticed; only that the days were colder, and the daylight hours fewer. A good deal of the time I didn't know what day of the week it was or what the date was. I only knew when it was Sunday because then the concierge walked out with her husband and little girl, the two of them in their best black, Niki in bright scarlet. I knew it was Christmas when the decorated trees appeared on the café terraces, slung with colored lights. I didn't see much of Helen. When I knocked off work I liked to sit by myself at a *bistro*, or on the terrace of one of the smaller cafés, turning various problems of the work over in my mind. I was completely absorbed in what I was trying to do and conversation about anything else was an intrusion. The only person whose visits and conversation I welcomed at that time was little Niki. She would come and skip about the studio, playing with the wood chippings or a piece of clay and talking away mostly to herself. She occasionally addressed some observation to me, knowing that I would not understand and not expecting an answer; it was quite the easiest form of conversation I'd yet encountered and it suited us both admirably. Helen came occasionally to view the work-in-progress, but I did not get the pleasure from her visits I'd got when she'd visited me when I was working on the Christ. Now she impinged on me, and I wished her gone. She reproached me with neglecting her, and begged me to go to the south with her to the villa of some American friends at Antibes. I told her I couldn't possibly knock off work at that stage, and she was angry and we quarreled. She went off and stayed on into the spring. She wrote me of almond blossom and cypresses, of violet fields and mimosa woods, of red rocks and umbrella pines, and wine-dark seas, and the burden of it all was "Come soon—soon." But I read all the letters and laid them all aside without reading them again, and I didn't answer any of them. I wanted only that she should leave me in peace.

But by the time she was back the doors were finished and I felt a restless need to talk and relax. I thought with voluptuous pleasure of waking with my arms full of red hair, and I set off one evening down the Boul' Mich' and along the quays and knocked on the door of her house. I think had she been out I should just have sat on the doorstep till she got back. But she was in, and not in the least pleased to see me. She said I had the cheek of the devil, and a damned nerve, and could go to hell. She added that she was going out and had to change. But while she was saying all this I was following her up the stairs and when we came into the studio I put my arms around her and tried to kiss her mouth, but she turned her head away and I got only her neck and that made me mad, so that I jerked her head around and made her do as I wanted. It was her turn to be mad then, and she rushed off to the bathroom and locked the door. When she came into the bedroom she found me lying on her bed smoking a cigarette.

"D'you want me to call the police?" she inquired coldly.

I laughed and got up and went over to her.

"Don't keep it up, Helen," I said, "it doesn't become you. It puts years onto you." I touched her hair, sliding down her neck and moist from the bath. Her shoulders, where the bath wrap slipped away, were very white against it. "Have a heart and forgive me," I said. "A heart for art's sake. Amen."

Her lips quivered and broke into a smile.

"You're preposterous, Tom!" Her hands went up into my hair, gripping it.

"You old devil!" she said, but her head went down onto my shoulder and an arm went around my neck. I stubbed out my cigarette in an ashtray on her dressing table, and my arms tightened around her.

We had to ring up to tell the people she was supposed to be dining with that she'd been held up and not to wait for her; that she would be along later.

So "there again were we." Caught up again in the same old war of passion and anger, "weaving to dreams the sexual strife." Love ought to be peace, I thought, but it was war. The problem was still "to make the Lion lie down with the Lamb," and to preserve love, "not by escaping or ignoring the enemy, but by meeting and suffering and surmounting him."

When we'd got over the honeymoon stage once again I got a beautiful piece of sycamore and set to work to reproduce a memory I had of her which haunted me with a curious poignance—her nude body stretched out face downward on the bed, her face, with the hair falling across it, resting on her arms. It was so she would roll over and lie sometimes when I had defeated her in an argument, or when, as on the evening I came back to her, I had made love to her, overriding her resisting will; it was an attitude in which defeat and resignation were combined, and because it was so difficult for her, there was something very moving in the final submission.

I didn't tell her what I had in mind when I had her pose for me like that, and when she saw that I was planning a recumbent figure she was puzzled. When it began to shape she began to see what I was at and would look at it ruefully.

"As long as you don't put my name to it," she would say, and, "I am glad my hair covers my face."

Once she asked me what I was going to call it. I told her, "Love bound down upon a rock."

"Isn't there any poet in the world for you but Blake?" she demanded impatiently.

"I'm a one-poet man," I assured her.

"Shelley might have something to say to you," she suggested. "Or Gerard Manley Hopkins. Or Francis Thompson."

"Not the last two," I said. "They were bound up with the black-coated ones—the priests of the Raven of dawn. Shelley was all right, except when he was skylarking. He was a natural anarchist, and at times he was a poet."

"Blake wasn't a poet all the time, either. 'Little lamb, who made thee? Dost thou know who made thee?' "

"Suits me," I said. " 'I a child and thou a lamb, We are callèd by His name.' It's art and it's religion. What more do you want?"

She would never go all the way with me over Blake. And I would never go all the way with her over abstract painting. As I saw it, it was trying to say in paint what was more effectively expressed in words. It failed to make communication with the beholder, and if art wasn't communication, I insisted, then I didn't know what we were all about. She would get a little angry, then, and talk about art being esoteric. To me that was all so much highfaultin nonsense, and I couldn't bear it. At times we seemed as far apart in our ideas as Tansy and I had been—even that Tansy and I had been closer. But at other times I would have a good feeling of comradeship and communion, and, all exasperations apart, my liking and admiration for her never faltered. I loved her, too, when she stopped being Mrs.-Helen-Shelmerley-the-artist and let her wonderful red hair fall about her bare shoulders and her soft beautiful voice become caressing. I loved her intensely all that spring when I was working on the sycamore figure of her; a new tenderness came into my feeling for her. So long as I was carving her she seemed all mine, nothing withheld, no intellectual pretensions coming between us. When I had finished the figure I felt a curious sadness; it was as though I had lost something of her. There was, too, the usual fallow period, with its mental, physical and nervous exhaustion, which I suppose for all artists in all media follows the completion of any big sustained creative effort.

5

AGAIN HELEN wanted me to go to the south with her, for what she called a "vacation," and again I refused. Paris, I felt, was my source of inspiration, and I wanted to stay by it. I was not in the mood for lotus-eating, with the Midi sun sapping my creative vitality. So she went off again without me, reproachfully as before, and I stayed in Paris and mooched along the quays and in the narrow streets of the Quarter. I made solitary trips to St. Germain-en-Laye and to St. Cloud and walked in the woods. I made what was for me in the nature of a pilgrimage to Chartres and stayed a few days in a cheap hotel and spent the greater part of the time just pottering about around or inside the Cathedral. It excited me as much as in my youth, and I felt I could gaze at it forever.

The first night back in Paris I was sitting alone in the Select, on the Boulevard Montparnasse, and wondering what the hell. I sat a lot at the Select when I was alone because it was quiet and warm and small, and I preferred its "dullness" to the clatter and chatter of the Dôme and the Coupole across the road. Since the war the old-time clientele of hunting-eyed young men which had made it attractive to people like Graham Carlton no longer propped up the bar. The people who went there now read the papers, wrote letters, played chess, or merely sat. Which was what I was doing, turning over in my mind whether it was worth while calling for *l'addition* and mooching off down to the Boulevard St. Germain and looking in at the Flore and the Magots—

because that is how it is with people who sit alone at cafés; had I been sitting at a café on the Boulevard St. Germain I'd have wondered whether I could raise the energy to get up to the Boulevard Montparnasse.

I had a glass of black coffee in front of me and a cognac, and was trying to make them last It was a warm evening, but I sat inside because the terrace was fairly full and I was in the mood to sit solitary in a corner. In the far corner, where I would like to have sat, was a party of four—three men and a girl, in their late twenties or early thirties so far as I could judge. They were all blond and I could not determine what language they were talking. I guessed them to be Scandinavians of some kind. The girl and one of the men played chess. Another of the men slept with his head on the table; the third slummocked in the corner with fair hair falling across a pale ugly intelligent face, and light blue eyes gazing blearily at everything or nothing. He wore a shapeless dark-blue suit and a high-necked dark-blue sweater and could have been a seaman, except that he looked too much like one. He held onto a mug of beer standing on the table which was puddled with spilled drink. The pile of saucers testified to the amount of drinking that had been going on between the four of them, though the chess players seemed sober enough. I looked at the young man because his face interested me. It was too flabby for his age, which I judged to be about twenty-eight or thirty, but it was an extremely intelligent face, and, I thought, a good one.

I pulled out of my pocket the small sketchbook I always carried, and in which I had notes of the gargoyles of Chartres Cathedral, and made a few thumbnail sketches of his head. Presently he got up and staggered over to me, still clutching the beer mug, which he swung wildly, slopping the contents. He stood swaying in front of me, six feet and more, and broad with it. He demanded, in strongly accented English, "Are you Josef Brenovska?"

I said, "Unfortunately I have not that honor."

The young man regarded me somberly from his nonfocusing pale blue eyes.

" 'A pard-like spirit, beautiful and swift,' " he stated.

I agreed with him and invited him to be seated. He collapsed into the chair opposite me and sat regarding me, shaking his head as though he would dislodge something entangled in his loose honey-colored hair.

"But you are an artist," he insisted.

"A sculptor," I told him.

"But you are not Josef Brenovska?" His tone besought me to be quite sure about it.

"He was killed in the French army in 1917," I said.

"It is what I complain of," he said. "Waste. Waste of life. Waste of genius. Everywhere in the world—waste. Whole civilizations running to waste." He waved the beer mug wildly, to the peril of all around him.

"You're wasting good beer," I pointed out.

He regarded me reproachfully, then staggered to his feet.

"Monsieur," he said gravely, "I apologize for intruding. You are not Josef Brenovska. I apologize. It is not your fault. But it is also not my fault, you understand? We are such stuff as dreams are made on." He bowed and sprawled across the table, his fingers parting company with the mug, which crashed to the floor. I straightened him up and he blundered back to his friends, where the man who had been playing chess was paying the waiter, and the girl was shaking the sleeper. On an impulse I scribbled my name and address on a piece of paper and as the party trooped past my table rose and addressed the girl.

"Mademoiselle, excuse me. I should like to meet your friend again sometime. I should like to discuss the sculptor Brenovska with him. If you would give him my name and address perhaps he would one day find time to call at my studio."

She smiled. "He is my brother. I will give it to him and tell him," she promised.

"You are Scandinavians?" I asked quickly as she turned away. She answered over her shoulder, still smiling, "Norwegian."

The next day and for a few days following I hoped for him, but he did not come. Then a very beautiful young Indian dancer sent me by the princess came for a portrait bust, for which she was paying. The young man had a charming, sympathetic personality and I enjoyed modeling him, and I thought no more about the Norwegian. Then one morning when I was putting the finishing touches to the bust I looked up and he stood looking in at me from the courtyard. I went over to the door and opened it. He had the same untidy, unkempt appearance, but his step and his gaze were now quite steady.

"I am called Bergsen," he said. "My sister tells me you wish to talk with me about Brenovska. Before I cannot come because I am finishing a book. When I am not working I am drinking. What I write at night when I am drunk I tear up in the morning. But still I finish the book." He smiled happily. He seemed to me like a big child pleased because it has finished its lessons and can now go out to play.

In my studio he only glanced at the head of the Indian dancer but went over to the carving of Helen and ran his hand along the broad planes of the back. He smiled.

"I was not quite wrong. Your name is English, but I think Josef Brenovska lives in you!"

I told him about the limewood carving and how I had first come to Paris in the twenties, and of my friendship first with Brenovska's mistress and then with his widow, who, I insisted with a rush of loyalty, was a very good painter.

"The American—Helen Shelmerley?" He moved his heavy head from side to side, judicially, noncommittally. "Talent is one thing; genius is another," he observed. "The souls of women cannot accommodate such a rash, fierce blaze of riot."

"You know your Shakespeare," I said.

"A little. Better I know Ibsen. Shakespeare, Ibsen, Rodin, Malliol—that is genius."

"Brenovska?" I suggested.

"The promise, perhaps. He did not live long enough. Henri Gaudier, too, perhaps. There are the intimations of passion. The rest is potentiality only."

He moved across to my panels of Life and Death and studied them closely. And I studied him. Something was stirring in me.

I asked him, "Why did you ask me if I was Brenovska?"

"There is a drawing of him which I have seen reproduced. I am drunk at the time, and I think you look like him."

"I am honored," I said, "but neither his mistress nor his widow saw the resemblance. Or if they did they did not say so."

"Women do not know what their men look like."

"Not even when they are artists, like Mrs. Shelmerley?"

"The female in them is always stronger than the artist. It is why they do not achieve genius. They see with their wombs—subjectively."

He stayed a long time talking, and though I did not always agree with what he said I found all that he said interesting. It seemed his father was a medical practitioner in Oslo, and he had himself studied medicine for a time, but his desire to write had been stronger. He had published some half dozen books—three novels, two volumes of critical essays, and a volume of poems. After the invasion of his country he had joined the resistance movement. At the time, he said, it had all seemed splendid, but afterwards the reaction set in. "I tell myself these men my friends and I take pride in killing have no wish to be in our country—perhaps even no wish to be soldiers. Many, perhaps, very much wish not to be. They had no choice. The war came upon them as it came upon us. There were things we did which I do not care to remember. When I remember them I drink, and I remember them very often. If I go to bed sober I have nightmares. It is always the same nightmare. There is a young German soldier who comes and stands at the foot of my bed. He could be my brother. We have the same hair, the same eyes, the same build. He shoots me in the belly for what I did to him. I try to cry out but I cannot, yet it is with screaming that I wake myself." But it was from more than this that he sought to escape; strong in him was the feeling that the world was not safer or nobler as a result of all the years of death and destruction, but more insecure, more brutalized, more bound and delivered over to the idea that killing is not murder so long as it is on a big enough scale. Life did not bear thinking about any more, so one thought about it as little as possible, and getting drunk was one way of putting the mind to sleep.

"My generation grew up into violence and horror," he said. "All around us civilization is destroying itself, and we also learn to destroy. The life of a man is not sacred to us any more. Universal death, destruction, suffering—we accept them as naturally as the wind and the rain."

I knew then that what I wanted to make of him was a study in *Weltschmerz*—the malady of his generation. When we sat together later in a *bistro* at the bottom of the Avenue de l'Observatoire I told him this. First I wanted to model a portrait bust of his head, but in wood, massively, I wanted to carve all that intolerable bitterness, pain, despair of his generation of which he was the embodiment. He listened with interest, but would make no promises, he said. He would come sometimes to my studio and I should do what I could—make what I could of him. There might be days, even weeks, he warned me, when he would not come at all.

I asked him what he was doing in Paris.

"Wasting my life," he replied laconically.

"Could you not waste it as well in Oslo?"

"I had to leave Norway. Too often I have nightmares there. The mental climate of postwar France suits me better." His brothers and his sister had come for a holiday to Paris to visit him and attempt to persuade him to return to Norway. He had convinced them that he would not return. Even if he could not continue to live in France he was not prepared to live in Norway again. In Paris he found it possible to forget what he defined as "the horror and emptiness of our world," the "anguish of nothingness" to which life had been reduced. He said all this with his charming smile, apologetically, but all that *Angst* of which he spoke was in his eyes. There was no escape for him in work because in his work he expressed his despair—gave the devils which possessed him full play. "And do not tell me," he said, "that love is the answer, because I cannot command love, nor can I give it."

He was fairly drunk by the time we left the *bistro*, and several times when he came to the studio he was several degrees less than sober, but drunk or sober he still interested me. Mentally and physically his shape interested me.

Helen called him my "tame existentialist," and was impatient of him as a neurotic egotist. She agreed that he had a "fine head" and she admired the portrait bust I made of him, which I had cast in a bronze with a verdigree patina, but the idea for the major work he had inspired in me left her cold.

"All this postwar *Weltschmerz* and *Angst* of the young," she said, "all this cult of Cocteau and Sartre and Anouilh, all these narcissistic children of the abyss of nothingness! An artist's function is to let in light, to illumine, to create—what is all this nihilism to do with him?"

"He can shed a light on it," I said stubbornly, for I felt that she was willfully opposing me, out of a kind of jealousy, because this new idea which was exciting me was as it were outside of her sphere of influence.

I had the good fortune to find a massive piece of gray poplar of exactly the right dimensions for what I had in mind. I was wildly excited as I had not been since I had made old Rintrah in teak. I had enjoyed making Helen in sycamore, but I could not deceive myself that it was a major work as the Christ-figure had been; and Rintrah, and even that now early work Negro Girl Dancing, had been more exciting to me. I suppose the Doors of

Life and Death would rank as a major work; they had taken me a long time and I had brought a great deal of thought and feeling to them, as I had to the stone bas-relief of the Eternal Horses, but no bas-relief would ever excite me like a work in the round.

So I got to work on my great poplar tree trunk, and Bergsen drifted in and out, and it hardly mattered whether he was there or not, for I had made a great many pencil sketches and even some clay small models before I got to work. When he came he would sit and smoke a pipe, sometimes not talking at all; or he would play with Niki, or even occasionally take her off out to the Luxembourg gardens. There was a kind of sweetness and gentleness about him, a lazy good nature, which drunk or sober immediately responded to the child's completely uncritical friendliness and trustfulness. I liked having the two of them around; they never intruded.

The great figure came along nicely. It was not recognizably Bergsen, except for the youthfully powerful body with the shapeless trousers and the high-necked sweater; the head was Bergsen's, too, and the fall of the hair, and the face was Bergsen, though it was not the face he sat with at cafés, or took with him into the Luxembourg gardens with Niki, or even the face that looked at me through the pipe smoke he exhaled in my studio. It was the face of all that *Weltschmerz* and *Angst* mirrored in his eyes, making all the external faces so many masks. The poplar was a beautiful wood to work, coming up with a beautiful smoothness under the tools, and the light yellow was as right for Bergsen's Scandinavian fairness as the lignum vitae had been for the Jewish darkness of the Christ. From the few remarks he made I realized that Bergsen understood very well what I was trying to say with the figure, and that he thought I was succeeding in saying it.

I never got to know him any better. He never added to the brief biographical outline he had given me the first time he had come to the studio, nor did he open any more casements upon the existentialist lands forlorn of his heart and mind. He came and went in my life with, as it were, a handful of intelligent observations on art and life, and a kind of lazy impersonal good nature. He was good company only in the sense that he was easy to be with; it was possible to be almost unaware of his presence. It seemed almost at times as though he sleepwalked through life. If he had any normal feelings for his mother or his father, his sister or his brothers, he kept them hidden from me. Only with little Niki did he seem to slough off some of that pervading somnambulance and become at least tentatively what we think of as "human." Yet sometimes even with her I would notice his smile play over her so dreamily it was as though he smiled in his sleep. When his family had gone back to Oslo I never saw him at the Select or anywhere else except alone, and invariably drunk or well on the way.

At the end of the summer when I had finished the *Weltschmerz* he stopped coming to the studio. The last time he came he looked up at the figure, like, yet unlike, himself and observed, "It seems my life has been not quite useless after all—since I inspired this!"

"There is your own work," I suggested.

"It has no value. I have done nothing that Jean Cocteau did not do better years ago. And which Cocteau and others will continue to do better. There is not merely no point in adding to the world's accumulation of mediocrity; it is a form of blasphemy. When one has nothing new to say, and is not even capable of an original reaffirmation of an old truth, the best is silence."

I did not agree with what he said, but I let it go. It was enough that he felt that he himself had nothing to say that seemed worth saying, and when a man feels that, he speaks out an inner despair and emptiness there's no remedying.

Shortly after this I saw him sitting inside the Select. I went over to him and sat with him. He told me he was making arrangements to go to Germany to live. He wanted to exist among the rubble, he said, and at the heart of the world-nightmare. Then the rubble of one's own life would become insignificant, and one's personal nightmares cease.

"But what will you do there?" I protested.

"Suffer," he said.

"You suffer here."

"There I shall become part of the general suffering."

"A self-imposed penance, in short?"

"Call it that. Call it masochism. Call it a short cut to self-absolution. Call it morbid insanity. Call it wisdom. Anything you like. Whatever anyone calls it it will be only part of the truth."

I couldn't stay long with him. I had to go to the Coupole American Bar to meet Helen and the owner of the gallery where it was proposed my work should be shown next month.

"Whatever the right label," I said, "I hope it will eventually prove creative for you."

He smiled. "Does nothing generate negation? Or negation nothingness?" he inquired.

I was impatient with him for the first time.

"You'll find in Germany that the questions don't arise. The empty belly generates a realistic approach to life. Starvation is positive, you'll find."

"Death, also. With this advantage over life, that it is permanent."

I was about to retort that death was the final negation when he turned away to catch at a waiter's sleeve, and I took the opportunity to get up.

"I must be going," I said.

"If we don't meet again," he said, "remember me when thou comest into thy kingdom." His usually gentle smile was ironic.

"If I were a Christian I'd pray for you," I told him.

"A Hindu or a Moslem would do as much. The Christians haven't the monopoly of prayer-heeding Godhead. But," he smiled again, "I thank you for the negative good-will."

"*Au revoir*," I said.

"Good-bye," he answered, and now his smile was empty of everything but charm.

He was right, for I never saw him again.

6

I HAD a fairly impressive amount of work for this exhibition, with the stone things, the bronzes, and my wood carvings of the last two years, and M. Perrot, Helen's agent, decided that it would be better if I had a one-man show following her exhibition. I was to get my Daughter of Los and my bas-relief of the Eternal Horses from London, and anything else which I considered of importance, including, on loan, anything from the London exhibition which I thought would enhance my reputation in France. I showed M. Perrot photographs of everything, and he did not want the Christ, which was a relief to me because I wanted my *Weltschmerz* to be the central piece of this exhibition. This figure belonged to the aesthetic and moral climate of the times, I felt. It could be said that the Christ-figure belonged to all time, yet to that immediate postwar world, I felt, everything I had tried to say through it was thrust into the background by that aftermath of misery and despair and chaos. Let Christ go. Well, in some two thousand years he could never be said to have arrived, so it was no loss. It might be that the world would have to descend into hell yet a third time before Christ would in fact drive the money-changers out of the temple. Those who survived the atomic holocaust would have to find a new way to live—if indeed the atomized earth allowed them to survive upon its barren surface at all. *Weltschmerz* was anyhow the present order of the day. Even the Daughter of Los did not rightly belong, poor girl, with her bright loins, gates to Paradise, and her brave assertion—"Everything that lives is Holy." But M. Perrot was very keen on the Daughter of Los, though I had the feeling he would have preferred her called something else—Eve, for example. He did not want Rintrah; it would mean nothing to the French public, he declared. I suggested that a good many Americans and perhaps a few English would come to the exhibition, but he pointed out that the critics were French. It was not even as though there was a possibility of selling Rintrah to an American, since it was sold already.

There was enough, though, without Christ or Rintrah, and I had enough to cope with in getting the Horses, and the Daughter of Los, and the stone carving of Tansy, over, and in arranging with the purchasers of the wood carvings of my first exhibition to loan them and ship them to me—there were Board of Trade regulations to be complied with, apart from the problem of packing and shipping. Graham Carlton brought the Negro Girl over in person and stayed over for the exhibition.

It was a nice modern gallery on the Boulevard Raspail. The lighting was extremely good, and the stuff looked well arranged along the gray walls, with *Weltschmerz* taking the floor in the middle. There was an elaborate flower arrangement of white and dark-red chrysanthemum blooms and goldening beech leaves on a table near the door, where the catalogs were for sale, and more flowers at the far end of the room, in a corner between Dryad and Eve. The busts were perched upon pedestals against the two long walls, and I must say I was surprised to see how well the heads of Niki and Lee stood out—they were quite the best things among the portraits, I thought, though I was pleased with the head of the Indian boy. The Doors of Life and Death had the wall at the far end to themselves and were effective, I thought. Tansy in stone wasn't as striking as I'd remembered it, and the Horses bas-relief was a bit lost near the entrance because people tended to buy their catalogs and just walk past it, their attention drawn by the Bergsen figure; they went on from that to the Daughter of Los, I noticed.

I attended the preview partly to please Helen, having disappointed her in London, and partly out of curiosity. It was a very grand affair, with all manner of distinguished persons present, including the English ambassador. The princess was there in full regalia of mink and diamonds and brought with her a gaggle or covey or pride, or whatever is the right word, of fashionable ladies and gentlemen of assorted nationalities. A number of Helen's American friends were there—some painters and writers, and people who were merely rich. M. Perrot and his secretary went around with glasses of champagne for everyone. You could tell the critics not only because they weren't so smart as the other people but because they were always looking for refills. Criticizing other people's work is evidently a thirsty business. Helen had been anxious that I should look what she called "respectable" for this important party, and after wearing down my resistance she had had a black velvet jacket made for me and some good black worsted trousers—the tailor had taken pride in assuring me that it was real English cloth. I didn't mind the jacket so much, though it was so damned fine and elegant I felt a kind of overgrown little Lord Fauntleroy in it, but I hated the trousers with their sleek hips and idiotic creases down the legs. The jacket would be all right when it got a bit old and shabby, I thought, but the trousers would never be anything but well cut and expensive-looking, however old they got. I had a pair of shapeless old flannels I would have been happy in and a pair of tweed bags, very baggy at the knees, which I had bought for ten bob in an old-clothes shop in Deptford High Street. Helen was right that they wouldn't go with the handsome velvet jacket, but then neither did I.

However, there I was, all dolled up in my black velvet and my English worsted, with a white silk shirt and black silk tie, also supplied by Helen, and all clean-shaven and washed behind the ears, and but for my manual-worker's hands I could have been a bank manager or a diplomat or a best-selling author—almost anything but what I was, which was a poor-but-honest carver.

The *Weltschmerz* figure attracted a good deal of attention, and the critics discussed it at length in the most learned and cultural terms. An artist hardly knows what he's up to in his work till the critics weigh-in to tell him about it. I knew what I wanted to express through that great gray poplar carving of Bergsen—the title I gave to the work was an indication of it; but I had no idea it was of such symbolic significance and cosmic content and the rest of it. It also gave the critics a chance to air their own *Weltschmerz*, sensitiveness, philosophic awareness, and general intellectualism. It seemed that Tom Rowse represented a force aesthetically and morally. There was similar highfalutin talk about the Doors and the Horses. It struck me that the critics were a deal more concerned to show off their own exquisite minds than to assess the artistic value of the artist's attempt to express himself in wood and stone.

However, it was what Helen called a Wonderful Press, and as soon as the reviews appeared Perrot received several offers by telephone both for the *Weltschmerz* and the Daughter of Los. Graham Carlton bought the Horses through a French friend. Nobody wanted Tansy or the Doors, but there were several offers for the figure of Helen which I had after all called simply Woman Weeping. The prices were high, and even when Perrot had taken his thirty-three-and-a-third per cent I still had enough to pay Graham Carlton what I had borrowed from him, with the equivalent in francs of several hundred pounds besides. In addition I received a great many inquiries for portrait-busts—had they not been sold I could have sold the Indian boy, Lee, and Niki several times over. I had more than enough commissions to keep me busy till the end of the year. I was also invited to a number of parties and receptions, none of which invitations I accepted. Helen urged that I should accept the most important of them at least—the princess's, for example, and the reception at the British Embassy; now that I had some good clothes, she urged, I could "go anywhere." I told her that I was quite prepared to go anywhere in such clothes as I had before then; I had been around with her and Graham in my old clothes, why should I have to dress up for princesses or ambassadors or anyone else? She replied rather crossly that there were such things as social customs, conventions, etiquette. I told her that I didn't recognize them, and that the sooner people stopped recognizing such artificialities the better for everyone and the sooner we'd get around to the real things. But it was no good; the only thing we were agreed upon was that we made each other tired.

We ended that year, Helen and I, a relationship that should never have begun. We had been good devoted friends, but we had been bad, quarrelsome lovers. She decided to take her own exhibition to New York at the end of the year, and mine was anyhow booked for London. She suggested that I should keep on the studio, since the owner was willing to let it for another year, and come back after the London show in January. She would be back from New York in the early spring, and perhaps this time we might really make the Riviera together—"give ourselves a real honeymoon," she said. She added that she knew we hadn't got on well lately, but urged that we had both done a lot of work this year and that we were tired and our nerves frayed.

I had to tell her: "It isn't that, Helen. Our differences are fundamental. You are an intellectual sympathetic to the theory of anarchism, but for you there's a world of difference between thought and living. Whereas I am an anarchist by nature—as my way of life demonstrates. You love money and want more of it for everyone. I regard it as an abomination and want it abolished. All this didn't prevent us from being friends because we weren't then personally involved with each other. As lovers it has mattered all the time—money has continually come between us—"

"My money has been useful to you," she pointed out bitterly.

"The mere fact that you say that is a money-wedge driven between us," I said. "I have resented your charity, and despised myself for having recourse to expediency—you know that."

"You have money of your own now—earned money. And you will have more. You won't look back now. If you're not careful you'll find yourself rich!"

"No one is compelled to be rich," I said. "At the moment I have enough to support myself in moderate comfort for another year while I work at the things I want to do—which is not modeling portrait busts!"

"Gratitude was never your strong point," she said, and the intense bitterness in her face and voice wounded me. I hated her to be so hurt and bitter, but I refused to sentimentalize the issue.

"You gave to me out of a very considerable surplus," I reminded her. "No sacrifice was involved in it. The money you have spent on me would not have been spent on yourself or anyone else; it would just have sat somewhere with the rest of your surplus, breeding more money—to no purpose."

Helen closed the discussion by saying that it was "sordid." She was hurt and angry, and we did not see each other for some weeks after it. When we did it was a chance meeting on the Boulevard Montparnasse. I had her come into the Select and have a drink or two. She looked old and unhappy and I couldn't bear it. I told her so.

"You mean," she said, with a small smile, "you don't like being made to feel bad about me." I agreed with her—I hated it; but it was also true, I insisted, that I hated her to be unhappy, whether I was the cause or not. We were obviously better suited to be friends than lovers, I urged.

"What is so bitter," she said, "is that I never wanted us to be lovers. That day in Greenwich when we were excited about the lignum vitae I suddenly realized that I was in love with you and had been for a long time, but I deliberately refused to answer the leading question you asked me. You had Tansy and I knew I was ruled out for you then and I was glad of it. I knew well enough that if I allowed myself to love you it would be a repetition of Josef all over again, and I felt too old and tired for it. I tried to love again, more peacefully, with John Shelmerley, who had no pretensions to being more than a businessman. He was good and kind and it was port after stormy seas. I mourned him very greatly when he died. There was no one else until I met you—with your passion for Brenovska, my one great love. Everything in me said Oh not, not all that, all over again! So I was glad you had Tansy, and glad when the war years cut us off from each other, and I thought we could meet again afterwards just as the good friends we'd always been. I thought myself quite invulnerable. If you hadn't stayed that night I might have gone on being. But you did stay—" she smiled ruefully, "and I discovered that my heart wasn't the shut-up shop I'd believed it to be."

I said, moved, "Your heart must never be that, Helen. It's the kind of heart that's meant to remain wide open until it closes down for good. But you haven't done with life yet, and life hasn't done with you, and while there's life there's love! For people like us, anyhow!"

We had several drinks and got a little sentimental and ended up holding hands and declaring with tears in our eyes that no doubt we should always love each other, as a result of which we felt close and peaceful and were able to go our separate ways without bitterness on her part or conscience on mine.

I went to see her off when she left Paris. I went to Cherbourg with her and we spent the night together in an expensive de luxe hotel for which I let her pay. I set myself out to please her, even to wearing the new jacket and trousers. We filled the room with hothouse white lilac, we had champagne sent up, and I laid myself out to be the romantic lover she had always wanted. I had already arranged for some red roses to be sent from Paris to the liner, to await her in her cabin—just to show her that her old scarecrow anarchist was capable of a gesture, and that in his own fashion he loved her. I wrote on the card to accompany the roses, *In love and friendship*, and I meant it.

So I sent her off happy, and soon after that I left for London.

7

I HAD written old Joe Snell from Paris asking him if I might come and stay with him until the exhibition had come and gone. He had replied with his usual phrase about my being as welcome as the flowers in May, the more so, he added, as *the missus has slung her hook. Gone off to live with the boy and his wife. Fed-up with the old man. Says I am a disgrace to her. Dear, dear. I live in great style now as a chore-lady comes in twice a week to do what she calls give me a clean-up, though it's the house she cleans up, not yours-truly, whom she calls Sir. Come when you like and stay as long as you like. I'm a dab hand at the cooking these days and we'll live like lords, and to hell with all the governments. Your old pal anarchy Joe.*

So to anarchy Joe's I went straight from Victoria, and a royal welcome he gave me, with his week's meat ration saved up and thrown into a pot he called "the dixie." The dixie stood on the kitchen range and we just took our plates over to it and ladled out the greasy mess, vegetables and all. We washed it down with a couple of bottles of beer, then sat with our feet up on the stove and lit our pipes and felt fine. Our plates with the grease congealed on them we left for his chore-lady, who would come in the day after tomorrow, by which time there would be plenty more, and she was never happy, he declared, unless she had something to grouse about.

Joe's flat over a shop in the main street was very noisy, and the only heated room was the kitchen in which we lived. The bedrooms had the coldness of rooms which have never had a fire lit in them in all their years. After the central heating of the last two years I felt the cold creep and creak in my bones, and going to bed and getting up were ordeals. Joe's ideas of living like a lord were peculiar; when there was no meat ration to throw with inadequately prepared vegetables into a pot he brought in fish-and-chips from a shop up the street. Sometimes we had a bit of corned beef and pickles. Joe didn't care what he ate. "What doesn't poison helps to fatten," he would say cheerfully. He was not much interested in the salads and fruit I'd bring in to balance our lordly meals. He would tolerate lettuce and tomatoes sprinkled with vinegar but considered that properly speaking they belonged to Sunday high-tea, when we would have what he called a "spread," with shrimps and winkles. Joe was very happy now that the missus had hooked it. He could wipe his fingers in his hair, pick his teeth with a pin, sit with his feet on the range, get up when the streets were aired, shave only once a week, read an anarchist paper called *Freedom* without being subjected to caustic remarks, and generally lead a peaceful, civilized life.

I was not comfortable at Joe's, but nevertheless I liked being there, and when I shivered in the refrigerator of a bedroom I thought with pleasure of the centrally heated studio to which I would be returning in a few weeks' time, this time paying my own rent and being free and independent, neither harassed by lack of money nor dependent on anyone's charity.

Meanwhile there was all the business of getting my stuff back from Paris and arranging for the loan stuff. Finstein wanted to make the Daughter of Los the center piece of the exhibition—there was not the same feeling of *Weltschmerz* in England, he thought, and he did not even mind whether we had that in the exhibition or not. From his point of view it was not a very satisfactory exhibition, as there were only the Doors and the stone bust of Tansy for sale. I pointed out that if we sold the Doors his commission would more than cover the cost of the exhibition, but he was not optimistic about selling them. Finally I offered to pay for the gallery myself, but warned him that if I did that I would feel myself free to have my next exhibition at any other gallery I chose—and that exhibition would not be a loan one but all new stuff. He read my Paris notices and wavered. "What we lose on the roundabouts we make up on the swings, eh?" he said at last. "More than," I assured him. All over again I thought what a loathsome business it was, this haggling over prices and commissions for what had been produced out of a kind of anguish in oneself. All over again I thought that exhibitions were a mistake, and that an artist must not place himself in the hands of shopkeepers, which was all agents, with their galleries, really were. Nor was an artist there for the critics, who had never made a piece of sculpture or a painting in their lives, to sharpen their wits on. I decided to pay for the gallery myself in the thought that this exhibition might be my last.

I had always thought that art should be applied, that artists should paint walls and ceilings for houses, schools, theatres, public buildings, rather than pictures for frames; that sculptors should co-operate with architects and town-planners; that art, in short, should belong to the people, to their homes, to their market places, to their life as a community; that it no more belonged in museums and galleries than animals belong in a zoo. There should be the village artist as there was the village carpenter, but when the village carpenters were dying out everywhere in the face of mass production what chance for the artist? An artist would always make the things he wanted to make, without reference to their marketability, of course, but in a society in which art had its right and natural place there would always be a demand for the authentic work of art—the demand, in fact, would exceed the supply. The town-planners of every new town and suburb would be looking about for painters and sculptors just as they look about for architects and builders. The artist would be a member of the community instead of an outcast from it, or at least a hanger-on. Art must cease to be a luxury for connoisseurs—and become integrated with life. Art, stripped of all the highfalutin jargon talked about it, is simply the thing well made, whether it is a piece of statuary for a garden or a public building or a church, a mural decoration, a chair, a poem, a piece of music, or anything else. The artist is essentially a workman, and a good shoemaker every bit as much an artist as a sculptor or painter.

Joe and I talked a good deal about all this the evenings we sat with our feet on the kitchen range, our pipes alight and the beer bottles handy. Joe would limp over to his bookshelf and take down Kropotkin's *The Conquest of Bread* and turn to the passage on Art and Society, to which he had recommended me in my apprenticeship days. I knew the passage he liked to quote by heart, and I think so did he, but just to handle one of Kropotkin's works gave him as much pleasure as I got from turning the pages of my battered old Blake. "*Nowadays*," he would read, smoothing his mustache along his upper lip as though to clear the way for the precious pronouncement, "*Nowadays the greatest honor a painter can aspire to is to see his canvas, framed in gilded wood, hung in a museum, a sort of old curiosity shop, where you see, as in the Prado, Murillo's Ascension next to a beggar of Velasquez and the dogs of Philip II. Poor Velasquez and poor Murillo! Poor Greek statues which* lived *in the Acropolis of their cities, and are now stifled beneath the red cloth hangings of the Louvre!*"

I had not much heart for this exhibition in London. Since I had nothing but my oak doors and a stone carving to sell, what was I having this exhibition *for?* To get myself known, to place myself at the mercy of the critics; for publicity in fact, self-advertisement. It was ugly, I thought, and vulgar. Quoth the raven. . . . I was glad Helen wasn't there to argue with me about it. I thought of her with affection. I was glad we had had that time in Cherbourg together, so that the ship of our relationship had as it were gone down with its flag flying—a rather tattered flag, perhaps, but still, a flag, and flying. . . .

Lee, with whom I would have liked to have discussed the matter, was with Graham on the Riviera. I attended the preview, and as Helen wasn't there I wore my old clothes and then realized that by so doing I was conspicuous in that smart crowd as I wouldn't have been in what Joe called the "glad rags" Helen had got for me. I saw people nudging each other as I passed—the artist, of course; who else would look so Bohemian? The bust of Tansy was bought the first day, by a dealer though we didn't know that at the time. An elderly woman all chins and chinchilla asked me if I ever modeled animals, because she had a very handsome chow she would like a small figure of in bronze. I took her card and promised to telephone her when I was less busy, and when I got back to Joe's that evening lit my pipe with the card.

I had a good press, on the whole, though the *Weltschmerz* did not create the sensation it had in Paris; the Daughter of Los attracted most attention, and the *Manchester Guardian* published a photograph of it. Nobody was scandalized by the Daughter of Los as they had been over the Christ-figure. The world had moved on that much, that it was no longer shocked by genitals. On the last day of the exhibition, just when Finstein and I had resigned ourselves to being left with them, a pleasant youngish man who wore a bowler hat and a dark overcoat with a velvet collar bought the Doors for his country house. His card revealed him as a peer of the realm, and Finstein looked him up in *Who's Who* when he had gone and was gratified to find that he was the eldest son of an eighth earl. "None of your jumped-up Labour peers," he observed, with satisfaction. I couldn't see myself that it mattered how his nibs had come by the handle to his name; I wasn't interested in handles; I was glad he liked the Doors and wanted to buy them, and would use them as doors, though I would have preferred him to have been the director of an Academy of Art wanting them as entrance doors for the inspiration of students, but I was glad he recognized the inscription from Blake and understood what they were all about. We talked Blake a bit. He had been to my first London exhibition. He invited me to what he called his "place" in Sussex to supervise the fitting of the doors to a barn he had had made into a theatre at which a local dramatic society performed plays under his direction. He urged that I should come for a week end and meet his wife, who "painted a bit," and his daughters who showed "considerable dramatic talent." He had a naïve, amateur's enthusiasm for art with a capital A in all its manifestations which I found rather appealing, and I thought I might go sometime. I ended by being quite happy about his acquiring the Doors, since he was evidently very pleased with them, and I quite liked him and would have gone to his place, but that half an hour before the exhibition closed Miss Hopkins turned up with a pale thin lad with glasses and a solemn expression singularly like her own.

"Good Lord, Hoppy!" I exclaimed.

She wore glasses herself now and her hair which had been light mouse was now graying. She looked plainer than ever, but her round brown eyes beamed with good-will, and she was all breathless with hurrying and with excitement, and was so palpably pleased to see me that I quite warmed to her, the creature.

"Such a rush to get here," she panted. "I didn't leave the office till five, and I met Willie outside Swan and Edgar's, and we ran all the way down Piccadilly! What do you think of Willie now? He got a scholarship for a commercial college. He's going to be an accountant. Anything with figures." Willie was goggling at the Daughter of Los and his mother added quickly, "Bookkeeping and that. He doesn't remember you, of course."

"Yes, I do," Willie declared, a little sulkily. "In Mr. Morton's room with the Spanish blokes." He turned away and stared fixedly at the Woman Weeping.

"Well," said his mother, "now we're here we'd better look at the statues! How've you been keeping all this time? I saw you had quite a write-up in the *Standard* the other night—in the Londoner's Diary. They said you'd been living in Paris. That's nice." She stared resolutely at the *Weltschmerz*. "Powerful," she added. She shifted her gaze along the row of busts and let it come to rest on the head of Niki. "Oh, how sweet!" she exclaimed. She beamed at me. "It's a great gift to be able to do all this. Wonderful, really. Willie was quite good at modeling at school, but they thought with his head for figures he should take a commercial course. Figures on paper, I mean, not this kind!" She giggled self-consciously. "You should come and visit us sometime," she prattled on, still darting her glance from bust to bust, carving to carving—the Horses and the Doors got no more than a glance—"I've got two rooms now—I took over Mrs. Hilley's room when she died. You heard about her, I suppose?"

"Yes," I said. "Lee told me in Paris—a heart attack during a raid, I gathered."

"That's right. And what did you think about poor Tansy?"

My heart plunged suddenly, then began to hammer.

"I hadn't heard," I murmured.

"Fancy Lee not telling you! Though of course they didn't move her to the place for incurables till after he had gone off to France, now I come to think of it. It's too awful. She's awfully young. Well, under forty's young, isn't it? Her mother's got the child. She's had two operations. But it's gone too far. They can't do any more for her."

"I don't understand," I said. "What's gone too far?"

Miss Hopkins glanced at the boy, but he had moved a little away from us and was bending down peering into the bas-relief of the trampling horses.

She murmured, "The growth. It was malignant, you see. It's usually operable. They take everything away, if you know what I mean, but once it gets into the glands—"

I said then, out loud, the word she shrank from saying. "D'you mean she's got cancer?" I demanded.

She flushed as though I had uttered an indecency.

"It's too awful," she said. She gazed at the bust of Lee, with the wreath of flowers at the base. "That's awfully like him," she observed. Then she turned to me. "You could go and see her," she said. "They let them have visitors almost any time. You could ring up. Not tomorrow—her husband goes Sundays. No matter what part of the country he's in on Saturday he gets back in time to see her Sunday, even if he has to travel all night."

"Where is it—this place?" I asked.

She told me, and added, "Of course she doesn't realize what sort of place it is. She thinks it's a convalescent home. I suppose they all do, but of course the hospitals only send them there when they can do no more for them, poor things. Look, the commissioner seems to be locking the door. I think we'd better go." She called to the boy at the far end of the room. "Come on, Willie. Closing time. Oh dear! Sounds like a pub, doesn't it? Well, it's been grand seeing you again, Mr. Rowse. Do come and have tea with us one Sunday. And do go and see Tansy. I'm sure it would cheer her up, as Mr. Tanswell can't go during the week. Her mother goes Wednesdays, early closing day."

"You really think she—can't get well?" I said, taking the hand she held out to me.

"Oh no," she answered. "Or she wouldn't be there. I mean they don't do anything for them there."

"Does she know, do you think?"

"I suppose so. Six women have died in her ward in the three weeks she's been there."

"Well," I said, "good-bye, and—thanks for coming."

"It's been a pleasure." She beamed up at me, then suddenly the brightness in her face disappeared, like a light switched off. "You look quite upset," she said. "I suppose it's a shock—as you hadn't heard."

"Yes. It's been a shock. Good night."

"Bye-bye. *Willie!*"

She and the boy went, and Finstein came out of his office and began talking about Lord Lake, and a Mrs. Someone-or-other who had bought the bust of Tansy, and about getting the stuff away, and how he would send my check on with the contra account for expenses and commission. I said yes to everything. It was all money, money, money. We could have been discussing sausages or underwear or any damn thing.

I got out at last and plunged about in the streets behind Piccadilly and washed up in a Mayfair pub, with a classy clientele in the saloon bar and the riffraff in the public. I joined the riffraff and began drinking. But nothing happened. I might as well have been drinking water.

"It's too awful," I kept hearing Miss Hopkins say, and then, reprovingly, "*Willie!*" to the pale boy who stared and stared pop-eyed at the white marble emanation of Tansy, at the bright loins that were golden gates, starry and glorious, my beautiful girl for whom they could not do anything more. Only I could not weep. I could not get drunk. "*They know not why they love, nor wherefore they sicken and die.*" The words swam about in my mind and I stared at them like fish in an aquarium tank. It was too awful. Heart and mind froze with it.

I was standing up at the bar, as I always did when I was drinking hard. The man next to me suddenly pushed his glass across the counter and looked up into my face. His was flushed and his eyes were bleary.

"Pore ole Gandy!" he said. "Wot you think about it, Guv'nor? Pore ole buzzer! The 'ole world respected 'im, say wot you like. I reckon they ought to lynch the bastard wot done it!"

The man at the other side of him muttered, "Good thing it was one of 'is own religion done it or there'd a bin a massacre!"

Something was ticking over in my brain, slowly.

"Gandhi?" I said. "Massacre?"

"'Aven't yer seen the papers? It was in lunchtime. Old Gandy's bin bumped orf. Shot at a prayer meeting or summin'."

"Assassinated," the other man corroborated, adding, "Musta bin a lunatic. It don't make sense otherwise. Wot would one of 'is own people want to bump the ole boy orf for? 'E was all but Gawd to 'em."

"P'lit'cle!" the flushed man asserted, with a hiccup. "Thass wot was—p'lit'cle!" He pulled his recharged glass toward him. "Pore ole buzzer," he repeated. "Respected the 'ole world over."

What was ticking over in my brain clicked like an automatic machine before the penny drops.

"It's too awful," I said.

I left the pub and walked out into what seemed a starless, lampless world wholly given over to evil—to envy, revenge, cruelty, a cold and desolate earth, in which man was a little, groveling root self-exiled from the light, as when the mob shouted for Barabbas and Christ was led away to be crucified.

8

I WAS glad that Sunday that I was living with old Joe. There weren't many people I could have borne to be with—no one else, really, except Lee. The impact of the double shock was overwhelming. The greatest moral force the world had known since Jesus had been destroyed in a fanatic moment; a light had been quenched that could not be rekindled. The whole world, it seemed, was profoundly shocked. Not since the dropping of the atomic bombs on Japan had there been such a universal shocked dismay; it embraced all classes and penetrated every degree of intelligence: people of the class and intelligence of old Tilley; people of the class and intelligence of the statesman who during the Mahatma's lifetime had derided him as the "half-naked fakir"; intelligent thinking people like Joe Snell, and unthinking ignorant people like the humble woman who cleaned for him. It was as though through all the degrees of human understanding ran a forked-lightning flash of awareness that such people occur only once in centuries and that not for two thousand years had there been such a one. The one positive power for good had disappeared from human midst, leaving the forces of evil in possession; the world was that much darker, that much less safe.

There was that major disaster in the outer world, and for that speck of protoplasmic energy that blundered about on the planet, its existence recorded as Tom Rowse, there was the disaster at the core of his infinitesimal private world. The death of Gandhi in terms of human values was everything; the death of Gladys Tanswell would be nothing, was of utterly no importance; she had not radiated any particular light even in her own small intimate circle. No one, really, would be any the worse off for her death. Poor old Bill would be upset; that would be the measure of his grief—he would be upset; and presently he would marry again, for sure; he was the marrying kind. And what had Tom Rowse got to be so harrowed about? She'd been dead to him for years.

"You got to get it into perspective, son, see," Joe kept on asserting.

Intellectually I could and did get it into perspective all right; I set the tragedy of Tansy side by side with the tragedy of Gandhi's assassination; unfortunately the intellect functions on one plane and the emotions on another. Supposing Tansy beat all the medicos and lived, I asked myself, what difference would it make to me? She had ceased to have anything to do with my life years ago. What good would it do me to know she still moved about the world—smiled and talked and brushed her hair and slept with Bill, and probably some fool lover as well? It was the wildest indulgence of irrationality to insist that she must live because the thought of her dead was intolerable; yet everything in me did so insist. Call her anything you like—a cheap little adulteress, a liar, a cheat, so much human rubbish not worth the shedding of a single tear; all that could be true, yet she was beauty, youth, life, love, inspiration, all joy, all peace, and all pain, and because of that the ugliness and cruelty of what had overtaken her was completely intolerable.

I spent a good deal of that Sunday walking about on the green hill, unpeopled and desolate with winter. Had we ever really walked there together in the warm and golden summer, my love and I, my golden girl, my white-limbed Daughter of Los? The wind was cold and gray, and the Lament of Enion moved in the bare branches of the little hawthorns and the great chestnuts.

> What is the price of experience? do men buy it for a song,
> Or wisdom for a dance in the street? No! it is bought with the price
> Of all that a man hath. . . .
> Wisdom is sold in the desolate market where none come to buy.

I took Joe drinking with me at the close of that interminable day. I drank hard and blindly.

"Take it easy, son," Joe urged.

But it wasn't a question of taking it easy or hard, but only of finding a way to take it at all.

I decided not to telephone the hospital to find out if Tansy would see me. I could not take the risk of her refusing. I had to see her once again; just once. I set off for the hospital in the early afternoon. I bought a few freesias because she had always liked them for their scent, and because they were expensive, and she had always liked luxury things. The first spring flowers, yellow and white narcissi and the first daffodils, were in the shops, but I rejected them. I would not mock her with the promise of a spring she might never see.

The hospital was more like a private nursing home, small, as such places go. It was free of the smell of ether, the familiar hospital smell. The significance of that didn't immediately occur to me. I asked at an inquiry office and was told the ward where I would find Mrs. Tanswell, and the floor. Oh yes, I could go straight up; visiting hours were from two till three-thirty; it was not yet three o'clock. The ward I wanted was on the first floor. I began to mount, slowly, my heart beating very fast. I had a sudden wild hope that someone else would be there—Hoppy, perhaps, or even old Bill himself. Even that at the door of the ward some stern sister would deny me admission. But when I hesitated at the door a pleasant-faced young nurse asked me kindly who I wanted, and when I told her said, "Up in the far corner on the right, by the fire."

I asked the girl desperately, "How is she?"

"Not too bad, really. She keeps up remarkably well."

"It's all right for me to see her?" I pressed, adding, "She's not expecting me, you see."

"You'll see for yourself how she is," the nurse said. "Some days she just dozes and doesn't want to talk. Other days she's quite lively. She varies." She repeated, smiling, "You'll just have to see for yourself."

She left me, and I went on up the ward to see for myself.

I was only vaguely aware of beds on either side of me and of some tables down the middle with plants and flowers. A fire burned in a grate on the far wall and I walked toward it; when I had almost reached it I stopped and looked to the right.

I saw a small head against a pillow and pale gold hair falling at either side a thin white face with deep hollows under high cheekbones. I saw dark hollows in which closed eyes were sunk. Her head was fallen a little to one side. Her lips were pink and childlike without any make-up, as I had seen them in the mornings we wakened together. I moved to the foot of the bed and stood there. Then I was aware that a gray-faced elderly woman in the next bed was watching me with a kind of eagerness.

"Wake her up," she urged.

"It seems a pity," I said.

"It won't hurt her. She sleeps all the time when there's no one here." She leaned across to Tansy's bed and called to her, in a shrill singsong: "Mrs. Tanswell! Mrs. Tans-we-ll!"

The small head moved restlessly on the pillow, from side to side; there was a gleam of blue in the dark hollows that held the eyes. Then Tansy was looking at me.

"A gentleman to see you," her neighbor said, and smiled from her to me.

"Tansy," I said, and went to the side of the bed. I laid the flowers in their white paper on the neatly folded sheet, where her hands lay limp. "Freesias," I said helplessly.

Now it's difficult for me to record what happened. Though every detail was burned deeply into me, her look, her words, the movement of the childish beautiful lips.

"What do you want?" she demanded.

I told her, "I didn't know you were ill. I'm not long back from Paris. Hoppy came to my exhibition, Saturday, the last day, and told me."

She did not take her sunken eyes from my face.

"What do you want?" she repeated.

"It seemed natural to come," I said. "I'd never forgotten you. I thought we could meet as friends now. Eight years is a long time."

"I can die all right without you, thanks. In fact I prefer to. Bill's the only one I want around. He's worth ten of you."

"I loved you," I pleaded. "I wanted you for myself."

"You don't know what it means to love anyone but yourself."

I was silent. What could I say? I could not at this stage make her believe what she chose to deny to herself. Whatever she had believed at the time, she was convinced now that I had never loved her. She had spent eight years building up Bill in her mind as the protagonist of devoted love and in drawing the sands of bitterness all over the memory of love as she had once known it with me.

She continued to stare at me, her mouth bitter, her hollow

eyes accusing, and at last I said, "Whatever it was I felt for you, I have cherished the memory of it. When I heard you were ill my instinct was to come."

"You heard I was dying. No one ever comes out of here alive, whether they're here three months or three weeks or three days. Now that your morbid curiosity is satisfied you'd better go."

She turned her face away from me and closed her eyes.

"Please go," she repeated.

I said, desperately, "I won't come again if you don't want me to, but don't send me away like that. At least say you forgive me —the things you have against me." I heard my voice crack as I said it and I had to fight for control. I forced myself to say in a lighter tone, "We used to be rather good at forgiving each other."

She answered without opening her eyes. "You remember what you said to me in the Ship that last time?"

"I don't remember—but whatever it was need we rake up an eight-year-old row?"

"You raked it up by coming here."

"That wasn't my intention—I swear to God! I came because I was—upset." I used the inadequate word because what else could I say—"I came because I was told you were dying and I had to see you just once again"?

"I was upset that night I came to the Ship to find you. You told me to go. For God's sake go, you said. Now it's my turn to say it." She turned her head and looked at me. "For God's sake go," she repeated tensely. I had the feeling that had she had the strength she would have screamed it at me.

"If you ever want to see me again I'm living with old Joe Snell over his shop in Deptford High Street. I'd always come, if you sent word to me there."

Her head drooped on the pillow again and her eyes closed. The paper of freesias lay untouched where I had laid them between her hands. I stood staring at her helplessly and then when she did not move or open her eyes I said, "Good-bye, Tansy, my love." I heard myself saying it, and it did not sound like my own voice, but loud and rough, like a roar of pain. Or perhaps I only whispered it. I don't know. I only knew that I was damned, finally and forever.

All next day I walked about dazed with misery, doing all that I had to do at the gallery and fighting the idea that I must go back and see Tansy just once again; perhaps she would have softened a little toward me, I thought; perhaps if I went now she would say just one small gentle thing, for old times' sake. Just say my name; or call me an old funny; or even if she would only say good-bye, if she would say it without that hard edge to her voice it would be a kind of absolution. I told myself I would just run up there for a few minutes in the afternoon; it would be worse than useless telephoning, I thought; if they asked her if she would see me she would probably say no. But if I just went there and begged her for just one kind word, so that I would sleep tonight. Then I thought no, I couldn't go again like that, after the way she had received me and what she had said. So it went on all the afternoon, would I, wouldn't I, till I was half crazy. It became an obsession with me; I had to see her, just once more. Finally I thought that even if she wouldn't look at me I would have to see her.

When Finstein closed the gallery at six I went into a pub and had a couple of drinks, telling myself alternately how I couldn't possibly go again today, how it would be completely useless, and that if I didn't go I should go mad. In the end I dived into the nearest tube station and in twenty minutes I was walking up the hospital steps. I'd stopped to buy some violets outside the station; I didn't want to go empty-handed.

There was no one in the entrance hall when I went in, and no one on the stairs. There were a few evening visitors in the wards to right and left at the top; here and there were gray faces on pillows and no bedside figures in attendance; some of the eyes were closed; some stared, vacantly. I noticed more that second time though my heart was plunging again, and I could not see at the end of the ward, the right-hand, by the fire; there all was a white blur. My pounding heart seemed to beat confusion up into my eyes.

At the fireplace I stopped with a vague sense of something wrong. There was no bed in the corner. I turned my head and saw the gray-faced elderly woman who had spoken to me yesterday.

"You're too late," she said. Her sunken eyes searched me. "Didn't anyone tell you? She died early this morning."

I stared at her.

"They always take the bed away," she added. Her eyes fastened on the paper of flowers I carried.

"Why don't you give them to Miss Lumly in the bed opposite? She's going on for eighty and they can't do any more for her. She doesn't have visitors—all her family are too far away. She'd welcome a few flowers—make her feel she had a visitor."

"Yes," I said. "Yes. I'll give them to her. In a minute. About Mrs. Tanswell—I didn't realize she was so ill."

"Didn't you? Didn't you know they only bring people here when they can't do any more for them in the other hospitals? You can't blame them—they need the beds. We get the medical attention here we couldn't have at home—not ordinary people, anyhow."

I said, painfully, "Mrs. Tanswell's husband should have been able to have afforded a nurse to look after her."

I couldn't bear to think of her dying in hospital.

"She'd have been left alone a lot, with her husband away traveling all the time. She had company here. I'd sooner be here myself. When you're left alone you get to thinking about yourself. In a place like this you realize there's plenty worse off. They could have done something for Mrs. Tanswell if she'd taken it earlier, but it had spread to her glands and it was too late. Same as that woman over there—Molly, we call her. We used to call your friend Tansy, by the way—she told us to. But Molly there, she's younger than your friend, thirty-five, and got six kids, the youngest only six months old. She's failing, fast. That's her young sister with her now. The family's always kidding her along she'll be home in the spring. Tansy thought that at first. She was always looking out of the window and remarking that the grass was getting greener in the square down there. The young ones are always hopeful. Living's a kind of habit with 'em and they can't seem to break it—but they don't get asked, for it breaks for them. Funny Tansy should go before me and old Miss Lumly, though. But there's no telling. We had a girl of twenty-five in last week—tumor of the brain. She was only here three days, then out she went, bed and all. I keep saying my turn next, but they keep carrying the others out before me, and matron tries to kid me she thinks I'm malingering."

"Perhaps," I forced myself to say, "you'll prove all the medicos wrong and walk out in spite of everything—when the grass is a bit greener!"

She smiled, displaying ill-fitting false teeth. The grin made her gaunt gray face seem more of a death's head than ever. Her gray hair was done in two small tight plaits which made me think of little Niki. It was possible to see through the furrows of age and the grayness of death that was upon her what she had been like at Niki's age—some sixty years ago. Her smile and her eager friendliness were somehow a frightful travesty of a child's smile and eagerness; a child's, and a young girl's, and a young woman's—all were imaginable. Only at the gray living skeleton in the bed did imagination balk, denying its reality.

"When the grass is a bit greener I shall be helping to grow it! You're like the chaplain—'Miracles have been known to happen, Mrs. Mac,' he says. 'We must have faith. God in His infinite mercy, etc., etc.' I told him if I was God I wouldn't strike a girl of twenty-five down with tumor of the brain, or give a woman with six kids incurable cancer—I wouldn't give it even to a cat, let alone humans, I told the chaplain—you've got it fixed up all right, both ways, I said; if anyone gets well it's God's mercy, and if they die it's also God's mercy. I hope I'm not shocking you?"

I shook my head.

"Mrs. Tanswell—Tansy—" I persisted, "was she alone—at the end?" Despising euphemisms I still could not bring myself to say "when she died."

"Must have been. She was there when the night-sister came on about ten, but when Sister walked around before going off this morning she was gone. Went in her sleep, I suppose. Best way, too."

"Yes," I said, and then, "Well—thanks for telling me. I'll just take the violets over to Miss Lumly."

"That's right. But she's stone deaf—no use trying to talk to her. That looks like my old man coming in at the door—"

She turned away and I crossed the small space of polished floor to the gray skeleton in the bed at the other side of the fireplace. I mumbled good evening and something about would she care to have these few violets, and about Mrs. Mac opposite having suggested it. I got an impression of extreme weakness as she raised a mottled hand to take the flowers. One side of her mouth twisted in a smile—she had had a stroke, perhaps—and her lips shaped almost soundless words of thanks. Oddly, she was not at all terrifying close to; there was something curiously gentle and refined about her. I think she said I was very kind. I mumbled something conventional and sweated with embarrassment. I wanted not to have to look on such pitifulness, on a human life guttering out like a candle before the wick finally collapses into the melted wax. I wanted to be gone from this place, and was ashamed of the fact; it somehow humiliated me. I turned to go, but the young girl seated by the bed of the woman called Molly smiled at me.

"She loves flowers," she said. "She only gets what other patients' visitors give her." She called across to the old woman, "You're in luck this evening, Miss Lumly!"

Miss Lumly smiled and her smile now seemed to twist the whole of her mouth. She raised the violets slowly and smelled them, then nodded and smiled in our direction.

"She can't hear," the girl explained, "but she lip-reads a bit."

"She's wonderful," the woman in the bed put in. "She lays there so patient with no one to talk to. She used to read at first—good books, not just novels. She's an educated person—you can tell that."

She wasn't a bad-looking woman, this Molly, with high cheekbones and rather pretty light-brown hair tied up with a red ribbon in a kind of mare's tail. She wore a bright pink bed jacket that seemed composed of loops, and a necklace of pale blue beads with earrings to match. She had large dark eyes which seemed to have receded far back into her head; a bright lipstick emphasized the gray-white of her hollow cheeks.

"I'm sorry your friend passed away," she went on. "We all were. She cheered us up, she was so lively at first, telling us about the lovely clothes she wore for mannequin parades and all that. But she failed these last few days, poor thing. She'd had her insides removed, but it was too late—she should have had it done years ago to be successful. We were the two youngest, her and me. She was about the same age, as a matter of fact, though she looked younger. Now I'm the baby!" She laughed. "Not but what I look a hundred since I've been in here. But you wait till I'm shoving the pram down Lewisham High Street again!"

"I tell her we'll have her home by Easter," the girl said. Her bright red lips smiled, but the eyes she turned on her sister were so troubled it seemed to me Molly could not be deceived by the confident words.

I don't know what I said—some amiable banalities, no doubt. I longed to be away, alone with my own shock and misery. A woman in a white overall at the door end of the ward rang a bell and visitors began getting up and saying their good-byes. I said good-bye to Molly and her sister and glanced in Miss Lumly's direction, but she lay back with her eyes closed, still holding the violets to her face. Mrs. Mac was still gabbling to her husband who kept looking nervously from her to the woman in white at the door.

On the stairs as we all trooped out a middle-aged woman remarked to me, "It's heartbreaking, isn't it? That's my sister right by the door. Each time I come she's weaker. She's suffered so terribly—three operations. They did all they could, but it was no use."

"Has anyone ever been known to walk out of this place?" I asked.

"Gawd knows," a poorly dressed old woman on my other side chipped in, adding wrily, "and he won't split!"

Just behind me a man's voice said over my shoulder, "Excuse me, I heard what you were saying. A woman did leave here last week, I understand."

"Discharged herself," the old woman said. "They never last, them that do that."

"You never know," the man said, with a kind of painful eagerness. "Nature perhaps sometimes defeats the doctors. Will-power is a big part of the battle!" I glanced around and saw a man of about forty, the city type, neatly dressed, neat mustache, haggard eyes; an accountant, perhaps, or a bank cashier.

"Prolongs the agony, that's all," the old woman said brusquely, and pushed on ahead.

The man came level with me. "It's my wife, you see," he said eagerly. "According to the doctors she couldn't live a fortnight when she left the hospital. She's been here a month now. She's so bright always it's hard to believe—to believe she won't recover. According to all the medical laws she can't. But I wonder—couldn't a body accommodate itself to—to a growth? A kind of adjustment of nature?"

His dark tormented eyes seem to burn.

"Perhaps," I said helplessly. "Who knows? Life itself is a miracle—so why not?"

"I'm glad you think so." The eagerness in his voice was almost unbearable. "My wife's only thirty, you see. A lovely girl. We have two lovely children. It's unthinkable that— I mean everything becomes meaningless if— Without hope, I mean. And with the better weather coming—"

"The grass is getting greener already," I said. I don't know why I said it. I suppose it swam up to the surface of my dazed mind, like a fish in a tank.

"Exactly," he said.

We came out into the drizzling gray of a January evening, and the gray stream of which we were a part merged with the greater flow on the crowded pavement.

I dived down into the light and warmth of the tube. When I got out at the other end I didn't go back to Joe's but spent the rest of the time, till the pubs closed, drinking. Between mental and emotional confusion and the drink I don't remember much about it. In the morning there was a letter from Miss Hopkins:

Dear Mr. Rowse,

I got your address from Mr. Finstein, over the phone. He didn't want to give it; he said he would forward it if I wrote care of the gallery. I suppose he thought I might be going to do a deal with you behind his back robbing him of his commission. I told him it was about a friend of yours who had died and the time and place of the funeral. Our poor Tansy died this morning. They had to bring her poor husband back from Birmingham. She was gone when he arrived. He is heartbroken. She is to be cremated at Golders Green on Monday next at 11 a.m. I am getting the time off from work and will be going. She was always so sweet with Willie when he was a baby, minding him for me often. I will always remember it. She was a sweet soul. I hope you managed to get along and see her. I am sure she would appreciate it. She was always so pleased when I went. I expect there will be a lot of flowers and wreaths, as everyone loved her. To think she was not yet forty, and so lovely—she never seemed to get any older; not a gray hair. I suppose it's the will of God, as they say.

Yours sincerely,

L. Hopkins.

I didn't go to the funeral and I didn't send a wreath. I didn't even acknowledge poor Hoppy's letter. At eleven o'clock that Monday morning I went out onto the hill and stood looking across to the Hampstead Heights. It was all lost in mist away over there, across the city, but somewhere over there a coffin containing the body of my love was sliding into a furnace and all that had been so beautiful and so vibrantly alive dissolving into ashes and rising in smoke, to lose itself in the sky. But it wasn't that I had to come to terms with, but the realization of failure in myself. So disastrously had I failed in my love that at the grave's edge she had been unable to grant me the absolution of her forgiveness. How terribly I had failed her I had not realized till then. I had always considered my love so much greater than hers, yet I had not made her happy, nor, when the time came to part, bequeathed her a legacy of anything but bitterness. I had never loved her enough; I should have been more patient with her, tried to understand her better, been more tolerant and forgiving. I had believed her to be a hypochondriac, but it seemed all the time there had been this dreadful disease germinating in her, spreading its tentacles in her flesh and tissues. I had been so damned selfish and egotistical that I had even wanted to keep her here to face the bombs; it was hubby-Bill who had been concerned for her safety. I had wanted only that she should stay with me. I was the one who had preached that love suffereth long and is kind, vaunteth not itself, is not puffed up, seeketh not its own—"beareth all things, believeth all things, hopeth all things, endureth all things"; yet I had not hoped, I had not believed, I had not endured; I had not accepted suffering patiently and humbly; I had not been kind, and I had sought my own—passionately. No wonder she came to despise me as a hypocrite and humbug and decided that Bill, in all his simplicity and unpretentiousness, was worth ten of me.

Afterwards they all tried to talk me out of all this—Lee and Joe and Helen. I was being morbid in my self-reproaches, they said, lacerating myself unduly in my remorse; they reminded me that she had deceived me as she had deceived Bill; they said she was shallow and trivial, and that emotionally and intellectually Bill was much more her level, and that her being dead didn't alter these facts. Because she was dead, they declared, I was sentimentally remembering only the good things about her and taking upon myself a burden of guilt I had no cause to feel. All this they said, wanting to comfort me, and I didn't blame them, even when they said hard and cruel things about my poor Tansy. Lee wrote me from the Riviera; Helen from New York. Joe was always taking out the philosophical line that I had lived without setting eyes on her for eight years so what difference did it make that she was now dead? But for her illness, and Miss Hopkins bringing me news of it, I might have lived the rest of my life without seeing her again—"You got to be reasonable, son," he insisted. But reason counter-insisted that it was unreasonable that the thin bright flame that had been Tansy should be extinguished forever, whether I was allowed to warm myself at that flame or not.

Helen wrote saying that she was renewing the lease of Graham's house and that I was welcome to use it for six months or a year, as suited me; as I liked the Ile St. Louis so much I might prefer it to the studio, and she promised not to return during that time and disturb me if I'd rather she didn't. *Whatever you are feeling now must be expressed in your work*, she wrote. *You have always said yourself that suffering was a good school for the artist. Perhaps the time has come now to portray the lamentation of Enion. "Eternity groaned and was troubled at the image of eternal death"—there's your theme.* Lee wrote saying that I should be glad to be released at last, finally, from the long "human bondage." He urged that now that the exhibition was over I should return to Paris and, as he phrased it, "start a fresh chapter"; I had probably my best work still to do. Graham wrote that he had been interested to hear of Lord Lake's interest in my work and this, he said, was well worth following up. Lake was one of the few peers with any real appreciation of art and the money with which to do something about it. While in England I should certainly avail myself of the invitation to go and stay at Lake House. Finstein wrote in a similar vein, with great plans for an exhibition of new works at the end of the year, he had had a number of inquiries for my work; and Perrot wrote in the same strain from Paris. Both agents sent me cuttings from shiny art magazines, English and French, in which my work was mentioned along with Erlich, Moore, Hepworth, as a modern sculptor fast establishing a reputation.

"You're on the up-and-up, son," Joe said. "More power to your elbow," he added. "They'll put a tablet up in Greenwich to you yet, to say you lived and worked here. I reckon as a Londoner born and bred you'll settle here yet."

I told him, then, that I had resolved not to return to Paris. He immediately suggested I should make a workshop at his place.

"You'd be comfortable enough," he said. "You could just pay for your keep. You'd be quids-in."

"That's why I can't accept," I told him, "just because I'd be comfortable and quids-in and everything made easy for me. I've got to get back to the rough-and-tumble of living. I've had two years of soft, easy, privileged existence, centrally heated and rent free, and hobnobbing with the so-called quality. I don't belong with that kind of life in that kind of world. I'm going back to my own world, my own class."

"You had a good few years on the bread line in Paris," Joe said, "surely you're entitled to a spell on Easy Street now."

"I'm not entitled to anything," I said violently.

"You worked for it," Joe said.

"I don't accept the idea of a privileged class," I said. "It's privilege enough," I added, "to be able to earn my bread doing the work I like to do. I've got to find a room again—the humbler the better. I'll probably make a good deal more than I need, but there's plenty of good use for surplus cash. I've got a bit in hand now needs redistributing."

"What's back of it all?" Joe asked.

I told him, "All the pain and misery of the underprivileged. Don't tell me in this beautiful welfare state no one starves. You can go hungry without starving. There are people living on the old-age pension, and men trying to support families on seven or eight quid a week, when the rent of even a council house or flat can be thirty-five bob."

"The wives go out to work, mostly. And there are family allowances—"

"Mostly they do, I know, and they manage, but they can't all do it, and none of them can do it all the time, and it's a mean sort of existence, always scraping and saving, and then the women are doing two jobs and wearing themselves out. But even if everything in this so-called Socialist England were as fine as it's supposed to be, I still don't want to belong to any privileged class. In that place where Tansy was I suddenly realized how soft my life had been these last two years, and even before then, all through the war—"

"Living in one room at the top of a ramshackle old house and doing odd-job carpentry?"

"Luxury compared with the way people were living in some of the German cities. And now with cities reduced to rubble, and the camps full of displaced persons, and the refugee camps in India and Pakistan—don't you realize," I almost shouted, "that two-thirds of the world lives on the bread line all the time? All those Asiatic millions that it's so easy and convenient not to think about! You meet people who tell you a Chinese coolie can live on a handful of rice a day. You bet he can! He has to! And the black

South Africans who if they're lucky earn two pounds a month—what do they live on? Don't tell me," I went on, "that my living in a slum room on the minimum of food doesn't help them. I know it doesn't. But the thing is it helps me! It helps me to come to terms with my conscience. It helps to reconcile me to the world's misery. To that woman of thirty-five dying slowly of cancer. To Tansy's death. To the misery of the camps. To the grubbing existence of the masses everywhere. To the tragedy and horror of our atomic age and the one shining light in it quenched. To the whole blasphemous iniquity of man's inhumanity to man, the ultimate sin against God—the sin against life—"

All this and a good deal more I said, of what had been going on in me since Tansy's death. I had somehow to come to terms with my own sense of personal failure. It didn't matter that even on her deathbed she had lied—characteristic pointless lies about her profession and her age. What did it matter that she lied? What right had I to despise this or anything else in her? What virtue in sticking to the verbal truth when there was no truth in oneself touching first and last things? I was lying to myself all the time about my great love and my intellectual and moral superiority; my love had been a selfish, possessive, intolerant thing; my superiority had been self-righteousness. I had always known, from the beginning, that by making her happy I could make her "good," but I was too busy grabbing happiness for myself, too busy being jealous and resentful, and allowing pride to get in the way of loving. And instead of enriching Tansy's life I had embittered it, so that at the end, to the grave's edge, her memory of me was bitter and she had died with her heart hard and unforgiving—Tansy, my love, my lovely girl, she who had been for me the bow of burning gold, and all the arrows of desire. Now the arrows were all steeped in the bitterness of regret and the anguish of remorse—that most futile of human emotions. But in the very futility lies the anguish.

Well, so I hunted about and found a room, in that same shabby square where I had had the room before, but in a much more squalid and dilapidated house. It was a ground-floor room and got all the noises of children playing in the square. The house had been blitzed and nothing had been done to it, though people still lived in it. The lathes had come through the walls, and there was a hole in the ceiling up into the roof. I patched it all up as best I could and cleaned it up and moved in, with the few things I had had before and had stored with Joe when I had stayed on in Paris. I went again to Lister's—still in their temporary premises in the Blackwall Road—for the first time for nearly ten years, and I ordered me an eight-foot walnut log around thirty inches in girth. I wanted something sizable. I planned a kind of memorial for Tansy; or perhaps for my love for her; my own particular interpretation of the Lamentation of Enion:

> Why wilt thou examine every little fibre of my soul,
> Spreading them out before the sun like stalks of flax to dry
> The infant joy is beautiful, but its anatomy
> Horrible, ghastly, and deadly: nought shalt thou find in it
> But death, despair, and everlasting brooding melancholy.

I was still working out the design for this on paper when Helen came back from America and having got my address from Joe came to see me.

9

SHE LOOKED as beautiful as I had remembered her; and she said all the things I expected she would say. Why was I living in this squalor when I could be living in civilized conditions in Paris, either at the studio in the rue Cassini or the house on the Ile St. Louis? Why had I deliberately thrown away such a wonderful patron as her old friend Lester Lake? How could I ever expect to do good work in this filthy hole where I hadn't even sufficient light? What, in short, was the meaning of this masochistic Francis of Assisi act? After all my years of struggle, what was the point of reverting to the old bad conditions just when I was beginning to become recognized and make some real money? She looked despairingly around the squalid room. She wore a round gray fur hat, and a gray fur coat over a mauve dress, with elaborate old-fashioned silver jewelry, and violets; she looked distinguished and striking as always, even to the big mouth too brightly painted and the absurd jade ring as big as a small egg on the little finger of her right hand. She was as magnificently larger-than-life-sized as ever, and all over again I marveled at the fact that for a time I had had the power both to reduce her to tears and make her cry out in ecstasy.

"What's the idea?" she demanded. "If it's because that poor girl died I don't get it. How does all this help?"

"It's me breaking with the twin bitch-goddesses, money and success," I told her.

"Don't you *want* to be acclaimed as an artist?"

"If you mean have a patch of conceited critics write a lot of claptrap about my work—no. Whether they praise or blame, it's equally highfalutin nonsense. When I made the Christ-figure I would have liked it set up outside a fashionable church or in the middle of Piccadilly or on the top of Tower Hill, for millions to see—for a revelation in their midst. They would look at it and *see*—with the inward as well as the outward eye. Or so I thought. But the critics wrote a lot of intellectual art-talk stuff about it and then it was bought and shoved away in some provincial municipal buildings, and I became one of the money-changers in the temple myself, since I took money for it. I made the *Weltschmerz* thing primarily for France, which, because of war and occupation and the resistance, is bound down upon that particular rock, but it was sold for dollars and taken to America, where they don't know anything about *Weltschmerz*—being young as nations go, and not having suffered by the war. It's success enough for me if I can make a living doing the things I want."

"And how do you think you can do that without having exhibitions and keeping in with people like Perrot and Finstein and Lord Lake? This thing you're designing now—who's going to buy it if you sit here in obscurity?"

"Lake might be interested. When it's done I shall ask him if he'd like to come and see it. What I'm not prepared to do is lackey to him—go out to his place and eat his meals and meet his friends and become part of his world, even for a week end."

"It's a perfectly good world—good food, pleasant company, a civilized atmosphere—"

"It's a world created out of the labor of others. I don't know where Lake gets his money, but I'm damn sure he doesn't earn it! Gets it from tenant farmers, probably—rents the land which is the Lord God's, since He alone made it—not Lord Lake or any other landowner. Charges a rent for it to the people who work it and make it produce food." I looked at her, sitting on my bed in her furs and jewelry, her perfumed elegance, and felt suddenly hopeless. Either she saw the basic immorality of landlordism or she didn't, and if she didn't it meant we didn't speak the same language, which I had thought so often in our Paris days. "Sorry if I'm tub-thumping," I added. "I mean only that his nibs and I belong to different worlds and I've no more stomach for his than he'd have for mine. He's pleasant enough, but so could the Devil be, no doubt, socially."

She laughed. "Poor Lester! But seriously, Tom, I don't see how you break with money by playing at poverty like that." Then, as I made an impatient movement, feeling I knew what she was going to say, "No, honey, listen. You still use money. You've still got more than the people all around you. But above all you're free of the continual anxiety which is the real curse of poverty. You're not working forty-four hours a week at a routine job for a small pay packet and always scared of being fired! You get up when you like, start work when you like, knock off when you like. As an artist you belong to a privileged class. You can't escape it. Even in your years of struggle you had freedom."

It was my turn to laugh then. "Freedom to starve," I said bitterly. "The privileges of one's profession are one thing," I went on, "the privileges of class, that is to say of money, another."

"But when you earn the money," she persisted. "When you earn it by your own labor, exploiting no one but yourself—?"

"That's where we both came in, years ago," I pointed out. "How are you going to assess the value of a wood carving or a chair or a poem or a bunch of flowers? Money values are all arbitrary. A thing is worth what it will 'fetch,' but what are the criteria for determining what a thing will fetch? Don't you see?" I pleaded with her. "Don't you see it's all such nonsense, all this money business? The price of diamonds is kept up by limiting the market—their value is purely artificial. The pearl diver who brings up the pearls from the bottom of the sea is a poor man who could never afford to buy his wife a pearl necklace. Even the loser in a prizefight earns more by that one night in the ring than a miner can earn in a lifetime. It doesn't make sense. It can't—because money is nonsense, and all ideas of it. I thought all this before I had any money. Now that I begin to have some I still think it. In fact it now seems all more preposterous than ever.

Only now there's something else. That second time I went to the hospital—"

I stopped because there didn't seem the words for what had grown out of that, working on my remorse, my sense of personal failure, and the deep need for atonement, and the peace of it—at-one-ment, the remedy for the disintegration wrought by the deprivation of forgiveness.

"We have to find absolution in our own way," I finished, with a kind of despair.

Of course she insisted that I had nothing to reproach myself with, that Tansy hadn't had it in her to be happy with anyone, that I had loved her a great deal more than she loved me—than she was capable of loving; that I was tormenting myself needlessly; that my denying myself social privileges wouldn't help the underprivileged; and that it was all self-dramatization and quixotic romanticism, and much else—all calculated to help me, to restore me to sanity, as she called it. She ended by proposing that we go out and have a drink together—at the Yacht, since the old Ship was gone—for old times' sake, and then perhaps we could go into town together and have a meal at some small place. She wanted that I should "cheer up."

Well, it was what Lee always called "drinksy time," though a long way off a quarter to sex. At that time I felt that it would never be a quarter to sex again. We went out and had a couple of drinks each and then I let Helen charter a taxi to the West End. I let her choose the restaurant, one of her favorite gourmet places, and then I took charge. We had the most expensive things on the menu and a bottle of fine wine. She recalled the meal we had had at the Laperouse in Paris with Graham; it was clear that she dwelled lovingly on the memory. "You see," she said—indeed she all but purred it—"there is a lot to be said for money." She smiled at me beseechingly. "Tom darling, just this once let us forget the absurdity of money and just enjoy having it!"

I pointed out, amiably enough, that it was not I who had introduced the subject, and began asking her about her exhibition in New York. There are artists who enjoy talking about their work, and artists who find it difficult and even embarrassing to do so; I have always found it difficult, particularly about the work in progress, though I could sometimes discuss a tentative idea with Helen. Helen herself enjoyed talking about her work

—it was all part of her enthusiasm and energy. She was always full of ideas, and always a jump ahead of what she was doing. She could discuss her work without egotism or conceit, and I always enjoyed listening to her. So I let her talk, and our differences were lost in the rich warm flow of aesthetic agreements. All over again I thought how much I liked and admired her, but I no longer wanted to run hand-in-hand with her through the starry darkness or a leafy sunshine, or loosen her wonderful red hair and let it ride her fine white shoulders. I wanted now only that we should not fight each other, we two Old Soldiers.

I settled the bill when she was away in the cloakroom so that we should neither of us be provoked into comment, and when we came into Soho we walked for a bit, taking in the foreign sights and sounds with a certain nostalgia, until she had had enough of it on her high heels and then—with a sense of it being for the last time—I called a taxi for her.

"The Dorchester," she said, as she climbed in. I leaned forward and put my hands on her shoulders and kissed her on both cheeks.

"Honey," she murmured, her voice caressing, and then—"Call me up sometime soon," she commanded. "I'll be here another week yet. Perhaps you'll change your mind and come to Paris after all?"

"Not in this incarnation," I told her.

She smiled. "I'll go on keeping a lookout for you in the Select, all the same. Good-bye-ee."

That soft singsong . . . but it had a dying fall, I thought. Was it some inner knowledge that made her say good-bye and not *au revoir?*

"Good-bye," I said, and suddenly seized her hand. "God bless," I said. There was the familiar quick pressure of her fingers, then she withdrew into the interior darkness; the door slammed and the cab moved off. I stood on the curb watching it, watching the dim blur of her face and the flutter of her fingers through the window in the back.

I walked on through the crowds with such a sadness in me as there are no words for. Not pain or any wild grief, only a deep-down sadness, of old joys folded and laid aside forever, of parting and change, of sand sown all over the ruddy limbs and the flaming hair. No more, I felt, would Rintrah roar and shake his fires in the burdened air, no more the hungry clouds swag on the deep. The days of exultation were over, the days of prophetic vision. The money-changers were still in the courtyard of the temple after two thousand years; now in the atomic era theirs is the kingdom, the power and the glory. In the holy of holies a still small voice still pleads that everything that lives is holy, but in the wild confusion of the universal den of thieves only.

A little sound it utters, and its cries are faintly heard.

I came to Piccadilly Circus and stood waiting for the traffic lights. The red turned to amber and the amber to green, and the people who waited with me moved on over the Circus to the safety of the island where Eros stood boarded up—as well he might be. I did not move on over with the crowd; I don't know why. It was as though I had exhausted the impetus which had brought me from one end of Piccadilly to the other. I had walked blindly, all directions the same to me, following only the labyrinth of my thoughts. But if I had gone on across the road with the rest of the crowd, the next few years would have shaped differently.

I stood waiting, and the lights moved around to red again and a fresh group of people waited with me. Suddenly a feminine voice exclaimed, "Why—Mr. Rowse! Well, fancy! They say you always meet everyone in London in the end. I always wondered if we'd bump into each other one of these days! You remember me, don't you?"

I looked into the smiling eager face, the soft bright eyes, of Norah Williams.

I took her by the elbow and when the lights were green again we went.

"Come and have a tooty-frooty in the Coventry Street Lyons," I said.

She laughed. "Fancy you remembering!"

"I remember everything," I said. It was true. I was right back at the plum tree at the gable of the house on a moonlight night ten years ago.

"You never looked me up."

"I lost your address," I said. In a sense it was true.

In the rattle and clatter of Lyons she asked me, over the top of her tall glass of tutti-frutti, "Did you marry your girl friend?" She added, as though to excuse so personal a question, "I often wondered."

"No," I said. I looked at her hands and saw that they were ringless. "She died," I added, to end further cross-examination.

She looked confused. "Oh dear," she said.

"Yes. But let's talk about you. . . ."

"Oh dear," she said again. "It's not very interesting. . . ."

She was quite right; it wasn't, though there was a lot of it. She had changed very little. She would still be only about thirty-one or two, I reflected. There was the same eagerness and warmth about her—that fresh-as-a-flower virginal quality.

For a long time, it seems, there are no traffic lights; then you come up with them again, and when they turn green, which eventually they are bound to, you go.

10

It is a commonplace of human experience that sometimes a chance meeting or remark tips the scales of decision. Meeting Norah again like that confirmed the idea which had been latent in my mind since that second visit to the hospital; she knew nothing of me as a sculptor, and asked me if I was "still in cabinetmaking," and when I said yes I realized that I had made my choice.

Perhaps I would have made the same choice without Norah's unwitting intervention; who knows? How can we ever know what we would have done had circumstances been other than they were? It is possible that had I crossed Piccadilly Circus that night the first time the lights changed to green, and so missed Norah, I might still have made eventually the decision I made in a moment by continuing to deceive her as to my profession. I might have made a detour instead of taking the short cut that presented itself. That part of my life might have been the same, by a different route; but about the rest it is impossible to speculate.

But because I did not go when the lights changed Norah caught up with me again, and by the end of the summer I had married her. Whether I would have done so had she not become pregnant I don't know, but it seems probable. It was as though I had not realized how innerly lonely I was until she lit and warmed and inhabited the gray chill emptiness of my world. She was the only consistently loving female I had ever had to do with. I had not known such simple loving affection since Helga, but whereas Helga threw herself in with her bed and board, from sheer sensual good nature, Norah gave herself to me in my drab room quite simply because she loved me and therefore, despite her physical fears and moral scruples, could not refuse the selfish demand I made upon her the very first evening I met her after the Piccadilly encounter. Had she refused I would probably have let her drift out of my life again; as it was I was touched, and contrary to all she had been taught to believe, respected her a great deal more afterwards than before. She reawakened not merely sex in me but tenderness and the capacity to love—not a great love but still, that tenderness lit by passion that serves most of us well enough most of the time. She was a good girl and gave herself lovingly and generously, and I loved her for it, with a gratitude that had never come into the picture with Tansy. But then Tansy had not so much "given" herself as committed herself to the *affaire* she expected and wanted to have with me. At the outset the question of love had not come into it. Norah had fallen in love with me in Cornwall; it was the first time she had fallen in love, and ten years later I was her first and, I fear, her last lover. It was very bad luck for her that I did not go when the traffic lights changed the first time.

She had gone home at the outbreak of war and got herself a job on a local farm rather than be conscripted into the forces or the Women's Land Army; she had not wanted to be cut off from her parents at that time; they had wanted her back and she had been glad to go, fearful of immediate bombs on London. She had had a dull war but a safe one, though with the R.A.F. in the neighborhood it could have been gay in the romantic sense, I gathered, had she chosen. But in an age when virginity as an ideal had become obsolete she cherished the memory of her first love and the hope that "when the war was over"—that phrase with which we were all in love—she would meet him again, and, as she put it, you never can tell. And now abided these three, faith, hope, and keeping yourself to yourself, and the greatest of these was purity—relinquished now for love's sake only.

If I appear to write mockingly of her simple faith and trust it is only because at this stage I shrink from allowing myself to be too deeply moved by the memory of her. So much has happened to us both since those spring and summer days when we made love so recklessly under the trees in the dells and hollows of Greenwich Park. It was her strength that she moved me by her innocence no less than she attracted me by it. At first she pestered me as to whether I loved her as much as "the girl who died," but I told her the question was unpardonable and must not be asked; that every love was necessarily different and I refused to make impossible comparisons; it must be enough that I loved her. And in terms of affection and tenderness plus desire I loved her increasingly, so that when with tears in her eyes she told me in August that she was already two months overdue it did not seem to me a hardship to marry her—I even thought that with the cold nights ahead it might be pleasant to tuck up two in a bed instead of camping out on the damp ground.

I might have reached that conclusion anyway. Perhaps something of the kind had been at the back of my mind in my not taking better care of her and ensuring that she didn't get pregnant. So I kissed her tears away and gave her a smack on the behind to cheer her up, and told her not to be a silly kid and daddy would do what was necessary at the registry office place and she would be an old married woman before she knew where she was. All I disliked in the idea was the concession to bourgeois morality it represented and the capitulation—for the first time in my life—to authority. At first I thought we might just live together and she could call herself Mrs. Rowse, if that was what she wanted, but I reminded myself that I had been prepared to marry Tansy legally and it seemed right and proper to do no less for Norah, who was anyhow bearing me a child in return for it.

The idea of the child both moved and excited me. I wanted it to be a boy. I was resolved to teach him to model in clay as soon as his child's hands were capable of it, and to carve wood as soon as he could be entrusted with a penknife. I had the feeling that a girl wouldn't interest me in the same way.

We were married at the end of August, with old Joe as one of the witnesses and the registrar's clerk as the other. We went to live with Joe at his suggestion. Norah would keep house and save the expense of the biweekly woman. I had been working for Joe since I had finished my Lamentation of Enion, that is to say since Easter. Joe had given me a solemn promise not to betray anything about my career as sculptor. With the Lamentation it was finished.

II

But it was not simply that I decided to carve and model no more in terms of creative effort, as a means of expression, in order that I might finish with the privileges inseparable from the life of the artist who contrives to live by his art. That decision I had taken, and I regarded it as irrevocable. But there was another sense in which the Lamentation was finis for me; it was my epitaph for Tansy, and for my dead life. Like Enion I could no longer, for love's sake, for God's sake, "see a god on every wind, and a blessing on every blast," nor "hear sounds of love in the thunder storm," as when I had fashioned the figure of Christ from lignum vitae, the wood of life. Once could my spirit so rejoice and thus triumphantly sing, in the days when I greatly loved, both as man and artist. Great paeans of praise had my spirit chanted creating the Daughter of Los, the shining image of gratified desire. These two works, the Christ and the emanation of Tansy, represented the one the passion of the spirit, the other the passion of the flesh. Where I had failed, I now knew, was to create anything which had united the two. Perhaps the nearest I had ever come to it, oddly enough, was in that early work, Negro Girl Dancing. Perhaps despite the major later works only in that had I come within measurable distance of the artistic wholeness of Brenovska. There is a lot to be said in favor of the artist dying young. Who knows to what banalities, to what mediocrities, Keats might have descended had he lived to middle age? And Henri Gaudier? And Josef Brenovska? The *Sturm und Drang* of living has a way of tarnishing the golden bow and blunting the arrows of desire—of both flesh and spirit. I who had made the Christ-figure, and the Daughter of Los, and the Eternal Horses, and Rintrah, and that apotheosis of life the Negro Girl Dancing, had been caught up in the end by the existentialist despair of the times and created the apotheosis of death—the *Weltschmerz*-figure. And in the end a lamentation that was as much a lament for the living as for the beloved dead. Where did the artist go from there, except into silence?

I could have gone on making portrait busts and carving animals and nude figures, both male and female, and children's heads, and once in a while, I suppose, some big symbolic piece—the East resurgent, or something of the kind, to balance the *Weltschmerz* of the West, and no doubt in the process increased the reputation I had thus far made. But I was not prepared, any more than Enion, to teach pale artifice to spread his nets upon the morning. What would have followed the Lamentation if I had not taken the decision I had could only have echoed the *Weltschmerz*, in a lesser degree, in purely personal terms of *ou sont les neiges d'antan*, and silence were better than that subjective repetition. Autobiography is not art.

Into the Lamentation I put the last passion of which I was capable—the passion of a wild pain. I made a great many sketches before I started work on this my only wholly symbolic work—since the *Weltschmerz* carried at least a recognizable likeness of one of the masks poor Bergsen presented to the world. For the lament I wanted wings, and I went to the Zoo and made a number of sketches of ravens, because Blake had a certain preoccupation with those somber birds. There was his Raven of Dawn of his "Song of Liberty" in the *Marriage of Heaven and Hell*, and his hungry raven crying in winter in his *Lament of Enion*, and in the *Lamentation* the raven cried and no eye pitied her. When I had got the drawings from life that I wanted I proceeded to stylize them until I had those downward sweeping planes that suggested what I sought to convey—a wintry, pitiless desolation.

My log was rich dark English walnut, with a beautiful grain. I was lucky to have got it, and so sizable, and I had got to like working in the harder woods. The planes of the wings came up beautifully in it; I don't think I had enjoyed making anything so much since I had carved the long flowing planes of the robes of the Christ-figure. Wood was the perfect medium for those winged rhythms, I felt. It was slow, detailed work, devoid of any broad free sweep, but the more I worked on it the more I became immersed in it and was almost reluctant to finish. And when it was done it had all of that "everlasting, brooding melancholy" I had wanted to express. If Tansy had had a grave I would have liked it to have stood there, but Tansy had no grave, and I was glad she had none—better that beauty be consumed in the fiery furnace than left to molder and decay in the wet earth.

If Graham Carlton had been in England I would have offered

it to him; as he was still abroad I wrote to Lord Lake. He came at once to see me, his car and chauffeur waiting outside the slummy house and causing a mild sensation in the square. His fair pleasant face kindled at the sight of the carving. His hands moved lovingly over the planes. "Beautiful," he said. "Beautiful!" He added that he would like to have it. There was a corner of his library into which it would fit perfectly in its "brooding sadness." He would go round at once and see Mr. Finstein. I told him that Finstein was out of the picture; that this deal was between producer and purchaser. Then as Graham had done over the Negro Girl he said that he found that embarrassing, because obviously it was impossible to assess a work of art in terms of money, since it was literally priceless. We could only accept certain commercial evaluations. He would therefore base his offer on prices obtained by my agent for other major works and suggest five hundred pounds.

"On that basis it's too much," I pointed out.

He smiled and took out his checkbook.

"It's all extremely difficult," he said, "but if the offer does not seem too little on an uncommercial basis . . ."

So I sold my Lamentation which was my farewell to Tansy for five hundred pounds, and as I had no particular use for the money at the time I put it into a post-office savings bank account. Later on, when I had married Norah, I thought of using it as a deposit for the purchase of a small house, but there were no houses of the size we wanted available, only names on long council-lists. However, Norah liked to think we had what she called "a nest egg tucked away for a rainy day," though what nest eggs had to do with rainy days I could never make out; she liked to think of it sitting there earning interest—that is to say, figures entered in a book accruing more figures, something which did not exist except on paper increasing the volume of its nothingness.

12

WHEN I finished off Tom Rowse, sculptor, I finished off his friendships, too. I wrote both to Lee and to Helen saying that I had decided to fade out of the artistic world, that I had married a simple young country woman who had always believed me to be a carpenter and who would be thrown into a great state of "chassis" to find I was anything more. I wrote them both that in the kind of life I was now leading their friendships would not belong, and they should not try to find me, I said, for I had left Greenwich, and not even Joe Snell would be able to tell where I was living and working. To give color to my story I posted the letter in southwest London.

At first I missed Helen and Lee acutely—almost intolerably. Old Joe had served me well enough as a boy, someone to talk to when my mind was hungry for new ideas and a kindred spirit with whom to share those I had; Joe who had only been middle-aged then seemed old with wisdom; now that I was middle-aged myself he seemed merely old and his mind to have got stuck somewhere with the late nineteenth-century radicals. I was still in agreement with everything he said touching politics and ethics; it was only that it seemed unnecessary to say it in this day and age, a wearisome laboring of the obvious, and I would be impatient and bored with the good old man. Yet sometimes I would deliberately start discussions with him, knowing in advance the string of platitudes I was thereby releasing, just as a sex-starved man will make advances to a woman who does not really attract him, in full awareness of all the dissatisfaction he is letting himself in for. Old Joe at least knew what I was talking about, however trite might be his observations on the subject.

To Norah I never attempted to talk, any more than I had to Tansy—only with Tansy it hadn't mattered because somehow there had always been so much going on between us, such an interplay of personalities, of provocation, curiosity, bewilderment, and general emotional excitement. Norah had voted Labour because she had been brought up to vote Labour. She was fond of referring to Churchill as "an old fool." Once when I said that on the contrary whatever he was he was not a fool, she was very surprised and said she'd always thought I was "Labour"; when I told her I despised the Labour Party she concluded I must be a Liberal; I let it go at that, but she was disappointed I was not a "socialist." Not that she knew anything about socialism, except that the Labour Party was "for the working class." She was startled when I said you bet they are—all those Labour peers.

I was glad when the child was born in March and she had something she understood to occupy her mind. I had my wish, for the child was a boy. Norah went into the hospital under the fine new health scheme in the fine new welfare state and came home with her prize. She took it for granted the child would be christened. I borrowed her prayer book from her and read her extracts from it—"forasmuch as all men are conceived and born in sin"—did she really believe that?—and about the mystical washing away of the "sins" of this scrap of humanity only a few weeks old? And was it fair, I demanded, to promise all this without consulting the person concerned? But she was quite happy about it all; it was "proper" to be christened, just as it was proper to be confirmed in due course. . . . I let it go; I had after all had my way about a registry-office wedding when she had hoped for a church one. It didn't matter, I thought, the boy would decide for himself when he was of an age. I had had a sentimental wish that the child should be called Martin, so that there should be a Martin Rowse again in the family, and as she liked the name we called him that, and Edward after her father. She raised some godparents among the people she had worked for, and Joe and I took ourselves off the day of the christening party.

We got along all right, Norah and I. She nagged me a bit about the house, but I didn't much mind; my mother had always done it; it's the price a man must usually pay for a clean and tidy home, I told myself. But motherhood made Norah a less loving wife; it was as though she had only a limited amount of love to dispense, and now the baby took the major part of it. Had I been in love with her I should have been jealous; as it was I felt cheated. I had been attracted by her in the first place by her loving sweetness; now this was withdrawn in favor of the child, and I found myself being increasingly bossed around in an uncomfortably tidy home and, as it seemed to me, very little but "tellings-off" coming my way. From time to time I would remind myself that the child frayed her nerves; he was a fretful child for the first six months, and we never had an unbroken night, so that my own nerves also became frayed. In the end I took myself off to sleep on a camp bed in the spareroom; Norah took the baby into bed with her then and seemed glad of the new arrangement. The baby worried her and she didn't want another, and such infrequent marital relations as we had were ruined by her anxiety as to whether it would be "all right." She no longer wanted me, and it was only a matter of time before, from forcing myself not to want her, in order to avoid being a nuisance to her, I ceased to do so.

Yet outwardly everything was all right. By the time Martin was three years old we had a little council house on the Maze Hill side, with lace curtains looped back from a plaster ornament in the exact center of the parlor window ledge looking onto the street, like everyone else. We had a bit of garden where I grew potatoes and tomatoes, and wallflowers and sweet peas, and some rambler roses on the trellis that was supposed to screen us from our neighbors. I minded Martin on Saturday nights so that Norah could go to the pictures with the young married woman next door, and on Sunday nights I went to the Yacht—where I had been with Tansy and with Helen. I put by out of my wages for a fortnight's holiday every summer by the sea—Hastings or Eastbourne or Littlehampton, because they were not too far, rail fares being high. Norah saved out of the housekeeping money I gave her for her fare to Cornwall to show her son to his grandparents; it took her nearly three years, but she managed it, and while she was away I went back to stay with Joe, which was a happy return to old times, with comfortably untidy rooms and meal-getting merely a matter of throwing the meat rations with a few vegetables into the big pot, which Joe still called "the dixie." Now that I was no longer living with him he didn't get on my nerves so much, and at times I felt again the old communion of being with someone of "mine own fashion."

He was getting frail now, in his seventies, and turned more and more of the outside work over to me. That was how he came to send me to do the bookshelf job in Mr. Harley's flat in an expensive block of flats in Mayfair. It was a mild spring day outside, but the steam heat in the entrance hall of the block nearly knocked me over. I suppose there was rubber under the deep pile carpet, because it gave under the tread like a spring mattress under the body. I had a row with the uniformed elevator man because he wanted that I should go out again and round to the back of the building and carry my deal planks up three flights of service stairs. He gave in when I said I had a weak heart and wouldn't be responsible for what happened if I had to walk up.

I looked at myself in the elevator mirrors and saw a gaunt dingy-looking workman with a lined face, a shabby raincoat, a neat clean darned shirt, and a faded cotton muffler to hide the absence of collar or tie. I carried the usual carpenter's bag of tools and there was the smell of dust and sweat on me. I was in a bad temper when I rang Mr. Harley's bell after the altercation with the elevator man, and hoped he would be out; I didn't feel inclined to have him standing over me telling me my job, as so many of them tried to do. They had a lot of impractical fancy ideas, too, many of them. When they were out there was often an amiable daily woman ready to offer a cup of tea, or even a nip of her employer's gin or whisky—when they offered sherry I always refused; a bottle of stout was another matter. Unfortunately in many places there would be some foreign girl come over from Germany or Austria to learn the language by working as "domestic help," and these girls, though usually easy on the eye and pleasant enough, didn't understand the customs of the country where workmen were concerned as our native charladies do. They don't understand about nice cups of tea and a bottle-of-stout-dear; the finer usage of the words *nice* and *dear* are lost upon them.

So as I stood waiting for Mr. Harley's bell to be answered I hoped, intensely, that he would be out, and that a nice homely woman would show me in and know what to offer me, and offer it forthwith. Then the door opened and I looked into the astonished face of someone who could not possibly be other than Lee.

"Good Lord, Tom!" he exclaimed.

It was nine o'clock in the morning and he wore a Paisley silk dressing gown over black silk pajamas. The fact that he had not shaved and a slight beard showed on his chin made him look older than I had remembered him; but he was as slim and golden as ever—though with a shock I realized that he must be forty by now.

"What on earth," I said, as he closed the door and we stood together in the overheated entrance passage of the flat, with a very Lee-like mass arrangement of tulips and white lilac and exotic foliage against the pale green wall behind us. "You've not changed your name to Harley?" I hazarded.

"Good heavens, no. You remember Gabriel Harley—of the antique shop? An aunt died and left him wads of money. He's only just come to this place, and I'm responsible for the redecoration. I'm staying here while he's away and getting everything done. When he said he wanted bookshelves I tried several people who couldn't send at once because they hadn't the timber; then I remembered your old friend Snell of Greenwich and wrote to him."

"Funny he didn't tell me—he would remember your name."

"I didn't sign my name—I put p.p. G. Harley. I nearly put p.s. any news of my old friend Tom Rowse, but thought better not. I *am* glad to see you! Fancy fading out on all of us like that! Look, do dump those planks in that empty room there and come into the sitting room and have a drink. I can't *tell* you how wonderful it is seeing you again, you wicked old thing!"

It was wonderful seeing him again, too, as I told him. He had got tired of his Chelsea basement, it seemed, and was living in a mews-flat now "behind Harrods." Why didn't I come and see it? Helen was back in Paris, on the Ile St. Louis. He and Graham had spent Easter there. Helen had had a "terrific press" for her last show, he said. She was probably the leading woman painter of the day. Graham hadn't been too well for some time and could, he said cheerfully, pop off any day. A clot or something. He ought to diet and cut out the drink, but of course he didn't, and who would—anyone, that is, with any feeling for living? Such a *bore!* He wanted to know about me, whom I had married, and why, and where was I living, and was I really never going to be a sculptor again, and if so, why, *why?* Any jobbing carpenter could put up bookshelves. It was all such a *waste*. . . . In *Apollo* he had seen a photograph of something of mine called Lamentation of Enion, in the collection of Lord Lake, and it looked terribly exciting. The article was on modern sculptors, and the writer seemed to consider Tom Rowse one of the most interesting. . . .

"How can you bear to fade out just when you're beginning to make a name for yourself?" Lee demanded.

"It was a matter of not being able to bear going on," I told him. "I made the Lamentation as a memorial to Tansy, and then I had nothing else to say."

With characteristic directness he objected, "Tansy had been dead to you for years before she actually died. I don't understand—"

"It's difficult for me to talk about it," I said. "If she could have forgiven me before she died. But she didn't. She told me to go. They were her last words."

I swallowed the rest of the drink and got up.

"I'd better get started," I said.

Lee did not move.

"I don't want to make you talk about anything painful to

you, Tom," he said, "but there is just this—so far as Tansy was concerned you've nothing to reproach yourself with. Anyone who knew her knew she wouldn't give up Bill for you. He was security for her. You were just a bit of excitement on the side. Why don't you face it? When she had to make a choice it was Bill she chose. I'd have thought any forgiving to be done would be from your side."

"I can't talk about it, Lee," I said. "Show me where the shelves are to go."

I worked till midday. Lee bathed, then while he shaved and dressed he put some records on the phonograph in the next room, leaving the doors open so that I could hear while I worked. I stopped hammering to listen, sitting on the floor of the empty room. He stood leaning against the door when he was dressed, his head lifted, smiling raptly. When the last record came to an automatic stop he was like one released from a trance.

"Brandenburg number five," he murmured, adding, with his old mocking smile, "I still play Bach to cheer myself up in the mornings."

"D'you need as much cheering up these days?"

"Oh my dear, more! *Much* more! I am no longer what Gabriel so delicately calls 'the sunny side of forty.' There would be silver threads among the gold—if I permitted anything so squalid. The mad rush at parties to hop into bed with one ceased *long* ago. So did the parties, for that matter. The *only* compensation for being forty is that one no longer sits at home crying one's eyes out if one isn't asked."

"You don't look forty, if that's any comfort to you," I told him, and I meant it. To me he looked very little different from when I had met him back in the early thirties.

"Of *course* it's a comfort. Positively the *only* one. Unfortunately it's only true with one's back to the light. The sag has set in . . ." he patted himself under the chin, "here, you know. And here. . . ." He pushed the flesh of one cheek up toward the eye. "One could be lifted, of course, but then there's that telltale tight look each side of the mouth. Gabriel had it done, poor pet. Went into a nursing home and gave out it was wisdom teeth. But I must get to Harrods. You'll be here for lunch, of course?"

"I've brought sandwiches," I said.

"Sandwiches are a bore—unless they're smoked salmon."

"They're fish paste," I told him.

"How very squalid! What shall I bring in? Perhaps we should just picnic with some smoked salmon and chicken in aspic—"

"You're as incorrigible as Helen," I said. "I shall eat my sandwiches. If you want to bring anything in for me make it a bottle of stout." I added, "You'd better hurry, too, if we're to eat together. I breakfast at seven and reckon to lunch at twelve."

"I don't mind eating at twelve, as I don't take breakfast—but couldn't you just this once eat the sandwiches for your tea when you go home?"

"Joe will be keeping something hot for me in the dixie."

"You're living with him?"

"Only while my wife's away visiting her people," I said quickly. "We got a house last year."

"In Greenwich?"

"No." Well, properly speaking Maze Hill isn't Greenwich.

He gave me one of his old speculative looks, then turned and went out. He got back shortly after twelve.

"I made it, you see! I just got a small cooked chicken and some asparagus in aspic and a half-bottle of Pouilly—"

He looked so happy that I hadn't the heart to refuse. He covered a small round white and gilt table in the sitting room with a handsome lace cloth, while I washed in a bathroom where all was green as the bottom of the sea and as damply warm as a tropical jungle. I thought of our cold stark little bathroom in the council house with the water closet beside the bath. But Norah was very pleased with our bathroom, even though when you got out of the bath you had to be careful not to knock your elbow on the door.

Well, I cleaned and tidied myself up as best I could and rejoined Lee in the beautiful room that was so like the one he had had in Paris—peach curtains, lavish flower arrangements and all. I admired the china and he told me that it was Spode and had come from Gabriel's shop, as had most of the valuable and beautiful things in the flat. It was all very elegant and tasteful and I could appreciate, aesthetically, that Sèvres dish, that Delft plate, that eighteenth-century flower print, each fine and beautifully and aesthetically satisfying object, but I didn't want any of it for myself, and I thought with another kind of satisfaction of the small cramped house full of ugly and vulgar mass-produced things, not because I approved of the mass-produced, for I loathed it as much then as always, but because such things made up the lives of the common people, the have-nots, the under-privileged, from whom I had sprung and with whom I identified myself. Norah, I thought, would have admired the lace cloth and the china, but even had she possessed such treasures would never have dared to use them, not even for "best," when she cautiously brought out the Doulton teapot her parents had given us for a wedding present and spread the table with the linen cloth edged with the deep lace her mother had crocheted at school. We had our own treasures, the lares and penates of our class.

"It's all very fine and handsome and valuable," I said suddenly, bringing my eyes back from a survey of the room's contents, "but I couldn't live with it."

"It is a bit much," Lee drawled, in his bored tone. "I always tell Gabriel it's like living in a high-class antique shop. I wouldn't mind having a few things here and there, though—that Chippendale armchair by the fireplace—that's the original needlework, you know. And that chandelier—eighteenth-century Waterford, hand cut. I've nothing much at my place—some Thornton prints, and a very nice Chippendale silver table that Graham picked up at a sale and gave me last Christmas, with some Georgian cream jugs to stand on it."

"Things," I said restlessly. "Things. Possessions. My Waterford chandelier, my Chippendale furniture, my Thornton prints, my Georgian silver—"

"Very nice too," Lee murmured, pouring wine into exquisite glasses with opaque twisted stems. "What's wrong with owning lovely things?"

"The fact that it takes money to make their ownership possible, so that they're for the privileged few. There's nothing in this room that anyone down our street could possibly afford to own—"

"Or with the exception of yourself—who shouldn't be there—would appreciate if they did own it," Lee said acidly. "The mass-produced is quite good enough for the masses."

"Unfortunately. So long as the masses live the lives they do they'll be the kind of people they are."

"What must they do to be saved?" Lee mocked.

"They must be given real education and leisure."

"Leisure to go to football matches and the dogs midweek?"

"Educated in the real sense they won't want to."

"Utopia!"

"Of course, and why not? Is man to be forever a little groveling root? Why shouldn't he gird himself up with a chain of stars to prevent himself falling into the abyss?"

"Try some of this gruyère," Lee murmured. "It's *delicious!*"

13

WE SPENT so long over lunch that I had to work late into the evening to finish the shelves. Lee wanted that I should leave them and come back again next day—in fact he recommended that I should spin the job out for a week; Gabriel wouldn't be back, and with his wads of money there was no need to count the cost. But I was determined that I should not come back. I had closed the doors upon my old life, and though one had unexpectedly swung open again I was anxious to close it—finally. I had chosen a certain kind of life and rejected another kind—the comfortable, leisured, privileged life—and I was not going back on my decision. I had never had great possessions to walk out on like Prince Gautama, the Buddha; or Francis of Assisi; what I had retreated from was the material promises of "the Accuser, who is the God of this world," and privilege not least among those promises. It was not the great act of renunciation that Helen and Lee seemed to see it. Like Saul of Tarsus I had set out along a certain road to achieve a certain object; his had been to persecute Christians; mine simply to live the life I wanted to live as an artist. Something had happened to Saul along that road, some experience of revelation so profound that the whole course of his life was changed. Along the road I was no less confidently pursuing something had happened, first blinding and then revealing.

I had served a long and arduous apprenticeship as an artist; I had served it on the bread line for the most part, and then for as long again I had lived a privileged life of doing the creative work which was the only real happiness I had ever known. I had done a certain amount of work that was not unworthy, and had I gone on I stood fair to possess a great deal more than my share of this world's goods. Only in a free world, where men are liberated from exploitation by their fellow men, from the profit motive, from the machine, from wage slavery, is the artist able to indulge his creative impulses without assuming privileges denied his fellows. I believed with Eric Gill—who was a considerable artist—that an artist is not a special kind of man, but that every man is a special kind of artist—given the conditions in which his special gift may find expression. I believed that then, and I believe it now. Whether without the shock of Tansy's tragedy, and her refusal of absolution for my sins against her, I should have continued along that road of success and money upon which I had walked only a short distance, who shall say? There is more than one road to Damascus, and the lightning of revelation may strike from any point of the compass.

But once the lightning has struck, and the scales have fallen from the eyes of the inner vision, there is no turning back. For a time we see through a glass darkly in our search for truth, for our own particular truth, but then face to face. Through the medium of wood and stone I had attempted for a time that illumination of life which is art. But all those facets of truth I had delineated, with the co-operation of hand and brain, the marriage of subject and material, the passion and vitality of the Negro Girl Dancing, the fecund power of the Daughter of Los, the wild anger of the Eternal Horses trampling the stony law to dust, the protest and plea of the Doors of Heaven and Hell, the contemporary despair of the *Weltschmerz* figure, even the impassioned and terrible figure of Christ driving the money-changers from the temple—all were in essence metaphysical, a theory of living and being; it took Christ crying out in agony of flesh and spirit upon the cross, "My God, my God, why hast thou forsaken me?" for the heavens to open in a lightning flash of revelation of ultimate, absolute truth.

Whether any manifestation can be so touched with the day-spring from on high, born out of the artist's personal experience of the moment of truth, I don't know. I only know that the truth shadowed forth from the eyes of death that looked out of Tansy's face that last time I saw her went beyond life to the threshold of eternity, and at that point, the edge of the infinite, finite expression retreated as life retreats into death. Death does not retreat or compromise. It can look with the eyes of forgiveness and reconciliation; or with the eyes of pitiless unforgiveness. In the eyes of death I had seen only that—the recorded reproach. Nothing I could create could erase that, or transmute it into mercy, pity, peace. That blessed trinity has to be sought in the labyrinth of living. The "woe and horror" of that deprivation of absolution could be erased only by living—as it were under another name—a quite different kind of life, purged of all pride, vanity, ambition, privilege, not as a penance but in the hope of achieving peace through humility, since it wears the human dress.

Lee urged upon me that last evening that we could still be friends even if I persisted in the life I had resolved to lead; if I did not want to meet him in his world he would come to mine; or could we not meet in some neutral territory, he suggested, such as—with a rueful laugh—a Lyons café? A cafeteria cup of coffee once a month wouldn't be all that un-Franciscan, surely? I didn't try to explain that I wasn't setting out in the imitation of St. Francis. I didn't expect him or anyone to understand what happens when you are thrown from your horse by the lightning flash on the road to Damascus. Or the mercy of that grace sought and found between the stirrup and the ground. And that it was this grace I was attempting to pursue.

"If we ever meet again it'll be by chance," I told him, and added, "It's better not to think about me—except as someone you once knew but who is now dead. The way I think of Tansy."

He looked so unhappy that I said, desperately, "You've still got Helen."

He looked away and I saw that there were tears in his eyes, and I damn near wept myself.

"You'd better go," he said. "Joe will be wondering what's happened to you."

I sought about for something else to say, something that would somehow help, but finding nothing laid a hand for a moment on his shoulder and went.

14

WHEN MARTIN was four, or thereabouts, I got him some clay and had him model birds and animals and human faces. He enjoyed it hugely, and I got the feeling he had a natural aptitude. Norah was much impressed by the things I modeled for his interest and amusement; I had a real gift, she declared, and if only I'd gone to the Polytechnic night classes when I'd left school I might have been able to have "gone in for it" and become a sculptor.

It felt strange to be making things again with my hands like that; it started a kind of restlessness in me, like the first birdsong in early spring; a kind of happy-sadness. Then, almost with a feeling of guilt, I went along to Lister's and cadged a few pieces of wood. I was touched that the foreman hadn't forgotten me; he asked me how I was doing, and laughed when I told him, in reply, that I'd taken out full-time employment as a husband and father. He told me he'd seen a piece about me in the papers a while back, some big pot, a lord or someone, having bought one of my statues, and how he'd said to his wife, reading it, that he'd known me, man and boy, since I was a bit of a lad coming round with orders from his boss and doing a bit of nicking on the side on his own account. . . .

So I nicked a bit then and there, when his back was turned, for old times' sake, and wondered how long it would be before young Martin would be around on the same errand. For I was all set to apprentice the boy to cabinetmaking and have him learn about timber and come to love the sight and touch and smell of it, and find his own way, as his dad had done. I had a sentimental romantic idea he might carry on where the old man had left off.

He was a nice bright kid, with a strong look of Norah about him, and a strong will. She was always declaring that he was a little devil and trying to make him "behave." She seemed to me to be always on at him with her don'ts and threats, and she accused me of spoiling him. Well, I didn't see why he had to be clean and tidy and say please and thank you, and I enjoyed the times she went off to the pictures or shopping and left him in my charge. Left to ourselves on Saturday afternoons when it was fine we would go off to the hill and play in the grassy hollows, or I would take him into the Maritime Museum where the models of ships always fascinated him, or we would potter about "beach-combing" on the bit of shingle below the terrace of the water-front. He got very dirty on his outings with me, but I would clean him up as best I could before we went home. There was a kind of conspiracy between us where the woman of the house was concerned.

I taught him how to handle a penknife without cutting himself and he chipped away at pieces of wood under my instruction and guidance, and it seemed to me he had the idea all right. I made him a number of small birds and beasts and little figures. I took him along to Joe's place sometimes and Joe showed him useful things such as how to tie different kinds of knots, and how to make a little ship and get it into a bottle, and how to signal with flags.

In the summer we would all three of us, Norah and the kid and I, make excursions to Epping Forest, with sandwiches and our tea in a thermos flask, and anyone seeing us sprawling on the grass would see in the group we made that of a happy little family. In a sense we were, since we didn't quarrel, and went on outings together, and I suppose we looked contented enough, playing with the kid, or Norah sitting knitting a jumper for herself or a pullover for Martin, and smiling and answering his questions, or listening to the rigmarole of real or imaginary happenings he was always recounting to her, and me sitting with my back against a tree trunk, or lolling on an elbow in the grass pulling away at my pipe or reading a paper. The man, an observer might say, was shabby but neatly dressed, the woman looked young and fresh in some pretty cotton frock, the child healthy and well cared-for—the typical nice little working-class family, in fact.

As a domestic façade it was all right, as good as many and better than some, but inside it was all bare, unfurnished, as you might say. Empty as a shell it was, and cold as a tomb. Which is what I often thought it was—a tomb for the living. Norah seemed content enough with her bright tomb, keeping it spick and span seemed to suffice her, and looking after the child. All sex seemed to have died in her after his birth; I believe it does happen with some women. Or perhaps it is just that biologically they have finished with that particular mate, like the female tiger when she has reared her cubs. Only unlike the tigress Norah didn't look around for a new mate, and her one young cub seemed sufficient for her.

As to me, I too was just a façade, hollow within. Perhaps if Norah had not withdrawn from me physically I might have remained at least alive in my body and some small flame have warmed my spirit. But I hadn't the power to hold her close to me; I suppose I didn't love her enough. Or perhaps I wasn't right for her and she had set herself against me and in time come not to want me in that way; this also, I believe, happens to women. Anyhow, whatever the reasons, there we were, so soon with all passion spent—there hadn't, it was evident, been much to spend, and I was out in the gray wastelands again, physically and in all other ways.

My one joy at that time was wandering about on the Observatory hill or in Epping Forest with Martin, and picking up bits of wood and chipping away at them with a penknife for him and showing him how to, and occasionally getting a bit of seasoned wood and making some small thing and teaching him how to handle a gouge; and helping him make things in clay, and teaching him to observe.

I didn't drink much at that time; I couldn't afford to; mostly it was just a Sunday night pint of mild-and-bitter with Joe down at the Yacht. Summer evenings we'd perhaps linger a bit on the terrace looking at the river growing shadowy in the fading light and then sometimes the memory of Tansy would stir in me with an intensity of longing that was a kind of agony. I could not come to terms with the fact that she existed nowhere except as dust and ashes. Perhaps after all, I would think at times, there was something to be said for earth burial; she should have had a tree planted on her grave, a blossoming tree drawing its live sap up from her dead heart—she who was my lovely myrtle tree. I took Norah occasionally to a pub for a glass of port, which she liked, but I could never bring myself to take her to the Yacht, though she often expressed the wish to go there; I would make an excuse that it was too crowded. It seemed that dead Tansy came closer to me than she ever had in life.

15

ALTHOUGH I had said good-bye to Lee "finally and forever," as I thought, I was fated to meet him once again, some eighteen months after my visit to Gabriel Harley's flat. The encounter was on a summer Saturday afternoon when Norah and Martin and I were sitting on the grass under a hawthorn tree, at the top of the hill, just below the terrace. It was a hot day and the city of London in the near distance, and the Hampstead Heights in the far distance across the river, were all one hazy blue shimmer. The heat was of the heavy sticky kind peculiar to the English heat-wave, particularly in London, and Norah was lying flat on the grass, her bare legs spread out, her head on my old jacket, rolled-up; Martin had rolled a little way down the hill and lay there, lacking the energy to get up and walk back; I sat up, my sports shirt open to the waist, gazing at nothing much and thinking nothing much except that when at last it was opening time a mild-and-bitter would go down well. . . . All about on the grass men, women and children sat and lay and leaned in inert groups, with the occasional solitary figure. The hill had a brown burned-up appearance, and was strewn with ice-cream cartons. Down at the pier there was a busyness of water buses and crowds of people continually disembarking, leaving the coolness of the river for the sultriness of the land. Every piece of tree shade was occupied. The proletariat sat about and sweated, and heavy thunderclouds swagged on the Hampstead horizon.

Lee and I saw each other at the same time. He looked cool, somewhat *recherché*, in wine-colored linen slacks and a gray sports shirt. He carried a slim lemon-colored volume with a gray spine—undoubtedly for effect.

He stopped in front of me and exclaimed, a little petulantly, "Oh, *there* you are! I've been looking for you all *over* the place! I went to Joe's and he told me you'd be somewhere about."

Martin came up the hill and stood staring.

"Hullo," Lee said. "What's your name?"

Martin hung his head and pressed the stick he was carrying close to his chest.

"I'm ig'oring everyone," he stated sulkily.

"Splendid idea," Lee said. "I only wish I could." He pulled a wine-colored silk handkerchief out of his trouser pocket and dabbed at his face.

"There's only one thing filthier than the English winter and that's the English summer," he observed; then, as Norah raised herself to a sitting position and regarded him, "Good afternoon. Mrs. Rowse, I presume? How d'you do?"

She nodded, blushing a little. "Pleased to meet you," she said, and looked inquiringly at me.

"Lee Morton," I told her, "an old friend of mine. I thought I'd dropped him for good, but old soldiers, we know, never die."

Lee said crossly, dropping down onto the dusty grass beside

me, "You don't suppose it gives me any *pleasure* to trek all out here after you in this heat, do you? I came on business."

"If it's another carpentering job the answer is no," I said.

"It's nothing of the kind." He held a handsome silver cigarette case, ribbed like fine corduroy, out to Norah. "Cigarette, Mrs. Rowse?"

"I don't smoke, thank you ever so much," Norah said.

He offered the case to me and I took one.

"Thanks," I said, and then, when he'd held the lighter, "I'm afraid you've come on a sleeveless errand, for no kind of business interests me."

"Five thousand pounds ought to interest you," he said. "Invested even at five per cent it would bring you in a nice little income, and then you could—"

"No," I cut in sharply. "You know my views, and you know the discussion we had at Harley's flat."

"I'm sorry," Lee said, "but you'll have to have it. It's been left you by Graham. He died last week—the clot reached his heart. He made his will several years ago. He's left the same amount to me. The rest of his estate to found a scholarship for sculptors—to be called the Brenovska Award. This money will come to you whether you like it or not. Perhaps your wife can suggest a good use for it."

"I don't understand," Norah said. "Why should anyone leave my husband money? We don't know any well-off people. There must be some mistake."

"There isn't any mistake," I said curtly. "The only mistake is thinking I've any use for it. It can be added to the Brenovska fund."

"Five thousand pounds?" Norah echoed, and her face looked foolish, and rather greedy, with wonder.

"We don't need it," I insisted.

She flared out then. "Of course we need it! Anyone would think we were well-off to hear you talk! We could buy a house with it, for one thing."

"There's nothing wrong with the house we've got," I pointed out. "It's small, convenient, and suited to our station."

Lee smiled ironically.

"I'll leave you to fight it out between you," he said, and got up, brushing the dust and dried grass from his slacks.

"I'll walk a bit of the way with you," I said, and stood up

beside him. "Don't wait tea for me," I added to Norah. "I'll probably have a drink with Mr. Morton."

Lee smiled at her.

"So glad to have met you," he murmured. Then smiling, "Between us we should be able to make your husband see reason. *Good*-bye!"

"Good afternoon," Norah said coldly, her eyes hostile—I couldn't for the life of me think why.

Lee ruffled Martin's hair.

"Good-bye," he said. "Or are you still ig'oring persons?"

The boy hung his head and ran to his mother.

"Say good-bye properly to the gentleman," Norah commanded.

"Good-bye properly," Martin sang out.

As we walked away down the hill I heard a yelp and knew that Martin had been smacked for not "behaving."

"Mothers will seldom accept the fact that children are noble savages," I observed.

"Did you say noble or natural?" Lee demanded.

"Both," I said, and then plunged into the business of the legacy. "Why on earth didn't you write me care of Joe?" I said. "Now I'm in for a high old row with Norah."

Lee said fretfully, "I don't see why you can't accept it and invest the money and have a little income and start work again as a sculptor. What right have you to withhold your creative gift from society in this way?"

"Look, Lee," I said. "It's no use going into it all over again. I've said all I've got to say as an artist—I won't be the first artist or the last to shut up shop a little early. It might be better if more artists did it, instead of repeating themselves year in and year out for the sake of the cash. Not to mention cashing-in when damn near senile on reputations made in their prime! Do you want me to hang on till I take refuge in abstractions which nobody can understand for the very good reason that they don't mean anything? I've said all I've got to say. It began with a paean of praise for life and ended up with *Weltschmerz* and Lamentation. Somewhere between the two comes my own particular vision of Christ. So long as the money-changers defile the temple with their squalid transactions, so long will art, love, life itself continue to be the debased thing it everywhere is. You've seen my Vision of Christ—

> And in His hand the scourge shone bright;
> He scourg'd the merchant Canaanite
> From out the Temple of his Mind—

Don't ask me to become one of the money-changers. You know what Jesus told the young man who had great possessions. And you probably don't know what Gandhi said on the same subject —that all who had more of this world's goods than they needed for their subsistence stole from those who had not."

Lee sighed. "You could anyhow let your wife have the money and get the house she wants and educate the boy—"

"Make a little bourgeois of him, you mean?"

"Well then, put the money by as an insurance for your wife in case you die before her."

"She'd hardly starve, if I did. She's good for work for another twenty or thirty years yet, and aren't we all insured, anyhow, from the womb to the tomb?"

"I can't help feeling it's bad luck on your wife, all the same. It must be embittering for her, poor girl, since she evidently doesn't share your views. Couldn't you let her have some of it to spend on clothes and a holiday at the seaside in a smart hotel?"

"She can have all the Lake money for the Lamentation—five hundred pounds. It's still sitting there. I can't touch this from Graham. I don't accept it. I don't believe in inherited wealth. What do you propose to do with yours?"

"Enjoy it," he said, shortly. There was an edge of irritation to his voice, and it didn't surprise me that when we came to Trafalgar Road he looked about for a bus, remarking that he had to be back in the West End by six. We parted this time without any emotionalism, each irritated with the other.

"I ought to have your address," he said, while I stood with him at the bus stop. "There'll be a lot of flap with lawyers. People create almost as many difficulties dying as living."

"Let the lawyers write me care of Joe," I said. "I'd rather not have letters coming to the house."

"You're still living in Greenwich?"

"Yes. But don't try to find me. It's as I said—we inhabit different worlds."

"I've no intention of forcing my friendship on you. Here's my bus."

"Lee," I said quickly.

He looked at me with his old ironic smile. "Well?"

"Oh, nothing," I said. "Hop on or you'll be left. Good-bye."

There was a slight inclination of his head, and I thought for a moment he was going to say something, then he was lost with the crowd on the platform of the bus. I looked after the bus and saw him mounting the stairs and his figure at the top, through the glass, but he did not look my way. "Last farewells should be softly spoken." Well, they should, but who knew what was a last farewell?

I turned and began walking in the Maze Hill direction, full of forebodings concerning the scene with Norah.

16

IT WAS not merely as bad as I had expected it to be, but much worse. I hadn't expected she would pitch into Lee.

"How on earth did you come to know that creature?" she demanded. "I swear he had powder on his face!"

"Probably. Touches his lips up too, I believe." It was stupid, of course, but it was what the politicians call unprovoked aggression, and while in principle I approved the turning-of-the-other-cheek tactic, and the soft-answer-that-turneth-away-wrath, I wasn't able for it just then.

"Loathsome creature!" She shuddered.

"On the contrary he's an extremely nice person," I said.

She demanded, "What's nice about him, I'd like to know!"

"If you'd like to know, he has warmth, generosity, and absolute honesty." I should have left it at that, but I added, "In fact he's the only really honest person I've ever met."

That, of course, sent the balloon up. She became hysterical immediately, saying oh so she wasn't honest, was that it? And perhaps that was what was the matter with me—perhaps I was really one of that sort, birds of a feather, etc. If I thought so highly of him and so little of her, why didn't I go off with my pansy boy friend, and so on, and so on, *ad nauseam*. Looking back I don't know whether I hit her to shut her up, or because the word "pansy" got me on the raw. Both, perhaps. She burst into a wild crying then and rushed upstairs and into her room.

I was deeply shocked by what I had done. I had never hit

anyone in my life—not even my brother in our childish quarrels. Not even Tansy at her most maddening. I was shocked and ashamed. I went upstairs and did what I hadn't done for about two years—took her into my arms. I brushed her hair back from her face and wiped her tears and kissed her wet eyes and quivering lips and begged her to forgive me. She clung to me sobbing violently, extracting the utmost ounce of emotion from the scene, I felt, demanding I take back what I had said about Lee and agree that she, my wife, was the one really true and honest person in my life. I took it back; I agreed to her proposition; I said that I had exaggerated about Lee, but that she had provoked me. She began to calm down, and then she reached up a hand and began stroking my forehead and saying she was sorry she had upset me, and how the shock of the news about the money had been too much for us, and we must think what to do with it for the best. Perhaps my friend's suggestion that we should invest it was a good one. Or perhaps we should buy a business—buy up old Joe's business, perhaps, and put money into it and make it into a real going concern, build it up for Martin so that one day it would be Rowse & Son. . . .

I let her talk. Anything to keep her quiet. Because I didn't argue with her she thought I was coming around to her view, thinking it over. She tidied herself and we went downstairs and she got tea and called in Martin from the street, and we sat around again, Norah flushed still, and excited, myself more silent than usual, and the child chattering eagerly. She put him to bed early so that she could sit with me and go on talking about what we would do with the windfall.

That night she came and got into my bed, snuggling up to me so that, as she said, we could talk cozily, putting her arms around me and punctuating the talk with kisses, and behaving as she had when we were first married and had shared a bed as a matter of course. In the end I responded to her, with a kind of suppressed anger, and afterwards felt that it was quite as shameful as what I had done to her earlier.

In the morning she wanted that we should lie in a little "like old times"; she was still being caressive and cajoling. I made the excuse that I had things to do in the garden, and got up. I had things to do all right, but not in the garden. In the evening she went off to the pictures with the woman next door, and I stayed home with Martin. I kept him amused till about nine modeling in clay, then got him to bed. He announced triumphantly, as I tucked him up, "Mummy says we're going to be rich and live in a big house and have a motor car!"

"Mummy was making up a fairy tale," I said. But I filled with a dark anger against her for corrupting his innocence. "What's the good of a motor car?" I went on. "You can't go up and down the hill in it or drive it along the beach. You don't need money to be happy."

"Money buys things," he said, and his tone challenged me to refute it.

"It doesn't buy you the things that are most fun. You can't buy the treasures you pick up along the beach, or the jay's feather you picked up this afternoon on the hill. It doesn't buy you the trees and the stars that you like looking at. It's only because people are silly we have to have money to buy food, because the food is there whether there's money or not; it grows up out of the earth, and if there was a famine and the earth didn't grow wheat and other things any more all the money in the whole wide world wouldn't give you enough to eat."

"Not all the money in the Bank of England?" he demanded.

"Not even all the money in all the banks of all the countries. Millions and millions of money wouldn't do it."

"Millions and billions," he declared eagerly. "Billions and trillions. What comes after trillions, Daddy?"

But in the disappointing way of grownups I suddenly refused to play any more.

"Go to sleep," I said. As I went downstairs I heard him murmuring in a little singsong, "Millions and billions, billions and trillions."

I sat at the kitchen table and wrote a letter to Norah:

Dear Norah,

This letter will no doubt come as a shock to you, but if you don't go rampaging off in the tracks of ready-made ideas it shouldn't be too difficult to be sensible about it. I have left home and I am not coming back. I'm clearing out like this because I can't stand any more futile discussion about that money which no power on earth will persuade me to keep. That ninety-nine people out of a hundred would keep it and be wild with joy about it doesn't interest me; I am, if you like, the hundredth person. I know that the majority of people, rich and poor alike, spend their adult lives wishing for more money than they've got; the poor go in for football pools and sweepstakes; the rich invest, and when they've made one pile go on to make another, and when poor people become rich they do likewise. But there must be somewhere a minority that thinks differently, and I am of it.

The legacy, though, has only brought to a head what has been festering below the skin for a long time—ever since Martin was born, in fact. Sometimes when the physical relationship in a marriage ceases people still remain mentally and emotionally married to each other, but we didn't. We became just two people with very little in common sharing a house together. What happened last night wasn't making love but making something that does neither of us credit. You needn't worry that you will get a baby from it, for you won't, which is perhaps a pity, because two children are better than one. Perhaps if Martin had had a brother or a sister years ago you and I might still be husband and wife, and our marriage a reality instead of a respectable façade with nothing behind it—just a few empty and cold and very lonely rooms.

You will be worrying about what the neighbors will think; you could tell them I have gone off on a job to the provinces and that you will be joining me. You could go and live with Joe again for a while, perhaps; you need not pretend with him as I shall be keeping in touch with him—though not seeing him—and shall tell him the truth. He may not approve, but he will understand. You will get your money just the same, and I will arrange for you to have the five hundred pounds. You could put it down as deposit on a house; what you will pay off on it won't be more than you'd be paying as rent, anyhow. Joe will help you with all that. You'll be all right. You don't need me. Presently, if you want, you can divorce me for desertion and get yourself a real husband. You are a good girl, Norah, and would make a good wife for the right man, which I wasn't. I did you a bad turn in taking up with you, but we made Martin between us, and he's a good kid, and I think he may have some talent. Don't try to make a gentleman of him. When he leaves school put him to the cabinetmaking, and encourage him to go to night classes and learn drawing and wood carving and modeling; he might turn out to be a sculptor, you never know. But if he doesn't, carpentry's a good trade. Jesus was a carpenter, if you remember.

Bless you. Don't try to find me; you wouldn't, anyhow, and it's better just to let me go like this and disappear just as though I had gone the first time the lights changed.

Tom

I left the letter on the kitchen table, then with my tool bag in one hand and an old suitcase with my few clothes and my battered old copy of Blake, I left the overclean, overtidy little domestic box that held all the happy-family equipment except the one thing needful.

17

I AM writing this now, as I have written all this history of one man's wanderings in the labyrinth of living, in which success proved a cul-de-sac and failure the way out, in a drab room in a tenement house at the other side of London. They don't build these dark ugly blocks any more, and enemy action in the last few years disposed of a number of them, but thousands of people continue to live in them, and children grow up in them. The standard of living has improved since these tenements were built, but having enough to eat, good shoes to your feet, and the price of the flicks once a week, can still leave you with a pretty mean sort of existence, when the conditions of living are themselves mean, as here.

The summer is the worst time, because then all the windows are open and you cannot escape the sounds and smells of enseamèd living. The world has grown a great deal noisier in the last twenty years as well as more barbarous. Here, as in all such mean human habitations, there is a racket of radios which begin at seven in the morning and go on, unremittingly, until late at night, and which know only two degrees—loud and louder. There is a fretful crying of children confined in stuffy rooms. and a shriek of children running loose in the bare, prisonlike yard in which the blocks of buildings stand. From the open windows come the shrill voices of women screaming at the children, nagging at the men, and sometimes the voice of a man raised in anger against a woman; the sound of blows and of a woman weeping. And all the time the tuneless tumty-tum and the crooning wail, the wailing croon, of the radios. And a smell of frying imposed upon the hot garbage smell from dark landings, and the smell of unaired beds and of human sweat.

By evening the air seems unbreathable in its staleness and used-upness and lies like a dirty rag across the mouth and nostrils. But the radios die away at last and there is quietness invaded by sounds muted by distance or muffled behind drawn blinds or curtains; in that quietness you can hear the night breathing. There is the call of a ship on the river, though the river itself does not touch this suburb. There is the clatter of a lorry in an empty street some way off. There is the sudden snarl and wail of cats, and a smothered human cry which could be ecstasy or pain but which is wrapped around impenetrably in the secrecy of the night. Secrecy there is here, but not privacy. Who cries out in the stillness of the night you do not know, but only that somebody cries and that in airless rooms the hot darkness listens and stirs. Sometimes a child cries, pitifully, and seemingly endlessly.

Everything goes on here, by night and by day, and one block of flats becomes the microcosm of universal life. Love and lust, tenderness and brutality, joy and misery, live side by side here. Here pity and cruelty both wear the human dress: all that is most contemptible in human nature and all that is courageous and devoted looks out of the human face. And life is not so mean in this ant hill but that the ants can dance and sing and enjoy living, especially on a Saturday night or a Bank Holiday, even though the singing be out of tune and the dance no more than "Knees Up Mother Brown." There are none of the finer shades of living here, but there is a vehemence and vitality of life which takes poverty in its stride and struggles upward to the light, come what may, come hell or high water, the rent collector or the tallyman, or the baby-too-many. It is the triumphant assertion of life at all costs, at any price—like maggots in a cheese, if you like, but still—life. *And everything that lives is holy*. Here there is nothing for it but to "learn to love without the aid of anything on earth."

The middle-aged couple in whose flat I rent a room—without "service," because I like to be solitary, and also catering for myself is cheaper, the way I live—have a boy of ten called Mickey. He is in and out of my room a good deal because I model things for him in clay, and sometimes chip things out for him in wood. He is a nice bright intelligent kid. One Saturday afternoon I got his mother's permission to take him to the Victoria and Albert Museum, where I showed him real wood carvings. He got excited about the wood carving of Jesus seated on the ass, and the lovely French fifteenth-century Angel Gabriel, with its beautiful faded paint on the crumbling worm-eaten oak. I showed him a lot of things and explained to him something of the technique of wood carving, and he took it all in eagerly. He calls me Mister, and it was an odd feeling when he exclaimed, "It's a wonder you didn't go in for being a sculptor yourself, Mister, knowing so much about it!"

Because this boy and I are friends I want to talk to him, but I am as pledged to silence as a Trappist monk. An elected silence and an elected poverty. Mickey has that quick bright eagerness which makes me think of Martin. Soon after I came here I had so intense a longing to see my own kid again that I went out on a Sunday afternoon to Greenwich and mooched about the hill in the hope of getting a glimpse of him. I'd planned to keep a sharp lookout and not let him see me. I just wanted to satisfy my hunger for a sight of him. There were a lot of kids running up and down the grass slopes and dodging about between the trees, but I didn't see Martin. Nor did I see him on the bit of beach below the waterside terrace. I wondered where he was that fine afternoon. Perhaps Norah had taken him to Epping Forest, I thought. Perhaps they were over at Joe's. I sat for a long time on a seat in front of the old Observatory, watching the people eagerly, but I didn't see my son. All I saw, continually, was the ghost of Tansy.

I never went back. I had renounced all that, and what you have renounced you've no right to try and get back even a part of. And soon I must renounce Mickey too and move on from here, deeper into my own particular journey to the end of the night, because I am self-committed to the renunciation of all possessions, even friendship and love. I must move on because I still have too much, materially and in all the other ways. I am rich in this child's love, and the comfort of it, and in his parents' good-natured friendliness, which manifests itself continually in all manner of small kindnesses—such as the fire ready lit in my room on a cold night, the odd cup of tea sent in to me, the odd job passed to me to help me along. Between them they are making living too easy for me, and my purpose is to be identified with those for whom life is unremitting sorrow and pain and struggle. Only so can I make my contribution, so pitifully, infinitesimally small, to that Vision of Christ in terms of mercy, pity, peace, which was for so long for me no more than a lost traveler's dream in a landscape sometimes dark, sometimes bright, occasionally exciting or beautiful, or both, but always confusing and labyrinthine.

When I leave here I shall sleep in common lodginghouses, then I shall have still more money to give back to those who have even less than I have. Such women friends as I have must be common prostitutes, not sweet women like Mickey's mother. Any thief I may meet shall be my friend, not a good man like Mickey's father. The prostitute and the thief are more in need of friends. According to Lee, and perhaps even more to Helen, and certainly to poor Norah if she knew about it, my walking out on everything like this doesn't make sense, but it makes sense to me. What can we do but seek truth in our own way—our own particular truth? I am under no illusions; I know that My Lady Poverty is a hag and a whore, but the hag needs pity, and often the whore has a good heart, and anyhow we are committed to travel together, intimately, to the end, be the journey long or short. And through her I am clear of possessions and privilege, and no man's need is on my conscience. I can look all men in the eyes, owning nothing, and if there's that Last Judgment the orthodox speak of and the black-robed ones would have us believe in, I shall stand there as one who for a long time saw through a glass darkly the everlasting Vision, but then in the lightning flash of revelation, on his own particular road to Damascus, face to face.

May 1st, 1952—Jan. 31st, 1953

London